BRUTAL BOYS CRY BLOOD

A SECRET SOCIETY ROMANTIC SUSPENSE

STEFFANIE HOLMES

Cover design: Seventhstar

ISBN: 978-1-99-115043-1

❀ Created with Vellum

BRUTAL BOYS CRY BLOOD

Don't get killed on Devil's Night.

I thought I was close to figuring out the truth about the mysterious death of my roommate. But Blackfriars University still holds her secrets close.

In the name of the Father...

Father Sebastian Pearce – my priest, my teacher, my friend. The man who tempted my into sin with that rich, commanding voice. The man who had me over an altar...in the biblical sense. The one man in the world I'm forbidden to love.

...the Son...

William Windsor-Forsyth – the dark prince who shattered my heart into a thousand pieces. He's as cruel as he is beautiful, and he's back to make sure I don't forget that he's royalty and I'm the freak.

...and the Holy Spirit...

In a moonlit ceremony of obscenity and excess, the Orpheus Society made me one of their own. But that doesn't mean I'll keep their secrets. I'm here to expose a killer, even if the price of justice is betraying the two men I love.

I've said my prayers,
and poured my libations.

The old gods are listening.
They demand *sacrifice*.

Amen.

Brutal Boys Cry Blood is a dark bully romance and part two of the Dark Academia duet. If you enjoy tales of clever heroines, ancient rites, secret societies, cruel princes and wicked priests, dusty libraries and decadent parties, twisted relationships and buried secrets, then prepare to enter the halls of Blackfriars University. You may never return.

Want to read chapters from William and Sebastian's POV? Get them in your free copy of *Cabinet of Curiosities* – a Steffanie Holmes compendium of short stories and bonus scenes – when you sign up for updates with the Steffanie Holmes newsletter.

A NOTE ON DARK CONTENT

I'm writing this note because I want you a heads up about some of the content in this book. Reading should be fun, so I want to make sure you don't get any nasty surprises. If you're cool with anything and you don't want spoilers, then skip this note and dive in.

Keep reading if you like a bit of warning about what to expect in this series.

- There is some bullying in this first book, but our heroine holds her own. No heroes in this story threaten or are involved in physical or sexual assault of the heroine.

- George is a sexual abuse survivor and she references this past trauma in places.

- George has also been at the side of her BFF, Claws, as Claws reclaimed her criminal empire in the *Stonehurst Prep* series. This means she sometimes references violent acts from that series, and the Dark Academia books contain spoilers for *Stonehurst Prep*.

- This book contains an age-gap, taboo relationship between George and her teacher/priest, Sebastian Pearce. If hot priests and sacrilegious altar sex aren't you thing, this probably isn't the book for you.

- There is some murder, violence, claustrophobic situations, and body horror in this and subsequent books.

I wouldn't call this book dark, but it's definitely a smidge 'grey.' I promise there will be suspense, hot sex, gothic ambience, and a clever heroine searching for the truth and finding her heart along the way. If that's not your jam, that's totally cool. I suggest you pick up my Nevermore Bookshop Mysteries series – all of the mystery without the gore and creepiness.

Enjoy, you beautiful depraved human, you :) Steff

The god on the cross is a curse on life, a signpost to seek redemption from life; Dionysus cut to pieces is a promise of life: it will be eternally reborn and return again from destruction.

— Nietzsche

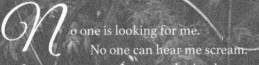

1

No one is looking for me.

No one can hear me scream.

I scream anyway, because that's what you do, isn't it? That's what you do when there's a monster under the bed and your dad is at a late-night film shoot in heaven and you have to face it all by yourself.

I scream, and my voice coils back on itself in the claustrophobic space. It grows talons that rake across my skin.

I scream, and weirdly, I feel better.

Okay, not *better*, exactly. Because I'm still walled into this pitch-black room with no way out. But I feel calmer. I stop screaming and lean my back against the wall and *think*.

I'm George Fisher. I've thought myself out of worse scrapes than this. None come immediately to mind, but still...

Claws didn't keep me around last year because of my excellent karaoke skills. We get along so well because she does the slaying and I do the thinking. And if I can help my best friend run a criminal empire, then I can figure a way out of this room.

Why am I in this room? Who put me here? Is it some enemy of

Claws, trying to blackmail her into submission? Or is this to do with the Orpheus Society? Or Keely's family—

No. Don't think about the why. That way lies only madness. I suck in a deep breath. *Focus on the problem in front of you.*

Right. How to get out of this cell.

I've already checked the room for possible tools I can use to break out. Nothing. I stood on my tiptoes and scraped my fingers against the ceiling, but it seems to be solid stone. The only exits from the room are the three windows – the one that faces into the church for receiving communion and the one the anchoress' maid handed food through are too small for me to fit through. But there's the third window, facing out into the walled grave-yard where the monks are buried.

I cross the room and examine the window with my hands. It has old wooden shutters that I might be able to break, but the window is covered by three metal bars that seem pretty fixed in place. If I can get the shutters off, I can call for help, but the graveyard isn't exactly frequented by people—

But the church is.

Even though the campus has emptied out, and even though both Sebastian and Father Duncan have gone to their priest summer camp for the next few weeks and there won't be services, the church can't remain empty. The college runs tours, the cleaners have to dust the holy objects...*someone* will come in.

"Help, help!" I beat my fists against the shutters on the tiny window. It's locked from the other side, but if someone is nearby, they'll hear me.

Please, hear me.

After a few frantic minutes, my arms aching and my fists bleeding, I collapse back against the wall. There's obviously no one in the church right now. I'll wait a little and try again.

I lean back against the stones and fight to calm the panic

rising inside me. Imagine being walled up inside this room for your whole life. Imagine *choosing* this.

The anchoress who lived here gave up her worldly life to make her home in this tiny cell, to commune with God and the angels. She became anchored to the church, a tether to the spiritual realm around which her community could congregate. But was it God's presence within these walls that made her holy, or was it her sacrifice? Did the very act of giving herself to God, of stripping her life of everything but these four walls, allow her to see the unseen?

Is God here, in this place?

It's a strange question for an atheist to ask, but what can I say? Gods have been showing up as a theme in my life lately, and the duality between Sebastian's faith and the Orpheans' rapture became obvious when he lay me on the altar and made me come so hard I could believe in God.

The anchoress' asceticism, the Bacchanalia, the cilice Sebastian showed me in the sacristy: it's all the same – humans eternally searching for *ekstasis*, for the joyous rapture of giving your body and spirit completely over to a god, to be possessed in every way until you are outside of yourself, until you're beyond the veil of human suffering.

It requires something I don't possess, will *never* possess – the ability to let go, to throw oneself over a cliff and trust in something you can't see or understand to catch you. I like being in control of my body. I like my mind doing its thing without divine interference. I need to hold back a little of myself to keep safe.

Having a god barge into your head uninvited is a terrifying thought.

Although not as terrifying as slowly starving to death in an ancient anchorhold.

And once a god is possessing your body, how do you make

him leave? How do you know he's not still there all the time, directing you like a puppetmaster—

That's it.

Why didn't I think of it before?

It's so simple. I leave the way I came in.

Whoever placed me in here couldn't have used the windows – the size and the bars prevent that. So unless they dropped me through some hatch in the roof (unlikely, since I don't have any broken bones), they must have removed some of the stones and pushed me through the wall.

The rough stones jab into my spine. I cast my mind back to when I first woke up in the cell. I heard a scraping noise – probably the stones being mortared into place. They probably used a quick-set mortar, but even so, I can't have been in here for that long. I might be able to wiggle the stones free somehow or—

Holy shit. Dad's toolkit.

I dig my hand into my pocket. As soon as I touch the case, my lungs fill with the familiar scent of my father – black coffee and fresh aftershave and prosthetic latex. I know it's my brain tricking me into conjuring a scent memory, but in the gloom, I can almost believe it's something more...that Dad's here with me, looking out for his little girl.

Thank you, Daddy.

How did I not remember I had this with me? How did whoever stuck me in here not think to check my pockets?

I click it open, my fingers sliding over the familiar shapes until I find what I need. A tiny screwdriver. I feel around on the walls until I touch mortar that crumbles in my fingers. It's set, but not hard as stone like the rest of the room. I set the screwdriver into the mortar, draw back my hand, and hit—

"Yeow!"

I suck on my bruised finger. *Ow ow ow.* Who would've

thought trying to chisel an ancient rock in the dark is so damn difficult?

I take a smaller, more precise swing this time. The screwdriver slides into the mortar. Chunks fall around my feet. I cough as dust swirls around me. This is going to be a problem. The more mortar I chip away, the more dust I'll create.

Keep going. If it becomes a problem, I'll bust through the wooden shutters to let in fresh air.

I pound the screwdriver until my arm aches and my eyes sting from the dust. I grab the stone and wiggle it, but it still won't move. Tears sting at the corners of my eyes, but I don't know if it's from the irritation or the sinking realization that it's going to take hours of work to get these stones free, and my throat is dry and my head's spinning and my limbs are starting to tremble from hunger. I fight back a coughing fit and move the screwdriver to the next stone. I bring my hand back. I swing, and the hammer hits the screwdriver, but the screwdriver doesn't sink into the mortar, because the mortar is no longer there.

The entire brick wall crumbles away.

Dust encircles me in a cloud so thick and complete that even though light penetrates the wall, I can't see what's on the other side. Stones drop on my feet and scrape my legs.

I stagger back, trying to scream but unable to push sound through my parched mouth, as a pair of monstrous hands reach through the dust and grab me.

2

I claw at the wall of my prison as the hands drag me through the rubble. *Who are you? What are you going to do to me?*

I scream the questions inside my head, but it's all I can do now to fight for breath as I'm dragged into the church. Bright sunlight burns through the faces of dead saints in the stained glass windows, blinding me so I can't see the face of the person holding me. Are they my rescuer, or are they dragging me off to some even greater torture?

The hands rub my back and push my hair out of my face so I can gasp in fresh, incense-tinged air.

"Who are you?" I manage to choke out between dry, retching coughs. "Why are you doing this?"

"She's a little disoriented," a familiar voice says. Female, it drips with concern and comes from somewhere on my right. Not the voice of the person holding me.

"But she's right as a trivet?" Another voice. Male. He sounds almost...frightened. "No injuries?"

Shapes move around me, crowding in on all sides, blocking the light – almost as claustrophobic as the walls inside the anchorhold. I shove and kick and cough and wail, trying to make enough space so I can understand. They clear away, and I reel back and finally, *finally*, open my stinging eyes enough to get a look at the man who pulled me to safety.

It's Montague Cavendish.

Monty grins down at me as he pats me hard on the back. "No hard feelings, George old chap? It was just a little fun—"

I slap him across the face.

Monty reels, touching his cheek. Something that might be shock or rage flickers in his eyes, but he doesn't do anything except whimper. My palm stings, but the pain fills me with righteous anger.

Behind me, Diana laughs, but it's high-pitched, a little manic. "You're fine, George. You're perfectly fine." She comes forward to wrap her arms around me.

I'm *not* fine. I'm shaking from head to toe. I'm dehydrated and my head pounds and I have no idea what the *fuck* is going on. I want to run. I don't want to be surrounded by them, not right now. But my legs won't work, so I sink against Diana, letting her vanilla and blackcurrant scent calm me.

"We were never going to hurt you, you do know that," says Richard. "This was just a lark."

"Every Orphean has to go through an ordeal as part of their initiation," adds Tabitha. "It's tradition. And you love traditions, don't you, George?"

"You already had your room trashed, so we needed to think of something else to mark the occasion," explains Percy. "We've done it before, but we see now that it's awfully cruel, and we're sorry."

Wait, what?

They all seem so penitent, their heads hung, their pale cheeks reddened with shame. But they've never felt shame about any of their pranks before. Monty didn't act like this after the men's bathroom, so why now?

What is this? Why are the Orpheans apologizing to me?

"George, we're so so sorry." Diana squeezes me so tight I taste vanilla and blackcurrant. The other Orpheans crowd in, talking over each other as they squeeze me so hard I worry my brains will pop out my ears. *Sorry, so sorry.*

"Back off her," a deep, familiar voice booms.

The Orpheans leap away like I'm rigged to explode. I turn toward the voice. As the dust clears and the diffused light hits a spot in the pews, I recognize the hulk of a man sitting there, his eyes narrowed with menace.

"Tiberius?"

The scarred face of Claws' number one enforcer grins back at me. "Little George Fisher." He strides across the church and wraps me in his enormous arms. "Are you hurt?"

"Not physically." My mind is still reeling from the sheer terror of waking up inside the anchorhold. "What are you doing here?"

"You know Madeline and I live not far from here." He sets me down on a pew in the chapel and checks me over to make sure I'm not hurt. "Claws sent me to watch out for you. She thought you might be in trouble, but you didn't want her help, so she told me to stay in the background and only step in if you were in serious danger."

He glares at the Orpheans, who all take a step back. Diana's lip wobbles.

"She was never in danger from us," Monty says with a pout. "We weren't going to hurt her. Honest. It's just a silly initiation stunt—"

"We've done this a hundred times before. The mortar in the bricks is old. You can slip them out and then wall them back up." Percy scuffs the broken stone pieces with his wing-tip.

I wrap my arms around Tiberius' thick neck. "Thank you. How long have you been following me?"

"Ever since you got back after the New Year. I saw this lot nab you and wall you in. They were whooping around, cracking bottles of piss while you screamed your head off." Tiberius cracks his knuckles, and the Orpheans shrink away from him. "My duty is to set them straight on a few things."

It's then I notice the dried blood on Monty's jaw, the fact that Richard's holding a bloody shirt up to his face, and that Tabitha's eyes are wide with fright.

I grin at Tiberius. "You made them set me free."

"No, no," Diana says. "We were already pulling the wall down, honest. We would never..."

Tiberius grins. Diana trails off. I turn to the Orpheans and study their contrite faces, and all the emotion of the last year rises up inside me. All the awful things they did to me, the way they went out of their way to make me feel less than them, and now they do *this*? And Keely, what the fuck did they do to my roommate?

"Why?" I demand. *Why any of this?*

Diana rushes forward and takes my hand. "You know why, silly. It's your initiation."

"My—"

"Welcome to the Orpheus Society, George." Monty holds out a bottle of Domaine Leroy. His arm trembles a little.

As one, the Orpheans throw their arms around me, laughing as they tell me how they planned this little trick especially for me, how I did so brilliantly, how much they were looking forward to having me as one of them. And though I should be terrified that they've decided I'm going to take Keely's place, thrilled that I am officially in the inner circle, that I'm closer than ever to getting justice for my roommate and Khloe May and the poor dead person in Paris, the thought that consumes me is—

William's not here.

These are his friends, his closest circle, and he's not with them. Surely he's supposed to be present when a new member is initiated. The Orpheans seem like the kind of secret society that expects current members to show up. So where is he?

And why, after everything he's done, does thinking of him make my heart clatter in my chest?

3

"*W*ow." I peer out the window at a grand country estate – a Georgian Hall covered in creeping ivy, like a house from a storybook. "Is that where Monty's family lives?"

It's a week after my initiation, and I'm squashed with Diana and Tabitha in the backseat of a Bentley, nose pressed hard up against a window as rolling hills and lush estates roll by. We're somewhere in the Midlands, heading toward the country estate Monty declared would be our home base for the summer.

I'm supposed to be meeting Leigh in London tomorrow to start our backpacking adventure, but when I rang her to say I'm now a member of the Orpheans and Monty wanted me to join the society at the estate, she said I had to do it. Monty declared that Leigh was welcome too, as long as she brought along some bottles of her famous mead. Aware that I still suspect the society of murdering my roommate, I don't exactly want my new friend mixed up with them, but I also know I can't keep Leigh away. Besides, I think they're unlikely to try anything now they know Tiberius will be hanging around. He's behind us right now, his bulletproof windows rolled down as he cruises along, banging his head to the heavy metal blasting from his stereo.

Just cruising down to the country estate with my secret society friends and my ex-enforcer bodyguard watching out for me. This is my life now.

The last week has been surreal. My quiet sojourn on campus turned into an endless parade of fancy-dress picnics, impromptu Greek oratory debates, and raucous partying until all hours of the morning. The Orpheans never seem to tire of each other's company. They're all intimidatingly clever and demand stimulation every hour of the day. I'm breathless trying to keep up with them.

I know at least some of them are dangerous. I know they're hiding something. But I have to admit, being part of their group is *intoxicating*. We went to a restaurant on a country estate just out of Blackfriars Close, and when they saw Monty at the door, they ushered us into a private ballroom. Richard has keys to all these strange, hidden places in the campus, so on Tuesday, he snuck us into an old WWII air-raid shelter underneath the cricket pitch where we drank twenty-year-old Scotch and played backgammon until the wee hours.

And Diana...Diana is like a mythological creature. She's the personification of her name – wild and ethereal. She makes even the most mundane activities feel magical – a walk in the woods, a shopping trip to buy soap. When she talks about Dionysos or Persephone or any of the Greek myths, her eyes sparkle with this inner light, like she knows things that she can only hint at to mere mortals. Hanging out with her can make even an atheist like me question if the old gods really exist.

Right now, she reaches across me and touches my cheek. "No, no, not that place. Look over there. That's where we're going."

I whirl around just as the car turns into a driveway, passing beneath towering stone and ironwork gates that look more like they're welcoming us to Jurassic Park than someone's home. My breath catches in my throat as we sweep around a wide driveway lined with pink and white flowers, taking in rolling fields filled with fluffy sheep before climbing around a forested hill.

The house comes into view – a sprawling mass of neo-gothic arches and leaded windows nestled into the crook of the forest. A majestic garden and cascading water feature that would make Louis XIV blush stretches down the hillside. Just when I think it can't possibly get any larger, another wing reveals itself. This is not a house, it's a fucking *palace*. It makes my friend Gabe's place, Blackwich Castle, look like a shack in the woods in comparison.

Monty lives *here?*

I mean, I know the Orpheans are all rich. I know that money in England is different from money in America. In Emerald Beach, I've been surrounded by wealthy kids my whole life – kids who live in tacky Barbie doll beach houses, drive showy cars, dress head-to-toe in luxury brands and gold plate everything. But this...this is...otherworldly.

It looks like the movie set for *Pride and Prejudice*. It looks like the kind of place that inspires peasants to lop off heads. It's a fairy tale made flesh. I wind down my window and breathe in the blossoming honeysuckle as we round the winding driveway through verdant market gardens and avenues of trees into a large parking area covered in English Heritage signage. The forest stretches around the hillside, encircling the house like a magician's cloak.

We pile out of the car. Tabitha smooths down her dress. An army of staff dressed in pristine uniforms circle the car and start unloading our bags, while Monty chases a tiny kitten around the parking lot.

We follow the staff through opulent reception rooms and an

armory, past meandering tourist groups and into the deepest
recesses of the house, where I have no hope of finding my way
out again. In the guest wing, I'm shown to a room that's larger
than my entire house back in California. The oak-beamed
ceiling stretches so high I have to squint to make out the mural
painted between the carved beams – satyrs and maenads dancing, drawn in a Renaissance style, all flowing skirts and sensual
hands. I run to the window and pull back the gauzy fabric to
reveal a view of the shimmering artificial pool and grand
fountain.

This is the kind of house William grew up in.

It's so different from everything I've known. I feel like I
understand him a little more, just being here. I touch my fingers
to the heavy brocade bedspread. I mean, this place is magical,
but it's like stepping onto a movie set. It doesn't feel like any of
this furniture is supposed to be touched. It doesn't feel like a
home in the same way my mom's dreamcatchers and salt lamps
and Dad's piles of old blues vinyl and horror film posters do.
How do you be a kid in a place like this? What happens if you
knock over a vase? Do you get sent to the dungeon?

When I first met William, I couldn't imagine him ever being
a kid. He rarely smiles, and looks like he came out of his mother
all grim and posh and serious. And now that I've seen this place,
I think I understand, at least a little. I mean, this is *Monty's*
house, not William's, so maybe it's different at his place. Less...
off with their heads.

And there are so many sides to William – he might be serious, but he's not at Blackfriars to become an investment banker.
He's a brilliant artist, and in his studies of water are all the
emotions he refuses to wear on his skin.

Plus, there are all those stories I read about his parents,
about their 'swingers' parties and wife-swapping and drug-

fueled escapades. So perhaps not all country estates are painted with the same brushes. Perhaps William is—

I shake my head. I shouldn't be imagining William anywhere or doing anything.

I'm not feeling sorry for the poor little rich boy who stomped all over my heart.

I'm *not*.

I fling open my suitcase, scattering clothes around as I hunt for something to wear to dinner. All my clothes feel so wrong for dining in a literal palace. Finally, I settle on a red tartan skirt and a men's Septicflesh t-shirt – which I tie into a knot at my stomach – and some socks with tiny dinosaurs on them. I'm so obviously the odd one out in the group, I might as well embrace it.

It takes me a good hour to backtrack my steps through the vast rooms to reach the dining room. Hundreds of glittering candles light the banquet table, glinting off the gilded ceiling decorations but unable to penetrate the darkest corners of the room. Even though there are only nine of us, the table is set for thirty, so we spread out and have to shout at each other along the table length. Staff move around us constantly, bringing in dish after dish of food until I fear a Mr. Creosote situation. Monty keeps eating long after the rest of us retire to a nearby drawing room, the candles burning low around him as he licks meat juices from his fingers.

The rest of us crowd around tables beside a large carved fireplace. It's too warm to light the fire. Instead, we throw open the enormous windows. Richard and Alfie pull their chairs over to the windows and smoke cigarettes, Percy collapses into an over-stuffed chair with a book of poetry, while we girls crowd around a table and Fatima deals a game of poker. There are five girls and four boys – plus William makes five – the same as when I first saw the Orpheans draped over the fountain the first day at Blackfriars.

"Is there a significance in the number of members?" I ask as I study my hand. Might as well get as much information as I can, now that I'm part of the inner circle.

"There are always twelve members at the school at any time," Diana says as she hands out rolls of poker chips. I breathe a sigh of relief that we're not playing with real money. "Like the twelve apostles. Ten students, two faculty members. Some members believe Benet saw himself as the Jesus of the group. And there are ten students because the number ten is worshiped by Pythagoras."

So I did take Keely's spot.

"Who are the faculty members?" I have a pair of aces, but I match the current bets, not wanting to show too much enthusiasm. "I'm guessing one is Father Duncan."

"Nothing gets past you, Georgie." Fatima deals the other cards. "The other is Madame Ulrich. Have you met her? She tutors a few of us in the fine arts department."

Oh yes, I've met her.

"George joined us for one of her figure-drawing classes," Diana says as she deals again. I smile at her gratefully because she doesn't bring up what happened in that class. "The Madame's involvement is purely to smooth ruffled feathers in the faculty, making sure we don't get in trouble with the college for any of the stunts we pull. She was a member when she was at school, so she's automatically tapped, but she doesn't come to the events or take an interest in our affairs. Not like Father Duncan."

She casts a glance at Monty that betrays some meaning I don't understand. My Miss Marple senses tingle. I knew from the photographs I've seen that Father Duncan attends Orphean events. At least, he was at last year's Devil's Night party, where Keely was last seen alive.

I pick up another ace, so when the betting begins again, I raise.

"You bluffing, George?" Matilda raises a perfectly sculpted eyebrow.

"I can bluff with the best of them," I say in a deadpan voice. It's clear that they've played a lot of cards together – they know each other's tells. But I'm new. And I want to clean them out. I raise again, and Tabitha drops out.

The rest of us show our cards. To my surprise, I win. We play a few more rounds. Tabitha keeps our wine glasses filled and the girls share gossip about people I don't know. I can't quite manage to steer the conversation back to Father Duncan.

"I'm bored," Diana gets to her feet. "I fancy a turn about the gardens. George, care to join me?"

"Sure." I set down my untouched wine and trail after her.

Diana leads me through the winding passages with the confidence of someone who's spent many summers here. She collects two pairs of rubber boots (Wellingtons, as she calls them) from a closet, and leads me out a narrow door into a walled kitchen garden. We follow the neat cobbled paths through rows of vegetables and herbs. Diana stops to pick a handful of strawberries that stain her lips pink. On the other side of the garden is a small iron gate leading to a forked trail.

"Would you like the formal garden or the meadow?" Diana asks.

"The meadow."

We turn away from the neat parterres and Classical statuary, meandering down an irregular cobbled path that snakes between towering oaks and fluttering aspen. We pierce the edge of the trees and come out on the edge of a gentle slope, dotted with wildflowers of impossibly bright hues. The meadow stretches on for an eternity, only finishing on the edge of a shimmering lake that curls around the edge of the forest, its glass-like surface disappearing into the woods. A Tudor-style boathouse sits on the edge of the water.

"It's beautiful," I breathe.

"We'll go boating tomorrow, if you want to," Diana says as she sinks to her knees, spreading her skirt around her and threading her fingers through the long grass. "There's a small island in the center that you can't see from here. We like to picnic there—"

"Where are Monty's parents?" I blurt out.

Diana blinks. "Who?"

"Monty's parents. Are we really allowed to just wander around like this? We've been here for hours, making a mess, eating all their food, smoking in their house. I thought they'd at least introduce themselves..." I trail off as Diana's husky laugh breaks the stillness of the night.

"Oh, but the Cavendish family don't live here," Diana says. "This is Forsyth Hall. It belongs to William's family."

What?

How can this be William's house? William never invited us. It was all Monty. He said—

Wait.

Fuck.

Monty never said we were going to *his* house. He said we were going to 'the summer place.' I'd made the assumption it belonged to Monty's family because I didn't know you could show up to your friend's palace unannounced and have their staff roll over themselves to provide for your every whim.

But apparently, that's exactly what you can do if you're Monty Cavendish.

"See that house over the hill, there?" Diana points. I plonk down beside her and follow her finger. If I squint, I can just make out a rooftop peeking over the tree line. "That's the Cavendish estate. Monty only goes there if he's summoned. His parents are *awful*. They're both sadists. They get off on causing pain. They used to come to Sir Henry's little soirees, but he stopped inviting them after they frightened all his friends. I cannot imagine the things Monty went through locked up in that house alone with them."

I can't resist this chance to learn more about William's childhood. "So is that how Monty and William became friends?"

Their relationship confuses me. Monty is a profoundly odd person – a brilliant visual artist who at times seems to have the mind of a child. He can switch from kindness to cruelty. William coddles Monty like an indulgent big brother, but he's also afraid of him. I have a sense the others are too, that they walk on eggshells around him.

"They're more like siblings than friends. We all are. Since Monty learned to ride a horse, he's been riding over here to spend time with William," Diana says. "He even has his own room in the hall, filled with things Sir Henry and Lady Isabella brought for him – birthday presents for all the birthdays his parents ignored. William's parents are like that – they loved to collect people, especially misfits, outcasts, those who don't fit in with what our world demands of them. My mother has been friends with Lady Isabella since their bon vivant art school days in Paris. We've been coming to Forsyth Hall for the summer for as long as I can remember, so I suppose it feels natural to just show up now. Although my parents don't come any longer. Not after the accident."

I assume she means when William's mother drowned. *In this lake.* I look over the shimmering mirror again. Its beauty has a disquieting edge.

How did a woman drown in water so calm?

I swallow. I have so many questions, but I choose the one

she's most likely to answer. "What was it like back in those days? Before William's mother drowned?"

Diana stares across the meadow, her face pensive. "I presume you know all about William's parents, about the swingers' parties."

I nod. There's no sense denying it. The Orpheans know me now. They know I do my research.

"Right. Well, it wasn't the way they portrayed it in the gutter press, as this sordid house of iniquity where our young minds were corrupted by our parents' sins. It felt like living in a fairy tale. Sir Henry had no mind for children, of course. He treated us like tiny adults, and grew frustrated when we didn't understand him or ruined his jovial parties with our tantrums and skinned knees. When you meet him, I think you'll understand where William gets his...Williamness. But Lady Isabella adored us. She spent all year planning amusements for us – once, she had her gardeners construct an enormous topiary maze, and stacked boxes of toys in the center as prizes if we solved her labyrinth. Another year, she transformed an entire wing of the palace into Charlie's chocolate factory, and we all got frightfully sick from eating ridiculous sweets all day and night. Once she brought in a menagerie of exotic animals. I still remember William's face when a monkey peed down his back. You would have laughed to see it."

I smile at that. It did sound fun. "What did William think of...all this?"

"He loved it and he hated it. William was frightfully lonely. His father barely spoke to him. Not out of malice, mind you. He simply didn't understand kids. William didn't have friends at school. He stood up to the kids who picked on Monty, and that made him a target, too. If you want to know why he tolerates Monty's odd behavior, it's because Monty was the only person his age who talked to him until we showed up in the summers."

"Oh." I twist a strand of grass between my fingers. I never expected my childhood of horror film sets and reading by myself in the corner of the playground to be similar to William, but I know loneliness all too well.

Diana continues. "William was close to his mother, of course. She was an artist herself – too flighty to make a career of it, but she had a decent eye. They'd spend hours out here, paddling on the lake, setting up their easels and painting the sky or the trees or the birds. But when his parents were together, no one else existed. They were so lost in their own world that they forgot about him. William did everything he could to get their attention, earn their respect. All those awards he won, those achievements he ticked off his list, it was all about getting them to see him. When his mother died, I think he dared to hope it might be better, that at least Sir Henry might cling to him. Instead, he clings to God. This house has become a pale shade of what it once was, and the ghost of Lady Isabella lurks around every corner."

Diana looks out across the water with such intensity I wonder if she sees something I don't. "It was better for William in the summer. The adults would disappear, sometimes for days at a time, but we friends had each other. It was many years before we realized our parents went to the island on the lake, or camped in the woods, or they were simply squirreled away in Sir Henry's sex dungeon in one of the far-flung wings of the castle, having their orgies. We thought it was all perfectly normal. We didn't know it was something to be hidden away, to be ashamed of, until we went away to our various boarding schools and the press started to get wind of it. William had the worst of it. He was at school with Monty, and the two of them were bullied mercilessly." She smiles sadly. "Sometimes, in order to save yourself, you have to become the very thing you fear."

It made a sick kind of sense. William said to me once that I didn't fit. I made myself a target because I reminded people of everything they were afraid of. William said he was trying to protect me, but all this time he's been a frightened boy trying to protect himself.

Is that why he broke us? Because he's afraid?

I shake my head. I won't entertain hope. Even if that's why he did it, it doesn't change the fact that we're broken. I can't put us back together again, and I don't want to try.

Then why is your heart racing like a raccoon on crack ever since you heard this is his home?

Why are you asking all these questions, if not to understand William's heart?

I turn off the tap in my mind, the dangerous drip drip drip of thoughts that lead back to William Windsor-Forsyth. And I focus on Monty. For the last year, he's been the bogeyman at my back, the source of most of my dread and anguish. And now I feel like I understand a tiny bit of who he is behind the monster. It doesn't mean I forgive him, but he doesn't seem so scary anymore.

Instead, he seems sad.

Except that sad boy might've killed your roommate. Don't forget why you're here. You're not making friends with these people. You're exposing their crime.

"—you should probably know that most of us were conceived right here on the lawns or in the summerhouse or one of those opulent bedrooms," Diana is saying. "It's one of the reasons we embraced the Orpheus Society. It feels like an extension of what our parents were doing, like we're reclaiming a piece of those halcyon days."

"And the other reasons?" I ask.

Diana laughs, twirling her auburn hair around her delicate fingers. "Why, there's an element of legacy to it, of course. Some of our parents were members – Monty's mother, my father. But mostly because it's just a bit of fun. It lends a bit of magic to the drudgery of life. Don't you love it, George? Don't you love being special?"

I smile despite myself. She's right. When I went to their Bacchanal (or more accurately, when they kidnapped me and *dragged* me to their Bacchanal), what I saw was a typical college party with the trappings of an ancient religious cult. But I have to admit, as cults go, this one has some awesome trappings. I *do* feel special. I feel *chosen*. And George Fisher has never been chosen for anything in her life.

But then I remember what happened to the girl chosen before me, and my blood cools to ice.

"So," I try to sound nonchalant. "Where is William this summer? Paris?"

"Where do you think?" Diana sips her drink. "Down by the pond, yearning dramatically."

"He's *here?*"

Diana points toward the boathouse. At first, I'm too transfixed by the shimmer of her ivory nail polish to see a thing. But then I spy a lone figure standing on the edge of the lake, hands in pockets, gaze turned across the water.

William.

The urge to call out to him overwhelms me. Why is he just standing there? Why hasn't he come to see his friends? But then I remember all those horrible things he said to me in front of them, and I lock my jaw. I won't be the one to go to him. If he wants to sulk by the water, that's his prerogative.

Diana reaches across and grabs my hand. "I know he hurt you, but he's hurting, too."

I open my mouth to say all the things I'm feeling, that I don't care, that I do care, that I don't know what the fuck I'm doing, that if she weren't here I might just throw myself into the water so I could drown while he watches, when Diana suddenly falls away from me. She squeals with delight as she rolls down the hill, her skirts flying around her shapely legs as she topples through the wildflowers.

"Come on, George!"

I lie down in the grass, breathing in the earthy scent. A delicate pink flower tickles my nose. I throw myself forward, laughing as the world bowls around me. Adrenaline sings in my veins as I roll over the soft grass. The meadow never ends, the gentle slope propelling me toward the lake, toward William.

I can't remember when I ever felt so free.

At the bottom, I roll to a stop. Diana and I cling to each other, laughing. Bits of grass stick out of her hair, and wayward petals dust her skin. Maybe the Orpheans are dangerous, but I feel good about Diana. She's kindness personified, a goddess of meadows and laughter.

Maybe she doesn't know?

Maybe not all the Orpheans know the truth about what happened that night. When I was in the Cloister Garden on Devil's Night, the only voices I heard were Monty, Keely, Tabitha, Abigail, and William. The rest of them were supposedly already at the party.

Or maybe I'm just indulging in wishful thinking. Maybe I don't want to believe that someone like Diana could be involved in this. Maybe...

The laughter dies on my lips. My eyes are drawn back to the lake. William is still there, although he no longer looks out toward the horizon. Instead, his body is rigid as he watches us, the surface of his blue eyes rippling with the poetry of storms.

4

"*O*i, wake up."

I open one eye. I've been having the most amazing dream. I drank a magical potion so I could grow wings and fly up to heaven like an angel, only I'm not dead. I just wanted to ask my dad a question. It was a very, very important question, life or death stuff, and I got there and I found him teaching all the other angels how to make Halloween masks for a themed party, because that's the kind of angel my dad is. And I go to ask him my question but what comes out is, "What do I do if I'm in love with an evil prince *and* a beautiful priest?" And he laughs his good-natured laugh and holds me and I could smell his unique scent – his zesty aftershave and the chemically tang of latex prosthetics. And then we fall over on a fluffy cloud and Dad starts jumping on the cloud and—

I pry the second eye open, and the shape jumping on me resolves itself. It's not Dad. It's Leigh.

"This place is mad boss," she says. "But d'you know where the kitchen is? I'm fixin' for some proper scran. The food on the train was complete rubbish."

I hold out a hand and she pulls me into a sitting position. I wrap her into a hug. "It's so good to see you. When did you get here?"

"I took the early train up from London, an' Monty sent a car for me." Leigh kicks her backpack off the bed and flops down beside me. "I had to see this place for real."

"I'm sorry we're not doing our backpacking trip."

"Are you kidding?" Leigh leaps off the bed and starts shuffling the antiques around on the bookshelves. "This is a hundred times better. We're literally staying in a *palace*. The maid gave me the room next to yours. It's got a marble bathtub. You have to see it."

Leigh bounces from foot to foot as I haul myself out of bed and shuffle toward my suitcase. Every item of clothing looks just as out-of-place as it did yesterday. I scope Leigh's outfit out of the corner of my eye. She's wearing a black racer-back tank top and a pair of torn skinny jeans. At least I won't be the only misfit anymore. I pull on a lime-green dress covered in red cherries, add my New Rocks, and run a brush through my short hair. Leigh's tapping the walls, looking for secret passages. She grabs my hand and drags me into her room, which is a similar size to mine but decorated in dark maroon. Her bathroom is head-to-toe black marble, including the tub, which is deep and square and looks a little like an ancient sarcophagus.

"I want to explore more. But first, I need to find decent coffee," Leigh declares.

We stumble downstairs. It takes us four false starts to locate the hallway that leads to the breakfast room Diana showed me last night. When we arrive, we find a gorgeous buffet laid out – hot porridge with an array of homemade jams and spreads, fresh sourdough still warm from the oven, mountains of scrambled eggs and boiled eggs and even eggs Benedict with strips of perfectly-pink salmon, trays of sliced fruit, a rainbow of different yogurts and cheeses.

"Do we just...eat?" I ask. "Are we supposed to wait for the others?" It's so weird being guests in this house.

"Help yourselves. Miss Clements and Miss Mortlock have already dined," says a server as he places a silver chafing dish on the table. Leigh lifts the lid and lets out a squeal of delight as she starts to pile her plate with bacon and sausages. "And Sir Henry, of course. He's entertaining a guest today, and they wanted an early start. You might see them at lunch."

"William's father is here, too?" I'd got the idea that he wouldn't be, that he'd gone somewhere for the summer.

"Oh, of course. Sir Henry is in the chapel with his guest."

We fill our plates and dig in. The serving staff bustle in and out, adding more food and filling our cups with delicious, steaming coffee. Leigh grabs a man in chef whites and goads him into an intense conversation about the food, while I stare out the window and think about the two men who still hold my heart – the one I pushed away so he could remain holy, and the one who told me he had to wash his mouth after kissing me. All the unanswered questions swirl around in my head, and it takes me a few minutes to realize Leigh is talking to me.

"—all that bacon is cured right here on-site," she says happily, rubbing her stomach. "This place is absolutely boss. Gareth – he's the assistant chef – says he'll show me the smoke-house and maybe the beehives after lunch. You can come too if you like, but it might be boring for you."

"Why do you say that?"

"Oh, only because you've been glassy-eyed since I started talking, thinking about a priest and a prince." Leigh burps. "S'cuse me."

The other Orpheans either aren't awake or have gone off on their own, and the public wing of the palace isn't open yet, so we explore the courtyards and downstairs rooms by ourselves. There's no trace of last night's festivities when we peek into the dining hall and drawing room. We wander into a long portrait gallery, and Leigh does impressions of all the stodgy-looking old white dudes frowning at us from the paintings. A set of wooden doors with gilded scrollwork open into a grand reception hall hung with tapestries that glitter with gold thread. And down a set of stone steps, past a series of paintings depicting scenes from the Lives of the Saints, we step into a grand nave.

"What's that?" Leigh cranes her neck to take in the narrow Gothic columns and the vaulted ceiling painted with angels.

"I think it's a private chapel." I gaze at the harrowing figure of Christ on the cross behind the altar. "William's family are Catholics—"

Leigh starts to head down the aisle. I throw out my hand to stop her. A figure kneels on the floor in front of the altar, head pressed into the carpet. Two candles burn in stone holders, and a fresh bunch of flowers sit in an urn.

Despite the figure's lanky frame and the russet hair falling in slack curls over his face, I'm positive it's not William. I don't have that plugging-my-arteries-into-an-electrical-socket feeling I get around William, and something in the figure's frame seems smaller, more hollow. He remains prone in front of the altar, making no indication that he knows he's no longer alone.

I remember Gareth saying William's father was here with a guest. I don't see anyone else, and I'm not about to interrupt the master of the house to grill him about his son.

I raise my finger to my lips. We back out of the chapel so as not to disturb Henry Forsyth's prayers, and wander back in the direction of the breakfast room. The Orpheans are awake now. They gather in a grassy courtyard overlooking the formal Tudor garden. Percy reads the paper through gold-rimmed glasses, while Monty and Diana leap between croquet hoops on the sprawling lawn. William still isn't with them, and I cannot tell if I'm relieved or gutted.

Tabitha approaches us, holding up a silver tray. "There you two are. Tea?"

"Sure." I take a teacup from the tray she offers. It's only when I bring it to my lips that I realize it's filled with pink gin. How can they even think about drinking at this time of the morning? Leigh accepts a teacup too, and gulps hers back as she chases after Monty, demanding a go with his mallet.

"You better watch out for your friend," Tabitha says, not unkindly. "Monty tends to break his toys."

I nod to Abigail, who is lounging herself in one of the wrought iron chairs, which is pointedly turned away from the direction of the croquet game. "Aren't Monty and Abigail dating?"

"Please," Tabitha rolls her eyes. "You're so *American*. No one *dates* Montague Cavendish. You're seen around with him. And then you're not."

I watch Monty chasing after Leigh as she swings the mallet at the croquet ball. She laughs so hard she snorts and falls over. Monty catches her and hoists her in the air, pretending to use her as a mallet the way Alice did with the flamingos in *Alice in Wonderland*. My stomach churns with concern, but I can't do anything except watch them. I make a mental note to talk to Leigh later. I mean, she knows my suspicions about Monty. That smile she flashes him might be fake.

It doesn't feel fake, though.

It feels like I'm not the only one falling under the spell of the Orpheus Society.

I sip my gin as Monty, Diana, and Leigh come racing over to the group. "I propose a game of *apodidraskinda*," Monty says.

Leigh shuffles away from him. "Yer what? Is that contagious?"

Monty crooks his mouth at her. "Pardon?"

"Your terrible ailment. Do you need to go to the Ozzy?"

"She means the *hospital*," I say when everyone looks blank.

Monty laughs his loud, braying laugh. He pats Leigh on the head like she's a puppy dog. "What an absurd notion. Oh, this one is top entertainment. I said that we should play *apodidraskinda*, the game described by Julius Pollox."

He doesn't elaborate, because it never occurs to Monty that some people in the group might not have an intimate knowledge of obscure second-century scholars.

"It's a popular Victorian parlor game," Diana fills in for our blank stares. "One person hides somewhere in the palace, and everyone has to look for them. When you find them, instead of yelling out, you hide with them. In the end, everyone ends up packed together in some tiny cupboard while one poor chap has to find them, and then he's the next person to hide."

"It's delightful fun," adds Tabitha.

"Especially in a place like this," says Fatima. "We play for hours."

"You want to play hide and seek in the house?" I ask. "Isn't that disruptive? What about the tours?"

What about the man praying in the chapel?

"Not hide and seek. *Apodidraskinda*," Percy corrects. "And you worry too much if you think anyone in this house cares what we do."

Diana picks several dahlias from the garden, making the stem of one much shorter than the others. She forms the flowers into a glorious bouquet, which she hands to Monty. He makes a great show of rearranging them, then offers the bouquet for us each to pick one. I draw the short straw. I can't help but feel that Monty arranged it like that.

"Will you be okay?" Diana pats my arm. "You have until the count of a hundred to find a hiding place. No area is out of bounds except for Sir Henry's rooms and the dungeons. You can hide in the formal gardens, but not in the forest or the orangery or down by the boathouse."

Are we really playing this game, like a bunch of kids?

To my horror, as one the Orpheans turn around, placing their hands over their eyes and ears. Monty starts counting loudly, in Greek, because this is my life now. Leigh pokes her tongue out at me before covering her own ears and turning away.

Alpha, beta, gamma, delta, epsilon...

My heart thuds in my chest. Is this another cruel game at my expense? I picture myself huddled in some dark, dingy cupboard for hours while the Orpheans party without me. I imagine William joining them, smirking his dark, arrogant smirk as he raises a teacup of gin to his lips. It's enough to make me kick Monty in the shins.

The air is still, buzzing with bird song and Monty's voice counting down to my doom. I spin on my heel and race toward the house.

I head back the way Leigh and I came, thinking about finding the portrait gallery. It contained a large cabinet of curiosities with enough space underneath for a few people to crawl under. Only I take a wrong turn somewhere and end up back at the chapel.

It's deserted now, unless you count the wide, tormented eyes of Jesus that follow me as I tiptoe across the lofty nave. I'm struck by the way the architecture reflects the purpose of the chapel – the stone columns sweep the eye upward toward the heavens, and the light pouring in from the stained glass windows bathes the entire place in holiness. It's an exercise in misdirection, something the church excels at – look *here*, kneel *here*, pray *here*, focus on the affairs of the heavens, so you don't see what's really going on.

But despite what I think about organized religion, I feel safe in these walls of stone and glass – as if I've been gifted divine protection from the cruelty of the Orpheans. I know this sense of safety has everything to do with Father Sebastian Pearce and the way he made me feel, but I don't have time to examine my thoughts.

I need a place to hide.

Surely the Orpheans won't do something awful to me if they find me in a house of god? I flash back to the scene in the woods, where I found Keely's hand sticking up from my makeshift body farm. To Monty leering over me as he tied my arms to a pipe in the men's bathroom. To William's strange, haunted expression as he painted my naked body in Figure Drawing.

The Orpheans will do *anything* to get their way.

I'm positive their plan is to forgo looking for me and force me to hide like a fool all day long. Well, at least this is a nice place to hang out. I search the nave for appropriate hiding spots. Around the edges of the nave are stone coffins containing William's ancestors. I'm not super eager to hide amongst the dead, so I head through an iron gate into the chancel. There's a small sacristy, accessible through a low, arched wooden door.

There may even be communion wine in the sacristy. I'm not above a little blasphemous imbibing.

Unlike the sacristy at Blackfriars, the holy items in here are neatly tidied away. A layer of dust covers everything. I know from the photographs decorating the hallways that this chapel is sometimes used for family weddings, but it must not have been used for a while.

I pick up a silver chalice. As soon as my hands touch the smooth metal, I'm transported to another church, another time, to Sebastian's smooth voice speaking the Eucharist as he tilts a chalice so wine-turned-blood touches the tongue of his supplicant.

Sebastian.

His presence weighs heavy in this holy place, even though I'm alone and I have no idea if he's even visited this chapel before. But I can't think of God or prayer or sacrifice without thinking of him – they're forever entwined for me. I know I did the right thing, even though I miss him with every breath I take. He is made for this world of rituals and ghosts and goodness, and I can't be the reason he gives it all up. I can't look at the altar without my cheeks flushing at the memory of that night—

Shit.

I hear voices outside. No time for a proper hiding place. I duck into the rack of dusty vestments, pulling my knees to my chest. I strain to listen for Monty's annoying voice or Diana's musical trill.

But it's not the Orpheans.

The voices rise through the nave, echoing off the carved stone balconies and piercing straight through my heart.

It's William. And he's arguing loudly with someone—

Not just someone.

He's arguing with Sebastian.

5

"—Shouldn't have come here." William's voice is ragged with anger. He's close, closer than I expect. They must be just outside the door of the sacristy, near the altar. But what are they doing here?

"Your father invited me," Sebastian says. "To be fair, I didn't know you were going to be here. You've been avoiding this place as much as possible these days. You're usually in France with your friends this time of year, but I see they're running wild just like they did back in those days—"

"And *you* were supposed to be at that poxy retreat, getting that holier-than-thou stick shoved back up your arse," William yells.

My heart hammers in my chest. I slide my hands between the robes and pull them apart ever so slightly, enough to give me a sliver of a view of the sanctuary. I know that I'm not with either of them any longer, that I lost the right to give a shit about Sebastian and I'm a fool for ever giving a shit about William. But there's some history between them that's led them to this exact moment, and I *must* know what it is.

William and Sebastian face off against each other on either

side of the altar. William wears a polo shirt and pair of shorts that somehow manage to look both effortless and expensive, and Sebastian's in his usual black shirt and trousers, his dress shoes polished to perfection. They're pretty much the same height, but all that fountain-swimming has broadened Sebastian's shoulders, so he commands the space. Dark stubble lines his jaw, giving him a dangerous edge despite the white collar nestled firmly at his neck.

"You seem awfully concerned with what goes on in my nether regions." Sebastian leans over the altar, splaying his fingers across the stone. I'm transfixed by those fingers, long and soft and commanding. My breath catches as I remember what he did to me on another altar, on a night that feels a million years away and yet...

And yet the sensation of his hands on mine seizes my body, as though I'm beneath him right now. My stomach clenches and hot, raw need flares inside me as the ghost of Sebastian's touch dances over my skin.

"I don't give a fuck about you," William says. His eyes flash, and it's obvious that he gives many, many fucks. "I want you off my estate."

"This isn't yours yet. It belongs to your father, and he needed me," Sebastian repeats to William. "I won't turn away from an old friend."

"You turned away from me," William mutters bitterly.

Sebastian sighs. "You told me you never wanted to see me again. I obeyed your wish."

"And yet you showed up at my school. I heard you were offered a position tending to the library at the Ferrara di Monte Baldo. A dream job for the great Biblical Scholar Sebastian Pearce, but you turned it down to be a university cleric?" William's lip curls back with malice. "You want to pretend that had nothing to do with me?"

"Of course I came to Blackfriars for you," Sebastian says, with that same casual affection he so often used with me. "I had to look out for you. If I left you alone with Montague…"

His words hang in the air. And I remember a night, many months ago now, when I'd fled the college pub after Monty stiffed me for a bill I couldn't possibly afford. I ran through the doors of St. Benedict's Cathedral just as William was running the other way, his eyes wild with fear.

He'd been to see Sebastian. But why?

"You can stop trying to protect me," William hisses. "I'm fine."

"You're not fine. You're a *mess*. You broke up with George. And what about everything you told me in confession that night? You're hiding something from me, and I won't stand for it." Sebastian studies William's face. "*Did* you kill that girl?"

"I wish that I had," William grinds out. "It would be easier to bear than this hell."

"What hell?" Sebastian cries. "It can only be a hell of your own making. George thinks the Orpheus Society had something to do with that student's death—"

"Don't talk to me about George." William whirls away, his face twisting with rage. My name on his lips sends a shudder through my body.

After all this time, after the heartache, he still has this effect on me.

In one fluid motion, Sebastian reaches across the altar and grabs the collar of William's shirt. William tries to twist away, but Sebastian jerks him forward, stretching him across the altar so he stands on tiptoes.

William's cry is cut off by Sebastian mashing his lips against his.

6

W *hat the fuck?*

Sebastian. Is. Kissing. William.

I can't breathe. I can't move. I'm fixated on the impossible sight before me.

They hate each other. How is this possible?

At first, William resists the kiss. He plants his hands on Sebastian's shoulders, and I think he's going to shove him off. But instead, he grips him tighter. They cling to each other, kissing like their mouths are the uncreased pages of a book they're desperate to devour.

And I *know*.

This isn't new. This isn't Sebastian throwing himself at the nearest warm body to cool the heat we ignited at the bacchanal.

This is what's been between them.

This is the unspoken rift that started many years ago, the reason they can't be in the same room together, the catalyst for the jealousy that tears through them every time I talk about the other.

I don't understand it. But as I watch them with breath

hitched and arteries on fire, I *believe* it. The rightness of them, together, feels baked into the stones of this chapel.

"You know what you need to do, Pretty Boy," Sebastian says, in that buttery, commanding voice of his, that voice that demands to be obeyed. "You know you need to atone for your sins."

William reels back, and I think he's going to slap Sebastian. But instead, he reaches for the priest's belt, his fingers fumbling with the zipper while Sebastian murmurs Latin words against his lips.

As I watch, I can't help the heat pooling in my belly, the delicious ache that clings between my legs. I know intellectually that this moment is not for me, that whatever exists between them is for them alone. But I've kissed both those mouths, and something about the way they cling to each other, the way Sebastian commands William with that rough grip and—

"Mew?"

What?

I tear my eyes from the pair of them to look down. A tiny ginger kitten peers up at me from between my legs, eyes wide as the full moon and just as blue. The kitten twitches her nose and drops a mouthful of some kind of wildflower in my lap.

"Mew? Meerrrw."

My nose itches. The kitten rubs against me, and my eyes start to water. I'm no Einstein, but I'm guessing I'm allergic to the pollen in the flowery present the kitten brought me. And she's probably been rolling around in the same pollen, so as she rubs her cheek along my arm...

No, no, no.

I screw up my face. The kitten takes this as an invitation to play, and stands up on her hind legs to sniff my nose.

I clamp my hands over my mouth, but it's too late.

I sneeze.

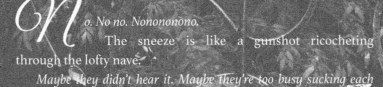

o. No no. Nonononono.

The sneeze is like a gunshot ricocheting through the lofty nave.

Maybe they didn't hear it. Maybe they're too busy sucking each other's faces to—

"What was that?" Sebastian asks.

It's just the wind. It's a bird caught in the rafters. It's the Orpheans playing some bizarre game—

The cat bops me on the nose with her paw. I sneeze again.

And again.

And again. Snot splatters across the intricately-embroidered chasuble. *Great, so in addition to being gross and sneezy, I'm going to hell for snotting all over a sacred robe.*

I dare a look into the chapel. Sebastian and William jerk apart, their passion exploding into panic at the possibility of being caught. Sebastian readjusts his trousers and slides his belt back into its loops, and they both storm toward the sacristy. I yank the robes back into place, obscuring me from view, but it's too late. I'm in the middle of sneezing my lungs out when Sebastian pulls the robes aside.

"Of all the gin joints," he smiles down at me. "William, look who it is."

William takes one look over Sebastian's shoulder, turns on his heel, and storms off.

His rejection of me stings just as much as it did back at school, when he told me I was disgusting. Tears prick at the corners of my eyes. Sebastian must've read my horror on my face, because his features transform into concern.

"George, are you okay?"

"I—" I open my mouth, but all that comes out is a sob. I bury my face into the kitten's fur, which only makes me weep more. I hate myself. I don't have the right to accept his empathy, not after I rejected him and the gift he offered me. "I didn't mean to—"

"Come here." Sebastian leans down and hooks his strong arms beneath my shoulders. He hoists me to my feet. I try to say thank you, but I'm sneezing and sniffling and why am I always such a mess around him?

Why does he have to be so perfect?

After all these weeks of not seeing him, I thought that the spectacle of Father Sebastian Pearce might've dimmed in my mind, that the reality of him would pale to the image I've built up, and so it would be easier to see him as a man, a mere mortal, and not anointed by the hand of his God. But he stands before me in those impeccable black clothes, stroking his soft fingers over my cheek to wipe away my fallen tears, and my resolve melts away.

The kitten circles Sebastian's feet as he rummages in the cupboard and pulls out a box of tissues. I take some wordlessly and blow my nose with a goose-like honk.

"I'm sorry, I'm so so sorry."

"Please, don't apologize." Sebastian glances over his shoulder as if he half hopes William is still standing there. "You probably did us both a favor. Not that I'm not delighted to see you, but what are you doing here?"

He asks the question so casually, like our last conversation where I told him that I slept with William and I can't see him anymore never happened. "I'm playing *apodidraskinda*."

"You're playing—" he looks momentarily flummoxed.

"*Apodidraskinda*. It's some kind of ancient Greek game, kind of like reverse hide-and-seek. It was Monty's idea. I have to hide and they find me."

Sebastian gives me this *look*, like, *you're rambling, George. You've got to give me more than that.*

I sigh. "They initiated me into the Orpheus Society. I'm one of them now. I've taken the slot Keely was supposed to have. To be honest, it's freaking me out a little."

Sebastian studies my face with an intense look, as if I'm some long-lost ancient tome filled with particularly thorny gerunds. "Have you done the initiation ceremony?"

I shrug. "Of course. I mean, they couldn't trash my room because they'd already done that, so they bricked me into the anchorhold, but I managed to get out—"

"No, the *ceremony*." Sebastian grips my shoulders. "That's why they brought you here. They like to do the initiation ceremonies on the lake. There's a little island there with a folly. Have they told you what that ceremony involves? George, you'll have to—"

"Georgie Pie," a singsong voice calls from somewhere in the house. "Come out, come out wherever you are."

The voice sends a shiver down my spine that has nothing to do with the possessive way Sebastian's looking at me.

"It's Monty," I say. "I should probably go back to hiding."

I'd rather be stuck on my own all day and night than have Monty be the first of the Orpheans to find me. The idea of being trapped in some small, dark space alone with my number one suspect for Keely's murder is more than I can handle right now.

Sebastian grabs my hand. "I know somewhere we can hide."

"But you don't have to—"

"Sssh." He drags me into the chapel, across the sanctuary, and into a shadowy corner. We duck beneath a low door, half-hidden behind a towering gold monstrance, and descend a narrow staircase into a gloomy space. I blink as my eyes adjust to the darkness. We're in a rectangular room, the floor laid in checkered black-and-white marble to match the chapel above, but punctuated with stone plaques and statues. Around the walls are brass plaques etched with names and dates. In the center of the room stands a grand stone sarcophagus, the lid carved with the likeness of a woman in repose. Fresh flowers adorn her feet.

"This is the Forsyth family crypt," Sebastian whispers. "The sarcophagus is the grave of William's mother, Lady Isabella."

When he says her name, his throat catches a little. I peer at Sebastian's eyes. Even in the gloom, I can see the demons dancing on the surface of the obsidian irises. He pulls me in front of a wall and points to one of the dark spaces not covered by a brass plaque.

"See this niche? That's where William's earthly remains will rest one day."

I turn away. Even after everything he's done for me, I don't like to think of William as a corpse in this lonely place.

Unfortunately, turning away means there's nowhere to go except deeper into Sebastian's dark, penetrating eyes. And as those inky pools draw me in and his sinful scent washes over me, I forget why I pushed him away in the first place.

Because he made a solemn vow to his God, and he *lives* to serve. That's why.

He's amazing to the students, helping them work through

their problems, and raising money for various student charities. Being a priest is his calling, it's what he's meant to do. I may not understand it, but I can't be the one who separates this beautiful man from his faith. I can't be the one to deprive the world of his holiness.

Father Sebastian Pearce doesn't look very holy now.

He looks *possessed*.

Sebastian backs me into a corner, pressing me against the tall statue of one of William's ancestors. We're tucked away from view, cloaked in shadow. You wouldn't be able to see us from the doorway, but if you stepped around the sarcophagus in the center of the room, we'd be obvious.

Sebastian's body covers mine. It's as if he hopes that if Monty does enter the catacombs, he will see a priest smushed in a corner and think, "move along, nothing to see here." Which... might just work on Monty. But it means I'm pressed hard up against a priest who smells like sin and salvation, and all my good intentions are rapidly dissolving. I can feel every inch of Sebastian through the thin fabric of my dress – the warmth pulsing through his skin, the tautness of his abdominal muscles, toned from swimming. The hardness pressing against my thigh.

"Hello," he whispers, his eyes boring into mine.

"Hello," I whisper back.

My heart hammers against my chest, and I know Sebastian can feel it. He can feel *everything* his proximity is doing to me. All those arguments about why I broke things off with him, why I set him free, crumble around the edges when he's so close, when I'm engulfed in frankincense and black narcissus and those bleak, haunted eyes.

When I just saw him kiss William like the haughty prince is his salvation.

Sebastian swallows, his Adam's apple bobbing. "Are you having a lovely summer?"

"Are we really going to small-talk?" I whisper back. "After everything that's happened, and after what I just saw—"

"You're right." His eyes glimmer. "I can think of much better things to be doing."

Then he kisses me.

It doesn't matter that I'm lost and confused and in way over my head. I don't care that I'm drowning when drowning feels this good. My lungs are full of Sebastian. My chest expands with him. He's in my mouth and in my soul.

Sebastian deepens the kiss. His fingers trail down my arm, grazing the underside of my forearm. His fingertips dance over my wrist, where my blood pounds close to the surface, where my skin burns for him.

His other arm rests against the statue, trapping me, holding my head exactly where he wants it. Sebastian's fingers graze my hip, pushing up beneath my skirt. He strokes gently over my cotton panties, so gently I might be able to close my eyes and pretend he isn't there at all.

Yeah, I'm not getting off this ride.

I whimper against his lips. *Resist. Just pull back and tell him this is a bad idea. It's easy. Resist—*

"No, no, you're not getting away from me again," he murmurs as he teases me through the fabric, stroking slow, languid circles like we have all the time in the world, like we're not pressed up against the wall of a tomb, hiding from Monty. I can feel the heat swelling inside me, the wetness soaking his fingers as he makes a little noise of appreciation. "That's my good girl."

"I—"

I want to be your good girl.

He tugs the fabric aside and pushes a finger inside me.

More. Please, more.

"Dear Lord," Sebastian whispers against my lips. It is a prayer, a liturgy.

He pushes a second finger in beside the first, bracing me against the wall as he twists his hand around for better leverage. He drives deep and hard and with the other hand he presses his fingers into the side of my neck – not enough to hurt or cut off oxygen, but with just enough pressure that I know I'm under his spell. I remember the way he grabbed William over the altar with that alpha possessiveness, and the way his eyes smolder when he gets that rich, commanding tone in his voice, and I wonder with a thrill if Father Sebastian Pearce has a dominant streak—

"Yoohoo, Georgie Porgie, Pudding and Pie."

The voice stabs through the haze of pleasure. *Shit. Monty is right outside.*

His shoes clomp through the chapel, echoing through the lofty space. My heart clenches in fear. I try to wriggle out of Sebastian's grip, but he holds me firm.

Sebastian's teeth graze my neck. My mouth falls open, desperate to tell him that we have to stop, that I can't have Monty see me like this. Instead, he presses his finger to my lips.

Quiet. I must be quiet.

Sebastian covers my mouth with his hand as his fingers dip inside me with a relentless pace. He curls his thumb over to rub my clit in hard, fast circles. Monty's feet clomp around outside, so close to the door. I don't want to lose control, but I can't help it. The heat builds and builds. I can't I can't—

I bite down on Sebastian's hand as my body rocks against the statue. Every inch of me is on fire, molten lava oozing through my veins. Sebastian holds me as the orgasm crests, clamping me in place so I can't move.

I can tell from the flames on the edges of Sebastian's eyes that he loves seeing me come undone for him. He waits until the last tremble leaves my body, then he removes his fingers from me and holds them to my lips.

"Lick," he commands.

I stare at him, wide-eyed. Did he just ask—

"I want to see you lick the taste of yourself from my fingers," he says. "Do it, or I will yell out and let Monty find us."

His eyes twinkle, and I know this is a game to him. We've never discussed this kind of thing, but he's giving me the space to refuse, to say no. But I can't refuse my priest.

Obediently, I open my mouth, and Sebastian pushes his fingers inside. I wrap my tongue around and lick and suck every surface. There's something *powerful* about obeying him, about tasting what he did to me, and the way his mouth twists and a furrow appears between his eyes like it's taking every ounce of holy spirit he possesses not to turn me around and fuck me against the tomb.

I'm the one in control. I'm the one who drives him to the edge of sanity.

Sebastian withdraws his fingers from my mouth. "I think our friend is gone." He gives me a shy smile, an innocent smile, the kind of smile that's completely at odds with the demonic, possessive way he kisses me.

I swallow, nod. I can't do anything else. My legs don't support my weight anymore.

"Let me help you find a safer hiding place." Sebastian steps back, gripping my arms and helping me across the crypt.

"We shouldn't have done this," I murmur.

"You're starting to sound like a true Catholic with all this guilt." Sebastian smooths down his trousers. "Do you want me to hear your confession? Or I could put you over my knee and show you how a good Catholic girl should have absolution."

My cheeks flush with heat. "No, I..."

His smile turns sad. "I appreciate you looking out for my mortal soul, George. But the truth is, I was corrupted a long time ago. I'm not sure God and I will be on speaking terms any time soon."

"But you and William—"

"That's his story to tell." Sebastian bows his head. "William and I have a long, complex history that's intrinsically bound up in this place. I think what happened today is just a reaction to the two of us being in close proximity to each other. And to you."

"Everything I said last term—"

"I understand what you were doing. You were trying to save me from myself. You're a bigger person than I could ever hope to be, George Fisher. And yet here you are, letting this naughty priest put his fingers inside you. I'm honored to be chosen by you. I'm not the person you should choose. I have little to offer you. I'm not..." he gestures around the tomb "—all this. But I'll be a guest here for as long as Sir Henry needs me. If you would like to spend some time together, I am happy to bare my corrupted soul for you again."

I swallow. I know I should refuse, but resisting is too difficult. William and I are already broken beyond repair, so what did it matter if Sebastian and I have a little fun? We're not at school, where this thing between us could cost him everything. Forsyth Hall is like a fairy tale, existing outside time, and maybe here, we can exist outside time and consequences for a little while. "I'd very much like that."

8

---

*T*wo hours later, Tabitha finds me in the chapel, alone, holding a book of Greek lyric poetry Sebastian lent me to pass the time. The two of us hide behind the altar until we're found by Diana, who carries an armload of supplies – food, wine, her blush-pink makeup kit, a deck of cards. She paints our nails and the two of them gossip about people they know while we wait out the end of the game.

Eventually, the rest of the Orpheans trickle in, no doubt drawn to our hiding place by Leigh's loud laughter. There are nine of us crammed in behind the altar, and it's impossible to stay quiet. Our clamor attracts the attention of Percy, the last player still searching, who sneaks up on us and sprays us all with Champagne.

Monty wants to play again, but a bell rings from somewhere in the house. Time for dinner.

It's such a fine day that the evening meal is served around a long table in the east courtyard, overlooking a view of the cascading water and the rows of classical statuary. It's an informal dinner without table service, and the table groans under the weight of delicious-smelling dishes. William and

Sebastian are already there when we arrive, sitting at opposite ends of the table. William scowls at his empty plate, while Sebastian heaps food onto his and digs in.

Sebastian smiles and waves when he sees me. He's still wearing his collar.

My cheeks burn. I'm certain that anyone looking at us could tell exactly what we were up to in the crypt. I press my thighs together, remembering the tightness of Sebastian's fingers plunging inside me and the taste of myself as he made me suck them clean. William's eyes flick over me, and his scowl deepens.

He knows.

Maybe no one else can see it, but William reads me like a volume of Byronic poetry.

A flare of anger burns inside me. William has *no right* to be pissed at me. I'm not his to possess. He made that perfectly clear.

There's another man sitting beside Sebastian, talking in an animated rush, his hands flying through the air like he's conducting an orchestra. He knocks his wine glass – Sebastian saves it before it topples over completely. He's the spitting image of William – the same dark blue eyes, clear and deep, like moonlight on a crystal lake. The same slightly-wavy russet hair, the same haughty slash of a mouth.

This must be his father, the man I saw earlier praying in the chapel. The infamous Sir Henry Forsyth. The man who spent his youth turning the royal family upside down, first with his conversion to Catholicism, then with his orgies, and finally with his wife's tragic drowning. All I know about him are the things Diana told me last night and the sordid tabloid stories.

"William, I'm so pleased to see your friends here again." Henry stands, pushing his chair over in his excitement. He's dressed in tan chinos and a designer shirt with the sleeves rolled up. The dark beads of a rosary peek from his throat. He runs over to us, wrapping Monty into a bear hug. Diana stands on tiptoes to kiss his cheek, and he greets the others in turn as if they're old friends. Which, in a way, I guess they are. I remember what Diana said about him, that he never knew how to treat children, but he was warm and welcoming to adults who shared his lifestyle.

"This is a new face." He turns to me, those moonlight eyes piercing me. I can feel the heat darken my cheeks, as if he can read what I've done with his son on my face.

"This is George Fisher," Sebastian says.

"Of the Californian Fishers," Diana says, trying to make me sound impressive.

"George's father made *films*," Abigail says, in that way she has of making things sound utterly alien and also beneath her. "And her mother...what does she do again?"

I stare at the platter of roasted pork in the center of the table. *She runs a vegan food truck, but I'm not going to say that.* "She's a restauranteur."

"Welcome, George." Henry encircles my hands in his. "It's a pleasure to meet William's friends. It's rare that I see my son or hear about his life, so I hope you can entertain an old man with tales of your carefree university days. Please, treat Forsyth Hall as if it is your own."

The way William talked about his father – or rather, *refused* to talk about him – I expected someone cold and unfeeling. But Sir Henry Forsyth seems anything but. His personality shimmers on the surface, an energetic antidote to William's seriousness.

"And this enchanting creature is new, also." Sir Henry turns to Leigh.

"Leigh Cho." Leigh pulls out one of the chairs and swirls it around so she's straddling, her chin resting on the back. "And before you ask, my parents won the lottery, so they don't do anything except buy Gucci purses online and yell at the telly."

"It's a delight, Leigh Cho. Everyone, sit down, sit down." Henry gestures to the table. "We've plenty of food. I presume you all know Father Sebastian Pearce, chaplain of St. Benedict's at Blackfriars. Sebastian is my confessor and an old family friend, so he often visits me here at the house."

Interesting. So that's why Sebastian is here at Blackfriars as Henry's guest. He's a friend of the family. But this doesn't explain what I saw back at the chapel or why they hate each other—

Sebastian gives a dark chuckle. "This lot don't exactly spend much time availing themselves of my services."

"You see George, though. Don't you?" William says sullenly from the end of the table. "You teach her Greek."

"Yes. George has an interest in the language, and she wasn't given another opportunity to learn." Sebastian leaves the pointed barb dangling in William's side – if the Orpheans hadn't tried to keep me out of Father Duncan's class, Sebastian and I might never have become what we are. "I took her under my wing. She's a fast learner; took first in Greek this year, Sir Henry, would you believe it?"

"I would," Sir Henry chuckles as he reaches across to fill wine glasses. "Sebastian was always a patient teacher. Even before he took the cloth he was teaching William Sunday School—"

"And you think that's an appropriate relationship to have with a student?" William interrupts, glaring at Sebastian. "Especially a female student? The two of you, all alone at night by the roaring fire—"

"Don't mind my son," Sir Henry says to me. "He's overly concerned with what's *appropriate*. Meanwhile, I've dedicated my whole life to not giving a shit about decorum. In fact, I *insist* that during your summer here, you all get up to mischief and impropriety. It would make an old man happy to know his legacy continues—"

"I'm not hungry." William pushes in his chair. He stomps toward the house, leaving an awkward silence in his wake.

———————

SEBASTIAN LEAVES the table with Sir Henry before I get a chance to talk to him privately. I hear them laughing together as they head down to the wine cellar. My face still burns from what William said at dinner. Thankfully, none of the Orpheans seem to have noticed my discomfort. I'm sure what we did on the altar is written all over my face, but bless my new friends who are too self-absorbed to deduce the truth in William's barb.

I crawl into bed that night with my belly full of wine and my head spinning. I thought I'd have the whole summer to avoid both of them, to get my head screwed on so I can survive my second year at Blackfriars University. But now they're both *here* and I'm more confused than ever.

The next morning, Leigh climbs into my bed and we alternate between sleeping off the remainder of our hangovers and guessing what strange games the Orpheans will foist on us today. Our growling stomachs eventually drag us from bed. We clamber downstairs to the breakfast room just as Gareth is clearing away the last of the food. I manage to snag some pastries and fresh strawberries. The Orpheans are in the courtyard, draped on the lawn furniture and nursing their own hangovers. Neither Sebastian nor William are amongst them.

The weather is beautiful, so we spend the day walking in the gardens, playing croquet, and drinking. The Orpheans guzzle pitchers of gin fizz like it's water and they've been in the desert for days. Previously, I'd only known the Orpheans as the people who tortured me, but here, away from school, they became real people.

Percy is a poet. He's very serious, hardly ever laughs. He

wears horn-rimmed glasses that make him appear permanently startled. Anytime we sit down somewhere, even for a moment, he pulls a book from his satchel and starts reading. But sometimes, when you least expect it, he joins the conversation with the driest wit I've ever heard. I can see why he and William are friends.

I know Richard is studying theatre at Blackfriars, and I also know he's Monty's closest friend other than William. I didn't know he has an impressive tenor that he uses at every opportunity, often accompanied by Tabitha. He knows the score of practically every opera ever written (which all sound the same to me), but he also randomly breaks out with The Smiths or Nick Cave.

Alfie is another actor. I remember seeing him around campus with Keely. He loves inventing limericks and sonnets on the spot – sometimes they're funny, often they're in poor taste.

Diana truly embodies her namesake, the Roman goddess of the hunt, of wild animals and the moon, of fertility and children. She prefers to be in nature, wandering the gardens or rolling in the meadow. Once, during a picnic, she held up her hand and a tiny sparrow settled on her fingers. He stayed there for most of the afternoon while she fed him bits from her lunch.

Tabitha can be a real bitch, but she's also one of those straight-talking people who'll always tell you what she thinks. Lies and liars make her uncomfortable, which means she loses hand after hand of poker.

Fatima shares many of the same fine art tutors as Leigh, William, and Diana. She shows me pictures of some of her work – big, colorful abstract landscapes done on bolts of fabric. She's the nicest of the girls after Diana, and she and Leigh are talking about a collaboration when they get back to Blackfriars.

Abigail hates me. She doesn't even try to hide the fact that my very presence annoys her. She sighs loudly whenever I sit down at the table, and makes faces at Tabitha whenever I talk, which isn't often. The rest of the Orpheans ignore her, so I try to do so, too.

She's a writer – but she's the kind of writer that sighs dramatically and talks about her muse a lot. She writes these visceral vignettes with lots of body horror and beautiful women staring out windows. She talks a lot of nonsense and uses phrases like 'existential ennui' unironically.

Monty...I can't figure him out. After everything I learned about him from Diana, I see him in a new light. He constantly seeks the approval of others – especially William – and when he doesn't get it, he turns nasty. He's always skittering around, leaping from one thing to the next, like he's not comfortable in his own skin.

William joins us after lunch. He sets up his easel in a corner of the courtyard and works on a painting with single-minded intensity. I find it impossible to focus on anything anyone says to me when he's so close. My eyes dart to him even when I give them specific instructions to ignore him.

And I'm also aware that I've spent too much time daydreaming about William and Sebastian, and not nearly enough time focused on my true purpose – figuring out what happened to Keely. If most of the Orpheans have been friends since childhood, why was Keely chosen to join their group? What might they reveal about her now that they're soaked in pink gin?

"I'm curious, what're the criteria for joining the Orphean Society?" I ask as we all accept slices of Victoria sponge cake, filled with cream and jam and fresh strawberries.

"At least one of us has to invite you," Tabitha says. "When a place opens up, as it did after Matilda finished school last year, we cast around for potential initiates. If it's someone we don't all know, we might invite you to a Bacchanal to see how you fit in."

I bite my tongue so I don't say that they didn't invite me to a Bacchanal, they *kidnapped* me.

"We have certain criteria we use to judge initiates." Abigail lifts the brim of her straw hat and frowns at my outfit, suggesting that whatever mysterious criteria they have for membership, I do not fit.

"And then we vote. We all have to agree," says Diana. "Sometimes that takes a while. Our last two initiates took months."

She says this with a pointed look at Abigail and William.

What made them agree to have me? I think I can guess. William said that he'd brought me close to them to try to protect me from them. Some of them, like Diana and Fatima, genuinely like me. And others, like Monty, want to keep me close so they can watch me. And then I wonder what was contentious about Keely's initiation. "Did you all know Keely before she started at Blackfriars?"

"Oh, yes." Fatima flashes a mysterious smile. "Her parents are Dublin crooks – small-time gangsters with aspirations. They've been flirting around the edges of our world for years. They'll get anything for you for the right price. Most respectable people see right through them, but Monty's father practically funds their enterprise with his taste for sadism."

"Yes, Daddy loves to buy people he can ruin. It's all so *boring*," Monty darts out his tongue to lick a piece of cream from his lip.

Daddy loves to buy people he can ruin. Monty's casual words send a cold shiver down my spine. I've met men like that before, men who brought women off slave ships in Emerald Beach so they could do whatever they liked to them. Men who had enough money to bury their problems beneath quick lime.

"Monty's father's proclivities aside, the O'Sullivan parents hate 'our sort' and didn't exactly approve of Keely's artistic temperament, so we enjoyed messing with them. Alfie met

Keely at the London Shakespeare Company Summer School, and she spent part of the summer in France with us last year. William doted on her in public so the press would think they were together, and that would stir up drama with her folks. At first, it was just to have a laugh at their expense. But the poor darling started to think William was serious, started imagining herself as Mrs. Windsor-Forsyth. It became rather sad. Still, we were prepared to put up with her – she *was* quite a hoot, but then tragedy struck, and now we have you instead."

"We all adored little Keely," Monty says. "It's such a pity what happened to her."

What you did to her, I think but don't say.

"We shouldn't talk about the dead when they're not here to defend themselves," William says stiffly. He doesn't look up from his canvas.

"Tosh." Richard spills crumbs down his shirt. "William is jealous that he was too prim and proper to take our bonny Irish lass to bed. I keep telling him that he can't keep moping around like a lovesick poet because some bint hurt him when he was a teenager—"

Not some bint, I guess. *Sebastian.*

"I'm not listening to this." William bolts from his chair and stomps off in the direction of the lake, easel and paints in hand.

"How can he paint out here now?" I ask. "It's practically dark."

"He's painted that lake so many times he can do it from memory," Tabitha says. "That's where his mother drowned."

I'd already guessed that. "Do you know what happened?" I ask.

I expect her to give me the 'it's not my story to tell' speech that Sebastian loves so much, but Tabitha can't resist gossip. "It's all so *very* mysterious, and William never talks about it, no matter how drunk he gets. Sir Henry and Lady Isabella had an open marriage. The summers our families spent here – they were so our parents could indulge their love of illicit drugs and moonlit orgies away from the prying eyes of the media. The Forsyths usually shared lovers and often had other couples living at the house with them year-round. That's how William and Monty know each other. William's parents were carrying on with the Earl and Countess of Cavendish for years, until they had enough of the particular Cavendish *tastes*. It was all very scandalous at the time, but to us, it was perfectly normal. We knew that when our parents made that certain look at each other, we were supposed to make ourselves scarce."

"But what happened to Isabella?"

"It was all so terribly sad," Diana says. "You know that priest who was at lunch? Father Pearce?"

"I know him."

In the most biblical sense.

"His mother, Carmilla, and Isabella were practically sisters – their families lived next door to each other and shared everything, perhaps even wives. After Carmilla's parents drowned in a boating accident, she went to live with the Windsors. Now, they're not titled, not *those* Windsors – they were a perfectly ordinary family from Dorset. Carmilla moved in when she was seventeen and started working to save money so she could get on her feet, while Isabella continued her art studies. The story goes that Henry met Isabella at a bar during his travels in Ireland and fell for her ethereal beauty and shimmering kindness. They married young, some say too young, in a Catholic service designed to annoy Sir Henry's family.

"Anyway, Carmilla's husband was a brute, and Isabella wanted to help her leave him, so she convinced Henry that Carmilla should live in the stables on the western edge of the property. William was about seven years old when Carmilla and her teenage son moved in."

So Sebastian and William lived here together. I hold this new morsel of information to my heart, hoping it will reveal all the things I desperately wish to know.

Tabitha continues, "Lady Isabella was wonderful. She could brighten a whole room with her smile. But she was also unpredictable. She fell into these terrible depressions where she wouldn't leave her bed for weeks. Sir Henry took her to every clinic and mental health expert on the continent, and her bouts of melancholia grew less frequent, but no one could help.

"I gather that while Isabella was undergoing a long stay at a French institution, Sir Henry fell hard and fast in love with Carmilla. They fooled around together behind Isabella's back, and couldn't stop themselves even after she returned to Forsyth Hall. Which is basically a hanging offense in a polyamorous relationship – trust and openness are everything. Henry and Isabella always shared everyone, and for him to not share this... Anyway, Isabella caught them at it, and the betrayal drove her over the edge. Or, as it happened, into the water."

"She killed herself?"

"No one knows exactly what happened, since William refuses to discuss it. The official story – the story in the press – is that she fell off the dinghy and drowned," Diana says. "A horrible, tragic accident. But it doesn't seem right, does it? She rowed blues at Oxford. She'd never tip off a boat, especially not on a quiet day when the lake was perfectly still and calm. Some say it was suicide, that she deliberately capsized her boat. Others say that she was in such a state that her usual reason left her. Still others say that Sir Henry killed her after she confronted him about the affair, or Carmilla held her under so she could get at Henry. Whatever occurred, the result is the same. William found Lady Isabella floating in the still water the next day."

Wow. That's horrific. I cannot imagine. And to not know the

truth of what happened...that would be the worst kind of nightmare.

I've never once thought myself lucky because of what happened to Dad, but at least I know the face of the demon who took him from me. Cancer ate my father from the prostate outward until there was nothing left of the vibrant man I loved. I have an enemy I can blame for my grief, but William has nothing.

Tabitha raised her eyes to the steeple of the private church. "After that, William...well, you know him. He became who he is. And Henry found God. All the gods. Instead of couples and families he intended to seduce, he started inviting all these kooky religious people to the castle – hippie cult leaders like Aaron Varney, snake oil salesmen, silent Buddhist monks. He settled on his old favorite, Catholicism, in the end, and he and Carmilla were never seen in public together after that. I think that Sir Henry can't bear the guilt of his part in his wife's death, so he pushed Carmilla away. She still lives on the property."

She does?

Is it weird that we haven't seen her at the house at all?

I mean, it is a big place. Big is not the right word. Emerald Beach is full of mansions. My friend Claws lives in one – Malloy Manor. I lived there for a time last year after her enemies sent heavies to my house and she stabbed one and he bled all over my kitchen. But her entire house – including the swimming pool and the weird succulent garden – could fit into the Forsyth Hall picture gallery with room for one of Gareth's impressive buffets. This is big on a whole different scale, so I guess it makes sense that we could hang out here for days and not see Sebastian's mother.

It still seems weird, though. Why has no one mentioned her?

My Miss Marple senses tell me there is more than one mystery to solve at Forsyth Hall.

9

I'm roused from a dream – a strange dream, where my father walks me through the endless tunnels and stacks of the library basement at Blackfriars and gives me life advice in the form of Pythagoras quotes – by rough hands shaking me.

I peer up from my blankets at a circle of faces bathed in cold moonlight. They're not wearing masks this time, but their white robes billow around naked flesh. "Wakey, wakey," Diana coos. "We're here to take you on a wee adventure."

"Do we have to do the kidnapping thing every single time?" I mutter.

"It comes with the territory," Tabitha says as she yanks off the sheets. I yelp as they clasp my wrists and ankles and lift me off the bed.

Outside the door of my room, Tiberius is slumped in a chair, his head against his chest. Loud snores shake his body, and an upturned teacup lies on the floor at his feet.

"Sleeping pills in his tea," Diana whispers as she pulls a blindfold over my eyes.

Even though Diana's giggling and Monty keeps slapping my

ass, the old fear creeps back. I'm here because I want to find the truth about what happened to Keely, and once again the Orpheans are dragging me somewhere without my knowledge or consent.

As we pass Leigh's room, I lurch to the side and kick her door. "Leigh, I'm being kidnapped." I say it in kind of a jokey way, but if she wakes up and hears me, she'll know I'm serious. That I might be in trouble.

Please, please wake up.

The Orpheans chatter as they carry me through the house. I try to map the turns we take, but the house is so large and confusing that I quickly lose my way.

We move outside. The crisp air caresses my skin, raising goosebumps on my arms. I hear the creak of the kitchen garden gate, and I can smell the sharp, dusty scent of the aspen trees on the way to the meadow. My captors set me down at the top of the slope. My feet sink into the soft grass.

A cool breeze blows off the surface of the lake, kissing my bare skin.

Someone rips off my blindfold. I'm not sure if I'm supposed to act surprised or not. They clamor around me, all talking at once.

"Come on, George. Follow me." Diana waves from the middle of the meadow. She takes off toward the lake.

I follow. With the Orpheans crowded around me, blocking my escape, I don't have a choice.

At the edge of the water, William waits for us. He stands on the prow of a wooden dinghy, oars poised above the water. Like the others, his head is wreathed in ivy and his white robe flutters over his naked skin.

"Life jacket," he barks, tossing an object into my lap. I pull it on over my sleep shirt. I try not to look in William's direction, but as the Orpheans crowd into the boat and I'm shoved up against him, that becomes difficult. His knees press against mine, and it's the most fucking sexual thing I've ever felt. He focuses on something over my right shoulder, and starts to row toward the center of the lake.

"Where are we going?" I ask, a tremor of fear creeping into my voice.

Diana leans her head on my shoulder, her pale eyes glinting in the moonlight. "Our secret place. You'll love it."

I swallow. "What about Leigh?"

"It's not that we don't like Leigh," Diana says. "But this is for Orpheus Society members only."

Our boat bobs across the dark water. William's lantern light dances patterns across the ripples, joined by more twinkling lights in the distance. The oars hit the water with slow, rhythmic cuts. Something magic tingles in the air.

Danger crawls over my skin. There's nothing out here except deep, still water. The same water that took William's mother from him.

Why have they dragged me out here? Did they steal my laptop from my room and find the files of my podcast? Are they planning to dispose of me because I'm too close to the truth?

How do I let myself get into these situations? The first rule of being kidnapped is don't let them take you to another location, because the other location means death. I've let days of partying and pink gin lull me into believing the Orpheans are my friends. But at least one person in this boat is likely a murderer.

We round the bend of the lake, and the twinkling lights on the horizon resolve into lanterns blazing on the edges of marble steps that lead from the waters' edge up to a towering marble edifice. A Greek temple – not a real one, of course, probably a Victorian folly – has been built at the water's edge, her steps extending down into the lake. Six slim Corinthian columns hold up a pediment carved with scenes of satyrs and maenads dancing with their *thyrsus* and passing around drinking cups.

A narrow door lies open, yawning into blackness beyond.

I recognize this place. Something about the color of the marble beneath the cool moonlight, the pattern of ripples against the steps. I've seen this temple before.

In William's paintings.

"Isn't it something?" Diana says.

I don't have words. It's breathtaking and terrifying in equal measure.

As William rows us closer, I notice the crosses carved into the columns, and my mind flashes with another memory. The underground temple in Paris with the same carved crosses on the columns. An Orphean temple. Behind the altar, a dead body, and the remains of a ritual.

Is that what's going to happen tonight?

I grip the edge of the boat, wondering if I can fling myself over the edge and swim for the shore. But we're already so far away and I'm not a great swimmer. There are more of them, and they'd be faster in the boat. I can't get away from the Orpheans, so I cast around for another plan. I notice that below William's feet is a waterproof box labeled with the symbol for a flare. I guess after your mom dies in a boating accident, you get serious about boat safety. If I can get to that box, I can use the flares as weapons or to put up a signal. If I managed to wake her, Leigh will be watching.

Leigh, if you're out there, please get help. Don't do anything stupid. I don't want you caught up in this, either.

We bump against the stone steps. William and Percy jump off and tie up the boat. William helps me onto the stone steps. His touch on mine is like jumping into the shower after swimming in the freezing ocean – scalding hot, but in the best possible way. The lake laps around my ankles. I'm surprised by how warm it feels. The Orpheans move over the steps, drop-ping the bags and items they carry. Percy drags a drum made from animal skin stretched over a wooden hoop, and starts beating it.

I'm terrified. I want to turn and run. I want to dive into the warm lake and swim for safety. But I grit my teeth and stay right where I am.

This is for Keely.

This is for the truth.

Diana takes my hand and leads me to the top step. I'm standing directly in front of the doorway, and I can't help staring into that gaping maw, wondering what horror might be waiting inside. The Orpheans surround me, their hands moving over my body. I yelp as someone rips my sleep shirt away. A soft robe falls around my shoulders. Something jabs into my skull. Warm hands rub some kind of fragrant oil on my skin, roaming unin-vited over the most intimate parts of my body. I'm raw with panic, my mind flicking between this present moment and another time, another starry night when I had my choices taken away.

William, help, please make them stop.

But it's no use. I can't see him. I'm too dizzy. William is lost to me.

Before I can scream, my jaw is yanked open and something stuffed inside my mouth. Hands spin me in circles so I can't see William's face. The world is a blur of laughter.

I bite down and taste a light, fluffy bread. It's some kind of cake with a sweet tang and a bitter aftertaste. Is it poisoned? I try to spit it out, but someone holds my mouth until I swallow.

The panic hits me and I lash out, kicking at anything that moves. I wrench my arms, trying to free myself. I know it's hope-less, but my body won't let me give up.

They let me go. I spin wildly, slamming into a column. I hear

Tabitha laugh, but it doesn't sound malicious. "Oh, George, silly. You don't need to be afraid."

"What do you think?" Diana giggles as she guides me to the edge of the step and points to the mirrored surface of the water. "Tonight, you are Dionysos."

I peer down at my reflection. I'm naked beneath a robe of brilliant purple, the fabric shot with golden thread that shimmers in the moonlight. My skin glistens from whatever oil they've rubbed on me, and the cake makes my throat dry. I don't dare spit it out.

Tabitha straightens the wreath of ivy on my head. "Ivy blooms in winter, and the grapevine blooms in summer," she says as she hands me a silver goblet overflowing with wine. "The vine of life and the vine of death. Drink."

I don't like the sound of that. I stare at the goblet. It smells like red wine, and the color is a perfect claret – but off the top of my head I can think of seven colorless, odorless poisons they could have slipped into this glass.

"It's perfectly safe," Diana whispers. "I poured it myself. I promise there will be none of Monty's tricks tonight. Do you trust me?"

I do. I do trust her. And whatever's going on tonight, it's going to give me answers about what happened on Devil's Night, and to the nameless body in Paris.

I have to do this.

For Keely.

I raise the goblet to my lips and take a tentative sip. It tastes like wine. No hint of bitterness. Not strychnine, then. Monty pushes the rim of the goblet into the air so the wine spills into my mouth. I cough and choke, but I'm aware this is some kind of test, so I keep going until the entire goblet is gone.

"Now, you must descend into Hades for the *katabasis*," Diana points me toward the black entrance to the temple.

Descend into Hades? Yeah, I'm not so sure I'm into that.

I've read enough about Dionysian myths to know what a katabasis is – it's a ritual of death and rebirth. If I'm Dionysos, then I'm recreating the myth where he descends into the underworld to rescue his human mother, Semele. And I know what else happened to Dionysos in mythology. He's dismembered by the Titans. In exactly the same way Keely was dismembered on Devil's Night.

The dark door gapes wide. The shadows within – they have form and substance, a malicious force that reaches for me with invisible fingers. My head pounds. Am I hallucinating this? Did they give me something in the wine?

Or the bread?

"You're not in danger. You've had a little something extra to make the experience more real. It's actually quite fun. Go on." Diana pushes me toward the temple. Percy's pounding rhythm assaults my ears as the Orpheans chant in Greek. I don't know enough to understand what they're saying, but I recognize one word that chills my blood.

Thusíā.

Sacrifice.

Yep, that's not good.

But I have to enter the temple if I want the truth. And they're not exactly going to let me go until I go inside. So I force my wobbly legs to carry me up the stairs. Whatever was in that bread swirls inside my head. Shadows dance on the edges of my vision. Nothing seems quite real, and yet my body tingles with an awareness I've never felt before. The sensation of my robe shifting against my skin, of the cool marble beneath my feet, mixes with the fear in my veins and becomes exciting.

I reach the darkened doorway. The air shifts, the temperature drops. A coldness yawns from within, reaching out with dead, icy fingers to take me. I can't see a thing, so I feel with my feet. Unlike a typical Greek temple with a level floor, the ground beneath me falls away. There are steps downward – an entrance to the underworld.

The drums pound in my ears. I can't turn back. They'll only force me back inside. I have to face wherever waits for me down there.

I descend the steps, aware as I do that the drugs I've taken make shadows lurch in the corners of my eyes. This truly does feel like a *katabasis*, like I am about to enter the world of the god Hades. I can smell the waters of Lethe in the damp air, and between the drum beats, the screams of souls tortured in the deep abyss of Tartarus.

I choke back fear as I feel for the step, and then another, and then another.

A pinprick of light pierces the gloom. I glance up and see a tiny crack in the ceiling where the light of the moon enters, dropping a few feet in front of me into the gloom. It glints off a metal object.

The object moves, becoming a form. A shadow.

And as the shadow steps into the light, I see he has a face.

William.

And he's holding a knife.

10

My fear escapes my lips in a choked scream.

I once had to hold down the trigger on a hand grenade to keep it from going off and blasting me and all the people I love into smithereens. And yet, I've never felt the kind of raw, abject terror that courses through my bones at the sight of William's face.

This is where I'm going to die.

He says something in Greek, but I'm too terrified to parse the meaning. I stagger back, my ankles scraping the rough stone steps. I trip on the hem of my robe and topple backward.

Why did I let them drag me off the boat without grabbing the flares? Can I get that knife off him? I try to remember all the self-defense moves I know, but they all float away on a current of drug-fueled terror. I can't make my limbs cooperate.

"George..."

"Stay away from me." I kick my foot to try and get him in the stomach, but he dodges easily. I scramble back up the steps as he advances on me. He grabs my wrist, and his touch lights my body up even as my mind explodes with fear.

"George, please." His voice cracks. "I'm not here to hurt you."

He drops the knife on the ground. It clatters on the stone.

I freeze.

And then something I never expected in a million years to happen. William drops to his knees on the step in front of me. "I'm so sorry. I fucked up."

"You..." I can't comprehend what I'm seeing. Is this another hallucination? How is it that William Windsor-Forsyth, seventeenth in line for the throne, is on his knees in front of me, his face such a picture of anguish not even Edward Munch could do it justice?

"I messed up everything," he says. "What I said to you that day...I didn't mean a word of it. I did it because I wanted to protect you. From me, from my friends, from all of *this*." He tugs the white robe at his breast, tearing a hole in the fabric and revealing the alabaster smoothness of his skin. "I thought that if you hated me, you'd be safe from me. And I thought I'd be safe from you, from the way you make me feel."

"And how's that?" I manage to choke out.

"Like you're a book where every word fills me with such wonder that I must close it in the middle of a chapter and turn off the lights just so I have something exciting to look forward to when I next crawl into bed. Like I wish that I had died before I met you, because living without you is like dying every day."

My mouth has gone numb. What can I say to that? William's eyes are like cut crystals, their surface shimmering with prisms of color.

He can't feel this way about me. He can't.

"All these days you've been here, in my home, being your beautiful, impossible self, they are the most exquisite torture because they have shown me all that I lost by being a selfish, cowardly oaf. You don't fit here, and it makes me see that I don't fit here, either. That maybe I never did, and that all I desperately want in the whole world is to be like you, to be proud and unashamed of not fitting, to be completely and utterly yourself. I've never wanted to be myself – I don't much think I'm a person worth being – and nothing I've done to you in the last year has changed that. But I'd like to be the man who worships at your feet. I've done nothing to deserve you, and I've done everything to destroy the trust you placed in me. But if you decide to give me another chance, I'll spend the rest of my days making it up to you."

"I don't understand," I say, as the shadows creep around William's face, and I see nymphs tugging at his hair, and the pool of water behind him turns red. The red of the wine I drank. The red of blood. "You're saying that—"

"—that I want you to take me back, if you'll have me." He pulls me closer. "I'm saying that I want to hold you in the moonlight and make you feel everything. I'm saying that if you wanted to run away from this house, tonight, and never look back, I'd follow wherever you lead."

"William, I—"

He kisses me, and in that kiss are a thousand promises. His tongue slakes across mine, speaking silent oaths. And perhaps for the first time, I believe them. Truly *believe* in something. The atheist in me quivers for a god, because in this holy place where a thousand wanton libations have been poured, I alone hold something sacred and fragile – William's heart.

The kiss hurts. It has to hurt, because nothing good comes without suffering. After all, repairing wounds often means cutting away dead, necrotic tissue. And we both have so very much to cut.

William crushes me against him, and our thin robes do nothing to hide the way our bodies fit together as if they're made for each other, as if we're two halves of Aristophanes' orbular people coming together, reunited where we had been so cruelly severed. I open my eyes and I see him, eyes shimmering like the water he paints, mouth twisting into a smile that's no longer cruel but hopeful.

And, behind his head, standing in the shaft of moonlight, the god himself. Dionysos, the horned one, with a leopard skin covering his shoulder, and his skin slashed with lines of rough stitches, like a Frankenstein's monster of limbs and spare parts.

11

"*W*hat the fuck?"

I jerk back. William's face crumples. I point a trembling finger to the god behind him. As William turns, Dionysos dissolves into shadow.

"What do you see?"

"I don't know." I rub my eyes. "The shadows...it looked like Dionysos, but that can't be possible—"

"It's the cake," William murmurs, touching my chin. "They're made from an ancient grain with hallucinogenic properties. You see things, experience feelings and emotions more fully, but apart from that, it's harmless. You're still in control of your body. But if you don't want me to touch you while you're under its influence—"

In response, I pull him to me and fuck his mouth with my tongue. I've been starved of the taste of him for weeks, and all these days in his presence have driven me wild with need. I'm a junkie for tortured artists, and he's my fix.

And yeah, maybe I'm hallucinating gods and not in the best frame of mind for decisions, but also, fuck responsibility. Every college student is supposed to wake up in the morning with a terrible hangover and a trunk of regrets. And I do always want to fit in.

But I am still George Fisher, which means that I'm starting to pull together the threads of this case, and I need answers. So as much as it feels physically painful, I draw back and cock my head toward the doorway, where Diana's laughter peals through from the party above. "What do they think we're doing in here? What's my katabasis supposed to be?"

"It is whatever your mind and heart want you to experience," he says. "In the Orphic tradition, Dionysos was first-born as the son of Zeus and Persephone. Zeus declares that Dionysos would be his successor, which angers his wife Hera. So she has the Titans dismember the child and devour him. Athena saves his heart and goes to Zeus to tell him what his wife had done. Zeus throws a thunderbolt at the Titans, burning them up, and the resulting soot covers the Earth, and from it emerges humans. The Greeks believe that although humans are mortal, like the Titans we are made from, we each contain a piece of immortality from Dionysos – our souls."

I know much of this myth from my reading, but I like hearing him talk, so I nod for him to continue.

"But Dionysos was to be reborn again. Some say that Zeus stitched his son's heart into his thigh and grew a new god, while others say that the god impregnated the mortal Semele, who gave birth to our god of wine. The new god was the trickster god, the wine-drinker, the merry-maker, but the first-born Dionysos – he is a god of the underworld, of feeding the dead through offerings of blood and wine, of *resurrection*."

I swallow. Yup, he sounds like an awesome god to chill out with.

"In the myths, after *Dionysos bromios* – Dionysos the roaring – rescues Semele, he ascends with her into heaven, where they both become immortals. When Benet of Blackfriars created the

Orpheus Society, he intended to honor the dual nature of the god in this ceremony of katabasis, the descent into the underworld where an initiate faces his or her own personal monster, followed by their resurrection and ascension. It's almost Christlike, which is why it appealed to the Black Monk."

"And you're my personal monster?" I ask.

William shakes his head as he touches his hand over my head. "That monster is inside of you – the piece of the god left behind. I'm here to draw out the monster and help you conquer him, in whatever way feels right for you. Some people fall to their knees and confess their sins, which was Benet's preferred ritual. Some throw themselves into the water and stay under until they're barely alive. When we initiated Monty, he took the knife and sliced open his arms and we had to call an ambulance."

"Okay, so I don't want to do any of those things," I say. "How do I get resurrected—"

The words are barely out of my mouth when William's lips are on mine again, hot and hungry and tinged with that magical elixir that makes my whole body tremble. He scoops me in his arms, and for the first time in a very long time, I feel *safe*.

"We can do whatever you want," he whispers. "If you're not ready to trust me, we can walk out of here now and I'll tell them what they need to hear."

It's tempting, and yet...I came here because I needed to get inside the Orpheus Society. And that means I need to experience every ritual as it's meant to be done. Which means I have a monster to slay...

Some people fall to their knees and confess their sins...

This is what Sebastian was trying to warn me about.

I think of the podcast episodes on my hard drive, and all the work I'd done to get in with the Orpheans in the name of solving Keely's murder, and all those private details about

William and Sebastian that I spoke onto tapes, not because they're clues but because I want to understand them, and me, and this *thing* between us.

The secret dances on my tongue. But if I speak it aloud, I'll lose my place here. William will never trust me again, and while I'm still brimming with the hurt of him dumping me, I know that I need him. I can always edit the podcast later, when I get to the truth, when I'm sure he's not involved. It's not even a big deal, really, just a kind of spoken diary that will never be shared.

And, fuck it, I want him.

There's more than one way to drive out a monster.

The drugs have heightened my senses, but my mind is clear. I know exactly what I want.

"I'm not ready to trust you," I say, my head swimming with him. "But I want you to make me feel good."

William's pouty lips curl into a wide, genuine smile. He carries me through the water to the opposite side of the pool, where he ascends three steps. Here, there is a stone altar, the sides covered with carvings of maenads and words that I recognize from the altar at Blackfriars – the Orphic Hymn to Dionysos. On top of the altar are several animal furs and cushions.

"Hmmm," I say with a smile. "It looks like someone had plans for how he wanted this night to go."

"To be fair, I also brought a knife, in case you planned to cut my balls off."

I raise an eyebrow. "You really would've let me turn you into a eunuch?"

"No. But I would have enjoyed watching you try."

William didn't know what I'd decide when I descended into hell and found him there, but he *hoped*. And that same hope clenches in my heart as he lays me on the cushions, as he lets the purple edges of my robe fall away, revealing my body beneath the dim sliver of moonlight.

Cool air tickles my chest, raising my nipples to hard points. William circles the table, reaching out his fingers to touch my skin. There's a moment before his fingers graze my skin where something else touches me, some pulsing sensation that's indescribable, and then he's there, his fingers painting my skin with fire and ice. Like he has not one hand but seven, and they are bringing dark and dormant parts of me to life. My skin ripples where he touches me – like I'm made of water, like I'm one of his paintings.

He bends down and sucks a nipple into his mouth. His lips are a hot rush against the cool of the temple. It feels like I have a hundred nipples, and he a hundred mouths, and they're each delivering pleasure that rolls up from my toes to claim my whole body. He grazes his teeth against the sensitive skin, and I can't help it – I arch my back and moan like I'm in a porn film.

From behind his head, the horned god watches.

William moves around my body, a lick here, a nibble there. He is everywhere at once, his fingers tangled in my hair, his lips against my earlobe or stroking the inside of my wrist. He kneels at the end of the altar, pushing my legs apart. Cool air rushes along my thighs, raising goosebumps on my skin. My belly pools with delicious need.

He lifts my leg over his shoulder and kisses the skin behind my knee. It's so sensitive I try to wriggle away, which only makes him kiss and lick and run his teeth over the skin until I'm a puddle of goo in his hands.

William trails kisses along my thigh. The god stands behind him, resting a hand on his shoulder, pulsing dark magic into my prince, into me. William's touch is almost too much. He's right – these drugs make me feel *everything*. His warm breath playing with the cool air, the edges of the robe shifting on my skin, the coal-black eyes of the god bearing down on me.

Why have I never taken drugs before? Drugs are *awesome*.

My dark prince buries his face between my legs, worshiping me with his tongue while his god presides over the ceremony. I'm so desperate for him that in only a few gentle strokes I'm gripped by a wild orgasm – the embrace of a magical ancient deity. William doesn't let me rest, doesn't allow me to ride out the waves of my orgasm in his arms. He digs his hands under my ass and lifts my thighs so he can lick longer and deeper, tasting every part of me and thrusting me into another *ekstasis* that leaves me trembling and momentarily blind.

When my vision returns, the god's face disappears and it's William who peers over me, looking every bit the Byronic hero, the haughty prince come to save me. And I can't help but think of the last man who had me over an altar. *Sebastian*. The priest who walks in holy light but whose tastes are so very, very depraved.

There's a rather Black Monkish duality in that.

I think William might have the same idea, the same memory burning inside him, because in one swift movement he digs his hands beneath me and flips me over. A hand firm on my back pushes me into the furs, as a thousand fingers of fire trail over my back.

"William," I manage to grind out as he massages the curve of my ass. "You should know that Sebastian and I—"

He freezes, his nails biting the skin of my thighs. The air around us fizzes with anticipation.

The god waits, listening, his breath scenting the air with sweetness.

William speaks at last, the words barely above a whisper. "You and Sebastian what?"

"When you left the chapel the other day, Sebastian stayed.

He showed me your family crypt, where we could hide from Monty. He pushed me into a corner and covered my body with his. And he..."

I trail off, my cheeks flaring. Even lying naked on an ancient altar with drugs coursing through my veins, I'm mortified at having to say the words aloud. *William won't want to know the details—*

William's fingers grip my shoulders. "Tell me what he did. Tell me everything."

I screw my eyes shut. I can't bear to watch his face.

"He put his fingers inside me," I whisper. "He made me come."

"And?"

I whimper.

"Tell me, George. I know that's not everything. That's not enough for him. It's never enough for him. He has to make it somehow profane. Otherwise, it's no fun."

William says this with such certainty, I know he's speaking from experience. That kiss Sebastian drew from him in the chapel was not their first.

Just how deviant is my priest?

I don't want to say the words. It was one thing to obey Sebastian in the moment, when his deep voice vibrated through my bones, but to say it aloud, to *William*...I screw my eyes even tighter, as if I might somehow squeeze out the humiliation of it. "He made me lick his fingers after."

William lets out a deep moan, like his soul is being torn to pieces and devoured by the hound of hell.

"This is what I deserve," he says. "This is my torture. I am Prometheus, sentenced not to have my guts pecked out each day by crows but to smell him on your skin every time I kiss you."

My eyes fly open. I watch him reel away from me, his face collapsing with disgust. But it's not disgust for me and my inability to choose between these two impossible men, but by his own actions. *He's punishing himself.*

"William, it's okay. If you must know, I don't know what I was thinking, doing that with him *here*. I told him I couldn't see him anymore, I can't be the reason he falls from grace—"

William snorts. "Sebastian Pearce toppled from the lofty heights of his Lord's favor a long time ago."

"—but I can't be done with him. His pull over me is too strong. I know it's the same for you, no matter how much you hate him. If this is too much for you, if you don't want me, then I understand—"

"Oh, I *want*," he catches my lips with his again. "I want it all so bad I feel it in my bones. His taste and yours are the most intoxicating poison."

"I tried to stay away from him, and I ended up coming on his fingers against your ancestor's tomb." I close my eyes. "I don't think I have the strength to resist him. And I don't want to. So if it's truly poison for you to know I'm with him, then we shouldn't do this thing. Because I don't think I can promise you monogamy, not in my heart."

"I tried to stay away from him, too," he mutters. "But his poison is in my bloodstream. He's part of our souls. I tried to save you both. I tried to keep my own sins from infecting you, but..."

I think back to what I saw in the chapel. I know it's too close to the surface to draw it from William right now. But there's another secret I need.

It takes everything I have to pull back, to sit up on the pillows and lay his head in my lap. The drugs, the god, and William's apology have made me bold, made me see myself not as a lowly peasant looking upon a god, but as his equal. I stroke his hair. "William, what is all of this talk about sin and punishment? I know something happened on Devil's Night, and

Monty doesn't want me to find out the truth. When you hid me in the garden, you were so afraid. What did you think would happen if Monty found me? What really happened to Keely? Tell me."

He screws up his face. "I can't."

"Why can't you?"

"Because." He looks to the door, to his friends outside. "I know they've been horrible to you, especially Monty, but in so many ways I love them. They're my real family. If I told you a secret that didn't belong to me, it would destroy everything. And I've already lost my family once. I've already died and been resurrected. I can't bear to do it again."

He's protecting someone. Someone in the Orpheus Society. Good. That's a good start. There are only eight of them – aside from me and William – so it can't be too hard to narrow it down and figure out—

I lean around and pull his head up to mine. He's tortured by this. I'm standing on a precipice with him, and we either jump over the edge together, or he pushes me over.

"Tell me," I cup his cheeks in my hand. "Did you kill Keely?"

"I swear I didn't touch her or hurt her, but—" William glances toward the doorway, where drums and laughter and cries of ecstasy pierce our gloom. As he looks, something passes over his face in a flash. And I see it's not love in his eyes. It's fear.

I finish his thought. *He didn't kill her...*

...but someone out there did.

"Okay. And you didn't kill anyone else?"

He shakes his head.

"Then I don't care about this secret."

The relief in William's eyes breaks my heart. It's like his whole body releases something. "You really don't need to know?"

I'm desperate to know, but I can't tell him that when he's flagellating himself over it. "I don't need to know. I'm choosing to trust you about this, so don't fuck with that trust. Your friends will tell you what happens when you mess with me."

"Yes. Your friend Tiberius has made quite a nuisance of himself with father's guards," William chuckles. "You truly trust me, after everything I did?"

Tears spring in the corners of my eyes. I'd never said those words to another person before. Since Dad died and I found out what happened to his remains, since Alec LeMarque tried to take advantage of me and nearly succeeded, so much of who I thought I was has been shattered. I can't just put those pieces back together. I'm supposed to be the rational one who holds my heart in check, and yet when I speak, the words taste like truth. "I trust you."

William kisses my fingers as he helps me up from the cushions. "Then you are resurrected."

That's my katabasis? I'm done? I've slain my monster?

It seemed such a small challenge and yet, as William helps me to my feet, my head spins and my tears wet his shoulder, and I know that nothing about tonight is small or insignificant. I've been torn open as surely as Dionysos was dismembered by the Titans.

He holds my hand and together we ascend the steps. When we pass onto the porch of the temple, no one notices or acknowledges our entrance. Percy is beating the drum while Tabitha lays in front of him, his naked cock fisted in her hand. Behind her, Richard pounds away in her pussy, his nails bleeding as he digs his hands into her plump ass.

On the other end of the porch, Diana reclines on a stone bench, as Fatima, Alfie, and Richard kneel around her, worshiping her body with their tongues. She rests her feet on Monty's back while he kneels like a table, stuffing grapes into his mouth. Overturned goblets and discarded robes litter the stone steps.

Percy shoots his load over Tabitha's chest. He waves at us. The end of his cock dribbles a little as he pads over toward us.

"George, you have ascended!" He pushes his glasses up his nose. Even amid Dionysian revelry, Percy wears his glasses. There's something so wholesome about that. He presses another goblet of wine into my hand. This time, I don't hesitate. I take a deep gulp.

William is protecting someone.

Someone who is at this temple right now.

But who?

The most obvious guess is Monty, but I can't afford to make obvious guesses. I need to gather evidence, follow the clues down whatever path they lead. That's how I got justice for my dad, and that's how I'll figure out who killed Keely, and how her death connects to Khloe May and those other dead women.

"Tell us all about your katabasis," Richard says, crawling over on his hands and knees. I stiffen as he slides his hand up my bare leg. William glares at him and he removes his arm.

"Yes, do." Tabitha picks up a bowl of meats and vegetables and starts threading the pieces onto a skewer, which she places over a fire burning in a brazier. "Mine was horrendous. I ran into the wall and hit my head and I was bleeding in the water. That's why we always have someone to act as a guide. In Benet's day, you went alone, and sometimes people didn't come back."

Didn't come back? Like how Keely didn't come back?

"We used to sacrifice a goat," Richard laughs. "Goats are supposed to be the manifestation of Dionysos, giver of wine, but they're also killers of wine, because they eat the grape harvest. You'll learn that everything has a dual nature."

"But then the school started getting antsy about us bringing livestock onto campus, and Fatima went vegan and it became a whole thing," Tabitha rolls her eyes as she strokes Richard's hair like he's a puppy. "So now we eat goat-shaped candies."

From the end of the porch, Diana cries out, lost in her *ekstasis*.

"George knows all this," Abigail sniffs as she stands up. "She did all that research on us."

I can tell by the way she says the word *research* she means the word *stalking*. My cheeks flare with heat, and I wish I could think of a witty retort. Surrounded by them all like this, I feel naked, like my thoughts are exposed along with my body.

I finish my goblet of the god's spirit. Percy, naked save for a pair of curling bull's horns attached to his head, returns to his skin drum and beats a relentless rhythm, while the others dance on the steps of the temple. Through the haze of drugs and the buzz of the wine against the inside of my skull, the beat worms its way into my veins, demanding movement, surrender. I sway softly in William's arms.

"Some music scholars believe there are certain rhythms that can be used to induce a trance-like state," he whispers. "They're used today by voodoo practitioners and other cults. Students of Benet believe these rhythms are present in the Orphic poems, in the prose of the Bacchae, and that they can help deliver us to ekstasis."

Ekstasis.

Ecstasy. The absolute surrender of body and heart and soul to Dionysos – the great primal chaos, the being before creation, beyond duality, beyond balance. Where the constraints of normal society are tipped on their head. For the ancient Greeks, this meant men and women dancing together, naked under the stars. For the Orpheus Society, this means rich, entitled prats unleashing their inner animals away from the prying eyes of the gutter press. And for me, George Fisher, it means that a guy like William Windsor-Forsyth looks at me like I draw down the moon.

William takes my hand. "Do you want to stay here? Or would you like to take a walk?"

I nod. "A walk. Please."

I know that if I stand on that porch another minute, I'll find myself kneeling at Diana's feet, tasting her flesh, and I'm not even bi. I'll say yes to anything Richard and Monty ask. I'll give myself over completely to the surge of pleasure inside me, to the overwhelming desire to lose myself in the ekstasis.

And that's not why I'm here, no matter how much William's warm hands and vicious mouth distract me.

I'm here to get to the truth. And I'm closer than ever.

We descend another set of stone steps, passing onto a path that winds through the center of the island. Owls hoot in the trees. My feet crunch over a bed of fallen leaves and soft earth.

"My great-grandmother had this island made," he says. "She was a member of the society, and Hierophant for the eight years she was at university obtaining her doctorate. For all the backward doctrine of the Catholics, Blackfriars always admitted women, something Oxford didn't allow until 1920."

"The society is unusual," I say, the words swimming around me with a life of their own. "Most collegiate secret societies are male-only."

"It's believed the Dionysian rituals started out as a female-only space, but of course the men couldn't let the ladies have all the fun. But don't ask Diana about this unless you relish a lecture on the entire history of feminism within organized religion." William nods at the temple, where his friends are now howling at the moon, deep in their *ekstasis*.

William helps me down a steep incline, and we step onto a stone platform on the opposite side of the island. Here, the edges of the lake pull closer as the land embraces us, rewilding the countryside into something ancient and primal, unbidden to gardening plans or agricultural needs. The manicured lawns of Forsyth Hall are obscured by the trees. In the center of the platform is a sunken pool, filled with lake water, with some modern-looking spa jets around the edges. William shows me how the pool works. "Water flows in from the lake, here. You can close these pumps and light this fire and it will warm the water, then you let it out when you're done."

"How cool." I sit on the edge, dangling my feet in the water. It's too cold to slip in, and I don't trust myself with large bodies of water anyway, not with the drugs and alcohol in my system. Not on *this* lake, where William's mother died with a similar cocktail of irresponsibility in her bloodstream.

William has no such qualms. He throws off his robe and slides into the pool, his alabaster skin shimmering in the moonlight. He pulls my knees apart and kneels on the stone bench that's perfectly positioned beneath me. His stiff cock rubs between my legs as he pulls me to him, shifting my body forward until I sit right on the edge of the pool.

He rubs his length against me, and raw, primordial need rushes me. My blood is boiling. My skin is burning from my bones, and the only thing that will sate this lust is for him to be inside me, *now*. His cock isn't enough. I want him to tear me open and crawl beneath my flesh. I want him to live in me forever.

"Sweet Georgie," William whispers against my lips as his hands tangle in my hair. "May I stay?"

"Yes."

"May we fuck?" The crass words come out in a ragged, needy grunt. "Because I'm so filled with drugs and poetry and need of you that if I don't back away *right now*, I won't be responsible for what happens—"

I kiss him. No, no, this isn't a kiss. The word cannot do justice to the way I consume William's mouth, the way I bite and flick and taste every hot corner of it. I kiss and I crave and I bend toward him and his cock teases my opening and he's not wearing a condom and I don't care and all I have to do is rock forward and—

A light flickers over William's shoulder.

At first, I assume I'm hallucinating another god, but the light bobs on the water in a very...ungodlike way. As painful as it is, I pull back from William and peer into the gloom. He turns and looks, too.

"Who's there?" I call out.

The light resolves itself into a flickering lantern attached to the prow of a small rowboat. *Have we died? Is that Charon come to ferry us over the river Acheron...*

Thankfully, no. A figure leans over the bow and peers at the island. "George?" Leigh whispers into the night, her voice trembling with cold. "That you, girl? You scared the shite out of me. Cor, it's absolutely Baltic out here."

"Leigh, what are you doing?" William sounds pissed, but he looks toward the temple, and I know it's fear that sharpens his voice. Who knows what the Orpheans would do to someone trespassing on their rituals?

"Quit your panicking, Lord Byron. I rowed over with the light off. No way did they see me. Looks like quite the antwacky party over there, but I couldn't see either of you so I came around and..." she waves her arms in wild circles, "...here you are."

"Yes, but why are you looking for us?" William huffs.

"I came to see if my friend is okay." Leigh folds her arms and glares at William. "It's a free lake."

"Actually, it's not. My family owns this land—"

Leigh skims her oar through the water and flings it straight at William. "I'm talking to George. You okay, girl? You sounded awful scared when you banged on my door. You need me to get you off this creepy island?"

William shoots me a look, like, *look what fresh hell you've visited upon us.*

I shrug at William. "I'm fine, thanks, Leigh. The Orpheans did kidnap me, but it turned out to be innocent."

"Innocent, eh?" Leigh nods at my naked body before picking up the oar again. "If you say so. I'm going back to bed. I'll keep dixie about all this innocence."

"Thanks, Leigh." I give her a little wave. "You're a good friend."

"Don't I know it." She pulls her jacket around her ears as she dips an oar in the water to turn the boat around.

As her boat bobs over the horizon, William turns back to me, his lips tugging into a wolfish grin. "Now, where were we?"

Without preamble, William shoves my legs open and plunges inside me. As he sinks his cock into my body, a gasp escapes his lips. He slides inside me and his cock becomes this living, writhing snake that slithers pleasure through my body without end.

Yup, drugs are *great.* Top-notch drugs.

I grip William's shoulders and come and come and come. I was told that women don't orgasm just from penetration, but apparently I got lucky, or maybe it only works if you're high on ancient grains and possessed by a roaring, double-natured, ivy-covered, horned ancient god.

Ekstasis. This is it. In William's arms, this is what it means to touch a god.

12

*R*AP RAP.

When I open my eyes, I'm back in my room in the palace. The curtains flutter at the open window and a square of diffused sunlight stretches across the bed. I sit up on the mountain of silk cushions and rub my eyes.

Did I dream it all?

The lake. The temple. The wine. The *katabasis*. William groveling before me. The couch. The pool. Leigh arriving in a boat to save my ass. The *mindblowing* sex. It felt like something from a movie – ethereal and wonderful, but tinged with yearning, because places and moments like that cannot possibly exist and I wish they did.

We didn't use a condom. *Fuck.* I'm on birth control but I shouldn't be that irresponsible. *That's what happens when you're off your head on psychedelic bread—*

RAP RAP.

And yet...

My thighs ache like I'd run five miles, which is to say, they ache a fuckton because George Fisher doesn't do running unless it's to a vintage sale. When I roll over, I see a wet, torn purple robe hanging over the back of the chair.

Rolling over makes my head spin and my thighs blush with pain. I collapse back against the pillows. The drug. The grain in the bread. Fuck. Why am I awake? I need to sleep for another seven years. What woke me?

RAP RAP.

Oh, right. That. Someone's knocking at the door.

RAP RAP.

"Come in," I call, my voice froggy and hoarse.

The door cracks open and Leigh's face appears in the gap. I smile at her and pat the bed beside me. She grins, shoving the door all the way open.

"I see His Royal Highness brought you back in one piece." She jumps onto the bed and thrusts something large into my hands.

"He did. Thanks for coming to my rescue," I say. "So how did you find us last night?"

"Please, for a bunch of hoity-toity toffs, they sound like a herd of stomping elephants. Monty was practically shouting outside my door as they took you away. I presume from the look of you it was for a night of debauchery." Leigh nudges the basket. "This was at your door."

"Debauchery...pagan worship...psychedelics – the trifecta of sin." I rub my temple, which throbs with snatches of memory, and stare down at the overflowing wicker basket. "What's this?"

"Present from lover boy." Leigh pulls out a box of Fortnum and Mason toffees and a package of ibuprofen. She tosses the pills to me and cracks open the toffees.

There's no note on the basket, but judging by the contents, it could only come from William. I remember the package he left on my bed after his friends trashed my room – clothing vouchers for companies like Vivienne Westwood that he knew

I'd love. And this morning, he's come bearing artisan toffee and hangover pills and—

"Do you like it?"

My head jerks up. William leans against the doorway, wearing only a pristine linen sheet tucked around his waist. With his smooth, alabaster chest and his taut abs leading down into that delectable V of muscle at his hips, he looks every bit like a Roman statue. Perhaps of Apollo, with that coy smile and that flop of perfect hair over one eye.

"Decent toffees," Leigh says, her mouth full of chocolate. "Next time, I could go for a bit of Russian fudge."

"Well, it wasn't for you," William shoots back, but he's still smiling.

"It's awesome, thanks." I rummage around in the wicker basket. Sandwiched between several bottles of fancy-looking French wine is a box of brownies that smell suspiciously like they contain THC, and a long thing that feels suspiciously like...like...

"Argh!" I drop the vibrator on my bed. Leigh chuckles as she picks it up and wiggles it at William.

"This thing could put an eye out!"

"Maybe that's the point," William says.

I cover my burning face with my sheet. "Why did you give me a basket with a vibrator and pot brownies?"

"It's our version of the 'sacred basket' given to initiates of the Orpheus Society," William explains. "In Benet's times, their baskets contained wineskins, bread made from hallucinogenic grains, and the phallus of the sacrificed goat."

"Remind me not to let the Orpheans buy me any Christmas gifts," I mutter.

"I came to see how you were feeling." William moves into the room, but he keeps his back against the wall. He's treating me gently, worrying that I might regret last night. *Regret my six billion orgasms and seeing William Windsor-Forsyth literally on his knees for me? Fat fucking chance.* "The others won't be up for several hours, but I thought you might like a picnic breakfast."

I bolt upright, my ills forgotten. "I'd love that. Can Leigh come too?"

William hesitates a second too long before saying, "Of course."

Leigh swings her legs off the bed. "You two lovebirds have fun. Don't worry about me. I've got a date with the assistant chef, Gareth. He's going to show me around the gardens, and I might have a forage around the house, see what rare mushrooms I can rustle up. If you need me, you'll find me in the kitchen, elbow-deep in jam."

Leigh skips off down the hall, stopping when she passes William to pinch his bum. His squeal of shock is so adorable I crack up laughing.

"She's something else," he says as he watches Leigh's retreating figure. "I've seen her around the art department, of course, but she hardly says a word. We've never crossed paths before I met you, and I'm honestly sad about that."

"You should be. Leigh's been a good friend to me."

Unlike you. My unsaid words hang between us. William swallows.

"Monty's fond of her. I think he wants her to join the society next year, after Tabitha graduates."

Leigh will join the Orpheus Society over my dead body, but I don't say that. Instead, I say, "Tabitha says that Monty likes to break his toys."

"That's true, but Leigh's tough, like you. She can handle him." William kisses my hand. "I know Monty's difficult, and I won't make excuses for the things he did to you, but he's been a good friend to me. I think if you knew the terrible things he suffered at the hands of his parents, you'd see that he's come a long way to taming his monster. You have friends like that, I think."

I think of my friend Claws, who boiled a man inside a brass bull because he hurt me. "Yeah, I know the type."

William takes my hand. "Come on," he says. "I wasn't kidding about going for a picnic by the lake."

He watches me as I self-consciously pull on an outfit – a rockabilly-style halter dress covered in lime-green cat faces, matching black and lime-green socks, my New Rocks, and a black military jacket I scored from an army surplus store Leigh took me to in Blackfriars Close. William takes my hand and leads me down another hallway to his bedroom.

His room is even larger than mine, which I didn't think humanly possible. The walls are covered in fussy Victorian floral wallpaper, and the bed is this giant carved oak monstrosity. The only things about the room that reminds me of him are the huge windows that overlook the lake and the mess of watercolors, sketchbooks, and easels arranged on a paint-splattered rug in front of them.

"Are these new?" I pluck a sketch from the easel and gaze at it. It's a girl in a purple robe emerging from the water of the lake, stepping in front of the temple. Something about the lighting makes memories of last night flutter in my stomach.

"I couldn't sleep when we got back this morning." William rummages in his closet while I look through his other work. Most of them are studies of the water, painted with the same dappled, careful application of color that is a signature of his work, but there are several sketches dashed off in a rough style – the lines frenzied, the pencil or charcoal pressed so hard against the paper that in some places it's torn through.

I hold one of these up to the light. It's a drawing of Sebastian. He wears the robes of the priesthood, the details of the chasuble and embroidered stole rendered in exquisite detail. The priest holds a chalice, which he tilts so a stream of water spills out. In the water are faces – human faces twisted in such agony that they appear demonic, their veins raised against their skin, their eyes sunken and mouths open in silent screams.

In contrast to their torment, Sebastian's face is serene, commanding. He has that same determined jaw that he gets when he demands I do something filthy.

The drawing is titled with a scrawl in the corner. *Original Sin.*

William takes the sketch from my hands. "That one is rubbish."

"But—" I cringe as he tears it in two and drops the pieces into an overflowing wastepaper basket. He's wearing his peacoat and has a fresh sketchbook under his arm. He takes my hand. "Time to go."

As we weave through the palace, William tells me stories about its history. It seems every famous king or queen of England has eaten, slept, or shat somewhere in these rooms – often in places one wouldn't expect. William holds open a door for me. "My father uses this wing as his private rooms, and for those of his *personal* guests. There's a sex dungeon hidden somewhere beneath here, where my father used to take his friends. Only spiders go there to get their jollies now."

"Can we see it?"

"You're asking if we can see my father's sex dungeon?" William manages to look both horrified and amused. "No, we absolutely cannot."

We stop by the kitchens, where Gareth presents William with a basket, a twinkle in his eye. I peer over Gareth's shoulder to see Leigh sitting at the long table with the rest of the staff. She has them in hysterics with some story. That's Leigh – her family may be richer than Croesus now, but she'll always be more at home with the people who prepare the posh food.

William carries our picnic as we stroll through the gardens

and across the meadow to the boathouse. A fresh breeze blows off the water, and I'm grateful for my warm jacket. His peacoat flaps around his long legs as he hauls a boat onto the water and helps me in.

William rows around the island. I lie back and let the sun warm my skin. In the daylight, the temple has lost a little of its magic. The pedimental carvings are coated in green mold. The god is no longer in residence.

We row past the temple and circle around the island, leaving the view of the palace behind us. As William turns the boat to take us in, I see a second boat already moored beside the pool. Steam rises from the water in the pool.

A black-clad figure waves to us from the shore.

It's Sebastian.

13

"*D*id you know he'd be here?" I ask William, awake of how squeaky my voice has gotten. "We can go somewhere else if you want—"

"I asked him," William says simply.

Sebastian wades out into the water and helps steer the boat close enough to tie up. He holds out a hand to keep me steady as I wobble over the edge to stand on the stone steps. His eyes lock with William's, and a moment passes between them that I don't understand. I have so many questions, and yet I know that what they're building here is fragile, and I can't smash my way into it with my typical Georgesque uncoordination. I bite back my questions and let Sebastian's strong hands deposit me on dry land.

"What is this?" I ask. Even though I'm carrying a picnic basket under my arm, Sebastian has already laid out an impressive spread. Three folding chairs are placed around a wooden table. A crisp white tablecloth flaps in the freeze, upon which sits an arrangement of wildflowers picked from the meadow, and white plates and teacups and silver cutlery. There's a platter of grapes and sliced melons, and a selection of cold meats and cheese beneath a clear cover. My mouth waters at the sight of it. Or maybe at the sight of Sebastian, shirtless, moving around the stone platform with casual familiarity. Maybe it's the possessive brush of his fingers against William's thigh as he helps him from the boat.

"I heard that your initiation went well last night. What did you bring for our picnic?" Sebastian asks us.

"Scones fresh from the oven, clotted cream, strawberry jam," I say. "Shortbread biscuits, cucumber sandwiches, and leftover Victoria sponge."

William digs around in the picnic basket and holds up a bottle of something French. "And three bottles of this, from the Cavendish chateaux in Bordeaux."

"Three bottles. Why, William Windsor-Forsyth, are you trying to corrupt your priest?"

Sebastian's tone is playful. A smile tugs at the corner of his mouth, hesitant to become a full-blown grin. He doesn't know how he's supposed to act around William. This moment between all three of us is new, uncharted territory.

William returns the smile with a nod. He's not ready to smile, but he's not stomping away, either. Progress.

Sebastian has the little wood stove bubbling. Not only does it heat the water in the pool, but he has a billy on top of it, which whistles to signal it's done. "Perfect. I'll think I'll begin with some tea. George?"

"Wine for me." I still haven't got the knack of enjoying tea like the British. Plus, I don't know what the two of them have planned, or why they've been able to put aside whatever exists between them to create this moment, but I have a feeling that to endure it I'll need fortification from the god of wine.

William casts his eyes over Sebastian's spread and huffs with annoyance. "I was bringing the food."

Sebastian shrugs. "I had to sneak into the kitchen to get the cutlery, so I stole a few things while I was there."

William looks like he wants to say more, but instead, he plops down in one of the folding chairs and sets about popping the cork. He pours the first drops into the earth – a libation – then fills our glasses. I sit down beside him, my gaze snapping between them.

"Open up." Sebastian holds out a grape. "These fruits come from the trees on the property."

Dutifully, I open, and he places the grape on my tongue, stroking his finger across my lip. I taste his skin, and it's even more delicious than the sweet fruit.

"Sebastian loves this place," William says. He stares across the lake, his eyes unfathomable.

Sebastian leans back in his chair, hands behind his head. He watches William, and so do I. The air sizzles, every atom on edge, waiting for something to happen.

"This is where my mother died," William says.

Fuck.

I reach across and knit my fingers in his. I'm surprised to see another hand do the same. Sebastian turns William's other hand over and traces his fingers across the palm. He smiles down at William in this indulgent way and I just...I don't know what the fuck is going on, but it makes my heart skip.

William swallows. He doesn't drop Sebastian's hand.

We sit in silence for...I don't know how long. I watch William as he watches the water lap against the stone steps and the side of the boat. I watch Sebastian as he watches William. The billy whistles, but no one moves to make the tea.

Finally, William says, "I should tell you about her."

I squeeze his hand. "Only if you want to."

He locks his jaw. "I know you've read all about my parents in the papers. You know about the wife-sharing, the swinging, the sex parties, the drugs, the Catholicism. You might see the company I keep and assume that I am my father's son, but it's more complicated than that."

"I believe you," I say. 'It's complicated' could describe my relationship with the Orpheans. I came here because I want to investigate them for Keely's murder, and yet with every day that passes, I'm falling under their spell. I like them as people, even Monty sometimes. They're spoiled, troubled rich kids, and I'm finding it harder to imagine them committing murder. And yet... I'll never forget the terror on William's face when he hid me in the garden on Devil's Night.

"My father always did things his own way. He converted to Catholicism when he attended Blackfriars, mainly to piss off his father, I think. His mother was an Orphean, but she was also an aristocrat in the '50s – she had certain duties and roles to fulfill. Father was a member at university, but after he left he didn't have much to do with the society. Instead, he made his own 'cult of Benet' here at Forsyth Hall, first with my mother – who was a barmaid and artist he met on his travels through Ireland – and Monty's parents, and then with anyone he fancied. I didn't like their friends. They'd stay up to all hours playing games, but they never let me join in. Monty would play with me, but playing with Monty is exhausting. If he didn't win, he'd turn nasty. Only my mother seemed to understand that I was lonely." He swallows. "She had a friend, a fellow artist, Carmilla, with a son ten years my senior. She'd invite them often for the weekends, and Carmilla would join my parents' revels, and her son would take me on wild adventures around the estate."

I glance at Sebastian. He nods.

"My mother was married to an evil man," he says, placing a hand over the Celtic cross tattoo on his chest. "I will never call that beast my father, for he doesn't deserve the word. This ink covers a burn from where he threw a frying pan of hot oil at me.

My mother worked and he looked after me during the day, so most of what he did to me was in secret."

I gasp. It's difficult for me – who grew up with kooky parents who loved me fiercely – to imagine fearing someone who is supposed to love me. Claws dealt with her evil uncle with a bullet to the head, which isn't exactly a healthy coping mechanism. And yet, when Sebastian speaks about this man, there's no anger in his voice.

And I understand something about my priest I'd never articulated before. That holiness that seems to shimmer on his skin is a battle hard-won. He's found the heart, the courage to forgive a monster who deserves no forgiveness.

Sebastian continues, "One day, he threw my mother against a wall. He broke her arm in three places. I think she'd known he was broken before then. I remember her asking me sometimes about my bruises, or when the school called to say I'd got into a fight again or said something so bitterly cruel to another kid that they'd be scarred for life. But whatever happened that night severed her love for him forever. She waited until he left for the pub, then packed our clothes and my stuffed penguin into a suitcase and ran here. Henry and Isabella took us in. They gave us a home in a beautiful stablehouse at the bottom of the valley. They invited us to meals and revels at the Hall and made us part of their family."

"And the two of you grew up as brothers," I say, understanding their connection at last.

Sebastian and William look at each other. The word *brother* carries a weight between them they're not ready to acknowledge, but they don't fight it, either.

"You have to understand that I see Henry as a father," says Sebastian. "He's the only male role model I've had. I was fourteen when I came to live here, so he and I have a different relationship than William. He could relate to me. He was never good with children."

"When Sebastian turned sixteen, my father started inviting him to their parties," William says. There's a bitter twist in his words. I caught their significance immediately. William had clung to Sebastian as an older brother, and then Sebastian betrayed him to hang with his father, leaving William alone again.

But that means... "You went to their sex parties?"

"I haven't always been a man of the cloth. At that time, I was a horny teenager with no higher thoughts of divinity," Sebastian says. "And it was a lot more fun than hanging out with a couple of six-year-old boys."

"I'll bet." I lift an eyebrow at him. "Is that where you learned...all those things you've done to me?"

William jabs his fingers in his ears. "I don't want to fucking hear this."

Sebastian raises a long finger to his lips. "A gentleman never kisses and tells."

Is that where you learned to be kinky? Is that where you honed that rich, commanding tone that makes me want to do anything you ask?

Is that where you realized you're bi?

William makes a face like he's going to throw up. Sebastian settles back in his chair and lets the silence of my unasked questions wash over us again. I press my thighs together, trying to ease the heat pooling there.

William clears his throat. "I suppose we should continue the story."

"Please do." I eat a handful of grapes just so I have something to do with my hands that isn't breaking the sexual tension sizzling between us.

William folds his hands neatly in his lap. "Meanwhile, my

father was sneaking around with Carmilla. My mother found out and it...it *crushed* her. It wasn't so much that Father chose her friend over her – they'd been part of the same parties, the swinger lifestyle. She didn't consider it cheating the same way a monogamous woman might. But instead of addressing their feelings in the open, they hid and snuck around and lied. And afterward, when she fell into one of her depressive episodes, he —" William glares at Sebastian "—took advantage of her."

"I comforted her," Sebastian says.

"You *fucked* her," William shoots back. "And she killed herself."

Sebastian closes his eyes. And I see that however much William blames him for his mother's death, he blames himself more. His god's forgiveness doesn't stretch to himself.

"The papers said it was a boating accident," I say.

"They are wrong," William snarls. "She rowed on this lake every day unless the rain fell so thick that it could sink her boat. The lake isn't exactly the wild rapids of the Amazon. And she came *here*, of all places, to the very spot where she found Father and Carmilla going at it like rabbits. It was no accident."

I move my chair against his and curl my body around him, allowing his pain to sear my own skin. My heart breaks for his loss. I know what it is to lose a parent, but my father died after a short, sharp battle with cancer. His parting words were an inappropriate joke that made his oncologist snort coffee up her nose. I cannot fathom the weight William carries on his heart, believing that his mother *chose* to leave him, that once again, one of his parents was so distracted by their own lives that they didn't see the child crying out for love.

All William has ever wanted is to be *seen*. And everyone – Henry, Monty, Sebastian, Isabella – they've left him behind. All those achievements he pursued, he did them to try to paint edges on himself, to make himself visible to the world. But all the world sees when they look at William is his father and this debaucherous house, and all his father sees was a strange little person who interrupted his fun. William feels like a ghost in his own home, and as beautiful as it is here, I understand how his feelings for Forsyth Hall, for Sebastian, for Sir Henry, are tangled around his heart, squeezing so he can't breathe.

"I couldn't bear to remain here after that," William says. "I went away to boarding school, and in the holidays I would go with Monty's family to France or to the Maldives with Diana, or I'd hole up in a pied-à-terre in New York and paint until my fingers bled. But wherever I go, this place stays with me, haunts me."

He's talking about his artwork, the studies of the water that he paints over and over, trying to understand what sent his mother into the lake that day. Trying to reconcile his love for her with her abandonment.

"And I couldn't bear to be away from this place," Sebastian says. "How can you not? I felt like I had purpose. After Isabella died, my mother needed me, and Henry needed me. As much as he'd grown out of love with Isabella, he still cared for her deeply. He believes her death is a divine punishment for his sin. He flung himself into the religion that had once been only a prop for his rebellion. I saw the comfort it brought him, and I wanted to be the person who brought such comfort to others who suffer. With Sir Henry's blessing, I went to college and then to seminary, and then took the job at Blackfriars two years ago."

Of course I came to Blackfriars for you. Sebastian's words from the chapel fly through my head. I know they haven't given me every chapter of their story yet, but that's okay. Sitting here with my head on William's shoulder and our hands clenched together, I know we're not done writing this tale yet.

"But what about your mother?" I ask Sebastian, dancing

around the question of the two of them. They'll tell me when they're ready.

"She still lives here," he says. "She has a beautiful home in the stables."

"And she and Henry—"

Sebastian hangs his head. "They haven't spoken since Isabella's death. It's why I come as often as I can – I'm the go-between for Mum and the Big House. The plumbing at the stablehouse needs redoing and she can't talk to Sir Henry about it."

I stare at Sebastian. He shrugs. "Ah, Miss Marple. You see right through me. I come for other reasons, of course. Sir Henry needs to make his confessions. He needs reassurance that he's on a path toward absolution, even though nothing I say to him can rub away the stain of his own guilt. I come for him, because he's the only father I've ever known. And I come because I need to stand at the altar and remember the time I laid a teenage prince upon it and took his innocence."

"Fuck you." William jerks his hand from Sebastian's. He tries to stand up, but I hold him firm.

"I saw you kiss in the chapel," I say.

Neither speaks for the longest time. Just when I think I'll have to give up ever hearing the truth of it, Sebastian says, "Isabella isn't the only person I took advantage of."

William's words come back to me. *He lures you in with smiles and prayers until you feel safe in his arms. But he's no godly man. He's a monster.*

William swallows. "I came to you. I wanted you."

He squeezes my fingers so tight that my knucklebones crack. It's hard for him to admit this, after so many years of telling himself he hates Sebastian for taking advantage of him, but really it's that he hates himself for trusting another person and getting his heart stomped on. Again. That's a feeling I can definitely relate to.

"You were fifteen," Sebastian says. "You were lost. You didn't know what you wanted."

"I wanted *you*." William bites his lip. A drop of blood appears on his flawless skin.

The tension between them is too much. I don't know what they need, but I have to do something or we will go round and round in circles. I get up from my seat and pad across the stones. My skin prickles from their eyes on me. I keep my back to them as I unfasten my dress and pull it over my head.

I step out of my underwear. The sun kisses my bare skin. I hear William's sharp intake of breath.

I slide into the water. The stove has taken the edge off – it's like relaxing into a deep, sensuous bath. Petals from the wild-flowers surrounding the platform dot the surface, scenting the air with heady sweetness.

I turn around and face them, leaning against the edge of the pool and letting my legs float out behind me.

"Here's the thing," I say. "I don't believe in God. Either of your gods. I don't believe in magic or tarot cards or ouija boards. Crystals are just pretty rocks. Astrology is a great joke the Babylonians played on the world. But despite this, I can't help but wonder if some higher power has pushed the three of us together."

"I believe that," Sebastian says. William snorts.

I swallow, my stomach tightening as I consider what I'm about to tell them. "I've never said this to anyone before, and after today I might not be brave enough to say it again, but here it is. I love you," to William. "And I love you," to Sebastian.

William's lips part a little. Sebastian shifts forward in his chair, leaning close so he doesn't miss a single word I say.

I touch my hand over my heart. "I love you both. And I can't separate my feelings. I can't love you as two separate parts. Plato says that to properly love someone, you must love them as a whole. You cannot love only a piece of them at the exclusion of the rest. And so it goes with us. I cannot love you apart. And the fact that neither of you has asked me to..." I hold up my hand, splashing a little water over William's boat shoes. "I don't know what to make of it, but I'm laying down the truth right here. If you want to do this...*whatever* it is...with me, then you have to do it together, too. You have to bury the hurt of the past and love each other as a whole. Would you do that, for me?"

"Plato says a lot about love," Sebastian says, leaning back in his chair and casting his dark eyes over William. "Much of it is nonsense."

"Every heart sings a song," William shoots back. "Incomplete, until another heart whispers back. Those who wish to sing always find a song. At the touch of a lover, everyone becomes a poet."

"So you did pay attention in my lessons," Sebastian grins. He leans across the table and grabs William's collar at the same time William cups his hand to the priest's cheek.

They come together, teeth clashing, lips hungry, tongues warring for dominance. The table overturns, sending crockery shattering and grapes bouncing over the stones. Their kiss is hard, violent – after so many years of yearning and hating, how can it be anything but?

Sebastian loops his fingers in William's belt and jerks him closer, pressing his body possessively against his. Sebastian walks backward with purposeful strides, dragging William to the edge of the pool, down the steps, into the rapidly heating water. William does not protest. Sebastian drags him until, clothes and all, they stand beside me.

I'm stuck mute by the beauty of them. Sebastian shrugs off his black shirt and collar, revealing his broad, naked chest. Droplets of water cling to the Celtic cross over his heart. William stands mute and awkward, his designer clothes ruined, his pouty lip stuck out and his royal hair all mussed. Sebastian reaches down and touches my cheek. He curls his fingers into my hair and pulls my face into him.

"Little George Fisher," he whispers in the moments before our lips touch. "You truly have no idea of the power you have, do you?"

He kisses me, slow and hungry, his tongue unfurling inside me like a flower blooming. He tastes like fresh grapes and sweet wine, like the sweet red apple the snake held out to Eve.

As Sebastian feasts on my mouth, warm hands circle my stomach. William moves behind me. He unbuttons his shirt and tears it away so he can rest his chest against my back. His hands slide all over me, the way he did in the temple just a few hours before.

I thought that I couldn't possibly handle any more sexual shenanigans after my initiation, but I am wrong. So, so wrong. Sebastian's hands join William's on my body, each of them touching my breasts, rolling my nipples between their fingers until I moan against Sebastian's lips. William reaches down and slides a finger into the hot heat of me, while Sebastian reaches around and kneads William's ass, jamming him against me so William's hardness grinds against my ass through his sodden shorts.

"William," Sebastian growls. "I suggest you get yourself out of those wet clothes."

William's eyelashes flutter against my skin as he pulls back only as far as he needs to fuss with his fly.

"I gave you an instruction," Sebastian's voice takes on that rich, fictive tone. "What do you say?"

"Yes," William murmurs, his lips against my neck. "Yes, Father."

Jesus fuck.

"Good boy." Sebastian coos as he reaches for William. He

breaks the kiss with me to lean over my shoulder and taste his posh boy again. We're all tangled together, hands and limbs entwined, and a craving burns inside me to be closer still.

Experienced fingers find my pussy, parting the lips and stroking my throbbing, desperate clit. I float back in William's arms as Sebastian works me beneath the water, his face in rapture as he regards my body.

"I know you've given William the pleasure of getting inside this tight, slick cunt," Sebastian says as he pumps two fingers inside me. "But would you do me the same honor?"

I nod. I'm too struck by him, by this, by both of them, to speak.

"George," Sebastian's voice grows firm, recriminatory. "I'd like a proper answer."

"Yes," I whisper. "Yes, Father."

Yes, Father. This is so wrong. But it feels so so right. I'm tired of being the one and—

"Wait," I whisper. "Did you bring condoms? I'm on birth control, but that doesn't mean—"

"I'm clean," Sebastian says. "My paperwork is in the basket, if you want to see it."

"Mine, too," William adds.

Jesus double fuck.

"You thought of everything," I whisper. "But when did you two have time to put this together?"

"William climbed in my window in the early hours of this morning," Sebastian says. "I must say, it was a surprise."

"He didn't throw a blindfold over your eyes and kidnap you?" I raise an eyebrow. "He's a big fan of that."

"No, no. I'm the one who does blindfolding around here," Sebastian clicks his tongue. "Such insolence. Let me show you how things will be between us."

He pushes me against the side of the pool, caging my body

with his arms. I can't escape him even if I wanted to. His cock brushes against my ass, huge and hot and hard, before sliding between my thighs to tease my entrance. For a moment, I freeze with terror, thinking that he's not wearing a condom, but then I remember what he said about being clean. I trust them both, and I've been having Depo-Provera injections ever since the Bacchanal, so we're good. *We're so good.* Sebastian holds me until I relax against him.

"That's right," he says. "Let us take care of you."

In a single stroke, he pierces me from behind, driving up inside me with such force it expels the air from my lungs. I gasp and grip the rocks as Sebastian draws back and slams into me again.

"Sweet Jesus," he whispers. "You feel amazing, George. You *are* amazing."

The way he says it, the hard edges of his voice blasted away, I *know*. He loves me, too. And the reality of that slams into me with his next punishing thrust.

Priests aren't allowed to fall in love.

I should have walked away from him when I had the chance. I should never have accepted his offer to tutor me, never allowed myself to fall under the spell of his brilliant mind and beautiful voice. But I *did*, and now he's trapped under that same spell and we're hurtling toward a doom neither of us can predict.

But Sebastian was doomed even before I saw him swimming naked in that fountain. He may have promised his soul to God, but he gave it to William a long time ago. But what did this, right here, mean for his future? What does it mean for me, to have a priest inside me, whispering the most deliciously blasphemous things in my ear as he fucks me against ancient stones?

I can't answer that question because Sebastian's fingers circle my clit and the hunger inside me demands to be fed. William climbs out of the pool, scooting around so that he's kneeling in front of me, his stiff cock rising from his body like a lewd Greek statue, the head wreathed in purple veins.

"Can you take him in your mouth, George?" Sebastian says. "I want to see his cock sliding between your pretty lips."

I would do anything Sebastian says right now. *Anything.* I tilt my head back and open my lips. William shuffles forward on his knees and places the tip of his cock on my lower lip. His eyes reflect the rippling waters as Sebastian thrusts into me from behind. He doesn't move.

Sebastian reaches around and guides William's shaft into my mouth. I love the feeling of this, both of us submitting, allowing Sebastian to command us, to do what he thinks will bring us the greatest pleasure.

William tastes warm and fresh, like lake water and sunshine, and a little bit salty. Sebastian strokes the shaft as I take in as much of William as I can. I'm pretty new to this and he's so big, he can't all fit in my tiny mouth. Sebastian pumps his hand down William's length, making our haughty prince's eyes roll back in his head.

"Yes," Sebastian purrs against my ear as I take another inch of William, as I feel his tip at the back of my throat. "That's it, George. Take all of him in. Take both of us in."

Through my body, they can touch each other, be with each other, and the pain is a little less raw. I can be the conduit that brings them home to each other.

Sebastian's thumb drums against my clit, sending me toppling over the edge. I pull my two lovers after me – first William, whose saltiness slams into the back of my throat, then our priest, who whispers a final prayer as his muscles tighten and he comes inside me.

We sink into the warm, healing waters, still tangled together, naked limbs and cracked hearts. We are in love. We are doomed.

After we climb out of the pool and enjoy the rest of the food, Sebastian rows back to meet Sir Henry for his confession. William and I stay on the island until the sun begins to set. I read a book and he sketches the water. It's peaceful, just being with him like this. I don't feel as though I need to fill the silence. We can just *be*.

We row back for dinner. I can hear the Orpheans in the dining room as we sneak through the house. William kisses me, long and hard, as he leaves me at the foot of the staircase to my wing. "Hurry down," he says. "I don't want to be without you for even a minute."

After a couple of false turns, I find my room. I hop in the shower and change my clothes. My thighs ache because I've done a lifetime of fucking in less than twenty-four hours, and I can barely keep my eyes open, but as tempting as it is to crawl into bed and sleep for seven centuries, I pop a couple of painkillers and pull on a pair of red cuffed pants and a Buzzcocks t-shirt.

As I brush my hair, I notice my podcasting equipment scattered over the bed where I left it. I'm hit with the desperate need to unload everything that's happened over the last couple of days, to make some sense of the things I've learned. Before I know what I'm doing, I've plugged in the mic and made myself a wall of pillows to create.

When I made the first season of *My Dad is a Gerbil*, I never intended to put it online. It wasn't about finding an audience or becoming internet famous. It was about recording my investigation, organizing my thoughts in a cohesive way, putting together all this complicated information into a story that might make sense to law enforcement. I just wanted them to listen to me, to do their jobs and investigate the funeral home. It was only after they refused to even look at the case that – in a fit of rage – I made the recordings into episodes and put them live on Apple Podcasts.

I'm doing the same thing with my investigation into Keely's death. I don't intend to ever make these episodes live. If I did, I'd have to edit it to take out the bits about William and Sebastian. But I feel comfort in talking to my invisible audience – that horde of people out there who care about solving murders and getting justice just as much as I do.

I hit record and start talking. "Hi, this is George. So much has happened since the last podcast. I'm now a member of that super-secret society, who count among their ranks some of the most influential people in this country. And they told me a few things about my roommate, Keely, that I think you should know..."

14

"Can you take the morning off?" Sebastian asks mildly as he pours tea for William.

It's two days since our picnic on the island, and I'm enjoying the subtle shift in Sebastian and William's interactions. They're still hostile to each other, but the barbs they hurl at each other drip with sexual tension, and I know when we can finally be alone together, the release will be explosive.

We're hiding our relationship from the others, but in moments like this, when Sebastian presents William with the perfect cup of tea, just the way he likes it, and his fingers brush William's shoulders, and the prince stiffens and spills hot tea on his trousers, that I wonder how they could ever doubt that they were meant for each other.

Luckily, the Orpheans are so self-absorbed they haven't noticed anything different, even though Sebastian is spending more time with us than with William's father.

"Why do I need to free up my morning, priest?" William demands. I love the haughty tone in his voice. He knows that in public he can get away with being insolent to Sebastian, and he plans to take full advantage of it. "Maybe I have extremely important things to do."

"I want to show you something. Just William and George." Sebastian holds up his hand as Monty leans forward. "Trust me, Montague, it won't be interesting to you."

"Pish." Monty pouts, but a moment later, he's forgotten Sebastian entirely, because Sir Henry bounces into the breakfast room and announces he's going horse riding if anyone wants to join him.

While the Orpheans chatter about horses and Sebastian fixes tea for Sir Henry, William and I peel away from breakfast to head back to our rooms to change. I go to turn into my hallway, but he grabs my hand, his finger on his lips. He pulls me behind a curtain, wrapping the heavy velvet around us as he lifts up my skirt.

"Someone might see us," I whisper.

"It doesn't matter," he says as he kisses me, and it's true. William and I are two college kids in a secret sex society. No one will give a fuck. It's Sebastian who will burn in hell for his sins. It's on the tip of my tongue to ask William if we should join together, if we should make a vow to each other that we'd resist our priest to save his soul, but the tip of my tongue is in William's mouth and he's caressing it in the most languid, panty-melting way and I'm only so strong, you know?

We emerge, freshly showered, our clothes in place, twenty minutes later to meet Sebastian in the courtyard. He surveys us with a warm smile, and I know he's guessed exactly what we were doing.

"Sir Henry has lent us the use of one of the farm vehicles." Sebastian leads us to a large ROV that looks like something from the set of *Jurassic Park*. "It's either this or horses, and I thought George has enough testosterone to handle without adding Lord Buckingham into the mix."

"You named a horse Lord *Buck*ingham?"

William shrugs as he helps me into the middle seat. "Let me tell you, he lives up to his name."

"I used to drive William around the estate in these all the time," Sebastian grins as he climbs into the driver's seat. "You're very safe."

"Don't let that priestly smile fool you," William says. "He's a maniac on the hills. I fear for our lives."

Sebastian gives a wicked grin and guns the engine. I grip the bars as we careen down the slope at an impossible angle, Sebastian yanking the ROV around a tree and onto a bumpy dirt road through the forest. Trees whir past my face as my priest whoops with joy. William's right – he *is* a maniac.

The estate speeds past – a blur of fields, glades, and wooded valleys. Beside me, William's body stiffens. I assume it's residual trauma from Sebastian's teenage antics, but then I look up and see our destination – a tiny, picture-perfect stablehouse nestled into the crook of the valley, with its own separate driveway leading to the main road.

Sebastian slows the vehicle to a crawl as we bump over the farm track. He looks over at William's stricken face.

"You don't have to go in if you don't want to," Sebastian says simply as he stops the vehicle outside a wooden gate latticed with ivy. "I wanted George to meet her and...I don't want to leave you again. You're just as important to me."

William swallows, his Adam's apple bobbing. "I'll go in."

"Are you sure?" Sebastian asks.

William brushes his hand away. "Do it, martyr, before I change my mind."

Martyr. Sebastian's eyes flash, and the air grows heavy with their history. I think this might be a nickname from their past. Of course – St. Sebastian the martyr, tied to a post and shot through with arrows and healed by St. Irene of Rome, only to return to Emperor Diocletian to warn him against sin, and Diocletian ordered him clubbed to death. The perfect namesake for our priest, our Sebastian, who returns again and again to the people who will be his undoing.

I know exactly where we are. I know who waits for us inside this gorgeous Tudor stablehouse, and I tremble with excitement and with dread.

Sebastian holds open the wooden gate, and I step through into the verdant vegetable garden. I notice statues peeking between the lettuces and melons – not the gaudy classical replicas of the Hall's formal gardens (or maybe they're not replicas), but modern, abstract shapes – languid, headless figures that seem to rise up from the soil.

A neat, trim woman wearing a flowing dress and quilted apron splattered with paint throws open the door and bustles onto the step. She's only a little taller than I am, with none of Sebastian's broad musculature, but her kind face, wine-dark eyes, and smooth, deep voice are every bit as enchanting as her son.

"Bastian." She holds her arms wide, and he stoops down to embrace her. Their love radiates from them, burning hotter than the sun. My heart stutters in my chest – a pang of homesickness for my own mother so many thousands of miles away. She would love this garden.

Sebastian's mother – Carmilla Pearce – untangles herself from her son and flits her dark eyes to the prince who stands frozen on her doorstep. "Welcome, William. It's been many years since I've seen you. You've grown into a handsome lad. And this must be George." Her eyes on me are kind but penetrating. "Come in, come in."

She holds the door open and we step inside.

The house is a shambles – it's crammed with wooden furniture in various stages of disrepair, stacks of objects I could only describe as 'trash' – old hubcaps, broken lampshades, boxes of broken crockery – cabinets crowded with books, rocks, crystals and bunches of wildflowers. From the ceiling hangs a million mobiles and wind chimes – they clang and tinkle as we move through the room. Sebastian sets to work clearing books and boxes of junk from the sagging sofa so we can sit down, while William circles the room, his eyes fixed on the artwork crowding the walls. I sit gingerly on the corner of the couch, not sure what I should say to the mother of the Catholic priest I'm fucking. Does she know he broke his vows for me?

Everywhere I turn, I see Sebastian. The photographs of him as a carbon-eyed baby crammed on the mantle, the boxes of British punk records spilling from beneath the table, the books stacked in messy piles, the icons of saints and crucifixes swinging on mobiles above our heads. Sometimes, the shape of him is defined by his absence – a couple of boxes labeled 'Bastian: Lego' and some childish doodles on the wall.

Despite the clutter, the house smells amazing, like freshly baked cookies and smoky incense. The converted stable is such a contrast to the big palace looming over it. I know where I feel more at home.

And it's weird, because I know William has never been here before, that he has complicated feelings for this woman who shares his greatest loss but who played such a vital part in it, but I see William here, too. He's in the haphazardly-stacked canvases leaning up against the wall, the stacks of art books being used as a tea table, the paint and resin splotches on Carmilla's apron. And he's very definitely in the dappled light of the large, abstract canvas in front of which he stands, mesmerized.

Carmilla slams cupboards and rattles tins in the messy kitchen. She returns with a tray of British hospitality – a bright teapot and cups, with a plate of what I'd call cookies but in the UK are always referred to as 'biscuits' because no one speaks proper English. I take a cookie/biscuit and accept a steaming cup of tea, because I need something to do with my hands or I'll knock over a dog statue and cause an avalanche that will bury us all.

A pair of big, yellow eyes peer up at me from the chair opposite. It's the tiny ginger kitten who gave away my hiding place in the chapel. Carmilla picks him up and settles him into her lap, stroking his fur with long fingers tipped with chipped red polish. "George, I understand you're one of Sebastian's students."

Sebastian's eyes crinkle at the edges. He's almost amused by his mother putting me on the spot. My ears burn, and I know they're turning beet red.

"Y-y-yes," I stammer out. "I took his history of religion class, and he's been tutoring me in Ancient Greek."

"He says you're one of the brightest students he's had in a long time." She leans back in her chair, her fingers playing with the cat's soft fur. "Probably a lot like him at that age. My son always loved to learn. He once tried to get me out of bed at *six am* to take him to his first day of school because he was so excited."

"Mother," Sebastian warns, but he's smiling.

"Don't worry, son, I won't tell them about the time you decoded a Latin inscription on one of Sir Henry's paintings and unlocked that secret chamber, and you thought you'd discovered some ancient treasure but really it was Sir Henry's sex dungeon," she grins at Sebastian, the love shining in her dark eyes as he makes a gagging sound. "I don't know where he gets his book smarts from. Certainly not his father, and I was always terrible at school. I couldn't sit still long enough. The only place I was ever happy was in the art room."

"You're an artist?" I ask, even though it's obvious. I want to know everything about her, this woman who raised such a beautiful, complicated man.

Carmilla nods. "For my sins. Sometimes I am also an online marketer, a shop assistant, or a blackberry picker on the local farms – whatever keeps food on the table. I paint a lot of murals for tech startups in London, sell a lot of wind chimes at local markets, and in between I paint and sculpt and do whatever takes my fancy."

"Mum is being modest." Sebastian holds her hand in that quietly possessive way of his. He's showing her that even though he's brought William into her space, he'll protect her from the simmering anger burning between our prince's hunched shoulders. "She's exhibited all over the world. She does a lot with kinetic sculpture and natural forms—"

"This is my mother's painting," William says suddenly.

We all turn toward him. He hasn't looked away from the canvas and doesn't seem to have heard Carmilla's comment about the sex dungeon. He's trapped within the pigment, between the wild splashes and wavering, elegant lines.

"It is," Carmilla answers simply. "Isabella gave it to me when we first moved into the stablehouse. It's from our time in Paris together, part of a collection of studies of the sidewalk cafes and open markets we visited. Your mother had so much talent – she saw the world in a way no one else did. She saw beauty in everything, and her work reflects that. It brings me joy to wake up every day and see this piece of her in my life. You are welcome to come and look at it any time you like."

"And you took these photographs?" William barks, jabbing his finger at a series of frames on the opposite wall. It takes me a minute to recognize the people in the pictures. There's Carmilla in one, much younger, her willowy frame a silhouette against the tall grass of the meadow as she poses for a self-portrait. There's Sir Henry – the subject of nearly every composition –

striding confidently in the gardens or laughing with his friends or nuzzling up to a horse. In one he has his arm around a heart-stoppingly beautiful girl with auburn hair and William's deep blue eyes. The photographs are taken at various places around the estate. There's even one on the steps of the temple.

"Those are mine." Carmilla stands and moves closer to him. "I did a lot of photography in those days. I even turned Sebastian's closet into a darkroom."

"I had to store my clothes in an old suitcase," Sebastian laughs. "No wonder I'm not so fond of traveling."

Carmilla touches a picture of Sir Henry balancing on the edge of the fountain, tousled hair wild about his face, arms splayed out, foot kicking the air, looking every bit like a carefree lord of the manor. Her lips move over silent prayers, and a different kind of love burns bright in her eyes – the love we have for dark, hidden things we know are bad for us but feel so very, very good. *After all this time, she still hungers for him.* "Your father was very different then, full of life and promise. He had this vision of how he could live, how we all could live, away from the rules and expectations society placed on us. He made us believe it was possible, that nothing or no one could hurt us within the walls of Forsyth Hall. But of course, we rotted ourselves from the inside out, like apples still clinging to a poisoned tree."

William leans his cheek against the picture of his mother and traces his finger over the glass, over the beautiful woman in the flowing dress with the smile so like his. I wish I knew what to say to take away the pain in his eyes.

William turns away. "Are you happy here?" he blurts out.

I dig my nails into Sebastian's thigh.

If Carmilla is shocked by his outburst, she doesn't reveal it. "I think that's one of the most important questions a person can ever ask themselves. Look around you. I've made a life for myself here. I have my cat and my art and my garden. I don't have to answer to a man or a boss. My boy visits me whenever he can. My life is full of love, even if it's not the great, windswept, Heathcliff and Catherine love I imagined in my youth. That kind of love burns so bright it eventually turns everyone it touches to ash. So yes, I am happy."

She kisses the top of Sebastian's head. But as she straightens, her gaze settles on the window. I follow where she's looking and notice a wooden window frame set into the overgrown hedge. The glass inside the frame looks handmade, with bubbles and imperfections, and the frame is decorated with jagged aluminum hearts. It's the only place in the house where we can see up to the palace on the hill.

After all this time, after everything that happened, she still burns bright for him.

Carmilla's eyes rest on me. She says, "Sometimes love means setting someone free, even if it's the hardest thing you've ever done. True love is sacrifice. That's what your Jesus would say." She pats Sebastian's hand.

"I have to go," William says. "I need some air."

"Wait—" Sebastian cries, but it's too late. The door slams against the wall as William runs outside. Sebastian lurches after him, but I throw my hand to hold him back.

"It can't be you," I say to my priest as I sprint outside after William.

"William?" I hurry down the path just as he crashes into the gate. He grips the top and leans over, gasping for air.

I come up beside him. I long to place my hands on him, but his face is red and blotchy and his eyes are made of thin, fragile glass, and I think if I touch him he might shatter into a thousand pieces. "William? Are you okay?"

He says nothing, just gasps for air, his eyes fixed on some spot on the horizon.

"William, please." My voice cracks. "I hate seeing you like

this. Talk to me. Is this about the painting? What she said about your father?"

William shakes his head.

"Then what? Is it too hard to be with Sebastian? I know what I said, but I've asked something enormous of you, to forgive him for sleeping with your mother. If you can't, then—"

"What's going to happen when we get back to school?" William snarls. The fire in his voice knocks the air from my lungs. "We keep sneaking around? We hide in a priest's bed and convince ourselves that we're not damning his soul with every kiss?"

"We'll be careful—"

"And when we graduate, what then? Where we go, he cannot follow. He'll end up like her, trapped in a tiny cottage somewhere with only a cat and his God for company, ignoring the fact that his love is turning him to ashes. If love is a sacrifice, then Sebastian Pearce is setting himself up to be the fucking martyr. And I don't know if I can bear it—"

"What's going on?" Sebastian charges up the path after us.

William sucks in a final breath and straightens up, squaring his shoulders. It's as if someone flicks a switch inside him. In an instant, his face is passive, the hunger and pain in his eyes replaced by cool, haughty indifference. He reaches down and takes my hand. His fingers feel cold.

"Let's go back to the Hall," he says pleasantly, as if nothing at all was amiss. "It must be getting close to tea time."

15

*T*he summer days blend into one another. I call Claws less and less, for it seems ridiculous to tell my friend the same story every time – I'm living in a palace with a priest and a prince (and a scarred bodyguard lurking in the background), and we walk in the meadow and memorize Greek poetry and fuck under the moonlight.

Leigh leaves Forsyth Hall after a couple of weeks to visit her family, laden with bags of produce from the palace orchard and jars of Gareth's homemade preserves. She promises to return to school with new batches of mead and fruit wine made from her booty. "See you in September," she kisses my cheek as she leaves. "If you get in trouble, give us a holler."

She's smiley and cheerful as she hops into the taxi, but the look she flashes me as the car pulls away sends chills down my spine. That look admonishes me, *don't forget the body count.*

Keely. Khloe May. The five other women who've died on Devil's Night. They may not be connected to the society at all, but I can't ignore the coincidences or the churning feeling in my gut.

I know that I should still be afraid, but it's hard to be scared of the Orpheans now I've gotten to know them. Even Monty isn't terrible. Okay, he is, but he also has the attention span of a gnat. He seems to have forgotten the animosity between us. And his terribleness comes from a loyalty to William that I can't help but admire.

Besides, Tiberius is still here. After he allowed himself to be drugged by the Orpheans, he's redoubled his security efforts. I don't know when or where he sleeps, but he's always close by, comically attempting to camouflage his bulky frame behind decorative urns or elegant topiary. He *wants* to be seen. Even though he knows I'm with William and Sebastian, he doesn't trust them yet. His job is to remind the Orpheans not to fuck with me.

In front of the Orpheans, William and I can be a couple, and I'm ashamed to admit just how much I love that. I've never been a part of a couple before, apart from a short-lived thing in high school with Isaac the adorable stoner metalhead. I used to sneer at the gross PDA of all the oversexed kids at school, but now I get it. I can hardly walk down a hallway in the palace without pulling William or Sebastian into a broom closet to make out, and there are many, many broom closets to choose from.

The whole summer is a dream made flesh. I spend the mornings with the Orpheans, playing croquet or arguing about Plato or re-enacting Sophocles or Shakespeare with costumes pulled from steamer trunks in the Forsyth Hall attic. After lunch, William and I head off toward the boathouse with strict instructions for the others not to disturb us, and we take a boat out and meet Sebastian at the pool. We eat foods pilfered from the kitchen and we drink sweet wine and we fuck and we talk. We talk about ordinary things, like the music we enjoy (William sadly doesn't share Sebastian and my love of old-school punk and metal) and the books we're reading, and we talk about things that matter, like why Sebastian slept with William's mother.

"Because she was hurting," he says. "And she wanted to chase the hurt away. And I wanted so desperately to be a person who did good in the world, who healed instead of hurt. I wanted to be the opposite of my father. I was too young to understand that prayer is a much better healer than sex. I understand why you hate me for what happened between us, but I do not believe she killed herself because of me. I've seen the look in a person's eyes when they care about someone, and she never looked at me like that. I wasn't a person to her – I was a void to fill with her sorrow."

William doesn't look at Sebastian as he digests this, but he reaches over and knits his fingers in his.

Slowly, achingly slowly, William's walls are coming down. He won't admit it to himself, but he's starting to trust Sebastian again.

When we get back from the lake, I have tea with Sebastian and Carmina in the converted stables. They talk, mostly, and laugh, and I listen, picking through the conversation for snatches of useful information as I build a picture of life at this castle. At one point, all of the Orpheans spent time here as children with *their* parents, who allowed the society's rituals into their everyday lives, who naively believed they could live in an endless Bacchanal away from the confines of the real world. Benet of Blackfriar's rituals are carved into the stone of this site. Whatever ended with Keely's death began here, I'm sure of it.

Carmilla fascinates me. She's so carefree and funny and wonderful and yet...whenever her memories return to those days, her gaze slips to that hidden window in the hedge, and her voice grows thick with yearning. How can she stand to be so close to the man she clearly still loves, and yet remain apart?

Sebastian and I could barely last a month before he's

fingering me in a chapel crypt, and she's lived in the shadow of Henry Forsyth for *years*. How? How can she stand it?

How will I stand it, when we go back to school and Sebastian has to be my priest again?

———

BEFORE I KNOW IT, the summer is over, and I'm riding in William's Bentley north to Blackfriars. He has one hand on the wheel, the other lazily dangling out the window, while I choose songs from my Spotify playlists in a vain attempt to educate him about British punk.

"Why'd you start the song again?" he asks. "I was just starting to enjoy it."

"No, you weren't. You were making a face."

"I was not."

"You were. One of the greatest musical movements of modern history came out of your country and you're poopooing it. And I didn't start the song again. This is a new song. We were listening to 'White Riot' by The Clash. Now we're listening to the Sex Pistols' 'Anarchy in the UK'."

"They sound exactly the same, like a squirrel trapped in a washing machine," he sighs. "And I *was* making a face."

"I knew it!" I thump the dashboard. "At least Sebastian appreciates decent music."

"This is why you having two boyfriends works for all of us. You and he can go to some smelly little club and get your eardrums blown out with this nonsense, while I can enjoy a performance of Bach by the London Symphony at the Royal Albert Hall, and we can meet up afterward at some devilishly expensive restaurant where we mainline saffron gin and debate your questionable music taste until the sun rises."

"Mainline saffron gin?" I quirk an eyebrow.

"Of course." He flashes me one of those rare William smiles, the kind that warms my whole body right to my toes. "Saffron is a potent aphrodisiac. So says Aristotle."

Sebastian left two weeks ago to prepare for the new semester. I've missed him terribly, and from the way William oh-so-casually slips his name into every conversation, I suspect he does, too. Since that day at Carmilla's house, we haven't talked about what will happen when we're all back at school. Every time I've tried to bring it up, either William or Sebastian change the subject or kiss me until I forget what I was talking about.

What's going to happen? Are we going to keep sneaking around and pretending our priest isn't breaking his sacred vow every time he sees us? Or do William and I try to live without him, even though the thought of it is like cutting off my own arm?

I guess we're about to find out.

We pull into the parking lot. I can already feel eyes on us. Students and their parents pretend to look away, but they're watching. Their phones are poised, hidden in the crooks of their elbows or behind stacks of textbooks. They want to see who William Windsor-Forsyth has on his arm.

One of the scouts rushes out to help with our bags, but William waves him away. "I've got these."

We only have a tiny suitcase each. My few worldly possessions are in storage at college, and William pays some insane fee to keep his things in his room over the summer. He picks up both cases and heads for the carved gates. Usually, the heavy wooden gates are shut, keeping the centuries' old separation of 'town and gown.' Only the wicket – the small door in the gates that admits only one person at a time – is kept open for students and staff to come and go. But today, to ease the flow of traffic, both gates are open wide. My suitcase wheels screech in protest as William drags our bags across the ancient cobbles.

Heads turn and whispers greet us as we enter the porter's office. It was like this with Claws, too. I'll never get used to it, to being an object of gossip not because of who I am, but because of who I'm *with*. I'm used to being ridiculed for my clothes and my...*Georgeness*, but even when my podcast hit big, even when I started hanging out with my best friend the mafia queen, people didn't recognize me in the street the way they do William.

The same woman who greeted my reports of Keely's disappearance with indifference lifts an eyebrow when she sees me on William's arm. She doesn't bat an eyelid, though. "Georgina, William, welcome back. I have your keys ready for you. You'll just need to sign in."

"Thank you, Victoria." William accepts a key from her and leans over to study the paperwork.

Victoria places a large, heavy key in my hand. It's very different from the modern key I had for my room last year. "—kept your room exactly as you left it," she's telling William. "George, you're in the Isabella Forsyth building this year."

Isabella Forsyth? As in...I glance at William, but he's engrossed in a conversation with the porter and not paying attention to me. We sign the necessary paperwork and collect our schedules and reading lists. Then William picks up our bags and it's back outside to the gawking crowds.

I stare down at my key as we wander back across the quad. "So, I have a room in the building named after your mother."

"That's correct."

"That's very odd. My scholarship only entitles me to a student room in Cavendish, because it's the cheapest quad. My loyal benefactor, the Duke of Blackwich, is a bit of a cheapskate. And even though he's dead now, his son has been a bit distracted touring his new album to force any changes through."

"Your point, Fisher?" The corner of William's mouth works, like he's trying to smile, but he enjoys holding it back.

"Any idea why I've been moved?"

"None whatsoever." That mysterious smile breaks free of its bounds, and suddenly I understand why people can't keep their eyes off William. They *should* be staring, because he's fucking beautiful.

William leads me to the Isabella Forsyth building, my new home for the year. We pass through a short passage in the corner of St. Benedict's Quad, and the medieval structure rises up to greet us. Built from darker stone than the surrounding buildings, the Isabella Forsyth building is a late medieval addition to the monastery – it was built in the fourteenth century to house visiting clergy and distinguished guests. Although the monks lived in austere cells in what is now Cavendish Quad, their guests had opulent suites.

Students call this building 'The Izzy,' and I've only been here a handful of times – the night of the Bacchanal, and then all those dreadful days when William wouldn't speak to me. The Izzy is small and awkwardly shoved between the south transept of the cathedral and the charred remains of the old refectory. It's a building of strange angles and crooked staircases, without a right angle or straight wall in sight. Students poke their heads out of arched Gothic windows and drag belongings up the worn stairs. Our suitcase wheels bump over uneven floors.

William has the same room at the top of the turret as he did last year. I notice that all his stuff is exactly as he left it. A painting of trees reflected in a body of water sits on his easel – the last thing he worked on before he left campus in the middle of exams. Left to avoid me. I recognize the scene as a view of the lake from the pool, a tiny boat on the horizon – a blur, just out of view.

We drop William's bag and head downstairs to look at my room.

It's directly below William, and across the hall from Monty. William throws open the door and I gasp.

This isn't the bare student room I expected, but a fully furnished *apartment*. I have a bay window overlooking the refectory. A mahogany desk sits beneath it – a stack of books and computer cords sit there beside the framed photograph of me and Dad. Posters of my favorite punk bands adorn the walls, and the marble-tiled bathroom brims with all manner of delicious-smelling products. An enormous bed almost as big as William's sits in the center, covered in a blood-red duvet screen-printed with tiny black skulls. On a reclaimed wooden cabinet beside the bed is a stack of true-crime novels. I swallow back the urge to cry as I realize the fiberglass cabinet in the corner isn't a closet, but a state-of-the-art podcast-recording booth, with my gear all set up.

The room is...it's *me*. Everything about it screams 'George Fisher, only with money.'

How the fuck did he do this?

"William, I—" my throat closes. "I can't believe you—"

"Diana helped," he says. "I don't exactly have an eye for this interior design stuff."

He's wrong about that. There are touches of William everywhere, from the portrait of me from figure drawing above the bed to the collection of fossils sitting on the bookshelf. I sit on the edge of the bed, trying to take it all in. *This is a dream. It can't be real. I can't get to live here.*

William stands over me, knitting his fingers in mine. A look of concern crosses his face. "Do you like it?"

"I love it." I can hardly get the words out. I'm in shock. No one has done anything this...this *lovely* for me before. *Except for the last time William decorated your dorm, after the Orpheans trashed your room.* "But, if this is some way of convincing me you're sorry for last year, it's not necessary—"

"See, this is the hard thing about having money. If you spend it on yourself, you're selfish. If you spend it on other people, you're trying to buy something from them. And if you don't spend it, you're a miser." William sweeps me into his arms. "That's why I never intended to tell you who replaced your laptop and gave you those clothing vouchers."

"Poor little rich boy." I swipe a stray curl from his forehead. "Seriously, though. I don't want you to spend the whole year walking on eggshells, feeling as though you owe me something. I'm trying to take a leaf from Sebastian's God on forgiveness and all that. It's hard for an atheist to grasp, but if you kiss me a little, I think I'll get there."

William obliges, tilting my face to his and meeting my lips in a long, sensuous kiss that tastes like summer wine and dangerous promises. "Maybe I didn't do this for me. Maybe I did it because I think you deserve it," he whispers against my lips, his finger stroking my cheek. "Maybe I wanted to see that sweet smile."

I fist his shirt and bring him closer, ready to pull him down into that insanely comfortable bed, when there's a knock at the door.

"Yoohoo, Georgie Pie. I'm ever so excited that we're floor buddies."

I stiffen at the voice. William pulls back and straightens his blazer. I plaster a smile on my face. "Hi, Monty. Come on in."

Monty pokes his head inside. Diana's golden halo of hair appears below him. "George, do you like the room?"

"I love it."

She beams. "William and I had so much fun doing it. We found that duvet set in—"

"You lovebirds joining us for dinner?" Monty asks. "I'm starving."

LEIGH and I usually avoid Formal Hall like the plague, preferring to grab something quick from the buffet or sit on the roof of her room, eating one of her delicious foraged stews or a steak and Guinness pie and sharing a bottle of mead between us. But tonight, as I walk inside the dining hall on William's arm, a zing of excitement shoots up my arms. My eyes are drawn up to that beautiful Christopher Wren ceiling and the gilt-edge portraits of past deans and masters and monks who watch over proceedings. Benet of Blackfriars looms down at us, his head wreathed in flames from the refectory fire. The flames almost seem to move. A little bit of the magic of my first days at Blackfriars comes back.

William leads me to the Orpheus Society's usual table. He waves Leigh over, and she joins us, along with the rest of the society and about ten other hangers-on. I notice a scary-looking guy with close-shaven hair and rumpled, paint-splattered black clothes staring at the back of Leigh's head with cruel intensity. I'm just about to ask her about him when Monty shows up, his arms around two first-year girls who look at me like I'm the answer to a puzzle 'what doesn't belong here.' My skin itches from the eyes that follow my every move. I'm so nervous I accidentally tip minted peas down my cleavage.

The Master clinks his glass and calls for silence. Sebastian stands to give the Latin prayer. He is so beautiful in his black academic robes, the white collar at his throat. His dark eyes search the room before landing on me and William. He bows his head solemnly, and I shiver to remember that this is the same man who slid his fingers inside me, who gave me my first ever orgasm spread-legged on an altar.

Sebastian returns to his seat, and the Master continues with the announcements, including the warning to the first years about Devil's Night. Monty starts the chant of "Kakodai-monistai," pounding the table with irritating malice. Gravy sloshes off my plate and splatters across my Clash t-shirt.

Last year, when I heard the Orpheans chanting, I thought it rude and a little terrifying. This year, I chant as loud as any of them, banging my utensils and ignoring the looks of intrigue and fear from the other students. I know I won't get into trouble because we are untouchable.

Sometimes it's good to be bad.

After he finishes his speech about Devil's Night, the Master retreats to the safety of the High Table and we dig into our roast beef. "Now that I'm a member of the society, you can tell me all about what you get up to on Devil's Night," I say to William as I slosh more gravy onto my Yorkshire pudding to make up for the losses sustained in Monty's exuberance. I keep my voice even, trying to not make it obvious that I'm fishing for information about Keely.

Panic flares in William's eyes, but Monty steps in. "Oh, Georgie Pie, you're in for a treat. It's the most wonderful night of the year. It's the night where we perform our most sacred rituals, where we invite the god himself to possess us—"

"Devil's Night has been an Orphean tradition since Benet of Blackfriars first founded the society," Diana explains. "It's where Dionysos is worshiped in his role as a divine communicant between the dead and the living, as the resurrected god. It's the night when the veil between the worlds is the thinnest. It's a time of trickery and games, of masks and mayhem. The pranks you saw last year are just the beginning, but they're an essential part of the ritual. It's also the only ritual where all previous members of the society are welcome to attend—"

"Why does the school let you get away with this?"

"Are you kidding?" Diana looks down the length of the table. "Do you know how much money the families of people at this table give to this school? If the Orpheans don't get their Devil's Night, then Blackfriars would lose its position as one of the most prestigious schools in the world."

"So what stunts are you planning for this year?" I ask.

Tabitha grins at me. "We were hoping our newest member might come up with some ideas."

I grin at Leigh across the table. "I bet we can think of something."

16

*A*fter I've licked clean my dessert bowl (British desserts are the literal best), William walks me back to Forsyth. Most of the Orpheans are heading to the Bad Habit to continue the merriment, but I want to get an early night before classes in the morning. I may be an Orphean now, but I'm still a newb, and I'd never dream of showing up for Professor Hipkins' Criminology class hungover and unprepared.

William and I climb the ancient, crooked stairs in silence. In the absence of conversation, the secrets we carry loom large. He's protecting someone. I'm investigating his friends. And we're both fooling around with the school's chaplain, who's supposed to be faithful and chaste.

My prince hovers at my door. I toy with inviting him in, but he bends down and sweeps a breathless kiss across my lips. "I know that look in your eyes, George. You want to study. I'll come by tomorrow to take you to breakfast."

I watch him climb the stairs to his room, my head full of fairy tales. When he's gone from view, I retreat into my room. I shower in my new bathroom and use a mountain of fancy products, mingling different scents together until I emerge smelling like a heady concoction I'm henceforth calling 'rich bitch.' I do an hour of reading and notes for class, then snuggle down into the soft blankets and pick up a book on Jack the Ripper, but I can't concentrate. I stare at the ceiling as the ceiling above me creaks. The soft strains of classical music waft down to me. William's still awake – no doubt he's painting.

William wants so badly for me to forgive him. Do I forgive him?

Do I?

Are soft furnishings enough to make up for the horrors he put me through last year? For the bathroom? For those things he said to me because he was afraid?

William has all the money in the world. Spending it on lavish gifts like this is easy for him.

And yet...that picnic at his house, telling me the truth about him and Sebastian, letting me see him open and wounded and vulnerable, those were his real gifts.

What he's done here, it's not about the money he spent. It's about the fact that every element of this room has been chosen for me. For *me*.

No one has ever seen me, truly seen me, the way William does. I'm George the freak, George the weirdo with the thrifted clothes and the cutesy tattoos. But with this room, I can be completely myself. And that's the gift William says I give to him, that just being around me makes him feel comfortable in his own skin.

I hold my fingers over my heart, then wave them at the ceiling. "I forgive you," I whisper into the night.

17

The first week of classes is brutal. It's as if Sebastian's God knows I'm secretly shagging his favorite priest and is determined to punish me. This year I'm taking more classes in Criminology and audio-visual art, continuing my Greek studies, and adding the history of crime and justice in Europe, because that sounds fun.

When William and I walk into the first of Father Duncan's Greek tutorials, he and Monty are already sitting at the table, cross-legged, a Turkish shisha pipe between them. The air smells of apple tea and spices. When he sees us in the doorway, Father Duncan abruptly cuts off mid-sentence and stands.

"We can discuss this further at dinner tomorrow," he says to Monty, turning to us and clasping his hands with glee. "George, William, welcome, welcome! Tell me all about your summer."

Father Duncan pours tea and sets out simple foods as the other students trickle in. We discuss the summer – not the sex rituals, but the books we read, the poetry we memorized, the places the Orpheans traveled. Diana spent the last three weeks in Greece, painting at the temple of Eleusis. She shows us pictures of the ruins and presents Father Duncan with a painting of the temple as a gift. Father Duncan holds her artwork in the light and gushes over the details.

"Remarkable," he says. "You are very talented, Diana. Of course, Eleusis is the site of the most famous mystery cult in Greece – the Eleusinian Mysteries. Very similar to the Dionysian and Orphic mysteries you're all so familiar with, these mysteries dealt with the abduction of Persephone from her mother Demeter by Hades, god of the underworld. The rituals haven't survived, but we do know that the cult was focused around a *katabasis* – a ritual descent into the underworld, a search for Persephone, and ascension back to Earth. It was a cult of the divine feminine."

"But it wasn't. Not in Classical Greece – it was used specifically to *control* women, to make sure they weren't doing immoral things without men present," Diana says. "The madness of the maenads is a manifestation of male fear over women having power."

"An intriguing idea," Father Duncan says. "Please elaborate."

"The mysteries were based on an earlier cult – a female-centric celebration of Demeter's gifts of fertility and the cyclical nature of all creation." Diana's cheeks redden. "Then men got involved and turned it into a quest for eternal life."

"That may be an overly simplistic interpretation of the shift, but you're correct. While priestesses played a vital role in the mysteries from the Classical period, they were secondary to the male Hierophant. The focus became having a happy afterlife, filled with the things that bring pleasure. Some scholars argue this change came about because the female body mirrors the cycles of that *katabasis*, and women live in synchronicity with nature, therefore they are more accepting of death and do not need the reassurance of a pleasurable afterlife. But the new male leaders molded the rituals around their fear of death."

"So it's a cult dedicated to fragile masculinity," Diana scoffs.

"Perhaps. I think it's more likely a reaction to the changing nature of the Greek world. The earlier agrarian festival was from a different time, and it didn't meet the needs of an increasingly complex, global, and warlike society. Thus, the Eleusinian rituals moved from being a local celebration to a centralized festival that drew practitioners and initiates from across the ancient world. A similar shift happened within the cult of Dionysos, of course. An early version of the festival was the biennial rites of Tristeria, held during the winter on Mt. Parnassus, where Dionysos' emergence from the underworld was celebrated with wild orgies, and women dressed as maenads would chase animals through the woods and tear them apart with their bare hands."

"Is this interest in the afterlife and resurrection why both these cults have their ritual spaces underground?" I ask, seeing a connection to the Orpheans.

"I believe so. The underground has long been important for mystery cults. Of course," Duncan touches the collar at his throat, "underground worship has been important to Christians, too. In times of persecution, Christians have always sought sanctuary beneath the earth – two common examples are the underground cities of Turkey, and the catacombs of Paris. Benet of Blackfriars was drawn to the similarities between Dionysos and Jesus, which formed the basis of his later, more unorthodox beliefs."

My throat closes as I remember the temple Leigh and I found in Paris with the crucifixes carved into the colonnade. Yet again, the duality of Christian belief butts up against the ancient mystery cults. This was Benet of Blackfriars' jam. The Black Monk got off on duality.

I look at Father Duncan, at the way his eyes light up when he runs his finger over the edge of Diana's painting. A ripple of something ancient scents the air with blood. Another Blackfriars' priest obsessed with duality. But what is the price of that obsession?

"Did you have a good summer?" Professor Hipkins asks as she sets down a tray holding...you guessed it, tea. All second-year students meet with their faculty advisors during the first week to determine they're on the right track toward their goals, and if they need any additional resources. That's why I'm sitting in Professor Hipkins' second-floor office, about to drown my tea in milk and sugar in a vain attempt to convince myself I like the stuff. We sit across from each other in two overstuffed chairs beneath an impressive Gothic window. Professor Melinda Hipkins is a research fellow, which means she lives at the college. Her suite of rooms overlook Martyr's Quad and comprise of a large office with tall bookshelves, and a small apartment and ensuite bathroom behind them. "You and your friend were going to backpack around Europe, isn't that right?"

"Our plans changed," I say as I fiddle with the delicate handle of my cup. For some reason, I feel weird telling Professor Hipkins that I spent the summer at Forsyth Hall. Perhaps it's because when I look across at her, I see myself in a few years. Or, at least, someone I hope to be – a clever woman who has dedicated her career to pursuing truth and justice, and who is wearing a Smiths shirt underneath her conservative blazer. She reminds me a lot of Madeline Drysdale, my history teacher at Stonehurst Prep, who's with Tiberius and who now lives close enough we can occasionally grab coffee together.

"That's too bad. You should definitely do as much travel as you can while you're here. It's one of the few regrets I have from when I was an undergrad – I spent my summers in unpaid internships while my classmates were off drinking absinthe in

Prague. It's important to work hard, but you should have fun, too."

"I definitely want to travel," I say. "It's tough on my budget, but we did manage to go to France over the term holidays. Leigh and I went all over Paris. We visited the Père Lachaise Cemetery, the Louvre, the Catacombs..."

I trail off as a shiver runs down my spine. I can't think about our Paris trip without seeing that body buried in the underground temple – a nameless victim of whatever dark ritual had been performed there.

"...and my boyfriend and I are talking about visiting Greece next summer," I add, trying to save the conversation from my odd lull.

"Your boyfriend is William Windsor-Forsyth." She says it as a statement. I jump, splashing hot tea on my shirt. She smiles. "It's a small school, George. The faculty are not immune to student gossip, especially not about our more infamous students. I didn't mean to embarrass you – I'm glad to see you making friends and participating in college life. Last year, you seemed a little...lonely."

"Right," I mumble, dabbing my napkin at the stain.

"I'll get straight to the point, George." Professor Hipkins crosses her ankles and stretches her long legs across the shaggy rug. "The courses you've chosen don't seem to be steering you toward a specific goal. You want to major in Criminology, but you're not taking any of the associated science papers. Instead, you've chosen Ancient Greek? There's not much call for Homeric Hymns in our field. Over the next few weeks, you'll be putting together your proposal for your colloquy, and I can't see you bringing together these disparate subjects. In first year we like students to cast a wide net, follow their interests and figure out where they'd like to focus their studies, but by the second year, when you start your colloquy, we expect a pattern of specialty to emerge."

The colloquy is a unique feature of Blackfriars' curriculum. During our second and third years, each undergraduate must put together a body of work that showcases their studies in a particular field. This is then presented to a panel of scholars and to the student body at large for feedback and debate. It's not as strict in terms of format as a thesis or dissertation, and it can be collaborative – the AV students often join forces with the theatre or fine arts departments to create multi-disciplinary work.

I'm terrified of colloquy, but I'll keep that to myself for now.

"I'm not going to be a scientist. I'm more interested in criminology as a background to my podcast," I mumble.

"That's fine, as long as you're certain you wish to pursue true-crime reporting as a career. It's unconventional, but that's what we do at Blackfriars, and I'm personally a big fan, so I support it. I might suggest you take a critical writing paper instead of Ancient Greek—"

Is she going to make me drop out of Greek?

The two podcast episodes burn a hole through my hard drive. "I sort of started a project," I say. "For my colloquy."

I can't look at her. I stare out the window. Monty and Leigh are in the middle of the quad. He leans against the fountain like he owns it. She opens a reusable coffee cup to reveal a pile of leaves that Monty stuffs hungrily into his mouth.

Oh, no, you don't, Monty Cavendish. Just because I'm sleeping with your friend doesn't mean you can steal mine.

"Why am I not surprised?" I hear the smile in Professor Hipkins' voice. "I was thoroughly impressed by your body farm project from last year, and your work with Dr. Grainger. I'm assuming your colloquy will have something to do with your roommate's murder?"

I nod. "It goes round and round in my head, that she was

killed right *here*, in the woods, and nothing's being done about it. It's not like on crime shows, where the police keep digging until they find the bad guys. So I want to get the justice Keely's been denied. Only, I'm not sure it's the right thing to do anymore."

She taps her chin. "There are many interesting ways with which to approach true crime. We've spent so long idolizing clever detectives in pop culture that we're all dying to be one. We like the puzzle, the mystery, the salacious *game* of it all. And what we might not realize is that our pursuit of the truth is as much about our own need for safety – that if we understand killers, if we bring them to justice, then we can keep ourselves and our loved ones safe. That's why consumers of true crime are overwhelmingly women – because we feel the most *unsafe* in our real lives. But combine this with a cult of personality and a human desire to be clever and well-liked and you get a double-edged sword – even the most well-intentioned true-crime reporter will send an internet lynch mob after the wrong person. Is that what you're talking about?"

"Sort of. I wanted to revisit the material in the Khloe May case," I say. "It has parallels to what happened to Keely. But is that crass? I wanted to explore it in a series of podcast episodes. Does it read as me trying to cash in on her death?"

"The fact you're asking the questions suggests that's not your intent, but I think you'll have to carefully consider the approach." Professor Hipkins shifts in her chair. "But Khloe May's body was never found. It's a missing persons' case, not a murder."

"I know that, but I think the parallels can't be ignored." I tick them off on my fingers. "Both are young women. Keely's body was found in the woods, and Khloe disappeared in the woods. Both students studied Ancient Greek. Both students were last seen alive on Devil's Night."

"Ah." Her eyes glinted. "Hence your interest in the subject."

I nod. "And there are suggestions of collusion between the university and the police to hush up certain aspects of both cases. I think there might be reasons the search for Khloe's body wasn't conducted as thoroughly as it should have been."

"You're talking about the Orpheus Society."

I jerk back, surprised she spoke so openly about the Orpheans' hold over Blackfriars.

She narrows her eyes. "I'm not so naive to assume that a group of students who can shut down the university for an entire night each year to conduct destructive pranks doesn't have some kind of influence at a faculty level. Aren't you friendly with the society members?"

"Yes. But they don't have anything to do with a murder from twenty years ago. Some of them weren't even born yet. And it means I can get inside information about how the society works, if it's connected," I add. "There are other angles. There might be an organized crime connection."

"Are you sure you want to use your friends for information?" she asks. "You're aware that your colloquy will be scrutinized publicly. They will find out."

I nod, certain. "If they have nothing to hide, they have nothing to fear. I found Keely's body. I feel as though it was a message, you know? She deserves justice."

"I agree with you." She steeples her fingers. "I'll accept this project, and your unorthodox schedule, on one condition."

I swallow a mouthful of lukewarm tea. It burns like acid on the way down. "Anything."

"I'm going to give you a warning, and I know you're not going to pay any attention to it because you are exactly like me when I was your age, but I feel it's important to give it anyway. Be careful. That society is a powerful force at this university, and not just among the students. If they have anything to hide, they will go to great lengths to see it remains hidden."

18

"*A*re you sure you're okay with me coming along?" William asks as we walk across the quad toward the cathedral.

I hug my Liddell and Scott against my chest, using it to shield the thudding of my heart from view. "Of course."

"Because this has been a private thing between you and him, and I don't want to—"

I fit my hand in his. Beneath his skin, his pulse quickens. "This might be the only time the three of us have together. I'm not going to hog it."

We enter the church, checking every corner of the nave and chapels are empty of students. I lead William through the nave and into the annex. The door leading to the underground baths beneath the church is locked, but a cold draft blows up from beneath. The door to the roof is locked, too. The key is hidden in a pocket in my organizer. Sebastian's door is also closed. I rap twice. "We're here—"

The door swings open before I've even finished speaking. "Welcome." Sebastian's frame takes up most of the door frame, his broad, swimmer's shoulders practically heaving with excite-

ment to see us both. He gestures to his cozy apartment.
"Come in."

I step inside the familiar room, and my whole body relaxes.
This place was my sanctuary all last year, the one place on
campus – besides the roof in Leigh's room – where I felt
comfortable being completely myself. I never had to look over
my shoulder, watching for the next Orpheus Society
humiliation.

Everything is exactly as I remember it – the books piled in
every corner, the messy bed pushed beneath the stacks, the desk
beneath the window buried under mountains of paperwork, the
boxes of vinyl and a Clash album spinning on the turntable –
except for one small but significant change.

Sebastian has pulled a third chair beside the crackling fire.
For William.

I turn back to the door. William remains in the hallway, his
feet rooted in place, his blue eyes rippled with fear.

"Come on inside," Sebastian beckons him, his voice taking
on that authoritative tone that vibrates in my bones. "You're
letting the heat out."

William takes a cautious step inside the room. The air thick-
ens, charges with energy. Sebastian's on him in a moment. He
slams the door and shoves William so hard against it that the
wood cracks. His hands tangle in William's hair as he pulls our
pompous prince into a violent, thirsty kiss.

I cross the floor to join them. I don't touch them. Instead, I
watch Sebastian fuck William's mouth with his tongue.
William's whole body relaxes as he sinks into Sebastian's cruel
embrace.

I, on the other hand, am everything *but* relaxed. My veins
hum with energy, with hunger, with a kind of Byronic *yearning*
that consumes every atom of me. Ever since Sebastian left us at
Forsyth Hall, I've been wondering if it was all a dream, a

summer distraction, and when we got back to school we would fall to pieces again. But as Sebastian's hand closes around William's throat, as he devours his haughty prince like he's the only water for miles around, I know that what we have is real.

We're on this wild fairground ride hurtling out of control toward a brick wall, but I couldn't get off even if I wanted to.

"Do you know how much I've imagined this moment?" Sebastian whispers, his teeth scraping along William's throat. "Watching you sit in church on Sunday, holding George's hand like butter wouldn't melt in your mouth. I've been hard as a rod beneath my robes thinking about the day I'd defile you again."

Such unpriestly words, and yet to hear Sebastian say them... he turns to me, and the fire wreathing his dark eyes burns all my worries to ash.

"You're so tempting, both of you. You are Adam and Eve, the fallen ones, cast out from the garden of Eden. Did you come here tonight to tempt me from the path of righteousness, or do you seek atonement?"

This is his game. This is what excites him – dancing on the very edge of his God's words, twisting their meaning to suit his dark desires. William's eyes shimmer, and I know that words like atonement are more than a game to him. He *needs* this. Sebastian always knows exactly what we need.

"Punish me, Father," William chokes out. "I wish for atonement."

Sebastian takes William's hand, and mine, and leads us across the room. I expect him to pull us into his bed, but instead, he stops in front of the fire.

"Kneel."

He shoves William's shoulders down. My prince slumps to his knees in front of the fire. He peers up at Sebastian with rapture, his whole body trembling with need.

"I have decided on your punishment. You will watch me and

George," Sebastian says. "You will not come until I give you permission."

William blinks. His lips part. A groan of assent rises from his throat. Sebastian presses his palm against William's cheek, and William leans into it, seeking the atonement that only our priest can provide.

"Obey, little prince," Sebastian coos. "Or I'll make this even worse for you."

I love watching this dynamic between them – William's arrogance reduced by Sebastian's dominance into this kneeling, keening creature. Sebastian's tenderness redrawn as this caring alpha. It's beautiful to see how they each give the other what they need – Sebastian's orders bring William back to himself, to his own body. He stops performing as this perfect, overachieving prince. He just *is*. He *is* the moment – the chafing of his hard cock against his slacks, the carpet burn on his knees.

And Sebastian...my priest doesn't live in our mortal world. His battles are those of the soul, of angels and demons. And when he strides toward me, his demons crawl out from their hiding places to lay their hands upon his skin.

"Sit," he commands. I rush to obey, plopping down in the chair where I've sat for so many nights with him, dreaming of a world where I might be able to kiss him and touch him and pretend he belongs to me. But the inky depths of his eyes make it clear that not even my wildest dreams can prepare me for what Sebastian Pearce has in mind.

He leans over me, his broad shoulders curling over as he tilts my head back and captures my lips in his. The kiss is a *devouring*. He attacks me with the same hunger he has for William, and I rise up to meet him with a hunger of my own. Cannibalism might be a sin, but he tastes too good to be wrong. A thousand butterflies in my stomach sizzle and pop as their wings touch the tips of his flames.

He kisses so hard and long and deep that I barely notice him removing my clothes. He rests his hand over my heart, naked skin on skin, and pushes me gently back. I sink into the chair, gripping the arms as Sebastian tucks my knees up and positions my legs wide apart. Warm heat from the fire kisses my pussy, promising more, more, more as fresh hunger gnaws at my belly.

With a look over his shoulder to check that William is watching without touching himself, Sebastian steps back. He slowly undoes his fly and pushes his slacks down his narrow hips to give me a full view of him, so hard and hot and ready. A bead of moisture dots the tip of his magnificent cock. My priest is enjoying this very much.

Behind him, William groans. But he doesn't touch himself. He won't disobey.

Sebastian takes his time with his shirt buttons, slowly revealing the planes of his chest and the Celtic cross tattoo over his heart. He slips the rosary from around his neck and holds out the beads, kissing the cross. As I watch, wide-eyed, he wraps the beads around the base of his huge, erect cock, tight enough that they dig into his sensitive flesh, reddening the skin.

"Today is Thursday, which means we say the rosary for the Luminous Mysteries," he says, stepping toward me. "Will you pray with me, George?"

"I don't know what to do, Father Pearce." My voice trembles.

"It's easy, you follow me. First, we make the sign of the cross." He takes my fingers in his and touches my hand to my forehead. His fingertips brush my skin, and just that touch alone in the charged and violent air sends a shudder of pleasure through my body. "And we say, 'In the name of the Father'."

"In the name of the Father," I breathe.

Sebastian moves my hand down my body, pressing my palm into my belly, splaying his fingers over my skin.

"—and the son—"

He draws my hand over my breast, his fingers sneaking around to roll my nipple between his fingers. I gasp at the sensation, at the way my heart blooms with fire.

"—and the Holy Spirit—"

Sebastian moves my hand to my other breast, his fingers expertly touching and teasing my skin. Behind me, William moans, one hand fisting his cock as he takes in the scene.

"—Amen."

He cups my hand over my mound. "Show us how you touch yourself," he whispers.

Oh, fuck.

I cannot refuse him. And from the way he smiles down at me, he knows it. My cheeks burn with heat, but I curl a finger and press it against my clit. I circle it slowly, my arm shaking from the embarrassment of it. Sebastian leans back, studying my technique with the inquisitive scrutiny of a scholar. Behind him, William bites his lip to trap his moan.

Watching my haughty prince go to pieces flips a switch inside me, and I'm not embarrassed anymore. I'm on fire. Sebastian may be the one with the dominant streak, but I'm the one in control. I'm the one with two men on their knees before me.

I swipe my finger through the juices leaking from me and rub faster, leaning my head back against the cushions and pressing my thighs apart to give them a better view. I drink in their desire as their eyes burn my skin. My breath comes out in hard rasps. I feel invincible, like Queen Boudicca staring down the Roman army.

"May I?" Sebastian asks, his voice choked with awe. I don't know what he's asking but I know I want it, *all* of it. I nod vigorously as my orgasm builds inside me, like a rollercoaster climbing the first incline, when your stomach sinks with delicious anticipation and you taste the salt of fairground snacks on your tongue.

Sebastian slides a finger inside me, curling up to press on my inner wall, rubbing a spot that drives me wild. His dark eyes draw me in as we work together to drag me up and up that incline and right to the edge and over over over, the pleasure spilling out of me as I hurtle into oblivion.

Orgasms are great, aren't they? I sort of wish I'd spent more time having them in high school, less time with my nose buried in books.

The rollercoaster slows and stops and I'm back where I started, lying in the chair with my priest staring down at me with those kind, luminous eyes, and a broken prince kneeling behind him, a hand on his cock and his heart all twisted up inside.

"Now, George," Sebastian raises my fingers to his lips and kisses them reverently, licking away the taste of me. "We will pray the rosary together. Have you ever done this?"

I shake my head.

He fingers the beads wrapped around the base of his cock. "For each bead of the rosary, we say a Hail Mary while meditating on one of the twenty mysteries of Christ. Today we meditate on the luminous mystery of the Eucharist. Are you ready?"

I nod. What else can I do when I'm spread out for him like this?

Sebastian leans over me, his teeth scraping against my neck as he prays. "Jesus says to his disciples, 'I have eagerly desired to eat this Passover with you before I suffer.'"

The tip of his cock teases my entrance. My mouth falls open to let out a faint moan as I thrust my hips up, trying to coax him inside.

"Say your prayers," Sebastian whispers against my lips. "There's a good girl."

I swallow. "Hail Mary, full of grace. The Lord is with thee—"

My words break off into a scream of pleasure as he enters me in one swift stroke. He sinks into me with a delighted sigh, his body wrapping around mine as his hips press down on my legs, holding me wide for him. His length fills me completely, and the rosary beads bite into my skin – not enough to hurt, but I definitely feel them. Oh, how I feel them.

Sebastian draws back, his breath ragged, his chest glistening with sweat, and says, "Jesus took bread, blessed it, and say: "Take this bread and eat it. This is My Body."

"Hail Mary, mother of God, pray for us sinners..."

He strokes into me again, and I struggle to get the words out because he's inside me, his sacred beads drawing all kinds of wet, delicious sensations from my flesh. Sebastian's teeth bite into my neck, and with a sharp jolt of pain I realize that he's bitten me, that the metallic tang from the trickle of blood from the tiny wound mingles with the heady scent of sex in the air – that this is our Eucharist, our sacred bonding, our cleansing ritual. That through his kiss, through the sharing of body and blood, we are all made anew.

Sebastian licks the blood from my skin. "This cup is the covenant of my blood, shed for you."

"Hail Mary, full of grace..." the words shudder on my tongue as he slams into me, again and again. The beads dig in and I'm on fire, I'm a ball of molten lava and I slip over the edge again and I don't know if I'm saying words or prayers or just screaming his name.

"At that eucharistic meal, Jesus celebrated the first Mass." Sebastian cups the back of my neck in his hand, his strong forearm lifting my back from the chair, bending me so that he can draw a nipple into his mouth.

White stars dance in front of my eyes. I don't have control of my body or my tongue any longer, but from somewhere far away I hear myself speak the prayer, "...blessed art thou among women and blessed is the fruit of thy womb..."

"Whoever eats my flesh and drinks my blood remains in me, and I in him." Sebastian grunts, his thrusts faster now, relentless, his eyes open but lost in a world beyond that which mortals can see. Behind him, I can hear William stroking himself, his lips murmuring the familiar prayers.

"In this mass, we offer ourselves to God, and God gives himself to us." My priest's tongue plunges between my lips, fucking my mouth as the beads drag across my most sensitive skin. My thighs clamp against him as another orgasm claims me, as raw pleasure floods my body and I imagine I see God behind my eyelids.

"Glory be..." Sebastian whispers against my lips as I scream my pleasure down his throat. "As it was in the beginning, is now, and ever shall be, world without end."

He pumps into me, his jaw locking as his shoulders tense and he lets go, he lets *everything* go. Father Sebastian Pearce in total rapture is a beautiful thing.

Sebastian grips the arm of the chair, his shoulders heaving as he brings himself back in control. He kisses my lips as he slides out of me, cupping his hand around himself, smearing my juices and his over his fingers.

Sebastian turns to William, cupping his cheek in his hand, tipping his mouth back to offer him the Eucharist. William's skin sheens with sweat, his muscles taut with need as he sucks on Sebastian's fingers. Sebastian withdraws his hand and fists William's cock. He pumps it hard, so hard I wonder if it must hurt, but William doesn't look like he's in pain. He looks serene, *free*.

Sebastian presses his lips to William's ear and whispers, "To thee we send up our sighs, mourning and weeping in this vale of tears."

"Pray for us, O holy mother, that we may," William chokes out. "That we may be made worthy of the promise of Christ."

"Amen. You may come."

William's face contracts. His whole body convulses, and he collapses forward as the tip of his cock jerks and explodes. Threads of his seed spill across my naked stomach.

"Fuck." William's chest heaves. He clings to Sebastian like the priest is all that keeps his body melting into a puddle. "*Fuck.*"

Sebastian kisses his hair, then leans over and touches my cheek. "Your atonement isn't over. George, lie on the bed."

I hurry to obey, scrambling across the room on shaky legs and crawling over the linen sheets.

"Lie on your back, place your arms wide, there's a good girl." Sebastian whips a leather belt from the rack beside the bed and loops it through the brass bed stand and around my hands so I can't move. A thrill runs through me. I never in a million years thought I'd be into this, but seeing Sebastian go full dom is so fucking hot. William comes to stand beside him, his features tense with hunger, his cock already hard again.

"William, on top of her," Sebastian commands. "You may enter her, if you're ready."

"Please," I moan, opening my legs as he kneels between them. I wrap my ankles around my prince, drawing him closer. William looks down at me with this expression like he can't believe he's so lucky. It's the same expression I see on the faces of Eli, Noah, and Gabe whenever they're in Claws' presence.

I never thought anyone would look at *me* like that.

William is still dressed. Both Sebastian and I watch as he unbuttons his shirt, lays it down, and folds it neatly, making sure the fabric is smoothed and the collar is turned just so. He does the same with his trousers, socks, and briefs, making a neat pile at the foot of the bed. He looks at Sebastian, who gives him a nod of approval that makes William's whole face glow with pleasure.

My prince climbs up on the bed, kisses me tenderly, and

slides inside me. After the punishment Sebastian gave me, it hurts a little, but a good, stretching kind of hurt. The hurt of a well-fucked woman.

Sebastian watches us as William plunges into me, moving around the bed for the best view. William's eyes flick to him briefly, then back to me. I know I should feel strange about what's happening. I'm having a *threesome*. With a priest and a prince. This should register somewhere on the George Fisher scale of weirdness. But it doesn't – it feels like I'm a broken loco-motive set right upon the tracks, like every moment in my life had been specifically engineered to bring me to this moment, where a dark prince lays reverent kisses upon me while a priest with love in his eyes looks on in awe.

"Yes." Sebastian strokes his fingers down William's spine. William shudders, and the sensation of that touch and what it does to him passes from his body into mine. The bed creaks as Sebastian climbs up and throws a leg casually over William. He presses his body into William's back and leans over his shoulder to kiss his tear-stained cheek.

"I've got lube in the top drawer, little prince." He tugs on William's earlobe with his teeth, making William shudder again. "Do you want me to get it? Do you want me to—"

"Father Pearce?"

Shit.

We freeze. Sebastian whips around to face the door just as someone bangs on it.

"Father Pearce? Are you still awake? I see your light is on."

Shit shit shit. I recognize that voice. It's Father Duncan.

"Just a minute," Sebastian calls. Gone is the blissful domi-nance. He looks terrified.

William withdraws so fast I gasp at the sudden lack of him. Sebastian slides off William and drops his neat pile of clothes into his outstretched hands. William scrambles for the bathroom, pulling the door closed behind him as silently as possible.

"What about me?" I wail, tugging at my trapped hand. My clothes are strewn across the floor in front of the fire, where we left them.

"I'm sorry, George." Sebastian throws the thick duvet over top of me. "Please, don't move. I'll get rid of him as soon as possible."

I feel him place pillows over my arms so his guest won't see the restraints, and dump books and papers over my legs. I'm trapped beneath the blankets, my arms aching in the restraints, unable to move or make a sound. My nose itches. My legs are still spread wide, my pussy begging for them to finish what they started.

Why did Father Duncan have to show up now? Why? Why?

The door creaks as Sebastian opens it. "Father Duncan? It's nice to see you. It's very late for a visit. I was just thinking about heading to bed."

"I won't keep you long. I came past earlier, but I heard you praying the rosary, so I hoped to catch you after you were done. May I come in?"

"Of course." The door creaks wider. "Would you like some coffee?"

A chair creaks as Father Duncan sits down. *Please let Sebastian have hidden all my clothes.* I hear cups clattering in the kitchen, the kettle boiling.

"Look at this," Father Duncan says. "You already have a tray of tea on the table. Three cups. The pot is cold, though."

"Oh, yes. I forgot about that. I had some students over earlier, asking for extensions on their history assignments, you know how it is. I made them tea, but then we got talking about Sumeria and we forgot to drink it," Sebastian says smoothly. He must've prepared tea things for us, but changed his mind when he saw us at the door. I hear clatter in the kitchen, the kettle whistling. When Sebastian speaks again, he's in the room. "Did you want to ask me something?"

"Oh, nothing in particular, really," Father Duncan says. "I've been reading about the differences in the textual forms in the Gospel of Nicodemus. Particularly, the significance of Pilate as a central figure in the first half of the account, but virtually disappearing in the second. I wondered what your thoughts were on this text?"

They talk a long time, about Coptic manuscripts uncovered by the building of the Aswan Dam, about the trial, death, and resurrection of Jesus, about sin and redemption and the immortal soul. It's a fascinating discussion between two learned men that I would've loved to participate in, if only I could scratch the goddamn itch on my nose.

Finally, Sebastian is able to lead Father Duncan to the door, fake yawning as he wishes his colleague goodnight. Just as the door creaks close and I dare to hope for some reprieve, Father Duncan lets out one last bombshell.

"I shall see you tomorrow for Lauds, Father. Get some sleep – you must be working too hard. That must be why you haven't noticed that your shirt buttons are done up unevenly."

He knows.

He knew exactly what we were doing in this room. He came here to catch us out, to torment Sebastian with religious discourse because he fucking knows.

Sebastian laughs. "Oh, silly me. Yes, I've probably been working too hard. I'll go straight to bed."

Finally, *finally*, the door slams shut. I hear the bolt slide and the key turn. My whole face is ready to explode from want of itching. My legs are numb. The duvet is thrown off my face and I gasp in fresh air. Sebastian bends down and brushes a kiss on my forehead.

"George, sweetheart, I'm so sorry." He pulls off the pillows and starts working the knot in the belt securing my arms. "You were such a good girl. I had no idea Duncan was in the mood to talk. Are you okay? Do you hurt—"

"Where's William?" I croak.

"He's gone. He fled out the window. I'll talk to him." Sebastian tugs on the belt. "I'll free you from these and—"

"No," I whisper. "Please. Finish what you started."

Sebastian looks down at me, those dark eyes of his hooding with shadows. "Are you sure? Aren't you sore from lying still for so long?"

I am, but I don't care. I shake my head. "Please?" I beg.

Sorrow passes across Sebastian's features – as if he's being wounded from the inside out, as if his heart is being weighed on the scales of justice and he's not sure which way it will go. I sense he's communing with his God, that he's making some sort of vow from which he cannot return.

His fingers hesitate on the knot. I hold my breath, expecting him to untie me, to send me away before I taint his soul further.

Instead, he snakes his hand behind my neck, tipping my head to his so he can drink my own soul from my lips.

He moves his hands over my skin, and it's like...you know when you're lying in bed, almost asleep, and then you get this sense that your body is falling or flying, that you're hurtling toward the sky or the ground and there's nothing to stop you? That's what it feels like to be touched by Father Sebastian Pearce. To be still for him, unable to move my hands or squirm away, to feel a creeping door open beneath me and know I'm falling, to know that eventually I will hit the hard earth and it will hurt, but I cannot care because the falling is so perfect. I have to feel everything, every touch, every caress, every sinful lick of that priestly tongue.

In his arms, I am worshiped.

In his arms, I understand what it means to *believe*. It's knowing about the pain at the end of the fall, but choosing to fall anyway.

He purrs against my flesh as he devours me. His tongue plunges inside me, tasting me, drinking his fill until I drop over the edge again, until my veins churn with adrenaline and ecstasy, until I'm filled with a much older and more capricious God.

As Sebastian enters me a second time that night, I know that I've fallen so far and so deep I'll never be able to crawl free again, even if I wanted to.

My immortal soul might be destined for hell, but my mortal body feels pretty fucking damn fine.

19

"*A*re you okay?" I whisper to William as I slide into the corral beside him in the library reading room.

I haven't talked to him since he ran out of Sebastian's the other night. He was conspicuously absent from the Orpheus Society picnic on Saturday, and he hasn't stopped by my room to escort me to the dining hall. I've been to his room a couple of times, but a knock on the door never produces an answer. He text me to say he was okay, just wrapped up in a painting, but I had a feeling that wasn't all that's going on.

"Hmm? Oh, yes. I'm fine." He finishes writing the line he's translating for Father Duncan's class. "Did you finish this? I find the optative mood rather tricky."

I place my hand over his. His fingers are cold. They curl away from me. "You're obviously not fine."

William glances at the door, where a couple of students had just walked in. He grabs my hand and yanks me into the stacks.

He pulls me into a corner where the Greek reference books are kept. Hardly anyone is ever in this section of the library, so we're safe from prying eyes and ears. William shoves me up against the stacks. The corner of the *Iliad* jabs into my spine, but

I don't care because William's hands rake over my body, his lips kissing a trail of fire along the edge of my jaw.

"Sebastian nearly got caught that night," he murmurs against my lips. "In fact, I think Father Duncan may suspect something."

"You could be right. When Father Duncan came into Sebastian's room, he made comments about his shirt being buttoned wrong. And the extra coffee cups. And he made a point of saying he heard Sebastian praying the rosary."

"Those could just be innocent observations." William frowns, and I know that even as he says it, he realize how, when taken together, they could very well be Father Duncan's way of telling Sebastian he's onto us.

"Why would Father Duncan suspect anything?" I ask. "He wasn't at the house over summer, and there's no way he can infer anything from a few torrid glances across a crowded church."

"Maybe someone told him," William says.

I catch his meaning immediately. "Monty?"

"I wouldn't put it past him. And they have been spending a lot of time together." William frowns. His azure eyes go somewhere else for a moment, and I can't help but wonder if he's thinking about the secret he's keeping from me, the person he's protecting. Is it Monty? Is it Father Duncan?

I ball my hands into fists. Why would William protect Monty when it could destroy Sebastian? "I thought Monty was supposed to be your friend."

"He is, but he's also...well, you've met him. He's *different*. We've been through a lot together. I was a safe place to run from his parents, and he was there for me after my mother died, when *certain other people* were nowhere to be seen." His jaw clenches. "Monty can't help what his parents made him. I might be the only person in the world who truly cares about him, apart from

Diana, but she cares about everyone. In some silly way, he might believe he's helping me."

I could buy that. I could also buy Monty trying to ruin our relationship out of some twisted sense of ownership. I wasn't sure he saw William as a person so much as a treasured possession that could be stolen away from him. I've come into William's life and completely thrown everything off-kilter, including their friendship. Monty was just the type of bastard who would blow up our lives to bring William back under his power.

"Okay," I breathe hard. "So maybe Father Duncan suspects. But he doesn't *know*. He can't have evidence because we haven't left any. And he can't just come out and accuse Sebastian of anything publicly. The scandal would reflect back on him. We just have to be more careful—"

"I don't know if we should do this with Sebastian. Not here. It could cost him everything, especially if—" William's eyes dart away again.

"Especially if what?"

"Nothing," he murmurs.

"Are you thinking about this secret you're carrying? Because if it's causing you this much pain, you should just tell us—"

"No." William's fingers tighten around my arm. "I won't burden you with it. I must carry it alone."

"If that's how you're going to roll, I know where you can find a genuine hairshirt. You can wear that under your blazer, get your skin all nice and red," I smile. "You don't have to keep punishing yourself."

"Yes." William shoves himself away from the shelves, his face stricken. "I do."

illiam is struggling," Sebastian says. He lifts an eyebrow at me, but it's not a question.

I nod.

Sebastian text me in the early hours of this morning, saying that he had to drive over to the York Museum to look at some of their archival material for a paper he was writing, and wondering if I'd like to accompany him. I pulled on some nondescript clothing and hurried down the forest path to Black-friars Close, checking the trees every few seconds in case someone was watching, and he picked me up in a college pool car.

We shared a pleasant morning exploring the museum together – there's a Jurassic exhibit William would have loved, and at one point Sebastian pulls me behind a pillar in the Roman exhibit and shoves his tongue down my throat.

Now, we're driving back to college, the stereo blaring The Smiths' 'Pretty Girls Make Graves,' and Sebastian has revealed the true reason he wanted me alone today.

"He refuses to talk about it," I say. "I think part of it is concern for you – that what we're doing might come back to haunt you. But something has been eating away at him ever since Devil's Night. I think he knows who hurt Keely, and he's keeping their secret. But I don't understand why."

"I do." Sebastian turns down the music. "I assume you think this secret concerns Montague Cavendish."

I nod. "I guess it could be any of the Orpheans, but what are their motives? Monty's the only one I can imagine actually *killing* someone. Keely was after William, and Monty can't stand the idea of someone taking his friend away, so he kills Keely in this bizarre Orphean ritual and burdens William with his secret."

It's the first time I've ever actually voiced my dark fear. I play back the words I overheard at the amphitheater when Monty told William how he'd been possessed by the god. And it would explain William's desire to keep me away from the Orpheans, and why Monty came after me so fiercely once he knew I was looking into them.

But if that's true, if Monty really did kill Keely because of his jealousy, then why has he suddenly decided to embrace me? And if Keely's death is a jealous rage, then it can't explain Khloe's disappearance or those other missing girls.

"George," Sebastian warns, his knuckles tightening on the steering wheel. "I hope you're not still trying to investigate Keely's death."

"I can't help it!" I glare at him. "I have a bad feeling about all of this. And if you know something you're not saying, something that could help William, you'd better not keep it to yourself."

"If you're referring to the sanctity of confession," he says. "I won't forsake that vow—"

"Why not? You have no qualms about breaking vows."

The car falls silent. I cringe at my callous words. Sebastian focuses on the road, refusing to look at me.

"Sebastian, I'm sorry. I didn't mean—"

"No," he cuts in. "You were entirely fair. I suppose we were destined to have this conversation at some point."

"What conversation?"

"The 'you're not acting very priestly, fucking me over altars and fingering me in crypts' conversation." Sebastian's lip curls into a friendly half-smile. "Have you ever noticed that even without religion, humans organize ourselves into groups? These groups usually focus around something or someone they despise – secular society is filled with groups designed to *other* something they are afraid of or do not understand, and they rarely move beyond that primary purpose. That's religion, even if we don't consider it thus. We are by nature a religious species; your religion can be a political movement or a particular heavy metal band."

I smile at that. "So why this group for you? Why Catholicism?"

"I am aware of the worst of organized religion," Sebastian says. "Not just the evil priests abusing their power but the small injustices made daily in God's name. Sir Henry used religion as a way to cast off his family. It was his permission slip to live a life of excess without his family legacy breathing down his neck. It was only when his wife died that he sought God for real. And I know that's fucked up William beyond repair. So the answer to 'why Catholicism' is both simple and complex – because it was there, in my face, accessible and yet utterly incomprehensible. And I'm like you in a way – I love a good mystery, only instead of true crime, religion is about mysteries of the soul. I didn't have a father and I was adrift – I wanted so desperately to understand suffering and salvation and forgiveness, and Sir Henry was there to teach me everything I wanted to know. When you're utterly lost, there's comfort knowing you can fall to your knees in prayer and you'll always be heard."

"You can be religious and not be a priest," I point out. "You have to admit, your life is quite...extreme."

"It could be worse. I could've become a Trappist monk. Although I do prefer beer to communion wine," he laughs. "When I look back on it, this vocation seems the most unlikely for me to choose. And yet God led me to the church and set me on this path. I spent a lot of time alone in the Forsyth family chapel, gazing up at those impenetrable saints and the son of God on his cross. I demanded answers, and I know you don't believe that God speaks to us, but I felt like I was given answers. William was too young to understand, and when he became old enough I..." he swallows. "I tainted my friendship with him with something darker, and I thought I had to take myself away from him for his own protection. I thought that I'd been poisoned by my father's cruelty, by Sir Henry's avarice. I thought I'd become the very thing that I feared. And so I went to seminary. I wanted to be closer to God, to claw my way to redemption."

"And did you find it? This redemption?"

Sebastian shakes his head. "Redemption isn't a destination, but a journey. What I learned was that I didn't have to be perfect. I didn't have to be Godly, because that was God's job. But I could be *good*. I believe that two thousand years ago, there lived a man named Jesus rocking around Palestine, and that he was the unity of human and god – the divine with human scars. I believe that he preached things I hold to be true, that he was crucified, and that he died and rose again. To walk with Jesus means to accept your own personal crucifixion. You and William are mine. I know this as I know that the sun rises each day and that Jesus died for my sins, and I do not know what will happen in the future, as none of us shares the secrets of death. But I believe that in your love I will die and be reborn."

"But redemption isn't only available for priests." I'm pressing this point. But I have to believe that there's some future for us.

He'd offered to leave the church once before, but I could not accept it when it meant he was chopping off his own limb, mutilating his soul just to be with me. But if there was a way for him to have what he needed without being a priest... "Isn't that the whole idea?"

"Walking with Jesus means walking with others, even if you don't always like or agree with them. Being a priest means learning that walk, and helping others along the way as they falter or fall. There's so much to learn, and so much I can change. And I need to be part of something bigger than myself. Making my vows to a centuries-old religious tradition has opened my eyes to some of the richest thinking and scholarly pursuits available. It's a pleasure for me to wear the robes of the priesthood, as it is to sink into your warm pussy. And I don't believe it's an accident that William started at Blackfriars and then the position of chaplain came up, and that I was uniquely and perfectly qualified for it. I don't believe it's a coincidence that you walked into the cloister that day. And—" he yanks the wheel hard, slamming me into the passenger door.

"What are you doing? What's happening?" I cry.

But Sebastian isn't looking at me. He's staring out the window, his shoulders rigid, his jaw tight.

Across the road is an abortion clinic, complete with the usual smattering of protesters holding gross signs. Leigh told me that clinics in London and some other areas have won the right to a hundred-meter exclusion zone (I don't know what a hundred meters is in feet, but it sounds like a lot) around clinics, but this clinic has no such legal protection. A group of protesters huddles around the doors, their faces red from yelling. But Sebastian isn't looking at them.

His gaze is fixed on a woman standing alone on the corner, her coat pulled high around her face. She stares at her shoes, her body braced against the abuse the protesters hurl at her.

"How can you do this to your child?" one yells. "You're a mother."

"You're a murderer."

"Give your baby the gift of a birthday."

Before I know what's happening, Sebastian is out of the car. He walks over to the girl, speaks to her gently. She looks up, sees the white collar clasped at his throat, and her eyes widen. She turns to run, but he says something else. He holds out his hand.

Tears stream down her cheeks. She takes his hand. Together, they walk across the road toward the clinic. He stays by her side the entire time, placing his body between her and the protestors like a human shield. They see them approaching and start yelling at him.

"What are you doing, Father?" one woman yells. "She's killing her child."

"Don't pay attention to them. Focus on me. I'll stay with you as long as you need me," Sebastian says gently as he escorts the woman inside. The doors shut behind them.

He comes out a few moments later. The protestors try to engage him, but he doesn't give them a single word. He opens the door to the car and climbs inside, folding his hands calmly in his lap.

"Miranda will be done in a couple of hours," he says. "I'll take you back to school and then I'll come back here to make sure she gets home okay."

Miranda. He speaks her name and treats her like a human being. He lets his own morals, his own vision of a righteous and just God, guide his actions, instead of religious dogma or regard for 'rules.'

Sebastian Pearce is holy, through and through. He's needed in the world as a beacon of light and hope and love.

William's right. We can't take his priesthood away from him. We can't take him away from the world.

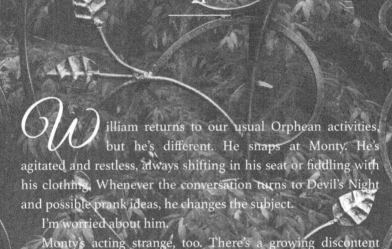

21

*W*illiam returns to our usual Orphean activities, but he's different. He snaps at Monty. He's agitated and restless, always shifting in his seat or fiddling with his clothing. Whenever the conversation turns to Devil's Night and possible prank ideas, he changes the subject.

I'm worried about him.

Monty's acting strange, too. There's a growing discontent between him and William, and he seems to have redirected his relentless energy toward recruiting Leigh as his new best pal. Every time I turn around, Montague Cavendish is right there. In the hallway outside our rooms, hovering around me in the editing suite, sitting at the table behind me at the Bad Habit, inviting himself along to Leigh's and my private study sessions.

Leigh's wary of him, but she also knows that keeping him close will give us the chance to bring him down. So she puts up with his off-color jokes and brings him little treats of things she's foraged, and enjoys the social clout of being seen around with him.

Now that we're back at school, away from the fairytale world of Forsyth Hall, I have to confront Keely's unsolved murder again. I know I've been slacking, but no more. I've submitted my proposal for my colloquy, and it's being accepted. No matter what happens with William and the society, I'm doing this.

This means that I need to stop being distracted by William's pouty lips and Devil's Night plans and get started on Khloe May's case. It means I have to do something I've been putting off.

I have to talk to her parents.

When I made season one of the podcast, I was dealing with my own pain. It didn't matter to me what I said or how I came across, because I wanted to get to the truth. But not all people are me, and some people – especially grieving parents whose only daughter disappeared – don't want to talk to nosy college students with true crime podcasts.

Professor Hipkins is right about the interesting moral issues around true crime. Sure, sometimes, attention on a cold case can help uncover new answers. But for victims and the families of victims, it can feel like raking over the gory details of their trauma for likes and clicks, and I don't want to do that.

But I have to tackle this investigation logically, and talking to the Mays is the first logical step.

It doesn't take me long to find Khloe May's mother online. She's divorced now, and she's been a panelist on a couple of true crime podcasts, talking about her daughter's case. She mentions in one of the interviews an email address where people can reach her if they have new information about the case. I send off an email, hoping I sound sincere, and she replies and invites me down to see her. She lives in a small village called Argleton, about two hours by train. Leigh offers to come with me, so after our morning tutorials, Tiberius drives us down to Blackfriars Close to catch the train.

"Look what Monty gave me." Leigh hands me a beautiful illustrated foragers guide. "It's kind of sweet, innit?"

I frown and hand the book back. "I don't like this."

Monty is always surprising William with little gifts. They're always thoughtful, but lately they feel somewhat...*pointed*. A statuette of Medusa, a book on crime and punishment in the Ancient World, a bottle of expensive Scotch named 'Cardinal Sin.'

"I don't like it, either," Leigh shudders. "I keep thinking about that skeleton we found in Paris. But maybe Monty didn't do it? Maybe there's another explanation. You're still looking at that organized crime angle, right?"

I nod. I've got Claws and her people digging into Keely's family and looking for connections to Khloe May. Keely's family didn't approve of William, and they might attempt to frame him for her murder out of spite. But it didn't explain the parallels between Keely and Khloe May's disappearance.

We step out of the train into Argleton village. It's absolutely delightful – a quaint circle of shops and an old English pub circling the village green. Down a side street, we find ourselves wandering around an enormous bookshop; that is, until Leigh notices a real live raven perched above the door. She quotes Poe at it and the bird thanks her by shitting on her denim jacket.

"Bloody bird," Leigh mutters as she stuffs her jacket into a trash bin.

"It might've been a blessing. Did you see the way the shop owner was looking at us? It's as if he didn't even want customers in his shop." I point to a beautiful Tudor cottage on the corner. "It's right here."

Before we even reach the front door, it's thrown open by a sandy-haired woman with a broad smile and eyes that crinkle in the corners. "George? I'm Vera May. Come on inside."

"Thank you so much for agreeing to talk to me," I say as Leigh and I take off our boots and follow Vera through a narrow hallway lined with pictures of Khloe and shelves of angel figurines.

"Are you kidding? When I saw your name on the email, I knew you'd been sent by the angels to help me." Vera bustles us into a cozy breakfast nook and heads to the kitchen to begin that essential British ritual of making tea. "It might seem macabre, but ever since Khloe went missing, I've been addicted to true crime. My therapist says that it's my subconscious unable to accept the fact that I'll never find out what happened. If I learn enough about other cases, especially ones the police can't solve, I'll see something I've missed and we'll find her. Milk and sugar?"

"Yes, please." I stare at Leigh across the table through the gossamer wings of a large angel statuette. The entire room is covered with angels – angel tablecloth, angel paintings, angel figurines crowded on the windowsill. *Sebastian would love this place.*

"I moved to the village after Reggie and I separated. It's hard to hang on as a couple, you know, after losing a child. I moved here for a new start, thinking the quiet life might do me some good." She laughs as she arranges biscuits on an angel plate. "Silly me! You wouldn't believe it, but there have been several strange murders in this tiny village. A girl at the local bookshop seems to be in the center of them all. And every time another villager is knocked off, it reminds me that somewhere out there, someone knows something about what happened to my daughter. It's enough to drive you barmy. Without my angels and my therapist, I think I'd be locked in a padded cell!"

Leigh gives me a look that implies a padded cell is *exactly* where Vera belongs.

"You can have those folders," Vera says as she returns with our cups and the plate of shortbread biscuits. She pushes a stack of ring binders toward me. They have angels on the covers. "It's all the research I've done on Khloe's case. It might keep you from heading down a dead end."

"Thank you." I flip open the top one and see scans of pages of Khloe's date planner, her class schedule, photocopies of receipts, and other items found in her dorm room. The margins are covered in illegible scribbles. "So I wanted to ask you some questions about Khloe. Are you okay if I record our conversation?"

"Go right ahead."

I check my phone's recording app and place it on the table in front of her. "I'm guessing you've seen that a girl's body was found in Blackfriar's Wood. The victim was Keely Sullivan, and she was last seen on the same night as Khloe. Devil's Night. I'm doing a school project, looking into what might've been going on. If I end up making another season of the podcast from it, I'll let you know in plenty of time, okay?"

"That's fine. I hope you do. If Khloe's story gets enough attention, I'm sure someone would—" she swallows. I know exactly what she's thinking. *Someone would find her body.* But voicing aloud that she believes her daughter is dead feels like a betrayal.

"You've never stopped looking for your daughter, even after the police declared the case unsolved," I say. "And you've always bitten back against allegations that your daughter killed herself—"

"I know my Khloe. She didn't kill herself. And the police are as useful as tits on a bull," she says. "I watch a lot of crime shows. The police are always chasing down every lead to get justice for a girl like my Khloe. Yet, the Blackfriars Close inspectors didn't seem interested in solving the case or sharing information with Reggie and me. I wanted to take them to court for negligence, but Reggie wouldn't let me."

She makes a face. I cut her off before she can launch into an anti-Reggie diatribe. "Did you notice anything unusual about Khloe before her disappearance?"

"I've been over this in my head a million times, especially when they suggested she killed herself. It didn't make sense. Khloe was happier than she'd ever been. She had new friends. A doting boyfriend. She converted to Catholicism, which is a little weird, but that's what you do in college, isn't it? You try on different personalities and find one that fits. She didn't kill herself, and she didn't just up and run away. Someone hurt her and got away with it. I *know* it."

I flip through my phone until I find a photograph of Father Duncan, which I show to Vera. "Do you remember this guy? He would've looked different, but he went to school with Khloe—"

"Of course I do." Vera pulls a folder from the stack and flips through the pages, before handing it back to me. "That's Patrick Duncan. He was Khloe's boyfriend. Why is he dressed up like a priest?"

"Wait, what?"

"I'll show you." Vera flips through the second binder and holds it open on a series of photographs. A young, fresh-faced Father Duncan together with a laughing, smiley Khloe May, sitting on the edge of Martyr's Fountain. Khloe and Father Duncan, dressed as Margaret Thatcher and Winston Churchill and holding giant beer steins at some event at the Bad Habit, the two of them with friends, playing cards in a cramped student dorm.

I pause at a picture of the couple lying on a picnic blanket. From the shape of the stones and the trees behind them, I can tell they're in the amphitheater.

Father Duncan was Khloe's boyfriend? How did he escape being questioned by the police? If a woman goes missing, the boyfriend is the first person the police look at. So why has there never been anything in the reports, the countless newspaper articles, and true crime podcasts about Father Duncan?

"I told the police all about him," Vera says, reading my mind.

"They said he had a watertight alibi for the time of her disappearance. So he's never been a suspect. But the look on your face—"

"It's just that he was near Keely on the night she went missing."

"That poor girl." Vera hugs herself. "Who would do such a thing to her? When I saw it on the news, I swear I had a heart attack. I thought they must've found Khloe, after all these years. But no, it was another girl. I asked my angels to look after her in heaven…"

I don't hear what Vera says next. I'm transfixed by a photograph in Vera's folder. It's shows Khloe and Father Duncan standing on the Martyr's Quad fountain with a group of friends. They're all wearing togas and holding Greek drinking vessels. "Khloe's Classical Studies society," the caption reads.

There, with his arm around Father Duncan's shoulders and a pair of curved goat's horns on his head, looking every bit like a smug Orpheus Society initiate, was a younger Inspector Jones, the officer in charge of Keely's case.

22

*A*s soon as I'm back in the privacy of my own room, I record a podcast episode of my interview with Vera. As I sit down to edit the raw files, I slip back into that calm, meditative state I remember from the months after Dad's death. When he died, I felt so helpless, and so angry. Angry because this horrible disease took my dad away from me and I couldn't do anything. But from the moment I had Walter Hart and his shady funeral business in my sights, I clawed back a modicum of control.

That's how I feel as I clip out awkward pauses and smooth the background noise. When I finish the file, I copy it and save one version into my colony project folder. The other, I climb into my custom-built podcast booth and record an introduction for a *My Dad is a Gerbil* episode.

"Hi, this is George again. Since we last talked, I've made some interesting progress on Keely's case, and my life has completely blown up. I'm back at school now, and it's strange how different Blackfriars is now that I'm an Orphean. I've been moved to a different dorm room...oh, wait, I'm sorry, it's less of a room and more of a 5-star hotel suite. I'm dating one of the society members and, well, it's wild. And there's this other guy we're seeing, too, but he's a teacher at school and there are so many reasons it's a bad idea...but you can't help the way you feel, right? So, anyway, we're planning the annual Devil's Night prank, and they keep throwing these insane, destructive ideas out like it's nothing, like their entire lives are without consequences simply because members of the faculty and the board and the police force are ex-Orpheans."

I take a deep breath and continue. "And thinking about Devil's Night brings me back. It's been a year since my roommate went missing and I found her body buried in the woods, and although the police have no answers and the world has moved on, I haven't forgotten her or the women who came before her. And so I'm continuing my investigations quietly, without arousing suspicions. And today I discovered something new that links Keely's death with the disappearance of Khloe May..."

I cut in the intro and save the files. As I set down my headphones, a wave of guilt washes over me. Just like last time, I've made the podcast deeply, almost embarrassingly, personal. I've revealed so much about the Orpheans, and William, and Sebastian, and our relationship – things I've been told in confidence by people I'm weirdly starting to consider my friends.

It's fine. Stop worrying about it. I'm not releasing these episodes. They're just for me, to organize my thoughts, not for public consumption. As for my colloquy, I have two years to put it together, to edit out the bits that aren't relevant.

I tidy everything away and I text William to see if he wants to walk over to our Greek lesson with Sebastian together. His reply is terse:

I'm not going.

I stare at the message, intrigued and annoyed. If William doesn't want to do this he should tell Sebastian in person, not sit in his room and sulk and make me do it. My fingers pause over the screen as I think of what to type in reply. A floorboard creaks above my head.

He's upstairs. I'll go and talk to him. Drag him out if I have to. We need to talk. The three of us *can* be in the same room, alone, and have a serious conversation without ending up in a hot, naked tangle. I mean, it's never happened before, but that doesn't mean we're not capable.

I push open my door and poke my head into the hallway to make sure Monty isn't around. Satisfied I'm alone, I lock my door and head upstairs to William's room.

As I approach the landing, I hear raised voices inside his room. I feel awful for spying, but I can't help it. My Miss Marple senses are tingling. I press my ear against the door.

"—can't keep acting like this." It's Diana's voice. She sounds upset.

"Like what?"

"Like you have something to feel guilty about."

"I can't help it." William sounds anguished. "I *do* feel guilty. And every time I see him, every time he makes some off-hand comment or pulls one of his stupid stunts or smiles that oafish smile, it's as if he's determined to make us as miserable as possible, as if he finds the whole thing *amusing*. All our necks on the chopping block and he's waving about the sword of Damocles. If he's not careful, he'll put someone's eye out."

"You know what he's like," Diana coos. I can picture her nuzzled up to him with her hand on his shoulder, their years of friendship holding her steadfast against the onslaught of his depression. "He doesn't mean any of it. He's brainwashed. He's sick. His father—"

"I know what his father is, thank you," William's clipped tone cuts her off. "I think we should go to the police, tell them everything. If we explain, then maybe it won't be so bad—"

"You know we can't do that," she says kindly. "You know what will happen if we—"

The door swings open. I grab at the frame, but I'm too late. I topple forward, landing in a tangled heap on the floor at Diana's feet.

"Oh, Hello, George." She reaches down to pick me up. "I was just seeing if William would lend me his notes for our Impressionism tutorial, but he's been an insufferable grump, as always."

As I dust myself off, I see her and William exchange a look. *What did she hear?* it says. *What does she know?*

Diana blows me a kiss as she breezes past, leaving me alone with William and the gaping silence between us.

William turns away from me and retreats into his room. He slumps down at his easel, in front of a half-finished canvas of water slicing around the prow of a boat. His tall, wiry frame is too large for the space.

"Well, then," he sighs as he stares at the congealing paints on his tray. "You heard everything. I suppose it's my own fault for dating Sherlock Holmes."

"I prefer Miss Marple." I slam the door. It rattles on the ancient hinges. "William, you need to tell me what's going on. You were talking about going to the police. What about? Why doesn't Diana want you to do that?"

He leans his elbows against the easel, dropping his head in his hands. "I can't tell you. I can't make you part of this."

"We're past that now. At the temple, I asked you to make me a promise. Are you telling me that you lied to me? You *promised* me you didn't kill her."

"What I did was a thousand times worse." William jerks his head up, his face contorting with misery. "I *ate* her."

23

I ate her.

What.

The.

Actual.

Fuck?

Did he just say what I think he said?

24

I ate her.
　　　I ate her.
I ate her.

The words loop over and over in my mind, but no matter how many times I replay them, I can't make sense of them. I pry William's hands from his eyes. "You're going to have to explain what you mean."

"What's there to explain? I'm a monster. There is nothing I can do that will atone for this sin."

He tries to hide his face again. I clamp my hand on his jaw, the way I'd seen Sebastian do. I hold his face so he has to look at me. "You don't get to hide behind the poetry of anguish. Just tell me, in plain words, what happened. I can help. We can figure this out."

"Not even you can help with this."

"All the same, I know the truth now, so you can unburden yourself of this secret. You've been carrying it alone for some time. I think it will make you feel better to share the burden. Tell me everything."

I've never demanded anything of anyone like this, my voice

hard and mean. But the words have an effect on William. He needs to be needed, and when I make it clear there's something I want him to do, he rushes to obey.

William takes a shuddering breath. "Keely was M-M-Monty's choice for our new initiate. She hung out with us at Forsyth Hall over the summer. She'd been interested in me for years, but that only made Monty even more interested in her."

I nod. I think I understand this. Theirs is a complicated friendship. Monty always wants what William has.

"Monty decided that Devil's Night was going to be the night we initiated her—"

William's words cut off as someone bangs on the door. He jerks away. I hold my finger to my lips.

"George? William? Are you in there?"

Sebastian. He sounds frantic. I look down at my phone and realize we were due at our Greek lesson twenty-three minutes ago.

I rush to the door and fling it open.

"I'm so sorry for turning up like this. You're always on time, but not tonight." He runs a hand through his long, dark hair and glances around frantically. "I worried something had happened to you..."

His voice trails off as he sees William's face. He crosses the room, slamming the door behind him. He plucks William from the chair and pulls him into his arms. William buries his face into Sebastian's shoulder, his body shuddering. Sebastian strokes his hair and looks to me for an explanation.

I offer the only one I've been given. "William ate Keely."

Sebastian frowns. "Be serious."

William jerks away from Sebastian, as if he can't bear touching either of us. He stumbles over the easel, scattering paints and knives and brushes across the floor. He doesn't move to pick them up but stands, shaking, his face hidden in his hands.

"That's what he told me." My own hands are trembling. I sink onto the bed and cross them in my lap, but I can't make them stop. "He's just about to explain what happened on Devil's Night."

William lowers his hands. His face is etched with sorrow. His eyes dart to Sebastian. "You shouldn't be here in a student's room like this."

Sebastian places a hand on William's shoulder. His whole body shudders beneath the touch. "My job on this campus is to listen to students in distress, to help them navigate matters of faith and the heart. It sounds like I'm exactly where I need to be."

He pushes William's shoulders until the prince perches next to me on the edge of the bed. Sebastian pulls over one of William's wingback chairs and sits down in front of him, placing one of his big hands on William's knee, the other over mine. The warmth is reassuring. It's risky that he's here after Father Duncan nearly caught us, especially with Monty's room right downstairs, but I'm so, so happy he came.

William takes a deep breath and starts his story again. He keeps his eyes locked on me, and his shoulders are so tense they're up around his ears. "Keely's initiation was going to happen at the party in the baths. We got the key to George's room from Father Duncan and went in to trash the place, as is tradition. Monty got carried away. Truthfully, he didn't seem interested in Keely's side of the room. He kept breaking your things, George, and talking about you."

"What was he saying?" Sebastian demands.

"Just…" William won't stop looking at me, like he wants to crush me to his chest or push me out the window and he can't decide which. "I don't want to say them aloud. I don't want to give his awfulness a voice. I didn't like the way he'd been fixating on you. I told him so, tried to make him stop. Luckily, Keely arrived and saw us all, and we took her away to get ready for the night.

"As you know, past members are invited to return to school for Devil's Night, so there were more than just the ten of us out that night. We had our robes on, and we were roaming all over the school, drinking and checking in on the various vignettes—" that's what the Orpheans call their pranks "—and I lost sight of her. It's hard to keep track of everyone in their robes and masks, and with so many of the old members taking part..."

I nod. That makes sense. I remember watching the white-robed figures from my window that night, trying to figure out who was who just by the shapes of their bodies.

William swallows. "I was heading back to the church after looking in at the dining hall, taking the shortcut from the theatre department through the Cloister Garden, and I saw you at the doorway, George. I saw Monty grab you. Keely was there, and Abigail, and after you slipped away I heard them whispering about you, about how they were going to make you pay. And I just...I knew Monty was taking this far too seriously. I knew that he and I know..." he swallows again. "I never told anyone, but the night I found my mother, I saw Monty run away from the lake."

"What?" Sebastian's eyes narrow.

What? "I don't understand. You saw Monty in the vicinity where your mother was killed, and yet you've remained friends with him, but you've hated Sebastian ever since—"

"I didn't hate him," William glares at the priest. "I hated myself. Only a man as good as Sebastian would let me treat him the way I did, and that's why I did it. I'm so sorry..."

His voice catches.

Sebastian squeezes his hand. "You've already been forgiven."

William's long lashes tangle together as he blinks back tears. "And Monty...it's complicated. He loved my mother, too. She was always so kind to him. He used to bring her gifts whenever he came over – bunches of wildflowers he picked, paintings he'd done, drawings of pretty things torn from books. I don't believe he hurt her but..."

"But?" Sebastian prompts.

"...but I know how he grew up, the things his parents tried to teach him, and sometimes, I'm afraid of him." William turns to me, the tears spilling freely down his alabaster cheeks. "If he caught you, George, he'd hurt you. So I hid you, and then I walked you back to your dorm so you'd be safe. But because of that, I was late to the party, and I didn't see what was really going on."

"William, what? Tell us."

"The party was in full swing when I arrived. Monty told me that I missed the initiation, that he'd done it down in the woods 'in the old ways.' He-he-he was leaping around, all manic, a completely different person to the one you saw in the garden. He had this tray of meat – little tiny squares of rare meat on crackers. He kept passing it around, declaring it a special treat to help our ritual and demanding we all try them. I thought it was just another of his larks. You know how he's always trying different exotic foods. He badgered everyone until all the meat was gone. Even Fatima had a piece. It tasted like roast pork. I asked him about the meat, and he said that Keely provided it. I thought he meant she gave him some raw venison from her family farm or something.

"And then, the next morning, Keely's missing. She's not passed out in the pools or sleeping off her hangover in anyone's room. She didn't leave with a past member. She's not *anywhere*. And Monty's swaggering around with this cat-ate-the-canary grin. And he tells us all that he knows where Keely is, that she's inside all of us. And he tells us that he didn't kill her but he wasn't going to let all that delicious flesh go to waste, not when it would bring us closer to the god. And we were reeling from the horror of it all, when you show up, demanding to know where Keely is."

I stagger away from him, my stomach lurching. "And you think—"

He nods, his face crumpling with misery.

"I should have been there that night," Sebastian growls. "Something *felt* wrong. There was a heaviness in the air. I should have stayed to protect you both. Father Duncan had set up a meeting for me with the deacon, and I had no good reason to refuse. I should have been there—"

"Don't you see?" William rages. "Father Duncan is responsible for all of this. He's been filling Monty's head with all these ideas about Benet of Blackfriars, about what the rituals are supposed to achieve. He's the one who killed her, I'm sure of it. Ever since we started taking Duncan's class, Monty's been pushing the society in this weird new direction. The Orpheus Society is supposed to be a drinking club – *Kakodaimonistai,* remember? It's supposed to be a bunch of rich toffs pulling silly pranks and helping each other get cushy jobs, but Monty's got this idea in his head that he wants to *truly* experience the ekstasis of the god."

"Didn't we do that at the initiation?" I ask. "With the...spiked bread?"

William shakes his head. "It's not enough for Monty. It's not what's described in the texts. He wants complete surrender, the *mainomenos* of the myths. He wants the spirit of the god to literally enter his body. And he believes that on Devil's Night, when he ate Keely's flesh, he achieved exactly that."

"But how? How do you get from fucking on the temple steps to cannibalism?"

"It has precedent," says Sebastian, his voice grave.

"Do you remember what Father Duncan told us in class about the Tristeria, the festival that predated the mystery cults?" William says. "The maenads would run wild in the woods of Mount Parnassus, hunting wild animals and dismembering them and eating their flesh. There are stories that animals weren't all that were hunted."

No.

"Humans," I breathe.

This isn't possible. It's the plot from one of Dad's cult horror films. This isn't real life. Real students in a prestigious twenty-first-century university don't believe they can eat their classmates to summon an ancient wine god.

"Benet writes about such rituals in vivid, gory details," Sebastian says. "And Benet was a Catholic. He's familiar with ritual cannibalism, with the use of flesh and blood to invoke the spirit of a god."

"This is insane," I moan.

"There's more," William says.

Sebastian kisses William's knuckles. "Please continue."

"That day I came to you in the woods, George...Monty followed me. He saw us kiss at your body farm. I think that's why he chose that spot to bury her. The same way he told Father Duncan his suspicions about Sebastian." William rubs his head as Sebastian turns sharply to face him. "Monty wants...fuck, I don't even know what he wants anymore."

"He wants you to himself. And George and I stand in your way. If Monty killed Keely, then you have to go to the police," Sebastian says. I nod in agreement.

"I can't." William screws up his face. "I ate the evidence. We all did. I have nothing to go on except my word and a wild story about ancient mystery cults. It will be my word against his, and everyone at the party – past and present members – ate a piece of her. He made sure of it. And that includes the investigating officer, Jones, who is a past member. This means that they all have a vested interest in keeping this quiet. If Monty goes down for her murder, then everyone in the Orpheus Society goes down, too, and that includes George."

Wait, what? "Why me?"

"You were there that night, out of your room. Monty saw you. Abigail saw you. And I can't guarantee that you're not on any of the security footage around the school. If you stand up for me, they'll close ranks against us. I think Diana would support me if I came forward, maybe Fatima, maybe a couple of others, but the rest...they have too much to lose. They can't risk a fucking cannibalism scandal getting out. They may even try to say it was us who did it. You and me. Her body was buried on your experiment, after all."

I rest my head in my hands. "That can't be the answer. There has to be other evidence. What about the murder weapon? What about the knife he used to butcher her? If he killed her in the woods, there might be DNA evidence. What about photographs from the party?"

"At the party, Monty's robe was covered in dark stains," William closes his eyes. "I thought it was red wine, but that was naive of me. He had us burn our robes at the end of the night. He threw other things on the fire, too. And he's no fool – the murder weapon he used is probably long gone."

I reach across and clasp William's other hand. Sebastian and I exchange a glance. The room spins. All those images of blue water blur together until a giant wave crashes over me, pulling me under, filling my nose and mouth with blood until I can't breathe. The faces beneath the surface peer out at me, trapped in the waves, their mouths open in silent screams.

"What do we do?" I ask.

"Nothing," William hangs his head. "We got away with it. Father Duncan got away with it."

"I don't accept that. You said there've been other murders," Sebastian turns to me. William looks up in surprise.

I nod. "Not murders specifically. Khloe May disappeared twenty years ago. And at least five other women that I know of over the last hundred years. All were found dead or disappeared on or around Devil's Night. And there's a body in an underground temple in Paris that has Orphean symbols on the pillars."

"What?" William leans forward. "How do you know about that temple? There's a *body* there?"

I nod. "Leigh and I found the temple, and the body. It's hard to tell because of the rodents, but it was probably a few months old."

William shudders. "We go to Monty's house in Paris and worship in that temple most years, but I don't know anything about a body. And Father Duncan wasn't with us. That temple is for current members only."

"But he knows where it is," I say. "And getting to Paris isn't exactly difficult. And get this – Khloe was Father Duncan's girlfriend."

Sebastian's eyes bore into me. "How do you know that?"

I explain to them what I know about Khloe's case so far, and what I learned when I spoke to Vera. They exchange a look – a 'here she goes again, Miss Marple-ing herself into trouble' look – which is actually quite adorable. I leave out the part about why I interviewed Vera. They don't need to know about the draft podcast episodes or my colloquy project.

"It sounds as though Father Duncan is connected to both these cases," Sebastian says. "And the Orpheans have conspired to cover up his crimes."

"I believe Khloe's body is somewhere in the woods," I say.

William looks at me with wide, hope-filled eyes. "If we find Khloe's body, if we can get Father Duncan for both crimes, then maybe we can get justice without having to drag the society through it, and we can get Monty out from under Duncan's influence."

I don't like it. Whichever way you slice it (excuse the pun), Monty is a murderer. But I also understand where William is coming from – if he comes out with the cannibalism, the tabloids will tear the Orpheans to pieces. (Argh, this is going to keep happening. I won't ever be able to look at roast pork the same way again.)

And the real evil behind these crimes – Father Duncan – will remain in the shadows, able to influence future students. But if we come up with irrefutable evidence of Duncan's guilt, the Orpheans will throw one of their own to the wolves to save their own skins.

Sebastian pats my shoulder. "This sounds like a job for our resident detective. What's our first move, George?"

25

"...And I love William, I love him, but when I bend up to kiss him I'm struck by the knowledge that he ate his friend, and I want to throw up." I lean over the podcast mic, my fingers gripping the edge of the desk. "That's not normal. I know it's not his fault, but I don't know if I can love a cannibal."

I hit stop and save the recording. I've been trying to make a new podcast episode about William's revelations, but it devolved into a brain-fart of all the conflicting thoughts circling in my head.

He knows where Keely is — she's inside all of us.
Benet writes about such rituals in vivid, gory details
It tasted like roast pork.

I shove my hands over my ears, as if that can somehow shut out the screaming voices. But all it does is make them shout louder. The man I love ate human flesh, and even though he had idea what he was doing, he will never forgive himself for it.

And I don't know if I can, either.

My phone rings. It's Leigh. "I'm dying for a bevvy. Want to go to the Bad Habit for dinner? They've got that new half-price Sunday special."

I cast a guilty look at the podcast episode sitting on my hard drive – William's darkest secret laid bare. Suddenly, I can't bear to be in the same room as it. "I'll see you there." I grab my coat. "As long as it's not roast pork."

"TELL us about your vignette idea, George," Abigail smirks as I set down my tray of breakfast food at the Orphean table. "We're waiting with bated breath."

She twirls a strand of her perfect hair, and I know she's hoping I'll deliver something lame so she can mock me. I glance down the table at the expectant faces and force myself to swallow the bile rising in my throat.

All these people *ate* a piece of Keely.

They're sitting around, going about their lives, arguing over stupid Devil's Night pranks, when a girl is dead and they *ate* her. And maybe they were tricked into doing it, but they've all chosen to say nothing, to let Keely's murderers go unpunished because they don't want a scandal.

I'll give them a fucking scandal. I have no intention of letting the Orpheans get away with this. But first, I need to move forward with the first stage of our plan. And that means I can't think about what these people did to Keely's body.

If I think about it for too long, I have to run to the bathroom.

And Abigail, who has literally eaten the flesh of her friend and covered it up, is giving me attitude because she thinks I won't come up with an exciting 'vignette' for the privileged wankfest of a Devil's Night party?

Fuck this shit.

But I have to keep pretending I'm in the dark. I have to remain on the inside of the Orpheus Society. It's the only way

I'm going to get to the bottom of this. And Devil's Night is going to play right into my plan.

"As a matter of fact, I have it all figured out. We're going to replace all the paintings in the college picture gallery with new art," I say. "We'll take down all those stuffy white men and replace them with something else."

"With what?"

I grin at William, Diana, Fatima, and Monty – the artists at the table. "It's up to you. You're in charge of creating new pieces to hang. I think this will be more fun if they're the exact same dimensions as the missing pieces, maybe they could even reference the current works in a satirical way. But we want them to really hit people in the face first thing in the morning."

"It sounds like a hoot," Monty smiles. "A genius plan, George old boy. I'm in. But how will we get past the alarms? The picture gallery is always locked up tighter than a nun's proverbial on Devil's Night."

I think of one of the contacts I have from Claws' network – a London hacking team who owes me a favor. "I can get the alarms shut off for the night."

William looks at me like he's never seen me before.

"Those paintings are significant English works. There's a Turner, and a stunning Gainsborough," Fatima says, drumming her hands nervously on the table. "I don't want our usual village thugs tearing them off the walls – they'll damage them."

"Tosh, it's all rubbish. What shall we do with it after we've hung our own masterpieces?" Monty's face perks up. "I say, a bonfire in Martyr's Quad. I'll bring the marshmallows."

"*No*," I say firmly. This is exactly why I'm offering this idea – it's big and bold, but if we do it right, it won't cause any property damage. I love Blackfriars – I don't want the Orpheans to hurt my school. "We're hiring a group of professional art movers to remove the current work and hang our new pieces. The paintings need to be stored in a temperature- and humidity-controlled atmosphere so they don't deteriorate while they're in our possession. I've got a team in mind."

Again, thanks to Claws and her contacts. I don't tell the Orpheans that this crew has more experience stealing priceless artworks than they do helping posh art-school kids with their pranks. That information is on a need-to-know basis.

I *also* don't mention that we'll be giving the curators of the portrait gallery a heads-up about our plans so that they don't panic and call the Art Squad. What we're doing is highly illegal – which is pretty typical for Orphean 'vignettes,' but this is a step up from property damage. I don't know how deep the Orpheus Society's influence goes, but it probably can't save us from charges of multi-million dollar art theft.

"This will be such a lark," Monty slaps my shoulder. "I can't wait. Good work, Georgie Pie."

My stomach tightens at his words. I'm taking a huge risk, but I have to know how deep the Orpheus Society's power goes at this school. The fact that no one else at the table seems afraid of the consequences should tell me everything I need to know.

Little does Monty know that this prank serves a secondary purpose. The distractions of Devil's Night give me the perfect chance to do a little sleuthing.

———

"YOU WANT to help me break into Father Duncan's office?" I ask Leigh as I kick her door closed and slump down on her bed.

"Sure." She sets down a wreath of leaves she's stitching together with thistles. Leigh creates these insane outdoor sculptures using only natural materials. Her current project is focused on circular forms. "Any particular reason?"

"I believe he helped Monty murder Keely. Or maybe he

didn't. But he's behind the whole thing, and if there's any evidence, it'll be in his office."

"You reckon he *just happens* to leave behind a note confessing his sins buried in his underwear drawer?" Leigh reaches for a bottle of mead and pours us both a goblet. (Mead, according to Leigh, should always be drunk from an earthenware goblet, never a glass.)

I bring my goblet to my lips and swallow a mouthful of the sweet, rich liquid. "I don't know what we'll find. He told us in class that legend says during the most ancient celebrations of Dionysos, his maenads tap into a deep atavistic state of madness, or Mainomenos, and they run wild in the forests, killing animals and tearing them apart with their own hands to consume the flesh. Keely was dismembered and Khloe May's body was never recovered and—"

"—and you think Father Duncan's a sadistic serial killer with a Bacchus fetish who might keep the bones of his victims lying around in his office?"

It sounds silly when she says it out loud. "Maybe. All I know is that too many women have died or disappeared around the Orpheus Society, and Father Duncan is behind it. And we're going to be the ones to unmask him."

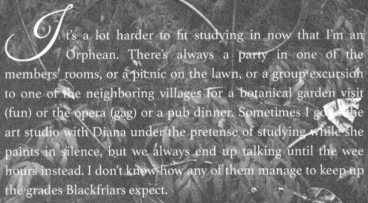

26

*I*t's a lot harder to fit studying in now that I'm an Orphean. There's always a party in one of the members' rooms, or a picnic on the lawn, or a group excursion to one of the neighboring villages for a botanical garden visit (fun) or the opera (gag) or a pub dinner. Sometimes I go to the art studio with Diana under the pretense of studying while she paints in silence, but we always end up talking until the wee hours instead. I don't know how any of them manage to keep up the grades Blackfriars expect.

Strangely, Monty often isn't with us. When I ask where he is, I'm told he's with Father Duncan. Once, when Diana and I head down to the amphitheater on one of the last sunny days of the year to listen to Richard and Alfie practice their lines for a new play, I see Monty and Father Duncan heading back up the path toward school. Father Duncan's trousers are stained with dirt.

"Hello, ladies," he waves as we pass on the narrow path. "It's a pleasant day for a walk, isn't it? As Aristotle would say, 'in all things of nature there is something of the marvelous'."

I watch them as they leave. Father Duncan holds Monty in

the crook of his arm, in a gesture that might seem to any passerby like the younger man leading the older. But I can see Father Duncan moving Monty, controlling him like a life-sized puppet. But you can't arrest a guy for holding someone's arm funny.

The next day, Monty is already seated at the table in Room 2C when we enter, and he rushes back to Father Duncan's office after class is over, claiming to have forgotten a book.

I don't know what they spend their time talking about – I don't think Father Duncan is tutoring him in Greek, because Monty's still the worst student in our class. And whenever one of us enters the room, they stop their conversation mid-sentence. Their words are not for us.

ON SUNDAYS, William and I rise at an ungodly hour to attend church.

You'd think Catholic services at 7AM at a university would be as barren as a nun's womb, but the combination of Father Duncan and Father Pearce is enough to fill the church to bursting. Father Duncan is a force of nature. His sermons are a rush of ideas so potent, they border on the supernatural. Monty sits in the front row, his mouth hanging open as if he intends to chew every ounce of wisdom from the Father's bones.

And when Sebastian speaks, he delivers a sermon so full of wry humor and moral insight you walk away feeling you've had the honor of listening to a visiting scholar, not a priest. Sometimes, when I listen to him, tears spring in the corners of my eyes for no reason, as if his God is trying to reach me through Sebastian's words.

William's face is such a picture of longing, I worry every

person in the place must be able to read our tryst on his features. Sebastian plays it cool, but sometimes he'll hand the proceedings over to Father Duncan and disappear into the sacristy, and a moment later my phone will beep with a filthy text message.

"Tell your friend William that when I hold the communion chalice, I'm imagining I'm gripping his firm cock."

Or once, "Put your bible over your knees and touch yourself underneath it."

I love it all, and I hate it, too. Because every moment feels like a betrayal of who Sebastian is, and yet I know he's never been more himself. He's endlessly busy with support groups on campus and organizing community projects and charity events. Tending his flock is as much a part of him as sticking my nose where it doesn't belong is a part of me. His vows were made to press him into a tiny box, because the church believes that he cannot serve God while he is in love, and William and I know that's not true.

When our priest calls for the devout to receive holy communion, William and I both line up, even though I'm an atheist and haven't been confirmed. William goes first. Sebastian touches his fingers to William's throat, applying a little force to tip his head back and kiss the chalice to his lips. William's Adam's apple bobs, his hands frozen at his sides.

I tear my eyes away from him to watch Monty, who has accepted his wafer from Father Duncan, and chews on it as he returns to his seat. He passes by us, watching William and Sebastian.

His lips curl back into a cruel, dark smile.

"I HAD no idea you had such a streak of criminal genius in you."

William carefully adds shading to his Holbein 'pastiche,' copying the artist's hand exactly. Except that instead of the serene monk who was the subject of the original portrait, he's created the perfect likeness of Benet of Blackfriars, naked beneath his habit, fornicating with a satyr.

"Oh, yes. Copying a master's hand is something many artists do as part of their training," William says. "It's the easiest part of a forgery. Even if I were doing a real fake and not a pastiche, this would never be mistaken by a serious collector for a real Holbein. The difficult part of forgery is sourcing the materials – paints in the correct pigments, canvases of the type and quality of the period – without accidentally creating anachronisms. Nowadays, a forgery doesn't merely have to pass a visual test, but it must undergo microscopic study and chemical analysis."

"You're more well versed in the art of forgery than I expected, Prince William."

"There's a student in my class who has some *interesting* extracurricular activities," William comments as he returns to his palette to mix pigments. "He's never been caught, but I've heard the rumors. You should watch out for Shane Kelly. He's often chatting to your friend, Leigh."

Leigh, you sly dog. I make a note to ask her about this art forger later. I spread out my books across the bed and work on my Criminology essay while William paints. Nick Cave's *Lyre of Orpheus* album plays softly in the background. William prefers to play Mahler while he paints, but we played a game of chess for control of the stereo, and I won.

I can hang out with William, and it's fine. It's fun. Wonderful, actually. But then out of nowhere I'll be hit by the truth of what he did, and it will make my stomach sink to my feet and I have to get far away. And as I watch his aristocratic features relax as he paints, the sick feeling bubbles up inside me again.

I'm in love with a cannibal.

And I want so desperately to be okay with what he did, because otherwise he will burn up in his own guilt.

I can't take it any more. I blurt out. "What are we going to do, William?"

"What do you mean?"

"About Sebastian. About you. About us. About what you did. We can't go on like this. Every Sunday you come back from church tied up in knots – and I know it's not just about Sebastian. It's killing me having to sneak around like this, pretend I'm in love with one man when really my heart belongs to two. And I can see it's killing him. But it seems like it's already killed you."

William is focused on a detail of Benet's foot. "Sebastian chose God over me a long time ago."

"Did he, though? He came here, to Blackfriars, to be close to you."

"Yes, and look where that got us." He rubs at the paint with his finger. "I can't change what I did. His God's forgiveness will not absolve my sin. Eventually Sebastian will realize his soul hangs in the balance and he will have to choose. Every day he wears those robes he chooses his God over us, and one day it won't be enough for either of us to be second best. If I can be with you every day, even when you can barely stand to kiss me, then the hole in my heart will heal. You're enough for me, George."

You're enough for me. Isn't that what every girl wants to hear?

And yet...I know it's not true. Ever since I've come to know both of them, my heart has expanded to fit them both. I understand that love isn't about edges, about boundaries. Love is filling your chest with fresh air until you think you will explode. It's riding that rollercoaster all the way to the end. And now that we're back at Blackfriars and we no longer have the safety of the temple, there's a deep, Sebastian-shaped hole in my chest where he's supposed to be. William wants to pave over his hole but I can't, I can't.

"I want to kiss you," I say. "I don't want it to be like this. But I—"

"I know," he cuts in, his words crisp. "I hate myself, too."

"I don't hate you. And neither does Sebastian. You could tell him how you feel, you know," I say.

"What would that achieve? He won't leave the church unless we ask him, and I'll never ask him to leave, so that's that."

"You can ask him," I say. "If it's what you truly want. You should always ask for what you want."

William shakes his head with such fury he steaks grey paint across his canvas. "I can't." He dabs angrily at the mistake. "Even if it wasn't his soul on the line, even if I'm not so soaked in sin that he cannot possibly abide me, Father Pearce is the only one holding my father together. Sir Henry lives in hope that if he spends enough time atoning, enough hours in reverent prayer, he will be rid of his guilt for what he did to my mother."

And suddenly, I glimpse William's future. Rotting away in that empty, joyless family seat alongside his father, his knees scraped raw from kneeling at the altar of his sins, begging for forgiveness that won't come because he will never forgive himself. And it tears my heart in two.

I lean over and pluck the brush from his hands. William looks up in surprise and I grab his cheeks and pull his mouth to mine.

He tastes like all the things he is – old poetry books and oil paint fumes and sea salt and desolation. I pour all my love into the kiss – a desperate flailing to hold on to him before he slips away forever.

"I love you," I whisper against his lips. "And we will get through this."

William cups my neck and pulls me closer, drinking deep as if I can fill the hole torn in his heart by his sin. And I know that I can't possibly heal that hole, that he needs to do that himself, but he needs my love to patch him up.

He needs me to keep fighting.

"*M*mmm, positively smashing." Monty pops a second raw mushroom onto his long tongue and chews it to mush with his mouth open. Watching Montague Cavendish eat is like watching two stray cats fucking – it's violent and terrifying, but you can't look away.

"Glad you like 'em." I back out of his room, ready to make a run for the stairs before he traps me with another foraging request. "I've got a tutorial, so I'll see you around—"

"Wait." Monty grabs my arm. It takes everything I have not to punch him in his posh snoz. If even half of what George suspects about this lad is true, he's dangerous as fuck and I shouldn't be within ten feet of him. But as long as I play nice, I get to stay 'in' with the Orpheans, and at Blackfriars, that's a good place to be.

Ever since George and I hooked up as pals and I've been seen around with the Orpheans, people have stopped with the 'Lotto bitch' bollocks. I thought I'd left that shit behind in Liverpool, but the people who go to this school care even more about money, if you can believe it. You can't just *have* money at Blackfriars, it's supposed to come from your great great grandpappy who looted Constantinople or gave Queen Elizabeth a bit of how's your father. My family didn't earn their fortune stomping on the backs of cowering peasants, yet *my* money is dirty? Go figure that.

No one takes me seriously, which means no one takes my *art* seriously, which means that I'll be stuck teaching fingerpainting at some posh reform school unless I can get some decent contacts in the art world, which the Orpheans have in spades. If collecting a few edible shrooms for Monty will give me access to the people he knows, I'll oblige.

While George and I try to take them down in secret, of course.

So I don't react when Monty's fingers close around my skin, when he pulls me against his chest so my racing heart thuds against his ribcage. "Won't you stay for a meal, Leigh Cho?" He licks his lips, and the glint in the eye makes it clear that I'm on the menu.

And knowing what George told me about Devil's Night, I don't know if he's planning to fuck me or fry me in butter. Probably both.

"Another time." I yank down on my arm, breaking his hold and spinning for the door. I'm halfway down the stairs when I yell back, "Enjoy the spores."

Footsteps clatter on the stone stairs behind me. I look back over my shoulder and there's Monty, following me with a diabolical smile on his face. "Where are you going?" he calls after me. "Are we playing a game? You hide and I find you. That's my favorite kind of game."

I reach the ground floor and hit the bricks, shoving students out of my way as I sprint across St. Benedict's Quad and duck into the Cloister Garden. Behind me, Monty laughs his high-pitched, serial-killer laugh as he strides after me on those long, praying mantis legs of his.

"Come out, come out, wherever you are," he calls as he swings on the creaking garden gate. Nowhere on campus is safe, except...

I slam my shoulder into the garden entrance to the art and theatre departments, skidding as the soles of my Docs slide on the polished marble floor. I turn down a dark, medieval corridor, and then another, until I reach a row of heavy wooden doors that were once cells for the monks. One door is different from the rest – while the others have the original locks that open the huge, old-fashioned keys, this door has an electronic keypad and a hefty steel lock.

I beat my fist against the door. No reply from inside. *Please don't let him be here. Please let me be able to get in.*

I scramble in my pocket for the key. My hands tremble as I fit it in the lock. It takes me three tries to get the thing in. I can hear Monty whistling a tune as he wanders the labyrinthine halls, looking for me. Any moment now he'll turn down here and see—

The key turns. I slam my finger onto the electronic pad. The door flies open. *Thank fuck, he's not here.* I throw myself inside and slam it behind me. The lock clicks into place, but I don't trust it's enough to keep Monty away from me. I reach down the length of the door, sliding five deadbolts and combination locks shut.

"You're lucky I didn't lock those," a voice calls behind me in a musical Irish brogue.

Shite, he is here.

The walls of the narrow, cramped cell close in around me. I press my hand against my ribs as I fight to regain my breath while Shane fucking Kelly glares at me from behind his workbench.

My first year, I arrived at Blackfriars the day after Michaelmas term officially began. I wanted to move into my dorm and get set up in the art department in the dead of night, which they wouldn't let me do, so I settled for a day late, when everyone was too busy with classes and freshers week to notice the Liverpool Lotto Girl show up.

Turns out, there are downsides to arriving late. As well as use of the large, communal studio spaces where most of our tutorials take place, the art department includes a suite of monk cells-turned-private studios that students rent by the term. They're in hot demand and they're all gone bar one by the time I show up to put my name down.

I'm standing in the hall in front of the last open studio door, glaring at my phone screen and wondering why it was blacked out as an option on the Blackfriars' app, when someone slams their hand into the door beside me, narrowly missing smashing my face.

"Oi, watch it." I jump out of my skin and whirl around to face the meff. "What the fuck do you want?"

My eyes meet a pair of startling green orbs. The color of them is so unique it drives the wind from my lungs. I've only ever seen that kind of green in nature – in the first buds of spring growth punching through the dreary, dead forest, in the translucent tendrils of fog that linger on the edges of the marsh at the estate. It takes me a moment to realize those green eyes are attached to a person – a lad about my age with close-shaved dark hair, a skull of exquisitely angular lines and panes, a smattering of abstract ink curling around his neck and around his ears, and a viciously mischievous smile tugging at the edges of full-red lips.

"Don't even think about using that studio," he purrs in a seductive voice, thick with Irish inflection – the kind of voice that vibrates in your bones. "It's reserved for members of the Orpheus Society."

I didn't know what that was back then, but I was pretty sure it was some toff thing. So I curl my lip at him and sneer, "You a member of this Orcish Society, then? Sounds like a Dungeons and Dragons group."

"*They wouldn't take the likes of me,*" he says, his voice taking on a hard, dangerous edge that makes my toes curl inside my Docs. He rubs the stubble on his jaw. "*But I've got space for one more person in my studio. If you're interested.*"

My sculptures are usually too large and ungainly to work on in my dorm room. This guy exudes trouble like it's his fucking eau de cologne, but I'm out of options. "*I'm interested.*"

"*There's one condition, though. I'm going to be working on some personal projects alongside my coursework. I need to store my tools there, so I'll be installing additional security. Whatever you see, you don't ask questions, and you don't tell anyone else. Got it?*"

As he speaks, his eyes travel over my body, taking in my slight frame, my dark hair, tiny nose, and tiny tits swimming in my oversized Iron Maiden hoodie. If he recognizes me as the Liverpool Lotto Girl, he doesn't say a word. Instead, he grins even wider, one of those heart-stopping, shit-eating grins that can topple a civilization.

He likes what he sees.

I want to kick the arrogant prick in the nuts for eye-fucking me, but honestly, it feels good to have someone look at me and see something other than the media circus that surrounds my family. For the first time in a long time, a smile tugs at the corner of my mouth.

"*Got it.*" *I hold out my hand.* "*I don't fuck with your shit, and you don't fuck with mine.*"

"*Deal.*" *He takes my hand, and as we shake, a strange, sizzling heat travels up my arm, through my chest, and pools in my belly.*

And that was how I ended up sharing a studio space with Shane Kelly, insanely talented artist, owner of two ethereal green eyes and one seriously hot Irish accent, and all-round arsehole.

He's the one who changed the lock and installed the deadbolts, so he can lock this place down like San Quentin from the inside in case one of the tutors decides they want to have a snoop around.

I usually have the studio to myself on Fridays, so I didn't expect him to be here. I wouldn't have come if I'd known he was here to witness me running from Monty, to see how afraid I am. I've worked hard to make sure Shane Kelly only sees the parts of me I want him to see, and now it's all coming undone. I'm coming undone.

I lean my back against the door. I can't stop trembling.

Shane's in the corner, wearing his apron and visor and fussing with his latest work. He's spent the last two weeks sculpting what looks like a Roman lion from a giant slab of *rosso antico* stone. After laboriously polishing the surface, he's now laying strips of wet cloth strategically over the surface, which he'll then pour liquified gas over to create mini explosions that blow off fine layers of the stone's texture. I've seen him do this before – it degrades the surface and makes the sculpture look old. I have my suspicions as to why Shane Kelly might want to make a perfectly finished sculpture look like it was dug up from a centuries-old Roman temple, but today is not the day to voice them. We have our agreement, and I'm staying out of his shit.

Someone bangs on the door. "Oh, Leeeeeeeigh," Monty croons. "I know you're in there. I won the game, so you'd better come out and join me at the pub, or I'll get someone to break down this door."

Shane takes one look at my face, and his playful expression turns deadly fucking serious. "Git out of the way." He grabs a tooth chisel from the workbench and stalks toward the door. I leap out of the way and reach up to grab his hand.

"No, don't let him in—"

Shane yanks open the door. When he sees Shane, Monty does a double-take but recovers quickly, pushing forward to get right up in Shane's face.

"What you doing in here with Leigh?" he demands imperiously, but his eyes flick nervously over Shane's face. If I didn't know better, I'd think Monty Cavendish – Hierophant of the Orpheus Society and king of this school – is *afraid* of Shane.

But that's ridiculous. Monty isn't afraid of anyone. People are afraid of *Monty*, and for good reason. I'm not the only one with stories about my family splashed through the tabloids. Rumor has it, Monty's parents kept their teenage maid locked in their dungeon torture chamber for six weeks. Only a substantial payout to the girl's family to cover up the scandal kept them out of prison.

"Leigh doesn't want you around here," Shane growls, grabbing Monty's collar and pressing the blade of the chisel against his throat. Up close, I see that Shane has several pounds on Monty – he's taller, broader in the shoulders, and downright meaner. There's something in those green eyes that's a little unhinged. "And nor do I. Now, feck off before I knock your bollix in. Go ndéana an diabhal dréimire do chnámh do dhroma."

Monty's eyes widen. Shane shoves him into the hallway. Monty hits the wall and crumples to the floor. Shane slams the door in Monty's face, cackling as he twirls the chisel between his fingers like he's Keith Moon about to break into an impressive drum solo. I press my ear to the door and listen to footsteps scrambling against the marble, retreating down the hall. And then, silence.

"He may be as thick as a beach ball, but he'll stay clear of you if he knows what's good for him." Shane drops the chisel onto his workbench and returns to his work.

"Thanks." I slump into the stool I keep in my workstation, wiping sweat from my brow. Now that it's all over, I realize I'm wet all the way through, my clothes clinging to my damp skin. "What's that thing you said to him?"

"Irish curse." Shane frowns at the statue as he removes one

of his cotton strips and replaces it along the lion's mane. "I told him that the devil will make a ladder out of his spine."

"Nice one." I feel strange as I sit down at my station, all light and giddy. Not like I've just run away from Monty Cavendish, but more like I've wiped my arse with a Tesla coil.

And I have no idea why.

Okay, okay, yeah. You got me. I *do* know why. I'll admit it. I have a ridiculous fucking childish crush on Shane Kelly. So sue me. It's the Irish accent that did it. You try being trapped in a box with a devastatingly attractive Irish artist with possible criminal intentions for three years and see how you fare.

I can barely stand to be in the studio with him because I can't work when he's here. His broad shoulders, his smoke and roses scent, his ghostly green eyes take up all the air, and I can't breathe and I drop things and I babble utter nonsense and make myself out as a right meff. So I try to only come in when I know he's not here.

And I haven't told him I'm into him because...well, look at me. Look at him. I'm the Liverpool Lotto Girl and he's a fucking scholarship student from Belfast with neck tattoos and a dark reputation. He doesn't go for girls like me. He's always got some bird on his arm – dumb girls from the village with tramp stamp tattoos and caked-on goth makeup who worship him like he's fucking Banksy.

And I don't go for lads like him, not if I want a serious career as an artist. Not if I want galleries to pay attention to me for the right reasons. And that's why I haven't even mentioned him to George.

Or it might be that I'm sick to fucking death of everything in my life being on display, right? When Pops won the Lotto, the tabloids circled like the vultures they are. "What are you going to spend all that money on?" they asked Ma and Pops in their smarmy voices, as if they already knew the answer and were trying to hold back their laughter.

Ma and Pops don't get it, of course. They think the whole thing was a lark, all their purchases listed in the papers, having the media camped out on the doorstep. "It's like I'm Princess Di," Ma would say as she watched two paps rooting through our garbage. She still gives them a queen wave every time she walks past.

I don't bother reminding her that things didn't turn out so peachy keen for Lady Di.

"What was that about?" Shane asks without looking up.

I snap my head toward him. That's the first time he's ever asked me a personal question about myself. In the years we've shared this studio space, he's been all business. I answer as casually as I can with my heart running a steeplechase around my chest cavity. "The usual nonsense – Montague Cavendish thinking he owns the world."

"I thought you were friends with that lot. The Orpheans." Shane's eyes search mine. I blink, trying to retain my composure as those liquid green orbs sweep over me with penetrating curiosity. In this light, they're the color of moss. "I heard they're planning some big stunt for Devil's Night, involving the portrait gallery."

I nod. "I think it might be your kind of thing."

"What's that supposed to mean?" His features turn hard, nasty. It's like someone's flipped a switch inside him, banishing the artist and turning on the thug. The planes of his face tighten, the vein above his eye throbs with barely concealed rage.

See? I told you he's all wrong for me.

"Nothing. Just that..." I shrug, nodding to his lion.

Shane slams his hose down on the workbench. He storms across the room and stands over my chair, looming over me like a loomy thing. He braces one hand on the wall above me and cups my chin with the other. Electric sparks ping against my skin as he wrenches my head up so I have no choice but to take him in.

"We have an agreement." The vein above his eye throbs. I'm transfixed by it – it's like a snake slithering beneath his skin. It's a better place to look than his haunting eyes or those fucking full lips. When he speaks, his breath kisses my face. It smells of mint and cigarette smoke and sweet rose petals. "You don't tell anyone what goes on in here."

"And you don't get all up in my shit," I shoot back. And just to show Shane that I don't take his shit, that getting all up in my face doesn't give him the upper hand, I give him a big moose lick right up his cheek.

"What the fuck?" Shane reels, touching his cheek, where a line of saliva clings to his stubble. I crack up laughing.

"Bitch." Shane storms out, the door slamming behind him. I lean back in my chair and will my heart to calm the fuck down. The taste of mint and roses still taints my tongue.

28

*D*evil's Night.

It feels like a century ago and also like yesterday when I sat at the window on my small Cavendish Quad room and watched a parade of rich wankers in white robes destroy a perfectly good historical well, since I wandered out into the darkness to search for my missing roommate and found a fallen prince in a garden instead.

Now, I sit at the window of William's room and watch as students scramble across campus to make it to the dining hall or buttery before they close. A year ago I was one of them, locking myself into my room while chaos and mayhem reigned around me.

Tonight is different. Tonight the campus belongs to me.

Well, it's not completely different. Because last year I snuck out when I wasn't supposed to. And tonight – while the rest of the club is off supervising our great art prank – Leigh and I will break into Father Duncan's rooms to try and find the answers to Keely's death.

William lies beside me, his fingers tangled in my hair. His thoughts are elsewhere – I suspect they're in a tiny cell in a hilltop monastery in Snowdonia where Father Duncan sent Sebastian for a week-long silent retreat.

"He's happy," I whisper to William. "He's breathing in the mountain air and praying the hours."

"I'm not worried about him." William pulls my face to his and kisses my nose. "I'm worried about my crazy mystery-obsessed girlfriend who is breaking into a murderer's office."

"I'll be fine. I've done this kind of thing before. Don't make me remind you of the time I—"

"—cleaned a henchman's blood from your mother's kitchen cabinets, I remember." William shudders. I've told him a few details about my life back in Emerald Beach with Claws, and all it's achieved is to make him determined that I'll never go back there. "I still don't like the idea of you going alone."

"I'm not alone. I'll have Leigh. And Tiberius will be skulking in the shadows, watching us." I know that's not what he means, but I can't let him change the plan at the last minute. "I need you to keep Father Duncan distracted. Keep him at the party as long as possible and text me if he leaves."

William pulls me to him, pressing his lips to mine. I sink into the kiss, even though I know it's a trick to keep me with him, to stop me from walking into the lion's den tonight. It's a pretty good trick.

I tear myself away from him and slide off the bed. I toss my clothes on the chair. William picks up the folded white robes and helps me into mine before pulling his over his muscled shoulders. The thin robes hide nothing, which is honestly a blessing when it comes to William, because I will never get enough of his body. His eyes roam over me with a mixture of sadness and hunger. "I wish we didn't have to go out there. I want to stay here with you. Make our own Devil's Night mischief."

I fist the front of his robe, bringing him close for a kiss. "Stop tempting me. We have a cannibal murderer to catch. This is every true-crime podcaster's dream."

At my words, William freezes.

I grip his shoulders. "Don't. Don't look at me like that. You know I'm not doing this because I want to make a spectacle of it. I want you to be free of this hold Monty has over you, and the only way to do that is to bring down the one behind all of this. If Father Duncan goes down for these crimes, it won't just be Keely and all of you who unwittingly ate her who get justice, but Khloe May and the body in Paris and all these old, unsolved murders."

The guilt pings against my skull, but I ignore it. I recorded those podcast episodes for myself, for my own thought process. I'm not releasing them, and if I tell William about them, it'll only confuse and upset him.

William adjusts my robe on my shoulders as I give my hair a final tease with my fingers. I slip my feet into my trusty New Rocks – they look ridiculous with the robe, but no way am I walking around campus barefoot – and we slip into the night.

William's fingers curl in mine as we walk across the quad. All is silent, save for the muffled pounding of bass from behind locked doors. My skin prickles from jealous eyes watching me from the dorm rooms above. The sun has disappeared below the spires, and the sky greets us with stripes of blood-red and royal purple. The thrice-born god is close tonight.

We meet the others at the fountain. Diana's breasts shimmer with body glitter and she smells like vanilla and blackcurrant. Everyone else is wearing masks or hoods pulled low. I recognize the eight other members of the society, and hanging back, enjoying the show, are a few older Orpheans. I scan their bodies, searching for Father Duncan. I think he's second from the end, wearing the curved horns of a ram, but I can't be sure.

Sagging breasts poke from the folds of robes, and dangly

bits...*dangle* between legs. It's kind of weird to have the ex-Orpheans here for Devil's Night. Why are a bunch of professional, upper-class British toffs interested in dancing naked around their old college campus? I hastily turn back to William. I wonder if I've just seen the wrinkly sac of a duke.

I'm handed a lantern to light my way to tonight's mischief. Percy beats his drum, and Fatima has a flute-thing that she plays, while we kind of shuffle around in an awkward dance. This ritual has a different vibe to what happened at the temple on the lake – we're all aware of the students watching from the windows, and the practically naked ex-members who might one day be our bosses or patrons, so the movements become performative.

Monty goes from person to person, muttering in Greek as he lights our lanterns. The opening ritual is complete. Champagne corks pop, and Richard waves a baggie of cocaine under my nose.

"No thanks," I wave him away. "Cocaine makes me sneeze."

Monty, Tabitha, and a few others crowd around Richard, eager for their sniff of the goods. Once again I'm struck by how cultish elements attempt to obfuscate perfectly ordinary college antics. We're just a group of students dressed in weird outfits getting fucked up in an empty quad. We're not special. There's no god here.

How many perfectly ordinary women have died on Devil's Night? How many more will be sacrificed so Father Duncan can claim to be possessed by an ancient god? It's all *nonsense*.

When the Champagne bottle is passed to me, I throw my head back and pretend to gulp down the sticky-sweet bubbles. I can't drink. I need my head about me tonight.

Monty finishes a single bottle himself. He tosses the empty into the fountain, where it smashes on the marble. Bits of glass float in the water. I wince, thinking of John the groundskeeper who'll have to clean that in the morning. I'm ashamed to be part of this, but at least I've stopped them from being as destructive as they might otherwise have been.

"Follow me to our sacred temple for the next ritual." Monty claps his hands, and the Orpheans follow him as he skips toward St. Benedict's cathedral.

As the group passes through the nave and down into the Roman baths, I cast a last, fleeting glance at William up ahead and duck off to the right. I flatten myself into an alcove so I'm not seen. When the procession has passed me by, I slide open Sebastian's door and creep inside.

"Leigh," I whisper, holding my lantern up, making shadows dance over the piles of books. "Please tell me you're here—"

I choke back a scream as a table lamp flickers on, illuminating Leigh and another familiar face.

"Surprise." Sebastian grins, standing from his chair. "Can I offer you a tea?"

29

I open my mouth and shut it again. I can't believe this. He's not supposed to be here. He's supposed to be at his silent retreat in Snowdonia, not arousing suspicion.

"George, I don't know if you know this, but your tits are hanging out." Leigh fingers the edge of my robe, her lips curled back in an evil smile. She tweaks one of the horns on my mask and laughs her loud, baying laugh. I press my finger to her lips, and she manages to muffle her voice with a cushion.

I turn to glare at Sebastian. "You're not supposed to be here."

"I didn't like the idea of you doing this alone," he says.

I sigh. "You and William are such worrywarts. You do know that I—"

"—once held your finger over a grenade trigger set off by a psychopath to prevent it blowing up your friends." Sebastian sighs. "I've heard. But that doesn't mean I'm going to let you walk into a murderer's office."

"You were supposed to go to the retreat like you do every year. If anything is out of the ordinary, we could tip off Father Duncan."

"The great thing about Trappist monks is that they're a silent order. They're not going to call Duncan to chew me out," Sebastian shrugs. "Shouldn't we get going?"

"You're not coming," I glare at him.

"I thought I was the one who gave the commands," he says with a coy smile. Behind him, Leigh chokes on her own tongue.

Heat flares across my face. "Sebastian, you can't—"

"This is not up for debate," he says in that forceful, rich voice of his.

"That's right. It's not. You're a faculty member, and you're not an Orphean. If we're caught, I'll get a slap on the wrist. If you're caught, you'll be up before the disciplinary committee. William won't be able to protect you. I won't risk your job."

"It's my choice to risk my job," he says. "I'm here now, and you know how much I love an intellectual debate. It will take you longer to talk me out of this than if we just got on with it."

I sigh. All along, he planned to come with us. He knew I wouldn't be able to win this argument. "Fine." I wave us onward.

As we shuffle back through the nave, the chanting voices rise up from beneath us. We exit the church and creep back through St. Benedict's Quad. We pass the entrance to the Cloister Garden and I feel a pang, remembering the moment last year where William pressed against me in the gloom, hiding me from Monty's wrath.

Monty, who seemed preoccupied with me, who hid his sordid act on my body farm site to fuck with me. Monty, who made a plan to take Keely into the woods and dismember her. Monty, whose parents raised him on lessons in cruelty and avarice, who doesn't know the meaning of the words 'no' and 'enough,' who wants to keep William all to himself.

Monty, who has fallen under the spell of an even more dangerous man.

We make our way to the Tower. The main doors are bolted, as per the Devil's Night rules, but as a teacher, Sebastian has the master keys, so he made sure the side door was left unlocked. We slip inside and climb the stairs carefully, trying to make no sound. Faculty members who live in college have their rooms here, including Professor Hipkins. If they hear voices in the hallway, they'd probably assume it was the Orpheans playing a prank in the building, but we can't risk anyone cracking their door to peek, or they might tell Father Duncan what they see.

We head upstairs as quickly and as quietly as we can. Sebastian tests the knob of Father Duncan's office. Locked. He looks to me as if to say, "what now?"

I yank two pins from my hair, and strip off the rubber knobs on the ends with my teeth. One I pull apart into a flat metal piece, inserting it into the lock to create a little hook on the end, then bending the other end back on itself to create a handle. The other I squeeze on the ends to bend it into a right angle – my lever. I insert the lever into the bottom of the lock, turn it slightly, and then push my pick on top of it and feel for the first seized pin. I push that up and hear it click.

"I could have just gotten you his key," Sebastian whispers, his warm breath on my ear sending a tremble through my body.

"I thought of that," I whisper back as I work on the next pin. "Duncan's precious about this office. That's what makes me sure there's evidence here. I couldn't risk him noticing his key gone and becoming suspicious of you, not with what I believe he already knows about you."

"Okay, I have a question now. How do you know how to pick a lock?" Leigh sounds both impressed and a little terrified.

"It's easy, especially with these old-fashioned locks. You just have to—" I bite my lip as the final pin lifts into place and the lock turns "—be patient."

I take one last look at the doors to the other offices and the staircase, making sure no one is watching. Then I usher Leigh and Sebastian inside and close the door softly behind us.

We stand in the sitting room where Father Duncan holds our Greek classes. Lit only by a square of moonlight at the window and the light of my lantern, it's a labyrinth of precariously-stacked books and eldritch shadows. It's also an absolute mess. Sebastian steps up to the table, shuffling through the scribbled translations and dog-eared textbooks we leave there each week, like the rings of a tree marking the passage of time.

"Let's see what snacks old Hannibal Lecter has on offer." Leigh yanks open a kitchen cupboard, riffling through crisp packets and glass jars of sugar and teabags.

"We have to put everything back exactly as we found it," I whisper, moving as silently as I can through the kitchenette. Although Father Duncan often served us sandwiches, cakes, or cheese and crackers like we were distinguished guests instead of students, only Monty has ever been permitted back into the father's private living space, to fetch a book of Greek lyric poetry Duncan left on the kitchen counter. That favoritism is significant.

I peruse the cork board pinned over the counter. It bulges beneath the weight of its contents – new papers pinned over old; pamphlets from local theatre companies and the York Philharmonic, faculty announcements, ticket stubs, train timetables, postcards. I pull off a stack of postcards and flip through them – mostly they're written in Greek, from students on their summer travels. I notice one from Diana; a picture of the temple of Eleusis. And several from Monty, written in his childish scrawl. His Greek is simple enough I can read most of it – rambling about his travels and his art, often written in the boasting tone of a son desperately trying to impress his father—

"Uh, Miss Marple, you might want to see this."

I whirl around. Leigh steps back from the pot cupboard, her face white. Inside the door is a series of photographs, newspaper cuttings, hand-drawn maps, and scrawled notes, most of them written in Greek. It looks a lot like the murder boards you saw in police dramas, or – in this case – the wall in the home of a serial killer.

Pictures of Khloe May, Keely, and five other women all peer out at me with young, innocent eyes. Words scribbled in Greek that chill my blood to ice – *sacrifice, Mainomenos, devour, Tristeria...*

Leigh peels another photograph from the murder wall and holds it up. "George, *look.*"

All I can see in the dim light is the face of a woman. I lift my lantern.

I stifle a scream.

It's a photograph of me.

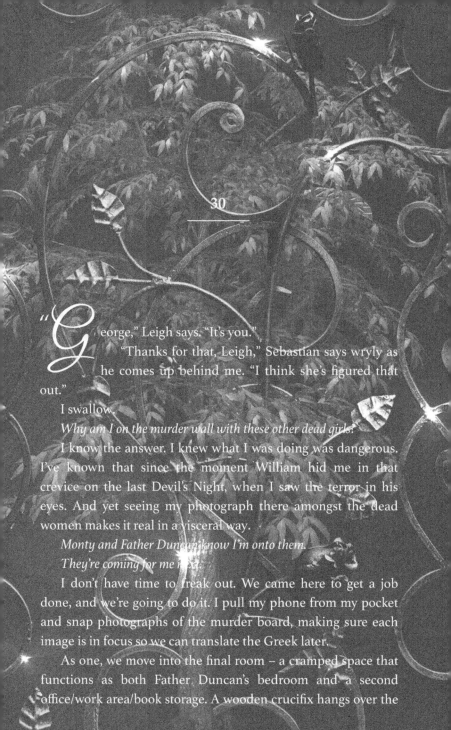

30

"George," Leigh says. "It's you."

"Thanks for that, Leigh," Sebastian says wryly as he comes up behind me. "I think she's figured that out."

I swallow.

Why am I on the murder wall with these other dead girls?

I know the answer. I knew what I was doing was dangerous. I've known that since the moment William hid me in that crevice on the last Devil's Night, when I saw the terror in his eyes. And yet seeing my photograph there amongst the dead women makes it real in a visceral way.

Monty and Father Duncan know I'm onto them.

They're coming for me next.

I don't have time to freak out. We came here to get a job done, and we're going to do it. I pull my phone from my pocket and snap photographs of the murder board, making sure each image is in focus so we can translate the Greek later.

As one, we move into the final room – a cramped space that functions as both Father Duncan's bedroom and a second office/work area/book storage. A wooden crucifix hangs over the bed. Rickety shelves along one wall hold an array of holy objects – prayer candles, a framed photograph of the Pope preaching in Vatican City, a couple of gold crosses inlaid with precious jewels, and some other objects I don't recognize but look both expensive and holy—

"What's this old thing?" Leigh pulls an object off the shelf and shakes it. Spindly gold angels with wings glittering with diamonds hold some kind of glass prism with something lumpy encased inside—

"It's a reliquary." Sebastian takes it gently from her. He turns the object over. "It's a box for holding religious relics, like pieces of the cross or the tongue of St. Anthony. This one is interesting. See the relief work around the base? It depicts Benet of Blackfriars' miracles. The man would have been canonized as a saint if he'd died with the other monks instead of escaping to Paris and setting up the blasphemous Orpheus Society. According to this inscription, this reliquary contains two of Benet's finger bones. This item was recorded as being part of the treasure of St. Benedict's, but it went missing from the church a number of years ago. It was believed students stole it. I wonder how Father Duncan came to have it in his possession, or why he's never mentioned it—"

"Um...Sebastian." I point to the glass casing in the center of the ornate gothic statue. "There are three finger bones inside."

"That's not right." Sebastian holds the reliquary up to the light and inspects the contents. "The records are very detailed, and when archaeologists X-rayed Benet's grave, they found only two fingers missing. How can there be three bones?"

"Because one of them doesn't belong to Benet."

"I doubt any of them belonged to Benet," Sebastian says. "The church has a long history of faking relics. There weren't enough saint's fingers to go around, so—"

"Sebastian," I say gently. "It's not the time for a lecture."

He swallows. "Right."

"Look at that third bone," I say, resting my head on his shoulder so I can see better. "It's clearly newer than the others. In fact, I'd say that's a recent addition."

"You think—" Leigh's voice rises in pitch. "You think this creepy bastard took a finger from Keely and shoved it in that little box?"

"Keely, or Khloe May. Only one way to find out." I grab the reliquary from Sebastian's hands and flip it over. "How do we open this?"

"You're not supposed to open it. It's sacred—"

But I've already found a tiny hinge in the plate-gold, which I swing open as I tip the reliquary upside down. The three bones drop into my gloved palm. I resist the urge to drop them. I shove Benet's fingers back into the container, and drop the mystery bone into a paper envelope I pull from a stack beside the bed.

"We can't take that bone," Sebastian says.

"We have to. I need to get it to the lab for DNA testing." I hand the envelope to Leigh, since I don't have pockets. "I need to know whose finger it is—"

We're interrupted by the shattering of glass. I wince as the sound pierces the silent night. It's probably just one of the Orpheans smashing a Champagne bottle. But I hear another smash, and another, like a tidal wave of destruction rolling closer.

Leigh runs to the window in the sitting room and peers out. "That gobshite."

"Who?"

"Monty Cavendish. He's got a baseball bat. He's breaking all the windows in the quad."

Shit.

I crowd in beside Leigh. Sure enough, there's Monty, accompanied by two others – I can't tell if they're present-day

Orpheans or alumni from this distance. Monty's yelling in garbled Greek and swinging the bat at the windows, while the man with him picks up loose cobbles and throws them at the upper stories, raining shards of glass down on them like crystalline snow.

"They're coming this way," Leigh hisses. "We should get out of here."

Damn right we should. Sebastian replaces the reliquary on Duncan's shelf while I slam the kitchen cupboards shut and try to replace the papers on the table the way I remember them. We scramble out of the room, sliding the lock into place. Hopefully, Father Duncan won't notice the finger is missing for some time, and if he does, what can he do? Report it to the police?

Down the steps we fly. I kick off my boots and hold them in my hand to make my footsteps quieter. Leigh copies me with her Docs. Sebastian reaches the bottom story first and reaches for the side door just as someone on the other side grabs the handle and shoves it open.

Sebastian throws his shoulder at the door, slamming it back. "Hide," he mouths to us. I grab Leigh's hand and pull her into a storage closet just as the person on the other side of the door manages to shove it open. We can't pull the door all the way shut without risking a sound, so I pull Leigh as far back amongst the mops and old paint cans and watch through the narrow cracks as a white-robed figure steps inside.

"Father Pearce." Father Duncan's voice lilts with surprise. "What are you doing here? Aren't you supposed to be in Snowdonia with our Trappist brothers?"

"The bus broke down," Sebastian says, the lie rolling smoothly off his tongue. "I'd have to wait until morning for another, and I thought I'd rather do that in my own bed than spend the school's money on a frivolous hotel. I had to scale the outer wall of the refectory, and when I landed on this side I saw some of the students in the quad and I didn't want them to see me. I tried this door and it was unlocked, so I thought I'd hide in here until they moved on..."

Sebastian's eyes roam over Duncan's bare chest, the white robe with the hem, the ram's horn mask tucked under his arm.

"You shouldn't be out of your room after dark," Duncan says. "You know what night it is. You know the rules."

The air sizzles with the threat dripping from his words.

"I'm aware of the rules," Sebastian says, raising his face to meet Duncan's eyes. His own threat is implicit. *You may know that I've broken my vow of chastity, but the school will not be amused to find out their favorite priest is running around naked, smashing up the school's windows in the company of a heathen society.*

If I fall, you fall.

Duncan places a hand on Sebastian's shoulder. "When I accepted you for this post, I knew you would be a good fit for Blackfriars. I see a fire inside you, Sebastian, a righteous fire that matches my own. Make sure you don't burn out that flame on the wrong hearth."

"Yes, Father."

Duncan moves into an office space. The walls are covered in cubby holes where tutors receive their internal school mail. He riffles in one of the desk drawers, and I hear the rattle of keys. "Take this," he says to Sebastian. "It's the key to an empty office on the third floor. There's a camp bed made up there. You'll sleep there tonight. It's not prudent for you to return to your rooms until morning. Is that clear?"

"Yes, Father."

"I think, Sebastian, that you should come by my office tomorrow morning. It's been a few months since your last confession." They move back into the corridor, into my line of sight, and Father Duncan places his hand on Sebastian's shoulder. "I think it would do you good to unburden your soul to God."

"Thank you." Sebastian takes the key. Duncan gives him one final nod before ducking out the door. I hear the scrape as another key is turned in the lock, and we're sealed inside the Martyrs' Tower.

Sebastian waits, staring at the window as glass smashes in the quad. When he's certain Father Duncan has moved away from the building, he flings open our door. "Come on out." I dive into his arms, so grateful that he managed to talk his way out of immediate trouble.

"That was close." Leigh dusts herself off, tripping over a mop handle as she untangles herself from the closet.

Sebastian leans against the wall, fingering the rosary beads around his neck – the same beads that had been inside me. "This isn't over. Not for me. I need to get to that room upstairs. He'll check on me, and the two of you can't be here when he does."

He pulls us into the office and locates a window. It faces one of the narrow alleys between Blackfriar's ancient buildings. It's a long drop to the ground, but it's the best we'll do. Leigh hops over the sill and drops. "Ouch," she cries as she lands in a spiky hawthorn bush. I slide out next. Leigh helps place my feet on the stone wall so I can climb down without falling or getting stuck with hawthorn spikes.

Sebastian peers down at us and presses his fingers to his lips before holding them out to me. "Be careful," he whispers. The rosary dangles from his fingers. I wave at him.

Leigh's room is in St. Benedict's, so we go there first, slipping her in through a ground-floor window we left open for exactly this purpose. Once she's safely inside and out of sight, I brush down my robes and head toward the church.

The party is in full swing by the time I arrive. Richard,

Percy, Fatima, and Matilda are fucking on one of the couches, while Monty chases Diana around in circles in the tepid bath, humming the *Jaws* soundtrack at the top of his lungs as she squeals with delight. Father Duncan sits in the smaller, hotter pool – the caldarium – chatting with two other older Orpheans. He looks up when I enter, and his eyes roam freely over my body. I yank the edges of the robe across my naked skin.

I find William near a table overflowing with food and bottles of mead provided by Leigh, talking to a woman who I recognize through her mask as Madame Ulrich.

"Georgina Fisher," she says. I can't believe she recognizes me. She clasps my hands in hers. Her breasts are remarkably perky for someone who must be in their sixties. "I am bereaved, positively *bereaved*, that you did not continue with my class. You have such talent for shock, for getting to the heart of a matter, that I'm sure you will be a great artist one day—"

William saves me from this strange conversation by pulling me through the altar room into one of the alcoves. This one is blissfully empty, save for some drug paraphernalia scattered across a small wooden table. William drags me down into a pile of silken cushions and covers my body in his.

For a few moments, I lose myself in him. Nothing exists except the dark prince, his skin like porcelain, his lips like liquid fire.

"Did you do it?" he whispers.

In breathless whispers, I tell him what we found in Father Duncan's room and how close we were to getting caught. His hands move over my body and I break off my story several times to gasp or moan as the pleasure rises inside me.

"What about Monty?" I ask. "Has he behaved himself?"

"He smashed hundreds of windows in the quad, which isn't great, but apart from that, he's been positively charming.

Remember, in Ancient Greece, the Tristeria happened every two years, so I don't think they're planning something this year."

As William pulls me back with another searing kiss, I spy Monty over my shoulder. He holds a kylix of mead in one hand and a stuffed wild mushroom in the other, and his cold, carbon eyes bore like daggers into William's back.

31

The next day, William and I watch from his window as students pour from the dormitories and hunt the school for the trail of destruction left by the Orpheus Society. I feel a little stab of sadness that I didn't get to see the portrait gallery after Claws' people finished with it last night. But we'll head there after breakfast, if we're even allowed out of our rooms. The porters yell at students to get back as they pick through the ancient leaded windows scattered in pieces across the quad. The college Master looks on from the door of his lodge, tears brimming in his eyes at the wanton destruction. At Blackfriars, windows aren't just windows – they're remnants of a long and august history, and now they're broken shards.

"I can't believe Monty did that," I say.

"I can." William's mouth draws in a tight line. "He didn't want your vignette to steal the limelight. Sometimes I don't know why I'm protecting him."

I know. I've seen the love burning bright in William when Monty's telling one of his tall tales. Monty was the only person there for William when his mother died, and William knows better than most just how childlike Monty's mind remains, how easily he can be led.

"You can turn yourself in," I say. "It's not too late. Tell the police about the meat he served, let them figure out the rest."

"And what will that achieve?" William hangs his head. "I've thought of it. Diana? Fatima? Their lives will be over because of something they didn't even do. And the Orpheans will band together to protect their secrets. No, we must cut Father Duncan off at the knees. Is he working alone? Is this something the alumni are supporting?"

My old scout, Sally, is down in the quad helping with the cleanup. She calls up to the students hanging out the windows. "All students in The Izzy and St. Benedict's Quad must remain in your rooms until we clear away the mess."

"I guess we're stuck here." William's lip curls back into a warm smile.

"However shall we pass the time?" I wrap my hands around William's neck and pull him down into the covers.

IT TAKES the cleanup crew a little over an hour to sweep up enough of the broken glass and put up barriers to funnel foot traffic. As we wander in the direction of the portrait gallery, I see John setting up scaffolding and nailing plywood sheets over windows to keep the weather out of the ancient buildings. All around us, students gripe about the damage.

"The drains overflowed last night and wet, filthy water dumped straight on my bed," one complains. "All my shit is ruined."

"It's colder than the arctic in my room." Another hugs her friend. "I'm going to get sick. My parents are making a complaint to the Master. The Orpheans have gone too far this time. Why should a bunch of students be given free rein for a night to do this kind of damage?"

An excellent question.

As we climb the steps to the dining hall, the grumblings turn to excited shouts. The portrait gallery is off to the right of the hall, and we left the doors open in the hopes someone will stumble in and notice our genius. Someone did, and they've alerted the whole school. Students mill around, admiring the new paintings we installed and snapping pictures with their phones.

The painting getting the most attention is definitely William's fornicating Benet. I hear a couple of students talking about buying it.

"Now *this* is a vignette." William kisses the top of my head as he watches people admire his painting. "I've never had this much excitement over my work before. My painting is even trending on Tiktok. Good work."

"I had an idea," I say. "We should auction off these fakes and give the money to charity. Do you think the Orpheans will go for that?"

"Diana and I will talk them around," William squeezes my hand. "And the real paintings are safe?"

"They're being housed in an off-site storage facility," I say. "The curator has been given instructions to leave the gallery unlocked tonight and everything will be back to normal by morning."

Leigh comes running up. "This is wild." She points to the large canvas William painted of Benet of Blackfriars. "Excellent work, sir. I particularly admire the brushwork around the Black Monk's dong."

William and Leigh start an intense art conversation filled with terms I don't understand. I feel a finger scrape across my hip as Leigh shoves the envelope containing the bone into my satchel. It's time to take Father Duncan down.

———

"Let me get this straight, you want me to run a DNA test on this random fragment of bone you just *happened* to find in the forest?" Lauren looks me over like she doesn't believe a word of my admittedly farfetched story. "What am I looking for, exactly?"

"What do you mean?"

"I can't just randomly go around doing DNA tests without consent, not unless I want to get this lab into a world of shit. It doesn't work like that. So what am I looking for?"

"You're looking to see if it's a match for Keely O'Sullivan."

CRASH.

I wince as Lauren slams shut a freezer unit. "You say something like that, you better have a fuckton of facts to back it up. Why is this bone being handed to me by a student instead of the police?"

I screw up my face. Professor Hipkins warned me that if I want any lab work to support my colloquy, I'll probably have to confide in Lauren. I don't want to bring any more people into danger with my suspicions, but I need to get this bone tested and I don't have the skills to do it myself. "Lauren, do you ever get the feeling that when it comes to the university, the police in this town look the other way?"

Lauren leans across the embalming table and narrows her eyes at me. "What are you suggesting, Fisher?"

"They don't interfere when the Orpheus Society pulls all their pranks on Devil's Night. Montague Cavendish broke over four hundred windows last week and didn't even get charged for it. And what has Inspector Jones done about Keely's murder?

Nothing, that's what, despite the fact that even a cursory look at the evidence draws parallels between Keely's death and Khloe May's disappearance twenty years ago. And I'll tell you why he hasn't done anything – because I saw Jones on Devil's Night, wearing Orpheus Society robes. If this finger gets into his hands and he figures out what I suspect, it'll be gone forever and so will the evidence needed to convict a killer."

Lauren looks at me like I'm crazy. "Just so we're clear, what exactly *do* you suspect?"

"That people connected with the Orpheus Society are ritually killing people and eating their flesh. And the police are covering it up."

Lauren's lips purse.

"Pleeeeease, Lauren."

She sighs. "You're a mad fish, but I trust you. I can do it, but you're going to have to wait a couple of weeks." Lauren points to a pile of folders on her desk. "See those? They're all current open cases from the county that need results like, yesterday. *Actual* crimes, not the farcical ramblings of a true-crime wannabe."

"I understand. Thank you so, so much. I owe you a massive favor."

"That's right, you do." Laura tosses a set of scrubs at me.

"What's this for?"

"Autopsy. A new stiff just arrived. I need an assistant and Derek called in sick," she grins. "You're up, Gerbil girl."

32

*M*y coursework gets so intense that I forget about the DNA results for a couple of weeks. I'm in the library until late every night, sneaking Walnut Whips and Fry's bars into the St. George Reading Room in my pockets while I work on Greek translations with William and Diana, or flipping through the school's history books, looking for information on the other Devil's Night murders and disappearances. There are a few resources stored in the basement stacks I'd like to look at, but I'm positive the librarian was the one who turned me in to Monty when I asked for Benet's diary. If she's involved in this, I don't want her to have an inkling that I'm connecting the dots.

So when I receive a phone call in the middle of AV studio time, I'm momentarily surprised to see Lauren's name on the screen. My heart pounds, but I can't answer it – not with Monty and Tabitha working on the class project right next to me, so I let it ring off, then send her a string of texts explaining that I'll call her back in ten minutes.

"Sorry, guys, I have to go." I throw my jacket over my shoulder and hope they can't read my nerves on my face. "That was Leigh. She's having some kind of boy crisis."

"You coming to The Bad Habit with us later, George?" Abigail asks as I gather my things. My phone buzzes impatiently in my pocket.

"I can't today. I haven't finished my Sophocles translation yet."

"Mine's a shambles," Monty says as he extracts a cigarette and rests it between his lips. He's not supposed to smoke in class but Professor Fletcher won't stop him. "The pluperfect is not my friend. I don't suppose we might be able to help each other, eh, Georgie—"

"Sorry, I have to go." I manage to untangle myself from them and sprint back to my room. I slam the door and check under the bed and in the closet for any spying Orpheans before I collapse on the bed and dial Lauren's number with trembling hands.

Lauren picks up on the first ring. "The finger bone isn't a match for Keely O'Sullivan."

"Then why—"

"The finger belongs to Khloe May."

Shit. "You're sure?"

Lauren scoffs. "You want to rethink that question."

"Fine, fine. I know you wouldn't lie to me. So it's Khloe May. And if someone's got her finger bone, it probably means she's—"

"Dead as a doornail? Yup. And now you've put me in the middle of a fucking ethical dilemma," Lauren says. "You know about the fruit of a poison tree?"

"You mean the William Blake poem?" It's one of William's favorites, about a protagonist who doesn't confront his foe about a quarrel, but rather feeds his anger to a tree that grows a poisoned apple, which his foe steals, eats, and then dies. "I was angry with my friend; I told my wrath, my wrath did end—"

Lauren lets out a sharp, barking sound that might've been a laugh. "Jesus Christ, college students are insufferable. *No*, I don't mean a fucking poem. I mean the legal doctrine that says evidence obtained illegally is inadmissible in court. This finger is tainted, poisoned. It could cinch an entire case against this guy and we can't use it because you broke into his room."

Panic brushes her poison wings against my chest. "But I'm not a cop."

"It doesn't matter. A good lawyer might be able to argue it into evidence, but we don't get those around here. And if we had someone like Judge Winklebottom...basically, I've done a morning's work for nothing. Meanwhile, whoever you got that bone from knows where the rest of Khloe is, which means you need to tell Inspector Jones."

"I know." I pause. "Except that he's in on it. I need someone I can trust, or enough evidence that he'll turn against the Orpheans. If Khloe May is dead, she's been dead for a long time. Nothing will change if we hold off for a bit."

"Not if this person finds out you have the bone," Lauren points out.

"I don't think they know." I have my eyes on Father Duncan. I know that as soon as he discovers the finger is missing, he'll change his behavior. He'll do something out of character to cover his ass. He'll probably come after Sebastian, because he'd put two-and-two together from their encounter on Devil's Night. And so far, day after day after day, his activities and behavior remain the same.

"We could put it back?" I say hopefully.

"Yeah, and risk losing a vital piece of evidence in a decades-old cold case? Not happening," Lauren says firmly. "If that's your plan, I'm not letting you have the finger back."

"Keep it. I'm a liability. Can you store it securely for me?"

"Sure." Lauren pauses, and I hear the freezer door scraping as she moves around her lab. "And what are you going to do?"

"Gather more evidence," I say. Lauren sighs. "*Legally,* this time. I promise. I'll do whatever it takes to bring Father Duncan down."

33

"Khloe loved the theatre," Ro says as she leans forward into a headstand, bringing her feet over her torso to touch her toes to her head. "She was in a few student films, and did advertising work during the summer holidays, but the stage was where she wanted to be. She was supposed to play the lead in our year's contribution to the Saint Benet's Day festival."

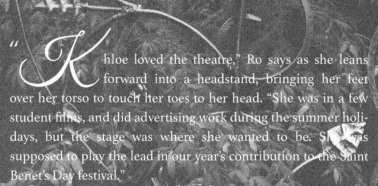

I'm sitting on the floor in a yoga studio in York, while Ro Wilson – Khloe May's best friend at Blackfriars – contorts her body into strange and terrifying shapes. Beside me, Leigh tries to copy Ro, but topples over and sends my microphone skidding across the floor.

"Oops, sorry." Leigh rushes to pick it up. I check that it's still recording and set it down again. Nothing we can't fix in post-production. Ro has changed positions and is now doing some kind of one-hand plank-thing she calls Wounded Peacock Pose and looks exactly as painful as it sounds.

"What was she like? As a friend?"

"Oh, she was the best," Ro says as she comes back to center, crossing her legs and placing her palms face-up on her knees.

"She was a real sweetheart, just nice to everyone, even when they didn't deserve it. No matter what she had going on in her life, she'd drop everything if a friend needed her."

"Do you remember her dating a guy? Julian Duncan—"

"Jules, oh sure." Ro frowns. "He was *weird*. Real intense. I didn't see as much of Khloe after they started dating. She spent a lot of time sneaking down around the woods with him. There's a shrine to one of those old pagan gods deep in the trees, down from that amphitheater in the woods. It was their secret snogging spot."

"Snogging?" I ask.

"Sorry," Leigh grins at Ro. "She's American. She can't talk proper."

"Snogging means making out. They went there to shag," Ro says with a smile. "To fuck. When she wasn't there or in class, she mostly hung out with Jules' friends. She'd invite me along, but I always got the feeling they were telling private jokes behind my back, you know?"

"Did you ever hear him being involved in a secret society on campus—"

"The Orpheus Society?" Ro scoffs. "A bunch of rich, entitled assholes who shut down the campus once a year so they can pull expensive pranks and drink the college's wine cellar dry. Yes, he was a member. Our last year there, he was the leader. Hierophant, I think they called him, because the Orpheans had to make everything special and mysterious. Jules wanted Khloe to be a member. The night she disappeared, I went to her room to see if she wanted to spend Devil's Night together, you know, watching movies and eating junk food and whatnot. We each had keys to our respective rooms. Anyway, I knocked and she didn't reply so I let myself in and the place was trashed. All her furniture broken, her clothes torn up, a designer lamp her mother gave her smashed against the wall. I'm told that's what the Orpheans do if they plan to initiate you into their little club."

I lean forward. "This wasn't in the police report."

"There's a surprise," Ro says wryly. "When she didn't turn up in class after Devil's Night, the Orpheans sent a couple of peons around to tidy up her stuff, repair the furniture, and put things back so it didn't look like it had happened. They even brought an exact copy of that lamp. They didn't know I had a key, that I'd seen her room. I definitely told the police about the damage."

But it's never been in the reports or the media.

"And you never told anyone else?"

"Nope." Ro pulls her ankle behind her head. "Because the day after I gave my statement, I found a dead rat stuffed under my door, with a note warning me that if I didn't keep my mouth shut, my sister would have an unfortunate accident. My sister was ten years old at the time, and she's everything to me. I kept my mouth shut and finished my degree and got the hell out of there, started my yoga studio, tried to forget that it ever happened. I've never heard another person even mention the Orpheans in relation to Khloe until I got your email."

"What made you tell me now?" I ask.

"Khloe's parents never got closure," Ro says. Her eyes swim with tears. "They broke up, you know? They were so in love, but it's hard for even great love to survive that kind of trauma. Vera left me a message last week and said that she'd given you my name, and that if you contacted me, I should tell you everything I know. She said you're on the side of the angels, and I believe her. She seems to believe that if anyone can find Khloe, it's you."

———

I FINISH out Michaelmas term without making any more headway on the case. But I do manage to keep on top of my studies at least. I clean up my interviews with Ro and Vera and submit those alongside some of my other research to Professor Hipkins, who gives me top marks on my colloquy project to date and offers me some useful advice on where to go next. Diana, William, and I tie for first in Ancient Greek, and my contributions to the collaborative arthouse film I made with my classmates gives me top marks in AV.

As much as I want to go back to Emerald Beach to see my mom for Christmas, when William invites me to spend the holiday with him at Forsyth Hall, I can't refuse. We travel down as soon as classes are done. This time, we'll be on our own. The Orpheans are spending their holidays with their families, except for Monty, who doesn't like to go home at all if he can help it. Diana's family took pity on him and invited him to the Maldives. I'm relieved that no one will be in Paris, adding another nameless sacrifice to the temple there.

A light dusting of snow covers the rolling fields and decorates the trees as we pull up to the gates of Forsyth Hall. A litany of staff rush the car as soon as we pull up, holding umbrellas and big wool coats to keep us warm and dry for our short walk to the house, and pulling our luggage from the trunk (sorry, boot).

This time, I can't help but notice that I've been given the room beside William's. My suitcase already waits at the foot of my bed, and there's a parcel of preserves and homemade salami with a personal note from Gareth the chef, asking that I deliver it to Leigh. I smile to myself, then remember that green-eyed guy watching Leigh in the portrait gallery, and what William said about an artist named Shane Kelly who'd been talking to her. She won't tell me a thing about Shane except that he's a 'massive pain in the arse,' which probably means she's in love with him and wants to have his babies. Poor Gareth doesn't stand a chance against a tattooed bad boy.

William meets me in my doorway, and we walk down to the 'Hunting Hall,' which the family use as their living room. By now, the snow is coming down in thick sheets, and a bitter wind pummels the mullioned windows. Sir Henry sits beside the fire, a glass of sherry in his hand. He frowns at the house phone, which sits silent on the table beside him.

"I've tried calling Father Pearce three times," he says, by way of greeting. "But his phone goes straight to voicemail. He should have arrived by now."

"It's probably the storm. It might've knocked out phone reception," William says with more gentleness than I've ever heard him use with his father. "I'm sure the good Father is fine. He's used to driving these roads in winter."

But William looks at me with concern. Sebastian is driving down to be with his mother over Christmas. We intend to sneak away for some time on the lake while we're all here. But he couldn't leave campus until a few hours after us because of his Christmas services. *If he's caught in this weather...please, let him get here in one piece...*

As if some God heard my silent prayers, my phone rings.

"Hi." It's Sebastian. He sounds far away. And blissfully, happily alive. "Did you make it before the storm hit?"

"Yeah, we're all snuggled up by the fire. What about you? Henry was wondering if you were facedown in a ditch somewhere?"

"I just arrived, but we've had a bit of a disaster. You know that big oak beside Mum's place? The storm tore off one of the rotting branches and it's crashed through her roof."

"Oh no." I press the phone to my ear, trying to catch every word. William's head whirls around, his eyes wide. "Are you both okay?"

"We're fine, but there's a mountain of snow pouring through the hole. I'm going to try to patch it with some things

Mum's got lying around but..." His words fade into crackling static.

"Sebastian?" I yell into the phone. "Sebastian, can you hear me?"

"What's happened?" Sir Henry sits bolt upright in his chair.

"A branch from the oak fell through the roof of Carmilla's house. Sebastian— er, Father Pearce says he's going to attempt some emergency repairs so they can wait out the storm, but—"

"Nonsense." Sir Henry waves his hand, forgetting he was holding his glass. Sherry sloshes over his shirt. "Tell him they must come up to the house for the night."

"Sebastian and...Carmilla?" William looks to his father in alarm.

"Of course. I won't hear a word to the contrary. I'll not allow that stubborn woman to freeze to death because she refuses to accept assistance from a Forsyth." Sir Henry pulls the bell cord. "Frazier, can you send Simon out on the side-by-side to pick up the Pearces? And tell Gareth there will be another two for dinner."

The staff leap into action. Before I know it, I'm seated opposite Sir Henry, my knee pressed against William's and a glass of warm mulled wine in my hands. Sir Henry keeps up a steady barrage of questions about school that William mostly leaves me to answer. Everyone is agitated, on edge about the arrival of our unexpected guests.

The butler, Frazier, enters the room. "Sebastian and Carmilla Pearce to see you, sir."

"Thank you, Frazier." Sir Henry leaps to his feet, running his hand through his russet hair and smoothing his trousers. He looks more like a nervous teenager waiting for his prom date than a literal Lord.

Sebastian enters the room, his arm looped in his mother's. In her other hand, Carmilla carries a cat basket containing a rather grumpy kitten. They're both soaked through, and look pretty windswept and bedraggled. Carmilla hands the basket to Frazier, who goes off to get the kitten some treats from the kitchen.

Heat pools in my belly at the sight of him. Trust Sebastian Pearce to make windswept and bedraggled look hot.

"Hello again, William. Hello, Sir Henry." Carmilla's eyes dart around the room, looking everywhere but at William's father. Her body poises, like she's going to run, but Sebastian holds her firm.

"Hello, Carmilla." Sir Henry stands transfixed. He can't take his eyes off her. "It's a pleasure."

"Yes, well." She reaches up and brushes snow out of her hair. "It's nice of you to take us in out of the weather. I'm afraid the stablehouse roof and attic will need some serious repairs, which I'm happy to contribute towards since I haven't thought to prune that blasted tree—"

"Father," William says helpfully. "Perhaps Carmilla and Sebastian might like a seat by the fire."

"Yes, yes, of course." Sir Henry bustles around, rearranging the chairs to make space and calling for Frazier to bring extra glasses of mulled wine.

Sebastian's shoes squelch as he crosses the floor. He lowers himself into the chair on the other side of William. Their eyes meet. I know this is an incredible moment for their family. Sebastian's mother and William's father have not been in the same room since Isabella's funeral.

Carmilla stares into the flames.

"I've had the staff make up your rooms. Father Pearce, you'll have the blue room, near the chapel. I thought you'd feel most comfortable there. And Carmilla..." Sir Henry reaches out a hand to her, but seems to think better of it and flaps it around in the air instead. "I've had Frazier prepare you the yellow room overlooking the rose garden. That was always your favorite."

Carmilla stiffens, her nails digging into the leather chair. "Thank you, Sir Henry."

"I'll get Simon and Jack onto the repairs immediately, just as soon as the storm allows. And don't trouble yourself with the bill; that roof was well overdue for replacing. In the meantime, you must make yourselves at home in the Hall. I won't hear of you sleeping out in the cold when I have rooms to spare."

"Thank you, Sir Henry." Sebastian sips his wine. His eyes lock with William, and a silent conversation plays out between the two of them.

"Will you join us for Mass tonight?" Henry asks, his gaze fixed on Carmilla. "And for Christmas lunch tomorrow?"

Carmilla spits wine all over herself. She whirls around to face him, her features visibly stunned. "I don't know. I—"

"Please. It would mean the world to both of us." He shoots a worried glance at his son. William nods.

"It would be an honor to have you both celebrate Christmas with us," William says. He swallows. I pat his knee. I know it's hard for him, but he's trying his best to forgive.

Sebastian reaches across and places his hand over his mother's, his finger touching the ring she wears. "We would be happy to."

34

The next night, we gather in the chapel for Midnight Mass, one of the most beautiful Catholic traditions. The storm has eased off somewhat and Henry's men have been out clearing the road and organizing a courtesy van for his guests. Sir Henry has invited the families of his staff and members of the nearby village to the service. Every pew in the chapel is crowded, the din rising through the nave as families catch up with the latest gossip.

Carmilla and William have combined their artistic talents to put together a nativity scene in the narthex, including straw figures of Jesus, Mary, and the three wise men. There are even little puffy sheep made of wool and painted with smiling faces. Families crowd around it oohing and aahing over the details. I help Sebastian hand out boxes of candles and printed booklets of carols. Sir Henry may not be good with children, but he went out of his way to listen to Sebastian's suggestions to make the Mass magical for them.

"Is that Carmilla Pearce?" an old lady whispers conspiratorially as I help her light her candle.

"She hasn't set foot in this chapel since Isabella's funeral," her friend says, loud enough for more old biddies to turn their heads and join the gossip sesh.

"What do you think it means?" one whispers.

"Probably nothing. After all, it's her fault Isabella took her own life. I always said she was bad news. She shouldn't be allowed within twenty feet of the Forsyth family. Sir Henry has already lost so much, what if she seduces his son next!"

"I think it's time to forgive and forget." One lady holds her black shawl against her crinkled cheek. "I think a love like theirs can't bear the separation a moment longer. I always say, you only get one life, and you shouldn't spend it regretting what might have been."

Her words stay with me as I finish handing out the carol books and return to the altar. Sebastian disappears into the sacristy. He's performing the service alone tonight, as the organist broke his leg trying to clean the snow off his front steps and is spending Christmas Eve in the ER. I assume we're going to make do with carol music piped through the sound system, but instead, after opening prayers, Sebastian dims the lights and sits down at the organ. I didn't even know he could play.

With his deep, rich tenor, Sebastian leads this motley congregation in an array of Christmas hymns and secular carols. He even puts on a blinking red nose for 'Rudolph the Red-Nosed Reindeer.' We take a break from the carols for 'In Splendoribus Sanctorum' while Sebastian administers holy communion. Again, William and I walk up with the devout. I feel a little naughty, since this is supposed to a sacrament for remembering the sacrifice of Jesus on the cross and not an opportunity for Sebastian to whisper something filthy in my ear as he tips the blood of Christ onto my tongue.

In splendoribus sanctorum, ex utero, ante luciferum, genui te.

In the brightness of the saints: from the womb before the day star...

The only lights in the medieval chapel are the glittering candles. Children gather on the carpeted area in front of the altar, scrambling around to pick up the boiled sweets Sebastian tosses around between songs.

Sebastian even does a few rockstar moves and – at one point – attempts to play with his feet. He has the children in hysterics.

It's 2AM by the time we say goodbye to the last of the guests. Frazier holds his sleeping daughter in his arms as he clasps Sir Henry's hand. "Thank you, sir, as always."

Sir Henry waves at Frazier until we can't see the car through the snow. Then he turns to Carmilla, the corners of his lips rising into a hopeful smile.

"The early morning is quite pleasant, now that infernal wind has died down. The snow on the northern side of the house is shallow enough to walk in without much trouble." Henry holds out his hand to Carmilla. "I wondered if you'd like to walk in the garden, under the moonlight? With me?"

Carmilla hesitates, throwing a look to Sebastian and William, who stand on the steps of the chapel, talking like old friends, like brothers. Her shoulders drop. "I'd love that."

She takes Sir Henry's hand and they walk off into the night, leaving only three souls behind in the vast, echoing chapel.

I step up to my two boyfriends. My broken prince and my forbidden priest. The air shimmers with Christmas magic. Snowflakes flutter past the windows.

Sebastian doesn't fuck about. He drags us toward the sacristy, one in each hand. I look over at William and grin a wild grin, which he returns.

Our priest stands behind the altar, caressing the stone surface with his long, sensuous fingers. William and I stand before him, clasping hands and waiting for our absolution.

"This altar was made as a place to offer sacrifice – to give gifts to God," Sebastian says, his rich voice filling the empty chapel with long-forgotten magic. "Never in my life have I had a gift that felt worthy of him. Until you. Until both of you. You don't know how many nights you've kept me awake, thinking about what I wanted to do to you upon this surface."

A quiet moan escapes my lips as his words drift through my body like smoke curling from a warm fire. Sebastian walks slowly around the altar toward us. His determined footfalls echo in the solemn space. I hold my breath, my heart pattering in nervous anticipation of what he might do next.

Sebastian reaches us. His obsidian eyes flicker over my face, then come to rest on William. The air crackles with heat, with the weight of a presence beyond our world, witnessing and blessing our ritual.

My heart slams against my ribs. For many moments we stand, letting the presence wash over us, feeling the tug of the invisible cords that bind us demanding we meet as one.

Sebastian surges forward and fists William's shirt, yanking our broken prince against his body. William yelps with surprise as Sebastian's mouth devours his, offering no escape, no chance for second-guessing. This is not Sebastian's usual game of dominance and sacrilege – this is visceral, mortal, *desperate*. My body swells with the same aching need for them. We've been without each other for so very long.

They kiss like starved lovers who've crossed deserts to meet each other. I watch and feel every stroke of their tongues, every lustful moan, every forbidden touch as if they were upon my own body. Sebastian shoves William's shoulders down until his ass hits the end of the altar. "Get up there and lie on your back," Sebastian commands.

William glances out into the nave, which only half an hour ago was filled with villagers and employees of the family. He bites his lower lip as if he has something to say, but he shuffles up, sitting on the edge of the stone altar and lying down on the ancient, anointed stone.

"Do you remember a night, all those years ago, when you were just fifteen years old?" Sebastian says as he undoes the buttons on his shirt in jerky, desperate motions. "You entered this chapel to find me in prayer. I was praying at this very altar."

"I remember." William's blue eyes shroud with darkness. His mouth twists a little as he gazes up at Sebastian, lost between this moment and one many years in the past.

Sebastian slides his shirt down his shoulders, revealing the sculpted planes of his chest, that holy tattoo over his heart. He makes the sign of the cross, then gets to work on William's shirt. "Why don't you tell George about it."

William bites his lip again. Sebastian's fingers tease his skin as they pull and rip at his buttons.

"I came to find Sebastian." William's voice trembles. His eyes lock on me, their surface rippled like water, bursting with prisms of color and light. "He was kneeling right here in front of the altar, right where you're standing, praying the rosary. I snuck up behind him. I didn't know what...what I wanted, exactly. Just that I had to come closer."

I hold my breath as fire licks my veins.

"I heard every hesitant step you took," Sebastian murmurs as he tugs open William's dress shirt, revealing smooth, alabaster flesh. "I heard the stutter in your breath, the frantic beating of your heart."

"I snuck so close that I was standing right behind him," William's voice trembles as Sebastian's fingers wander over his skin, rolling one of his nipples between them. "He was murmuring his prayers, and I thought that perhaps he didn't see me—"

"And then what happened?" Sebastian says, his tone conversational as he trails his fingers over William's skin.

"Sebastian whirls around. He's still on his knees, and before I know what's happening he has his hands on my hips, and his mouth pressed against me through my jeans and I..."

"What did I ask you?" Sebastian says quietly.

"You asked me if I wanted to make a confession. You asked if I had sin in my heart. You asked if I'd ever touched myself under the covers at night and thought of you." William's eyes flutter shut. "And I said that I had."

"And I took you into my mouth right then, didn't I?" Sebastian purrs. "And you tangled those long fingers in my hair and moaned as the head of your cock touched my throat. You watched with those heavy-lidded princely eyes as you slid in and out of my lips, as my saliva made you so wet, so silky..."

William moans. Sebastian shoves down his trousers and starts on William's fly. William lifts his hips so the priest can pull them down. Sebastian tosses the offending material away, followed by his boxer shorts. William is now completely naked, his back against the cool stone of the altar. Sebastian places his hand over the tattoo on his heart, then presses his fingers into William's chest.

"God sees into our hearts," Sebastian says. "It doesn't matter if we lie to him or if we lie to ourselves, he knows the truth. And he forgives us before we even sin. He asks only that we forgive each other, and ourselves."

William's eyes screw tight. "I forgive you. I don't blame you for her death anymore. How can I, when you loved her as much as I love her?"

Sebastian smooths William's hair. When he gazes into our prince's eyes, he wears the kind face of a holy man once more. "But you haven't forgiven yourself. You think that you have done something so beyond the pale that you're not worthy of forgiveness. And it's true that there are such reprehensive acts that we must be watchful for them, lest they pollute our souls. But we do not have to forgive the act to forgive the soul. To forgive ourselves is a truly human act – it feels what Derrida calls 'a madness of the impossible,' and yet without it we will wither and rot. God cannot give us absolution until we offer it to ourselves first. Can you do this, William? Can you grant yourself mercy for your mother's death, and for Keely's flesh?"

William's whole face contorts. I step forward, knowing instinctively that a great battle is taking place within his soul, and that I need to help him win it. I place my hand over Sebastian's, upon his heart, and let my love for him flow through my fingers, hoping it's enough to give him the strength to find absolution.

"You are a good person, William," Sebastian says. "You have done bad things, as we all have, but you are so very, very good."

Tears stream down William's cheeks. He opens his eyes and looks up at Sebastian, then me. Two pools of deep misery regard me, begging for the absolution that only he can give himself. His hands tremble at his sides as he turns back to Sebastian. "Even if I can forgive myself for those things, every day that I love you, I'm bringing you closer to ruin. I know it's wrong, I know I'm rotten for what I want to ask of you, so how am I to forgive myself for that?"

Oh, William. Sweet, tortured prince. These are the thoughts he uses to torment himself, to break his spirit the way an ascetic broke their skin in obedience to god. And suddenly I'm so goddamned *sick* of an invisible deity coming between us, laying down black and white decrees about what's good and bad as if the world isn't painted in shades of grey.

"Does this feel like sin?" Sebastian tips William's head up and plants a reverent kiss on his lips. "Does it feel wrong or rotten? Or does it feel like the perfect expression of God's love?"

He doesn't wait for an answer. Sebastian pulls on William's lower lip, chewing lightly on the puffed flesh as he fists William's cock until William groans into his mouth. Transfixed by the moment, I step closer, pressing my palm against William's chest, feeling his heart come to life, the forgiveness blooming inside him.

Sebastian comes for me next, moving around the altar to cup my face in his huge, protective hand.

"Who knew that what we were missing all these years is a little George Fisher," he murmurs as he strokes my cheek with his finger, pulling me in for a kiss that curls my toes. While his tongue draws all sorts of dark pleasures from me, he undoes layer after layer of clothing (hey, Britain is *cold*), pressing his hands against my needy flesh.

Sebastian pulls back, and when he looks down at me with those obsidian eyes, so full of love and holiness, I melt into a puddle. "George, climb on top of William," he commands.

When he uses that voice, I have to obey.

I'm too short and uncoordinated to pull myself up onto the altar, so Sebastian lifts me easily. I throw a leg over William and crawl up his length. The cool air kisses my naked ass.

William pulls my head down and kisses me, slow and long and deep. "This forgiveness thing," he whispers against my lips. "If I'd known how much fun it was, I'd have done it sooner."

I laugh as Sebastian's hands wrap around William's cock, guiding it inside me. I love it, this sense that he's in control, the puppet master pulling our strings. He's exactly what we both need – someone who loves us as we are, who makes us feel like we're special, like everything will be okay.

I sink back onto my heels, filling myself with William, enjoying the way the hard lines of his face soften as he sees, truly sees, that he is loved despite the horrible things he's done. Because he is *not* his sin.

He is William and he is ours.

My prince grips my thighs and thrusts into me, his face

contorting as he rides the edge of pleasure and absolution. He's searching the depths of his soul to draw the strength and the love to forgive himself, and if grinding myself against his glorious cock helps him do it, then sign me the fuck up.

Sebastian climbs up behind me, his knees pressing against the outsides of my shins, hemming me in. He curls his body over mine, and his thick, hard cock rests between my ass cheeks.

"I want to be inside you, George," Sebastian growls. "I want to make this beautiful ass mine and I want me and William to fuck you so hard that you can't walk for a week. I want us to share you in every way possible. I want you to feel the power of being the vessel of our worship, the goddess upon whose altar we both pray. Is that something you'd be interested in?"

I nod as I ride William, as the filthiness of Sebastian's words stoke a fire inside me that licks the inside of my skin, desperate to escape.

"Good girl. Pass me that anointing oil."

William reaches over his shoulder and hands Sebastian the container of sanctified oil, which he uses for anointing the sacred objects. Sebastian dribbles the oil on the small of my back, using his fingers to trail it between my ass cheeks.

I gasp as he pushes an oiled finger into my back entrance. "Don't fight it," he coos in my ear. I nod, trusting him even though it feels strange and full and stretched. Sebastian waits for me to get used to the sensation, until I'm grinding down on William's shaft again, relishing the way his finger presses against William through the thin wall inside me.

He adds a second finger, turning his hand to rub the oil everywhere, making me gasp and moan and thrash. William grips my hips, holding me in place.

"Don't move," he whispers. "Give in to it. Let us do the work of worshiping you."

A third finger joins the first, pushing past the ring of muscle to reach deep inside me. I feel so fucking *full*. Not just my pussy and my ass, but my heart is utterly brimming with them. Sebastian's fingers rub against my inner wall, pressing against William's cock on the other side as William thrusts his hips upward, throwing his head back with wild abandon.

Sebastian removes his fingers, and I'm temporarily sad until I feel something else, something huge, pressing at my entrance.

He's so big. How will he ever...

A hand snakes around my body, soft fingers pressing against my lips. "Bite me," Sebastian whispers. "Make me bleed."

I bite down on his hand as he thrusts inside me, first the head, then more and more of him until I'm so full and tight I think my heart will burst out of my chest, but still he seems to find another inch. And another. And another. My teeth dig into his flesh and I taste metallic blood, and I couldn't move even if I fucking tried and I want it I want it I want...

I'm caught between them, exactly where I most want to be.

They start to move. William pulls out slowly as Sebastian settles in, their cocks rubbing against each other. William makes the most delicious face, and I know this isn't just about him and Sebastian pleasuring me, it's about the two of them coming together again, touching each other in all the ways that had been forbidden to them.

William sucks in a deep breath and thrusts inside me just as Sebastian pulls back. It's so...I don't have words to describe it. I can only *feel*. I'm no longer a brain with limbs but this writhing, gibbering mess of nerve endings and raw, primal pleasure. I think I'm screaming. I think Sebastian is laughing and William is smiling his beautiful bright smile.

I think that over his shoulder, in a darkened corner of the chapel, a horned god watches us, and smiles, too.

They pick up speed, one thrusting forward as the other pulls back, so it's as though I'm being impaled on one long, monstrous cock. They hold me in place as orgasm after orgasm slam into my body, until I can't tell where one wave of pleasure ends and the next begins, until all three of us are a sweaty, babbling mess of limbs tangled on the altar.

I'd give anything, *anything,* for this moment of perfection to last.

35

*L*ent term at Blackfriars passes in a flurry of parties and studying and desperately missing Sebastian. With Father Duncan and Monty breathing down our necks, William and I can't risk seeing him outside of class and church, so we squirm in our seats through his Sunday sermons and then race back to William's room to fuck the desperation out of each other.

The sex is good, but it's not the same without Sebastian. Without him, a piece of us is missing. But whenever one of us tries to broach the subject, we go around and around in circles and don't come up with any answers.

Sebastian is a priest. It's part of who he is. It's baked into his soul, like the glaze on one of Leigh's clay pots before it's fired. And he cannot be a priest and be with us, so we exist in this between state – not apart, but not together – and we all suffer.

At least I have my colloquy project to distract me. I don't have to ask Professor Hipkins to know that I can't put breaking into Father Duncan's rooms to steal Khloe's finger bone into my project. I have to uncover his guilt in a different way. Instead, I record everything I know so far into two more podcast episodes. I don't know why I bother. They're not a public record of my sleuthing, but a diary of my feelings for William and Sebastian. But after I lay my soul bare on the tape, I do feel better. My form of absolution, I guess.

I'm convinced that Father Duncan knows where Khloe May is buried. He kept that bone. It means he's the kind of killer who keeps souvenirs. I start building a profile of him and comparing it to other killers and master manipulators, to people like Charles Manson who used their cult of personality to conduct their followers into a frenzy of violence. I dig into Julian Duncan's life, everything about him I can find, to try to see the pattern.

After four weeks, I have precious little to show for my work, so I decide it's time to step things up. I start following Father Duncan everywhere. If he notices me, too fucking bad. I want him to be afraid. I want him to slip up. It's a long shot, but I wonder...if he keeps souvenirs, does he also return to the scene of his crime? Does he stand over the spot where Khloe May died and remember the feeling of being consumed by the god's spirit?

A righteous man like that, of course he does.

So every morning, I scramble out of bed to be in St. Benedict's Quad, Bad Habit coffee in hand, with eyes on Father Duncan's windows as he moves around his office. I watch him cross the quad to make it to church in time to pray Lauds, then Sebastian keeps an eye on him so I can go to classes, and I'm back on the job after Vespers. Father Duncan usually partakes in Formal Hall, where he chats animatedly with the other dons as if he's not a cold-blooded psychopath. After dinner, he usually walks through the woods, sometimes with Monty, often alone, leaving Sebastian to perform the Compline prayers.

I follow at a distance, and what I notice over time is that

when Father Duncan is with Monty, they stick to the public path that leads down to the village. They often stop to feed the birds or talk to other students. Monty always laughs too loud and scares the birds away.

But when Father Duncan is alone, he strikes out in the direction of the amphitheater, sometimes splitting off to the left and following a similar route to my old body farm site, and other times he follows the crest of the hill. The tree cover thins out there, so it's difficult to follow him, but one day, during one of the last snowfalls of the season, I loiter in the amphitheater, pulling my coat around me and holding a book to my face so he can't see me. He walks briskly down the hill with a small bunch of flowers in his hands – picked from the arrangements from the church altar, at my guess, since few flowers can penetrate the snow at this time of year.

He disappears into the misty white.

The air is still.

My ass freezes to the stone.

He comes back thirty minutes later, hurrying along at a nice clip, each footfall perfectly preserved. I hold my breath as he passes the amphitheater without noticing me. When I'm sure he's well on his way back up the path, I hurry back to school and find Leigh huddled by the fire in the junior common room.

"Come with me," I whisper. "Father Duncan just left the forest. I think if we hurry we can follow his footsteps, find out where he goes."

"But it's warm in here," she mumbles. "And so very, very cold out there. Can't you get your prince to do it?"

"I would, but he's in the studio, working on serious art while you're faffing about in here." (Faffing about is my new British slang Leigh taught me. I'm quite proud of myself for using it in a sentence.) "And besides, you're Watson to my Holmes."

"Fine, fine." She hauls herself up from the fire. "But let's leg it – I want to spend as little time in that as possible."

We stop by Leigh's room so she can grab her coat and boots, then tramp across the campus to the wooded path. Once we move into the trees, the snow is thicker, soaking the bottoms of my jeans. Several pairs of footprints head to and from the amphitheater, but only one set continues on down the slope.

We follow. The air is crisp and dry, and our breath puffs in front of us. His perfectly formed footprints lead us along the hill a way before—

"What's that?"

Up ahead, right in our path, is a lumpy mass rising from the earth. It takes a few moments for me to understand I'm looking at the ruins of some sort of stone structure. All that remains is one corner and a large slab tilted on its side to create a kind of triangular cave. The footprints stop in front of this structure.

"I think this an old Roman altar," I say. "Sebastian told me there was one here."

"Look." Leigh points to some Latin text carved on one of the broken stones. It's too windswept to make out, and I can't read Latin anyway. I kneel down to peer under the altar stone. The flowers Father Duncan was carrying are pushed inside the dark crack.

I pull a pair of nitrile gloves from my pocket. Leigh frowns. "You carry those around just in case you need to riffle around in a crevice?"

"Sure. And they make a great snapping sound that freaks William out. Go on, snap them." I demonstrate. "It's satisfying."

"You're a strange bug, George."

I reach into the crevice and pull out the flowers. They're tied with a piece of paper twine, which has already started to go soggy in the snow. I pull out a few other objects – a couple of ribbons, a Blackfriars' pin, some blackened twigs that were probably more flowers, and a little plastic Shakespeare figurine.

"Look at this." I pull out a rectangular object. It's a piece of card folded in half, but it was pushed far back into the crack and wedged between the stones, so it wasn't as damaged or water-logged as I expected. I pull the edges carefully apart. It's a ticket for a play – Shakespeare's *Julius Caesar*. The dates on the ticket are from twenty years ago.

"What do all these things mean?"

"They're offerings," I whisper. "These are all things that mean something to Khloe May. This ticket stub and figurine, because she's an actress. The Blackfriars' pin. The ribbons were probably something she wore. And he came today to leave these flowers."

"Doesn't that seem odd?" Leigh asks. "If he killed her, why leave things for her? Isn't that what you do if you're mourning someone?"

"You're thinking like a protestant. Father Duncan worships a much older god – these are *offerings*. Which means—"

"Which means what, George?" Leigh cries. "George?"

I claw at the earth, but it's no good. The snow stings my hands through the gloves, and the dirt beneath is frozen solid. I can't break through. I lean back on my heels, my heart pounding against my ribs.

"I'm certain this is it," I whisper. "This is where he buried Khloe May."

THE SNOW THAWS.

The first growth of spring appears on the tips of branches. Wildflowers poke between ancient cobbles. Color bursts forth from blackened trees. I hang my wool coat in the back of my closet.

I'm desperate to return to the altar and dig up the softened ground, but Sebastian and William convince me to wait until the term's over. "Duncan will be away, giving the public lecture series at Cambridge," says Sebastian. "That gives us time to dig. We don't know how long it will take to find Khloe."

If she's even there, he doesn't say, but I know from the look he and William exchange that they're both thinking it. But I feel it in my bones. Khloe is near, waiting to reveal her secrets.

The end of the term is marked by Saint Benet's Day celebrations. This is a tradition where the different societies and faculties at Blackfriars put on plays at the amphitheater, followed by a bonfire in the old refectory and lots of boozy parties to celebrate the end of exams. The students refer to it as 'Saint Benet's Day' because it's held yearly on the day where Benet would have been celebrated as a saint, had he not gone all blasphemous and started worshiping a pagan god and luring impressionable youth into a life of sin and depravity.

"It's another tradition that comes from Benet's fascination with Dionysos," explains William as we wander down the path to the amphitheater. He carries a couple of pillows under his arm – he's attended enough Saint Benet's Day celebrations to know that not even the illicit port flask stuffed in my shirt can numb the pain of spending several hours sitting on hard Roman stone. "Every year in Athens there was a dramatic festival in the god's honor. Playwrights like Aristophanes would compose comedies, tragedies, and satyr plays to compete for a grand prize. There was also a parade where giant phallic artifices were carried throughout the city and much wine was drunk, but the university isn't so keen on that part."

"This festival isn't part of the mysteries?" It hadn't come up in my reading.

William shakes his head. "The mysteries are for initiates – those who wanted a close, personal relationship with the god. The city cults and public festivals were for everyone – it's the difference between people who go to church at Christmas and Sebastian."

We emerge into the amphitheater. It's strange to see this place that's always so peaceful and deserted teaming with people. Groups of students mill about, yelling to their friends as they spread out jackets and cushions to save seats. A row of food stalls run by various social clubs are scattered amongst the forest, and the smell of warm pies and hot chocolate wafts over the space. The wooden stage platform is festooned with garlands, and a temporary structure behind it houses the actors and sets. Costumed students and backstage people rush around, adding the last-minute touches before curtain.

William and I grab seats on the topmost row of the *cavea*. I wave to Diana, who's standing behind the backstage ropes, holding a cup of coffee and laughing at something Monty is saying. She's dressed as a maenad – barefoot, in a flowing chiton with fawn skin around her shoulders and a wreath of snakes in her loose, flowing golden hair. She jabs Monty – dressed as Dionysos – playfully with her thyrsus. Even though there's a crisp breeze and no sun penetrates the grey British sky, neither of them appears to feel the cold.

That's probably got to do with the five gallons of mead supplied to the actors and crew by one Leigh Cho.

Under Father Duncan's insistence, our Greek class are performing scenes from Euripides' *Bacchae*, which is about as meta as it gets. William and I got out of embarrassing ourselves on stage by being in charge of costumes and sets, and I'm quite proud of my efforts with the grotesque satyr masks I made for the guys.

Leigh's skills as an artist of large-scale sculptures have been in high demand, and she's currently rushing around five different student groups, checking things are ready for the metaphorical curtain to come up.

William slinks away and returns with two pies on paper plates, a cone filled with chips drowning in vinegar (weird, but when in Rome...), and steaming hot chocolates. He tells me more about the traditions of Saint Benet's Day, and some of the hilarious acts he's seen on this stage. I listen as I watch the crowd, looking for Sebastian. He said he'd be here. We can't sit together in plain view of everyone, but maybe when we go back to school for the bonfire—

Wait, what's that?

Father Duncan stands off to the side of the backstage area, hidden by the trees to anyone who doesn't have a bird's-eye view. He's talking with Monty. No, not talking. *Arguing.*

"George, are you listening?"

I hold my finger to my lips and lean forward, wishing I thought to plant some kind of hidden microphone so I could hear what they're saying. Father Duncan jabs his fingers into Monty's chest, his face red with anger. I've never even seen him raise his voice before, unless you count his vibrant sermons. Monty gets right up in his face, and he's got that mean glint in his eyes, the look he got when he tied me to a pipe in the men's bathroom and pissed on me.

And then the pair of them turn and disappear into the woods.

I don't know what that was about, but I know something is wrong. Terribly wrong. "I have to go." I stand up, spilling hot chocolate all over the student in the seat in front of me.

"Hey, watch it," the guy snaps, tugging at his sodden shirt.

"Sorry." I start to shove my way toward the end of the row, aware that with every moment passing I risk losing sight of them. There isn't a lot of space on the rows, and I tread on feet and kick people's backs as I scramble for the aisle.

"George, wait." William grabs my hand. I jerk away as I fly down the aisle, crashing through the crowds waiting at the food stalls. I head for the trees at speed.

"George, it's good to—" Sebastian's smile blurs into a concerned frown as I fly past him. "Where's she going?"

"I don't know," William says to him. I hear him fall in step with William as the two of them follow me into the trees until the sounds of the crowd become background noise to my own pounding heart. I can't see Father Duncan or Monty, nor can I hear them, but I'm pretty sure I know exactly where they're going.

"George, talk to me. What's going on?" Sebastian puffs as he catches up to me. My priest is fit from all that fountain swimming.

"Father Duncan and Monty were fighting. They went this way. I can't explain it. I have to—"

"I know." Sebastian takes my hand, squeezing my fingers in his. And I know it's dangerous for him to be seen with us, but I'm grateful for his steady presence as we ascend the steep slope leading to the altar.

The stone structure comes into view. Even though my chest is burning, I break into a run. Sebastian and William are right beside me, scanning the tree line for signs of life. The woods are eerily silent, the only sound the crunch of our footsteps on fallen twigs and the puff of my breath.

"I didn't even know this was here," Sebastian breathes as we approach the altar. "It's probably a Neolithic site the Romans turned into an altar. It's not on any of the archaeological maps of the university—"

"What's that?" William points to a lumpy shape on the other side of the stones. I rush around to look.

My hand flies to my mouth.

"Holy Father." Sebastian makes the sign of the cross.

A body lies facedown in the dirt, his hand above his head as if he's thrown himself at the altar from above. A dark stain spreads beneath him, staining the dirt a dark claret.

It's Father Duncan.

36

"*I*'m going to have to ask you to move along, miss."
Inspector Jones waves at me impatiently as he walks along the perimeter of the crime scene. "We can't have students contaminating the evidence—"

"George is with me," Lauren says without looking up. "Hand her that spare oversuit. I could use her help."

Inspector Jones frowns, but he hands me an oversuit, over-shoes, gloves, and a mask, and holds up the edge of the crime scene tape so I can climb underneath. I step carefully where Lauren directs me, and the officer turns away to continue his work elsewhere.

Father Duncan's body has already been photographed and moved to the morgue, which is good news because I didn't exactly want to face his corpse again. Lauren gets me working on the quadrants of the site, scanning the ground for evidence that needs to be photographed or examined. When the detectives move away to let her team do the work, she crouches down beside me, leaning her head close so we can talk without being overheard.

"The dead guy is the one, isn't he?" she says. "Father Julian

Duncan. He's the one you think is involved in Keely O'Sullivan's death."

I nod. "And I think that you should look in that little crack in the stones there, and if you can, get this whole site dug up."

She screws up her face. "Please don't make me do that. I'd have to get the county archaeologist to supervise the work, and they're a real pain in the—"

"I think Khloe May might be buried beneath this altar."

"Jesus Christ, kid." Lauren shakes her head. "You should stick around Blackfriars. You're going to single-handedly keep me in business."

LAUREN MUST'VE BELIEVED ME, because in the second week of Trinity term, a team of archaeologists arrives on campus with surveying equipment. I'm overjoyed to see them until I head to The Bad Habit for a post-exam snack and discover they've bought up the last of the pies.

Sebastian texts me to tell me he's down at the dig, and that the ground surveys have shown up a range of interesting features so they're going to open up a test pit. They know him from his interest in the Roman fresco in the library basement, so he's working with some of the school's archaeological students to do the grunt work.

I race down to the altar to find the woodland around the site littered with survey pegs. A small group of students gather to watch, but they quickly fade away when Katie, the county archaeologist, insists they pick up trowels and get to work. I accept a trowel and help Sebastian clear away a flat section of the test pit. We don't dare say a word to each other in case we give away my suspicions.

The test pit yields some promising artifacts and no bodies of murdered teenagers. The archaeology students are interested in making the altar their colloquy project, and Katie's excited to supervise them and receive funding from the school to keep digging, so we open up the rest of the site and divide it into quadrants.

Sebastian stays on the team, working every day between his classes and clerical duties. I go down to help when I can get away, which isn't as much as I like because it's the last term of my second year at Blackfriars and the work is piling up.

Fascinating artifacts are pulled out of the ground – a couple of Roman coins, some pottery shards, the edge of what might've been a large Neolithic structure. And then, one cool May morning, as I scrape away at the dirt and consider that I should be in the library finishing my Criminology reading, a student named Tania cries out from one of the nearby pits.

"There's a disturbance here."

Katie rushes over to see, and a few minutes later I hear her say, "Step back, those are human bones."

I rush over, my heart in my throat. We all crowd around as Katie brushes away the earth, revealing skeletal remains hung with frayed pieces of cloth.

"This isn't a Roman burial." She lifts away the ulna and a shiny object slides off into the dirt. A very un-historical watch.

A watch I recognize from the police reports on Khloe May.

"Get back, everyone," Katie shoos us away. "This is no longer a dig. It's a crime scene."

FATHER DUNCAN'S funeral is held on the last day of classes, the same day Khloe's bones are exhumed and sent to Lauren for analysis. The funeral had to be delayed while the school waited for the verdict of the coroner, and then they had to track down

Duncan's family, who tied things up with arrangements for a grand affair. Sebastian performs the service, and when he speaks of Duncan's commitment to his faith and to the school, I have to bite my tongue so I don't cry out the truth.

I can't help but notice that Benet's once-lost reliquary now has pride of place on the cathedral altar. Sebastian touches it sometimes as he speaks, as if reminding himself that all this really happened.

The Orpheans huddle together in the first pew. Monty stares straight ahead, his face unusually still. Tears roll down Diana's cheeks. Even when she cries she manages to look like a nymph. My skin burns with the injustice of it all.

Duncan is buried in the graveyard alongside monks from centuries past. As he's lowered into the earth, a wave of anger passes over me. It feels like a sacrilege to allow a murderer to taint the ground of these holy men. Father Julian Duncan goes to his grave an innocent man, and no one will ever know that his crimes have cost the lives of at least two young women.

William places his hand over mine.

We must bear the burden of our silence.

Keely and Khloe can never have the justice they deserve because the man responsible for their deaths slipped on a crooked stone and dashed his brains open. The coroner had ruled – an accidental death. The final blood sacrifice on the altar of Dionysos.

The autopsy on Khloe May's remains revealed much the same story as Keely – she'd been dismembered, both before and after death. She was missing one arm and both her thighs. Lauren says there were marks on her bones that looked like a wild animal gnawed at them.

I know the truth.

But the police don't care. I laid out all the clues for them. I've even pointed them toward the bone I gave to Lauren. I wait and wait for the story to break, but I hear from Vera that the police have no leads and are officially closing Khloe's case once again.

Which is bullshit, but even in death, the Orphean Society protects their own.

Thinking about it makes my blood boil. And then I remember those files sitting on my computer.

My podcast.

I've done it before – I pursued justice through the court of public opinion, and I won. The authorities wouldn't listen to me about the body brokering and the crooked undertaker. I don't blame them; it sounded so farfetched. So I released the podcast and the world took notice. And it didn't bring my dad back, but it got him the justice he deserved.

Even if I couldn't get corrupt cops and faculty to tell the truth about Khloe and Keely, I could get the public to take notice. I could make the Orpheus Society more infamous than the Illuminati, and ensure that whatever happened at Blackfriars would have the world watching.

But I can't do it.

If I release the podcast, William and Diana and everyone I've come to love will be on the hook for Father Duncan's crimes. Even Monty seems better now that Duncan is gone, more serene, less apt for cruelty. When Father Duncan died, he took with him the ritual of the Tristeria he was trying to resurrect. William has only just forgiven himself for what he unknowingly did to Keely. He couldn't live through a public flogging as a cannibal.

No. The podcast must stay buried. But I'll keep looking for answers. I'll keep digging.

After the funeral, there's a meal in the dining hall in Father Duncan's honor. I can't sit through students extolling his virtues without snapping, so I excuse myself from the Orpheans under the guise of grief and return to my room. I sit down at the computer and stare at the podcast files, my finger hovering over the delete button.

There's a knock at the door.

I open it. Leigh leans against the doorframe, holding a bottle of mead.

"All this sadness over a priest." She rolls her eyes. "He did it, didn't he? He killed those girls?"

I nod.

"And then someone killed him?"

I shrug. "He hit the rocks and split his head open. Lauren says it's difficult to tell whether he slipped or if someone pushed him. There was no sign of a struggle, although there was a strange mark on his skull near the fatal blow, and we didn't see anyone else walking away from the altar. I find it hard to believe too, but it is the most logical explanation."

"What about Monty?" Leigh strides into the room. I head to my bedside table to find two goblets while she flops down on my desk, throwing her jacket over my laptop. "You said he was with Duncan after they argued—"

"The timing doesn't work. When we called for help, Monty came from the amphitheater with the others," I say as I hold out the goblets and she pours the mead. "Diana says he came back about ten minutes before Sebastian ran up the hill to raise the alarm. Best I can figure timing-wise, Monty left Father Duncan sometime before he reached the altar and emerged further up the slope, where I might not have seen him. And that tallies with what the others were saying. I may not like Monty, but I can't see how he could possibly have done it and got back in time."

Leigh slumps in the chair, staring at her hands. Multi-colored paint blotches cling to her nails. She doesn't say anything for a long time, which is so unlike Leigh that a hard lump of worry churns in my gut.

"What is it?"

Leigh avoids my eyes. "Why aren't you releasing your podcast?" she asks the painting above my bed. "It's safe now. You're not in danger from Father Duncan. You can tell the story, tell the truth."

I shrug. "It's complicated."

"It's not, though. Everyone thinks Father Duncan is this saint. You should have heard them at the dinner. I was so sick of it I had to leave. I thought you were sick, too." She turns then, and I see the tears streaking her cheeks. "But you're fine. You're honestly *fine* with him getting away with killing them."

"I'm not fine, but it's pointless. Father Duncan is dead, and his sins die with him. When I did the last podcast, I was so consumed with finding the truth, I didn't think about the consequences. I was still grieving, and it felt like I'd been given this blessing, this puzzle to solve so that I didn't have to think about how much I missed my dad. I hit UPLOAD, and they were live and my life and the lives of hundreds of people whose loved ones had been cremated by Memories of the Hart changed forever. And mostly it was good – a bad man went to jail and people got closure. But not all of it was good."

"It was the right thing to do." Leigh's lip quivers.

"It was, but I'm not sure it would be this time. There's a lot of private stuff in those episodes. I can edit them, but I can't release the evidence I have against Duncan without incriminating people whose only crime was trusting Montague Cavendish—"

"You mean William," Leigh says flatly.

"Yes, I mean William, the man I love, the man who has been tearing himself to pieces with guilt over what happened. I know what the Orpheans did is wrong. They've done a lot of wrong things. But they didn't know what they were eating when Monty served them. You know Monty – hell, you spend half your time bringing him snacks. I don't think he even knows what he's doing. I don't think they're the ones to blame for what happened. Can you imagine if the media got a hold of this story? The student cannibals – it'll follow them for the rest of their lives."

"I get it," Leigh sighs. "You're protecting your boyfriend. You think a bunch of rich toffs deserve to get away with covering up these crimes because they're afraid of a little bad press. Well, I want to know when my friend stopped giving a shit about the truth, about getting justice for the victims. I thought you were different, George, but you're *exactly the same* as they are."

She picks up her coat and storms out.

37

I only see Leigh once during exams. I'm returning to The Izzy from my Greek exam, hurrying across St. Benedict's Quad with noun declensions and irregular past participles dancing in my head, just as she emerges from the art department, head bent low, chatting to that guy with the impossibly green eyes and the fuck-it-all smirk. *Shane Kelly.* I know without knowing this is the artist William warned me about. Shane wears a black hoodie pulled low over his face so he's completely in shadow. She's got on a pair of bright yellow overalls covered in dirt and leaves, and has her foraging bag slung over her shoulder – it looks as if she's just got back from the woods. She lifts his hand in hers and squeezes it.

Needles jab into my heart. I'm dying to run over and hug her, tell her all about my exam and ask her about the goodies she's found. I especially want to know about Shane fucking Kelly. He looks dangerous in all the right ways.

I don't even realize I've stopped in my tracks and I'm staring at them like a complete goober until Leigh meets my eyes. She jerks away and makes a run for it, sprinting toward Cavendish quad so she doesn't have to deal with me. Shane watches her go, then turns with a laconic air and heads back toward the art department.

I notice he's clutching something in his fist. Leigh gave him something just now.

He stares after Leigh's retreating figure with a twisted sneer on his face – the kind of smile that's not a smile at all, the kind that turns my blood to ice.

THE NEXT DAY, I can't bear the thought of facing anyone, so I stay in my room to study. Fat lot of good it does. I read the same chapter of my Criminology textbook over and over again as thoughts about the podcast and what Leigh said swirl around in my head, and I get angrier and angrier.

Why do I always have to be the one who makes the sacrifices?

Claws taught me that sometimes justice comes at the end of a blade. Keely and Khloe and Father Duncan are all dead. The victims from years ago are dead, their stories so poorly recorded that it's impossible to draw any parallels between them. I *won*, dammit. I cut off the evil at the roots so it can never grow back. The Orpheus Society will be nothing more than a posh drinking club. I did more than anyone else ever tried to do to help those girls.

So why should I volunteer my life or the lives of the people I love as fodder for the gutter press? Leigh's so good at dealing with them, she doesn't realize that 'just ignore them' doesn't work for people like me. It will never work for William. And Sebastian...even with editing some of the details in the podcast, it's clear he's broken a gazillion school policies, not to mention his solemn vow is in tatters. If I told this story, it would have to be in a way that kept him out of it, and I don't know how to do that yet.

Sometimes, you can't get justice.

Sometimes, you have to walk away.

I'm okay with that. I'm happy. I just wish that she could be happy for me.

Anyway, this isn't getting my study done. Come on, brain, focus.

I'm halfway through the chapter for the eighteenth time when my phone beeps. Thinking it's Leigh texting to apologize, I whip it out, but it's from Sebastian.

Can you come to the church? We need to talk. I don't have much time.

Hmmm. That sounds ominous. I throw my coat over my shoulders and leave my room. There's something in the air – a nervous, jerky energy that makes me want to dive under the covers and stay there forever.

But Sebastian needs me, and I always obey.

I step into the quad, and that strange energy gets stronger. I can't put my finger on it, but...it's almost as if...

No, not almost. Everyone *is* staring at me. Conversations stop and heads turn as I take a few cautious steps toward the cathedral.

I must be imagining it. It's a side effect of being bullied most of my life. If I hear people laughing cruelly nearby, I think they must be laughing at me. I think everyone's looking at me but really—

Nope, they're really looking. Their eyes follow me as I walk around the fountain. I touch my hair and try to surreptitiously feel my ass as I walk. Have I accidentally tucked my skirt into my tights?

No, no, everything is fine. So what...

My feet stop moving. I stand frozen, letting the unease settle on my shoulders. I can't move until I know what's going on. I swallow. I'm going to have to ask someone.

"Nice podcast," a girl smirks as she ambles past me.

"Oh, um...thanks?" My podcast came out a few years ago. It's well-known, sure, but it's weird that she'd choose this exact moment to mention it...

Don't worry about it. It's probably some joke. Monty's in fine form. All you have to do is get to the church and you can sink into Sebastian's arms and find your sanctuary.

I square my shoulders and keep going, picking up the pace because I have somewhere important to be and not because I'm terrified of them. When I walk past another group, one of them makes a sucking noise between their teeth, like Hannibal Lecter after discussing eating a census-taker's liver with fava beans and a Chianti. His friends laugh that cruel laugh that churns my stomach.

They're laughing at me, I'm positive.

I hurry toward the church, so certain that stepping across that invisible boundary will give me sanctuary from their stares. To my absolute horror, Abigail and Tabitha are sitting on a picnic blanket on the grass, blatantly violating the STAY OFF THE LAWN signs dotted all around. Abigail is dressed in the widow's weeds she's worn ever since Father Duncan died – short black velvet dress with a peter pan collar and cuffs, and a black feather fascinator with net veil. They're staring at Abigail's phone. When they see me, they start laughing uncontrollably.

A sick, churning feeling settles in my gut.

"Give me that." I tear the phone from her hands and stare at the screen. They're playing a podcast.

My Dad is A Gerbil, Season 2. Episode 1.

My voice comes out of the speakers, telling the story of how I infiltrated the Orpheus Society, how I intended to find Keely's murderer, and all those rambling, angst-filled questions about how I felt about William...and Sebastian.

It's *my* podcast.

Someone has taken my podcast and put it out, unedited, for all the world to devour.

38

I drop the phone in horror. Abigail and Tabitha collapse with giggles, toppling over in the grass.

It's my podcast.

But how is this possible? I never released these episodes, so how did—

Leigh.

Bile rises in my throat. I don't know how she's done it, but it has to be her.

She's the only one who knew about the podcast. I remember when she came to my room. She sat at my desk and placed her hoodie over my laptop, over my external hard drive. Then we argued and she bundled up her hoodie and left. I know that if I go back to my room now, I'll see the hard drive isn't on my desk. I can't believe I didn't even notice it was missing.

But Leigh's not technical. She wouldn't know the first thing about mastering the files or—

I swallow. Shane Kelly. He had something in his hand when he left the quad. Something square and black that I'd bet a million billion dollars is my hard drive.

I pull out my own phone and stare at the screen full of

muted notifications, the skyrocketing listen numbers and the hundreds of 5-star reviews. "I thought George's life couldn't get any crazier," someone wrote. "But I never expected a secret society of rich cannibals."

I sink to my knees right there in the grass. A whistle blows as a scout waves at me to get off, but I can't move. I'm stuck. Abigail's triumphant eyes blaze over me.

"Don't worry, George," she says, her lip curling. "When my lawyers come after you for defamation, I won't take *everything* you own. You can keep your weird clothing and grotty priest boyfriend. Oh, I'm sorry, he'll be an *ex*-priest now."

I look to Tabitha, but she's a stone wall. She won't come to my aid, not when her ass is on the line now. I don't know if they've listened to the whole podcast, but they know enough to know that I've brought a rain of hell down on their heads. They whirl on their heels and storm away.

I'm left in the middle of the quad, collapsing in upon myself like a black hole swallowing a star. A figure looms over me.

"George Fisher?" It's the porter, Victoria. She glares down at me with a look of utter disgust. "Get off the grass. You're coming with me."

I have to see Sebastian.

I scramble to my feet and try to step around her, but she blocks my path. I try again and end up slamming straight into her. She's built like a brick wall. She grabs my wrist and jerks me toward the office.

"What are you doing? I have to go. I going to meet someone."

"I'm afraid that will have to wait." Victoria tightens her iron grip. "The police are here and they need to talk to you."

$\mathcal{V}$ictoria drags me into the porter's office, behind her desk and through to a filing room crammed with people. A detective I've never seen before commands the space. Beside her, Lauren meets my eyes and nods. Scattered around – leaning against bookshelves or crouched in the windowsill and looking every bit like they intended to be there all along and not that they're being held against their will by three uniformed officers – are the Orpheans.

The temperature drops three degrees as they all turn to face me, as they read my betrayal on my face.

I didn't mean to do this, I want to shout. But it doesn't matter, because it's done. I can't undo it. I can't unmake those podcasts and all the things I said. I can't stuff the genie back into the bottle.

William sits in the window. Diana's hand rests on his knee. His head whips around. His blue eyes fix on me, cold as arctic winter. From the look on his face, I know he's listened to every episode, heard every sordid suspicion I had of him and every second thought I had about kissing lips that had tasted human flesh.

He knows I forgive him for all of it, right? He has to know that those words are me figuring things out in my own head. He has to...

"Right," the inspector says, glaring at me. "Now that we're all here, we can get down to business. I'm Inspector Claire Baddeley, and I'll be heading up this investigation from now on. I want to be clear that there *will be an investigation*. At least two students at this school have been killed, and a priest is dead, too, and I'm not going to let some entitled brats stop justice being done. I cannot be bought, got it?"

"Where's Inspector Jones?" Abigail asks, her tone wheedling.

"He's temporarily suspended pending a full investigation." Inspector Baddeley folds her arms and glares at Abigail. "We've discovered numerous instances of negligence – shoddy work, evidence going missing, leads not followed up, as well as some large sums of money deposited into his personal account. But you wouldn't know anything about that, would you, sweetheart?"

Her implication was clear. I was right all along – Inspector Jones was being paid off to look the other way by the Orpheans. And thanks to the podcast, he's going down for it.

Inspector Baddeley eyes every student. When she stops on me, her face is murderous. "We have a situation. Everyone in this room has been implicated as accessories to murder and desecration of a body. This story is out now, and I need to get to the truth before this school is overrun with press wanting all the ghastly details."

"It's all lies," Abigail spits. She points a trembling finger at me. "The Orpheus Society is just a student supper club, nothing more. George makes all the stuff up because she's so desperate to be interesting. She wanted to be in with our group, since she first started at school, and now that she's realized she'll never be one of us, she's determined to ruin our lives. You should arrest *her*, not us."

Her words cut me. I look to William, desperate for him to back me up, to show me that he stands by me no matter what. But he remains frozen.

Abigail continues, "George can't handle the fact that we're richer than her, cleverer than her, better than her in every way. This is her way of getting back at us. I mean, who ever heard of something so preposterous? Do I look like a cannibal?"

William, why won't you say something?

Beside her, Tabitha smiles such a pitying smile. "Personally, I just think it's sad. George, you need professional help. I can recommend an excellent therapist in London. She works wonders with complete head-cases, and she specializes in personality disorders—"

"I do not have a personality disorder," I shout back. "It's not a personality disorder to have a fucking problem with people *eating* their friends—"

"Silence!"

The room collapses in on itself. The inspector's red face and fearsome tone knock the wind out of our altercation.

"Now, rest assured, I will be investigating *every* claim made on this podcast, and every piece of evidence in this matter will be re-examined." The inspector nods at me. "And I'll begin with our podcaster. Georgina Fisher, we'll be escorting you and your little club to the station, where you'll need to answer some hard questions."

40

---

here's no clock in the interview room, which means I
have no idea how long I've been here. But judging by
the scratch at the back of my throat, I've been talking for hours.
Inspector Baddeley wants me to tell the story from the beginning, not missing a single sordid, personal detail.

The words drop like lead balls off my tongue. All I can think
about is William. Where is he now? Is he in another room like
this one, being forced to admit all the awful things he tried to
keep secret?

He'd just learned to forgive himself, to accept that he's not
perfect and never will be, and that that makes him more worthy
of love, not less. And now...

Everything Abigail and Tabitha said swirls around in my
head. I hate them so much because for all their self-preserving
cruelty, they see right through me like I'm made of glass. I was so
happy when they accepted me into their group. I wanted college
to be different. I wanted friends. I wanted to fit in. I wanted
people to look at me with a little bit of awe and envy. Well, I
fucking got what I wished for.

When Inspector Baddeley finishes the interview, I'm

escorted to the cells. I'm given a square room with a narrow slit of a window high on the wall. It reminds me of the anchorhold, and a sliver of cold terror slices through my heart.

I'm allowed to make a phone call. I try Leigh, but she won't pick up. I glance at the clock on the wall. It's the middle of the night in America. Mom will be sound asleep, but...

I bite my lip as I call Claws. She picks up on the second ring.

"What the fuck happened now?"

Tears stream down my cheeks as I tell her what happened. When Tiberius left me at the end of last summer, I thought I could stand on my own two feet at Blackfriars. I don't want to run to her every time I have a problem, because she's likely to solve my problems with knives.

But the sound of her voice makes my stomach churn with homesickness. I miss Claws. I miss Emerald Beach. I miss my mom and my friends who've always had my back and would never betray me.

I miss my dad. So, so much.

If he was here now, he'd find some way to make me laugh. He'd be on the phone singing, 'Working on the Chain Gang' and 'Folsom Prison Blues' and concocting brilliant schemes to tunnel me out with a plastic spoon and I just wish I could talk to him one more time and see him smile and feel like the world isn't falling apart around me...

"—stay calm, George," Claws is saying. "I know you're afraid, but you've survived worse than this. Remember Alec LeMarque? Remember when my sister tried to blow us all to pieces, and you saved us? All you did here was tell the truth and try to get justice. You're not at fault here, and the world will see that."

I nod, but my stomach churns, and I'm not so sure she's right. I'm not blameless. I'm not the good girl.

After I hang up the phone, I'm escorted back to the cells. I struggle to choke down my dinner of cold sausages, bread, and tomato sauce when the door swings open and I'm joined by Lauren.

"Hey," she says, standing gingerly in front of the door as if she's afraid I might bite. "I thought you might appreciate a friendly face."

You can say that again, I want to say. But if I speak I'll burst into tears, and I can't bear the humiliation of it after the day I've had. So I pat the thin mattress I'm sitting on.

"If it's all the same, I'd rather stand. There are all kinds of germs on those things." She makes a face at the mattress. "Right, so I've been able to observe some of the interviews. None of the Orpheans are talking about Devil's Night. There are so many penguin suits out here I could start my own zoo. This is gonna be bad, kid. They're closing ranks so it's your word against theirs. I've got the forensic evidence, but all that shows is that both women were mutilated. The finger ties Khloe's death to Father Duncan, and the school already cleaned out his office, so there's no chance of more evidence there."

I nod. I knew the Orphean alumni would get on that immediately. "What else?"

"The street is swarming with press. Your podcast is on every news channel in Britain. They may not go to prison for their part in it, but the Orpheans won't be able to set foot outside their castles ever again. In short," Lauren says, "you got justice."

"This doesn't feel like justice," I say.

"On the contrary." Lauren pats my shoulder. "This is exactly what justice is – a hollow feeling inside your chest because the system is completely fucked and a bunch of rich bastards get away with murder, again."

She leaves, swinging the door shut behind her.

A FEW HOURS LATER, the door opens again. A uniformed officer props it open with her arm. "Fisher, you're free to go."

I try to leap to my feet, but my legs have cramped up and I kind of slither off the slab. "I am?"

"You are. Your podcast is going to bring down a world of shit on your head, but the guv doesn't think you had anything to do with the murders of those two girls. And as for the cannibalism, that's a legal minefield. Your friends have already been sent back to school." She studies me as I drag myself out of the cell and collect my things from the desk as if I'm some interesting exhibit in a school.

She drives me to Blackfriars and drops me by the front gates. It's mid-morning, and the school buzzes with the news of my return. Whispers and stares follow me as I march across Martyr's Quad. I'd better get used to this, because it's my life now. Once again, I'm George the freak at the center of a scandal.

Only this time, I can't see this as black and white. I'm not the heroine and William isn't a villain.

I drag my feet to The Izzy. All I think about is getting to my room, having a shower, and going to see Sebastian. I didn't know why he didn't answer his phone when I called. He had to have heard what happened.

When I clamber up the stairs, I'm surprised to see a pile of stuff crowding the narrow landing between mine and Monty's doors – *my* stuff, to be specific. My clothes dumped in a messy pile, my computer cords snaking across the floor, the painting William did for me leaning against the wall, the glass smashed out and the canvas torn, like someone has slashed it with a knife.

I riffle through the broken items until I find the only thing I care about – the photograph of me and Dad. The frame and glass are smashed, but the photo is still intact. I hug it to my chest, heaving in great gasps of air to get my tears under control, when I hear a voice behind me.

"We should pat ourselves on the backs for our civil service, old chum. As the Americans like to say, someone had to take out the trash."

I turn. Monty sits on the stairs, chortling with high-pitched laughter as he slaps his knee. Another figure sits beside him. William.

He looks resigned, like he expected this. Like he's been waiting for it to happen, waiting for me to screw him over.

And that's when my heart truly breaks. I feel it crunch in my chest, the ventricles tearing from the arteries, the blood gushing freely into my chest cavity.

"William," I choke out his name. "Please, I can explain—"

"Is that so?" he says casually, as if he's discussing the weather. "You can explain how you convinced me that you loved me, how you fed me lies and made me believe I was actually a person worth a shit, when all this time you were using me to get fodder for your podcast?"

"It was never like that. I never lied to you. I've been so confused. In the beginning, I knew you were hiding the truth about Keely, and about Sebastian. And then after you told me, I had to figure out... I was never going to release the episodes, they were just for myself, but Leigh—"

He scoffs. I have to agree that it's a pretty sorry excuse. If I never intended to release it, then why did I keep making the episodes? If they were for me and me alone, why did I talk as if I were discussing the case with an invisible audience?

I've told myself all kinds of stories about why I was making the episode, but the truth is that I kept them on the back of my laptop just in case. They were my bargaining chip, my safety net.

In case they broke my heart.

If William hurt me, then I could use the podcast to hurt him.

Well, achievement fucking unlocked. William looks at me with such devastating hurt and revulsion that I don't think it's possible for a human being to hate themselves more than I hate myself right now.

Monty pats his friend's shoulder. "There, there, bonny Prince William, don't you fret about little Georgie Pie. She's just a fly we can swat away."

I have to get out of there. I can't look at William's face a moment longer. I grab my favorite denim jacket from the top of the pile – the one covered in patches from my fave bands – and I tuck Dad's photograph under my arm and throw myself back down the stairs.

I need to talk to Sebastian.

I can think of nothing else except getting to him. I need to fall into his arms and cry out all the loss. I need my sanctuary more than ever.

I don't even remember arriving at St. Benedict's. I crash through the church, my feet pounding on the marble. Father Howard – the kindly old man sent to replace Father Duncan – glances up from his breviary with shock, but I don't stop to talk to him. I crash into the annex. Sebastian's door is open and I throw myself over the threshold, desperate to fall into his arms.

"My podcast is live," I cry as I run into his rooms. "Leigh published it and William heard it and I'm—"

I stop dead.

The room is bare. The rumpled bed and desk piled high with books are gone. The boxes of records and creaky old chairs and that musky, sacrilegious, Sebastian smell that permeates everything, *gone*. All that remains of the cozy chairs where we spent all those nights studying Greek are eight tiny dents in the carpet.

Sally, my scout from first year, looks up from the window, where she's been scrubbing a stubborn stain in the glass.

Cleaning products and buckets are dotted around her, and a tiny dog winds itself between her legs.

"Hi, George. I haven't seen you around in a while. Are you looking for Father Pearce?" she asks, setting down her pail. "He's gone."

I manage to choke out a word. "Gone?"

"Aye. Packed up his things and left late last night. I don't know much about it, only he's broken some kind of priestly rule so they've sent him away to think about what he's done. He's gone for good – they want me to scrub this room down for the new priest to move in."

No. It can't be.

But it is.

And I caused it.

The podcast had details about Sebastian. Not a lot, but enough. Enough that anyone on the faculty could listen and know that their chaplain forsook his solemn vows, that a teacher had been carrying on an illicit affair with not one but *two* students, that the altar of their ancient church had been desecrated...

He's gone.

Sebastian is gone.

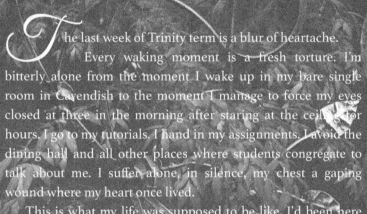

41

The last week of Trinity term is a blur of heartache. Every waking moment is a fresh torture. I'm bitterly alone from the moment I wake up in my bare single room in Cavendish to the moment I manage to force my eyes closed at three in the morning after staring at the ceiling for hours. I go to my tutorials. I hand in my assignments. I avoid the dining hall and all other places where students congregate to talk about me. I suffer alone, in silence, my chest a gaping wound where my heart once lived.

This is what my life was supposed to be like. I'd been here before – the outcast, the loner freak with the weird clothes and the obsession with truth. The difference is that I've fallen madly, deeply in love with two incredible men, I've found a best friend who understood me the way no one else did, and I hurt them all.

I broke their trust. I became *exactly* the kind of person I despise.

It doesn't matter that Leigh released the podcast without permission. I was angry about it at first, furious at her betrayal. But now I see that she was braver than I could ever hope to be.

She knew it would destroy our friendship, but she did it anyway because it was the right thing to do. I admire her more than ever.

Leigh, I know you'll never talk to me again, but I forgive you.

But I can't forgive myself. I made the podcast. They were my words, my thoughts, my secrets to keep that are now spilled to the four winds for carrion birds to pick over.

I don't remember a word of what I wrote in my exams. I know I won't have done as well as I hoped. If my grades are too low I could lose my scholarship, but I can't bring myself to care.

Instead, I stay glued to the online news sites where my podcast is dissected in minute detail. Gleeful reporters and true crime writers pick over the nuggets. Paparazzi start showing up at Mom's house in Emerald Beach again, looking for me, clamoring to pick over the ashes of our lives the way they'd done in the early days of the first season, after the Memories of the Hart story broke.

I text Sebastian. He never replies. I have no idea where he is or what's happened to him. I think about him, and William, every minute of every day.

Claws sends some of her heavies around to Mom's house to scare off the reporters. Tiberius is back at college. He stands guard outside my room and escorts me to my exams or the library (Claws must've been paying a lot to make the school turn the other way), making sure that the few intrepid journalists who sneak past Blackfriars' security don't escape with their bones intact. But he can't protect me from the words printed in every paper and on every news site across the globe.

THE RICH YOUNG CANNIBALS, one headline reads. I'd appreciate the pun if it didn't make me feel sick.

All those things I said when I was alone and scared, all my secret thoughts and fears are out there in the world. And words destroy lives quicker than fire. Quicker than biblical plagues or the wrath of any ancient god.

Words have always been my allies, my friends. But now they carry William and Sebastian far away from me.

42

"*B*ring the buckwheat muffins, will you?"

I make a face behind my mom's back as I carry a platter of hockey pucks through to the living room, grateful for the Fry's Chocolate Orange bar burning a hole in my pocket. It's the last of the candy stash I brought with me from England. Bless the UK's superior candy. (I'm sorry, Twinkies, but you've been dethroned.)

I'll need sugar to sustain me for the challenge ahead – we're about to embark on an eight-hour horror movie marathon. My friend Eli is manning the food truck today so we could do a little mother/daughter bonding. Every year since Dad died we have a little tradition. On his birthday, we stuff ourselves with his favorite foods and watch his movies. The last couple of years, we've had to do it over Zoom, and I've never felt so far away from Mom. This year it's right and good that I should be back at home, on the couch where we spent so many nights hanging out as a family.

As well as the buckwheat pucks, Mom's tried to make healthy versions of Dad's favorite foods. There's nothing on the table that looks remotely appetizing. Lentils should not be allowed anywhere near hot dogs.

Mom flicks through the channels while she waits for me to get settled. "I know last year we went in chronological order, but I thought this year we could try in order of the lowest ratings on Rotten Tomatoes."

"Excellent idea. That means *Shunned* is up first." It's my favorite film of Dad's – it's based on a book series by this author Steffanie Holmes, about a scholarship girl going to a fancy prep school and falling in love with three possessive a-holes. And an ancient Lovecraftian god lives under the school that causes all kinds of chaos and mayhem. I'd been hoping to show it to Leigh one day – I knew she'd love it.

I've text Leigh a couple of times since I got to California. No reply. She unfriended me on all her social media. I try not to think about her because if I do, I start crying. I suck in a deep breath and focus on Mom.

"*Shunned* it is." Mom crunches on a salt and vinegar Pringle – one of the only non-healthy snacks she's permitted me to include. "God, I've forgotten how amazing these taste. It must be all that MSG—hey, isn't that your school?"

"Huh?" I turn to the television just as Mom pumps the volume. It's a national news station. The camera pans around St. Benedict's Quad before circling up to take in the grey sky and the cathedral's gothic spires as ominous piano music plays. One of the college ravens flutters past in the corner of the frame, as if it had been queued.

"—the prestigious, exclusive university is once again the scene of controversy, as William Windsor-Forsyth shook the British media today by breaking the silence surrounding the cannibalistic secret society on campus."

The camera cuts to William, standing on the steps of the chapel at Forsyth Hall, with his father and about a gazillion lawyers clustered around him, addressing a gaggle of reporters. I notice to my surprise that Vera and Ro are also in the crowd. "I have done a terrible thing. Two years ago, at a party on the 30th of October, I was offered a platter of meat. I took a piece and ate it, not knowing at the time that it was the flesh of my friend, Keely O'Sullivan.

"Although the fact that I ate this is shocking, and I am deeply sorry that I desecrated Keely's remains in this way, it's not the part of the story for which I am most ashamed," William says. "I was given the meat and ate it without knowledge of what it was. It was only afterward that I was made aware. I should have come forward when Keely's body was first discovered, but I did not. I acted in a cowardly and selfish manner. I was afraid of what the public reaction would do to my already broken family, and to my friends and their families. I put our reputations over the need to learn the truth about my friend's killer.

"It took a woman much braver than I to uncover the truth. Georgina Fisher kept digging into Keely's death long after the police gave up. She discovered that Keely wasn't the first girl to die on Devil's Night. She never stopped questioning everything. She didn't even let the fact that Keely bullied her deter her from the truth." William looks into the camera. "If we were all a little more like George, no crime would ever go unsolved. No victim would be denied justice."

"That's you," Mom jabs me in the shoulder. "He said your name."

I can't acknowledge her. I can't speak. I can't move. I'm fixated by this brave prince as he takes a moment to consult the papers in his hands.

"—Even after George's podcast was released, the members of the society tried to hide the truth. We knew we had the power to change the narrative, to bury this story. We knew we had to do it to protect one of our own who was vulnerable, who had been manipulated by a man with power over him." William shuffles his papers and raises his head. "That silence ends today. I will be cooperating fully with Inspector Baddeley and the police on this case. Together, I hope we can bring to light answers that will give both Keely and Khloe May's families some closure."

William clears his throat and continues. "I know the media will fixate on what happened at the Devil's Night party, but that's not the story here. The story is of a young woman, full of life, who was taken too soon by her trusted teacher who thought that pain made him a god. Keely O'Sullivan deserves to be more than a footnote in a sordid tale. She will be missed."

"George, are you okay?"

When I don't answer, Mom flicks off the TV. She places her hand on my knee as the tears spill down my cheeks. The tears become giant, heaving sobs. She pulls me into her arms, and I sob and snot all over her kaftan until I give myself the hiccups.

"You...hic...listened to the...hic...podcast?" I manage to get out.

"Of course I listened to it. I'm your mother." Mom's fingers close around my shoulder. "Honey, look at me."

It takes every ounce of self-control to lift my head. I promise myself I won't cry anymore, I won't give her any more reason to worry about me when she should be thinking about herself, on today of all days. But as I raise my head and see the love in her eyes, I burst into tears again.

"Oh, George." Mom rubs circles on my back. I lie on her shoulder, burying my face in her neck and breathing her familiar patchouli perfume, and I let myself cry my big, messy tears.

I let it all out. I cry because I'm not the person I thought I was. I cry because of everything I've lost, because of a beautiful priest and a broken prince who are so far away, hurting so much, because of what I did. I cry because my dad should be here and we both know it, and we've both been trying to fill the void he left in our lives with podcasts and food trucks and threesomes and nothing is ever, ever going to bring him back.

Finally, Mom leans away. She swipes a strand of hair from my tear-stained cheek. "After your dad died—" her words catch in her throat.

"Mom, you don't have to—"

"I *do*," she rasps, clinging a little tighter. "After your dad died, I didn't know how to help you grieve. I'd lost the love of my life. There was so much that had to be done, and you were coping so well. I think that I was so relieved that you hadn't done all the things they warned me about in grief counseling – you weren't acting out or taking drugs or falling in with the wrong crowd—"

I dare a little smile, thinking about Claws. *I'm not so sure about that.*

"—that I didn't check in with you as much as I should have. And then your podcast came out and I realized what you'd been doing all this time, that you'd been falling to pieces as only my clever, beautiful daughter can, but by then it was too late. Our lives – your father's life and his death, were front-page news."

"I'm sorry," I sniff.

"Don't be sorry. Don't you for one minute apologize for what you did. You got the truth. It wasn't so much about what you gave me, but what you gave to all those other people who were searching for answers was nothing short of a miracle. But George, honey," she strokes my hair. "You don't have to do this alone. When I listened to your podcast, do you know what I heard? Not all the stuff about cannibals and murders. Not even the bits about you falling for a priest, although after seeing his picture on the news, I can say I understand. It was when you said how you couldn't believe that people like them would ever want to be friends with you. You've been so lonely for so long that you just assume that's the way your life will always be, and it's not true, George. It's *not true*."

"Mom, I—"

She cups my face in her hands. "You, my daughter, are a brilliant, funny, and unflinchingly kind person. You deserve every good thing in life. And to think you've been carrying this loneliness for so long and I didn't see it. George, you're not alone. You have me. You have your friend Claws, who might be a little insane—"

I stifle a laugh. Insane is an understatement.

"—but I have no doubt that girl would die for you." She kisses my forehead. "And this friend, Leigh? I think that you will make up with her. I think the two of you will be friends for a long time to come. You don't have to carry the weight of the world on your shoulders. There are so many good things in life waiting for you."

I sniff. "Thanks, Mom."

She pulls back, and as she draws away from my body, it's as if she lifts a heavy stone from my chest – a stone I'm so used to carrying I stopped noticing its weight.

Mom clicks the TV on again and starts the movie. I stare at the screen but I don't hear a word of dialogue. The first head rolls across the screen and I don't even react. I can't stop thinking about William standing up to the press, admitting the truth with head held high and forgiveness in his eyes.

He's learned to forgive himself. He's found absolution in the truth. And maybe, maybe, he's forgiven me too. Maybe I can learn from him and accept the madness of the impossible.

Maybe I can forgive myself.

A HUFF of exasperation explodes from the lounger beside me. "You're doing it again."

"Am not."

He still hasn't called. Or text. Or emailed. Or sent carrier pigeons. After all those things he said at the press conference, why doesn't he want to talk to me? Why does he still hate me?

I try to slip my phone back into my pocket without her seeing it. But I should know not to try to pull one over on Claws. She grabs my phone and holds it over the pool. The shimmering water beckons, threatening to devour my only line to the world outside Emerald Beach.

My mind flashes back to a day, two years ago, when this pool had been empty, the tiles cracked and coated in grime. A starved, man-eating lion circled at the bottom while a psychotic crime lord dragged me toward the edge. I touch my face where the cool metal of his gun pressed against my temple—

"I'll drop it." Claws' lips curl back into a smirk as she wiggles my phone. "You know that I will. It's for your own good."

"No, please!"

"You told me that I wasn't to let you spend all summer looking at the headlines in England," she says. "And if I have to destroy this perfectly good iPhone to protect you from yourself, I'll do it. That's the kind of friend I am. Or are you ready to stop pretending and admit to yourself that you still care about the priest and the prince?"

"I don't care," I say.

Claws lets go with two of her fingers. She's now holding my phone only by the corner. I stretch for it, but I'm such a shortass I'll never be able to grab it without falling in the water.

Curse my stumpy arms.

"*Fine.* I care, okay? But it doesn't matter if I care. Sebastian and William are both lost to me. And after all the scandal, I'll never be allowed to return to Blackfriars." I flop back on my lounger. "So, all caring does is make me feel sick all the time. Happy?"

"Not even remotely." Claws retracts my phone from above the pool. "But we can fix that. I can send some people to—"

"No. No people. William isn't going to magically forgive me because you cut off his thumb."

"Okay, so if it's really as bad as you say, then you don't go back. I have plenty of jobs here for you. And I know you've had offers from other universities. You have options, George. It's not Blackfriars or bust."

It's true. Since Leigh published the podcast, I've been contacted by the likes of Cambridge, Oberlin, and the California Institute of the Arts, all offering me generous scholarship packages to switch to their programs. It's tempting, especially since the idea of running into Leigh or William or any of the other Orpheans at school makes me feel ill. But leaving Blackfriars feels like admitting defeat. And one thing Claws has taught me is to know when it's time to sharpen my sword and march into battle.

Claws steps back and drops my phone into my waiting hands. "Do you want to know what I think you should do?"

"Sure. Give me the Mafia Queen's guide to unfucking my life."

Claws tosses her golden waves over her shoulder, her piercing blue eyes completely serious. "I think you should enact a little poetic justice. Carve a chunk out of William's leg and feed it to him. Get that friend of yours to fry it up with some butter and—"

"Claws!"

"What? If that prince tastes as delicious as he looks..." she licks her lips.

"No cannibalism," Noah snarls as he walks past with a tray of drinks.

"But—"

"No cannibalism."

On the other side of the pool, Gabriel looks up from his *Metal Hammer* magazine and stares at us over his designer sunglasses. "Now that's a rule for life if ever I heard one. When in doubt, try not to be a cannibal."

I WRAP my arms around myself. It's a hot day – a typical dry Californian stunner – but the breeze blowing off the ocean carries a sharp chill. Or maybe that's just how you feel when you hang out in a graveyard.

Usually, when I come to see Dad I lean against the mausoleum in the opposite row and stare at his modest stone. I never say anything, because it's never felt like he's here. He's *not* here – I know that scientifically, empirically. His earthly remains were never recovered from Memories of the Hart. All we had to bury were the ashes of a gerbil. Everything that I loved about Dad is gone – his hearty laugh, his wicked sense of humor, the way he had some macabre and disturbing story for every occasion, the smell of zesty aftershave and latex prosthetic on his skin when he returned from a long day on set and snuggled onto the couch beside me.

But something of Sebastian has rubbed off on me. Today, when I approach the grave, the hairs on my arms raise.

I *feel* him.

I sit on the grass, crossing my legs beneath me the way I did when I sat on the couch with him and watched a movie. I breathe in deep, and I catch the faintest hint of black coffee and zesty aftershave and latex on the breeze.

"Hey, Dad."

No answer apart from the relentless crash of the ocean against the cliffs below. My neck prickles.

"So, I fucked everything up."

I wipe a tear rolling from my eye. I've never cried here before. *Never*.

I take a deep breath and keep going. The words pour out of me like they've been waiting for a faucet to be turned on. "After you died, I got so caught up in trying to solve the mystery of your ashes that I don't think I ever stepped back to grieve. And then when I got to Blackfriars, I was so lonely, and in the loneliness, the grief crept in. I thought about you all the time, about how much you would have loved the place, and about how much more fun it would've been if you'd been there with me. Then when Keely disappeared, I jumped at the chance to throw myself into investigating because I knew it would distract me. I knew I could push the grief back into that box in my head, lock it away and not think about it. I could *not* feel for a while. And I thought, this is my chance to do it all *right*.

"I've been chasing distractions for so long that I...I realize I used the podcast to put up a barrier with William and Sebastian. And Leigh, too. With her I think doing the podcast made me feel like I was making a difference, but when it came down to it I wasn't willing to make sacrifices for the truth, and she was. She blew up her own life and incurred the wrath of the Orpheans, and I know she hates me because I made her do that alone.

"And William and Sebastian...I didn't allow myself to truly commit to them, because that would mean cutting my chest open and feeling all those things I've been trying to repress. I was afraid of falling for them because I could love them so easily and then I could lose them, the way I lost you. But then I *did* lose them and it's all my fault and I..." I suck in a breath. "I'm in pieces, Dad. I feel like you died all over again. How pathetic is that?"

No one answers, but a weight falls around my shoulders. Not an oppressive weight. More like the weight of two arms wrapping around me, holding me tight. The sensation is so real that I raise my hands, half expecting to feel Dad's hairy arms clutching me tight.

I touch my skin.

There's no one there.

*a*s I step through the gates to Blackfriars to begin my third year, the rickety wheel on my suitcase finally gives up the ghost and flies off.

Groaning under my breath, I chase it across the cobbles, picking it up from the gutter just as a tall, lanky shadow towers over me, and my fingers are crushed by a shiny Oxford shoe.

"Oopsies," Monty Cavendish says in a singsong voice. "I didn't see you, Georgie Pie, down there with the slugs and *rats*."

I stand up, refusing to rub my hand even though my fingers *sting* from where Monty ground them into the cobble with his heel. I study Monty with his hands thrust into his pockets and his blazer misbuttoned and a natty bowtie loose at his collar. The same sticky smirk that haunts my dreams plays across his face.

"You came back to school?" I meant it to be accusatory, but my voice comes out high, afraid. I hadn't prepared myself to see him again. I thought after William's confession, after Inspector Baddeley's promise to bring Keely and Khloe's killers to justice, that Monty would go down for his part in the murders. We don't know how much of the actual killing he did, but he was the one who prepared and served the meat. Turns out, the UK doesn't even have laws against the desecration of a corpse, so they had to let him go.

"You can't keep a Cavendish away from his rightful place." Monty glances up at Martyrs' Tower, whistling a little tune through his lips. "My great-something grandfather helped to build this school. Anyway, Georgie Pie, I *do* hope we'll see you around." He reaches down and ruffles my hair, like I'm a fucking dog he's met on the street. "We'll have ever so much fun."

He ambles away, whistling his annoying, terrifying tune. I stand in the gutter, my fingers stinging and my whole body shaking – with anger, with terror.

Monty is back. Monty got away with it.

But without Father Duncan, at least he won't be persuaded into any more deadly rituals. Right?

THAT NIGHT, at dinner, the Master stands to give his usual speech. Instead of the instructions about Devil's Night, he gives a short speech about Keely, emphasizing that student safety is of the utmost importance and urging us all not to get involved with illegal and dangerous activities on campus. Keely would have hated it, but it makes me smile.

The Orpheus Society table is taken over by Leigh and her bandmates and a bunch of guys from her sculpture course, including Shane Kelly. I long to go and sit with her but one filthy look from Shane and I know I'll be risking my life if I do. My ex-friends are scattered about the room. I can feel their eyes boring into me as I count all eight of them.

Not William.

The broken prince hasn't returned to Blackfriars. I can't say I blame him, but at the knowledge, a tiny butterfly with hope for wings that had taken up residence in my heart fluttered away and died.

———————

IT'S A BIG UNIVERSITY, I remind myself. *You can avoid Monty most of the time.*

It's little consolation. Monty is still in my AV class, and I have to work with him on our group projects. Every time he looks at me, I get jittery and drop expensive equipment.

Around every corner is another Orphean. They're posed around campus like perfect vignettes of collegiate life. Tabitha glares at me from her place in a circle of girls sharing cigarettes on a picnic blanket under the oak trees. Diana gives me a shy wave from across the quad as she sets up her easel and works on a sketch of the fountain. Richard tips his beer over my head when he passes me in The Bad Habit.

I never see them together anymore. The papers report that they've all fallen out, that the Orpheus Society is disbanded and gone for good. But I know better.

The network of ex-members who've infiltrated the most powerful positions in Britain got them out of this mess. They greased palms and paid bribes and got the papers to focus elsewhere and the police to conclude they didn't have enough evidence. Again.

The Orpheus Society still exists. It's merely gone underground.

And while the old George would have dived back into bringing them down, the new George turns the other way when she sees Percy approaching across the quad. She resists the urge to type her thoughts into vitriolic attacks that any paper would've paid her thousands to publish.

Instead, the new George reworks her colloquy. Instead of

being about the Khloe May murder, it's about the concept of forgiveness. As a human trait, a philosophical idea, and a facet of the criminal justice system.

"You're learning an important lesson," Professor Hipkins says during our first supervision meeting, after I tell her everything that happened over the summer break and that the Orpheans are back at school. "As an investigator, you have to know when to dig for the truth, but you also have to know when to walk away before you lose your humanity."

So I stay away. It's easier than I expected. Without William or Sebastian at school, and with Leigh not talking to me, my life is sheened over with grey.

Mom didn't want me to come back, and I'd *almost* accepted a place at the California Institute of the Arts. Professor Hipkins called to tell me she'd interceded for me with the board and they'd renewed my place for the year, so I felt that I owed it to her to show up. And then she offered me a part-time job as her research assistant putting together information on Victorian press sensationalism of murders for her new book.

Things are the same, but different. This time, even though I'm alone, I don't feel lonely. I talk to my mother and Claws every day. I tape the photograph above my desk and look at it often, and when I close my eyes, I can smell a little black coffee and latex wafting in the air.

I may not believe in God, but I do believe in *something*.

I believe my father is watching out for me.

I started seeing a therapist back in America, and I decide to continue. I go to a sunny office in the student medical center once a week, and I talk to this nice woman about how wonderful Dad was, and how much I miss him, and I cry a lot, but every time I cry it feels like a bloodletting, like all the shadows inside me are pouring out, leaving only light.

I'm finally beginning to sit with my sadness, to grieve.

I think about Sebastian and William a lot in those moments. William, who has been through the same as me. We both lost someone we loved too soon, and we both let the pain of it close us off to our true feelings, our deepest desires. We missed the opportunity to be there for each other, to help each other heal.

And Sebastian...who's being punished for the sin of refusing to feel shame for his deeds, when all along he was the holiest man you could ever meet. Sometimes people don't fit inside the box they're given. The world isn't ready for a priest like Father Sebastian Pearce. I only hope one day it will be, because what a blessing that will be.

Thinking about them isn't always healthy, but if I hold their faces in my mind – during their brightest moments, where their love for each other and for me shimmered on their skin – I am comforted. I do not feel alone.

Whatever happens, I can handle it. I am strong.

Bring it the fuck on.

———

WITHOUT MY WEALTHY BENEFACTOR, I'm back in cheap digs in Cavendish Quad under Sally's dominion. Since I'm a third year, I get a room to myself – it's on the first floor level with a large bay window that looks out over the monk's cemetery. From my desk, I have a perfect view over Father Duncan's grave, reminding me that even if he was never brought to justice, the truth about him has finally come out. Maybe my life is fucked, maybe Monty will get away scot-free, but the spirits of Keely and Khloe May and all those other women can at least begin to rest in peace.

It's a testament to Sebastian's power of belief that the thought gives me comfort.

Whispers follow me between my classes, tail me as I stop by the student mini-mart for snacks. I return to my first-year routine of avoiding the dining hall and eating at a shadowy table at The Bad Habit, or alone in my room, staring at my books. It's worse than first year, because I don't even have my weekly Greek classes with Sebastian to look forward to, but I keep going.

I fucked up, and I lost every friend I ever had here.

I'm determined that I won't waste this year feeling sorry for myself. I will graduate, and I will keep fighting, and one day I will be able to look at myself in the mirror and say I forgive myself.

The Orpheans may think that I've forgotten them. They will assume I've given up. And one day in the future they will let down their guard.

And I will be ready.

44

*D*evil's Night. Again.

There are murmurs around campus about some new group who might take over the pranking – some kind of radical art collective who I suspect might have something to do with Shane-Kelly. They can have it. Devil's Night has been the dominion of the rich and well-connected – it's time for the rabble, the 'unwashed hordes' as Monty would've called them, to take over.

It feels wrong *not* to mark the night in some way. If I were back in America, I'd be in full swing for Halloween plans – decorating the house, stocking up on candy, and planning which horror films I'd watch. I might be far from home, but I can have my own Devil's Night celebration.

I splurge some of my hard-earned money on a projector screen for my room. I spend all afternoon setting it up and downloading some of my fave horror films – movies Dad and I loved, and a couple we loved to hate on. I ask Tiberius if he wants to join me but he says he'd rather gouge his eyes out with a rusty spoon than watch horror films. So I leave him to run surveillance in the quad and head out to source the all-important snackage.

First stop is the college mini-mart to stock up on Fry's bars, Walnut Whips, and Walkers Crisps. As I leave, a rowdy group dressed in costumes enter and hog the narrow aisles. Diana is with them, dressed as a maenad with wild hair and a deerskin around her shoulders. She calls out to me but I don't stop.

As I wait at The Bad Habit for my takeaway pie and chips, I glance at the booth in the corner where two friends are sharing a pint. They're passing a phone between them and cracking up laughing. First years, by the looks of them. I think of all the nights Leigh and I spent in this dimly-lit room, solving the world's problems. All the times she made me laugh until I couldn't breathe.

I'm doing it again.

I'm cutting myself off because I'm afraid of getting hurt. I'm back at Blackfriars, the place I dreamed of being the entire time I was in high school. Yet I'm walking the campus like I'm a ghost. So what if I take a risk and get hurt? My heart is already an open wound. How much worse can things be?

I can't stand this anymore. I need to see Leigh. I need to ask her to forgive me.

"Can I get a second pie?" I ask Kit. "And maybe two servings of sticky date pudding?"

Kit bags my takeaways, then I go back across to the mini-mart and purchase a couple of bottles of cheap white wine. On the way to Leigh's room, I slip into the Cloister Garden and pick a bunch of dahlia flowers for her.

I climb the stairs to Leigh's room. She's one of the few students who's had the same room for her whole three years – that's what having money at Blackfriars means. Leigh could have her pick of the fancy suites in The Izzy, but she likes her quirky attic bedroom with the dormer window she can crawl out of and sit on the roof.

I'm puffing by the time I reach the top of her staircase. I bang on Leigh's door, shifting my packages nervously.

She doesn't answer.

Shit. In all my excitement to apologize for being a terrible friend, I didn't think that Leigh might have better things to do on Devil's Night than mope around in her room. I turn away, feeling deflated. I guess I could check in the studios...or maybe she's practicing with her band...or...

This is a bad idea. I should just go back to my room.

As I head for the stairs, a girl leans out of the opposite room.

"You looking for Leigh?"

I nod.

"She went out about an hour ago with her foraging bag over her shoulder. I dunno if she has her phone on her—"

"That's okay. Thanks." I hurry past her, my heart soaring. If Leigh's out foraging, I have a good idea of where she's gone.

I stop at my room to drop off the food and grab my coat, then head down toward the wooded path. I don't see Tiberius behind me but for an enormous, terrifying dude he's excellent at hiding. I pass a couple of students heading back from the village, their heads down, collars pulled high against the cold, even though by British standards it's a mild day, with low, heavy grey clouds and just a few drops of rain hitting my face.

At the amphitheater, I turn into the woods, following the ridge where we'd foraged so many times before. The bullace bushes are heavy with fruit, and I notice a few ripe nuts in their bristly cases on the lower branches of the beech trees. "Leigh?" I call out.

No answer.

I stop in front of the bullace and look down. There, in the damp earth, are perfectly preserved footprints – Leigh's combat boots stomping on top of her previous prints as she picks the wild plums. And over there...

Another set of prints, lighter, with square toes, like dress shoes. They come from the trees and march right behind Leigh and then...

I follow the two sets of prints deeper into the woods. The impressions are on top of each other, and many are smudged – they're not walking side by side, but more like Leigh's being led.

Or dragged.

My heart hammers against my ribs.

The footsteps take a long, meandering route, and often seem to turn about in circles or stomp over themselves, like they're looking for something, or continuing to forage together.

I clamber over a rotting log and spy something bright red poking out of the dirt in front of an ancient oak. A pile of bullace berries spill into the mud. They've fallen from a filthy canvas satchel. My hand flies to my mouth as I realize what I've found.

Leigh's foraging bag.

Covered in blood.

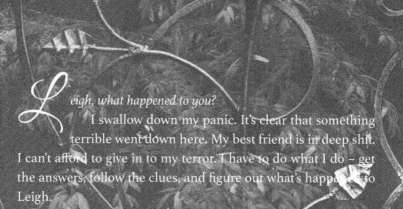

eigh, what happened to you?

I swallow down my panic. It's clear that something terrible went down here. My best friend is in deep shit. I can't afford to give in to my terror. I have to do what I do – get the answers, follow the clues, and figure out what's happened to Leigh.

I pick up the bag gingerly, looking carefully at the ground around it, at the branches snapped off and the divots in the mud. There was definitely a scuffle here. I find more footprints, too smudged and trampled to make out shapes and treads.

Tiny mushrooms poke through the dirt around the roots. I gaze up at the tree, at the Greek letter Alpha scrawled into the bark of an ancient oak, and a chill runs down my spine.

I know what's happened to Leigh.

It's Devil's Night.

It's the biannual anniversary of Keely's death and dismemberment.

Time for the Tristeria to return.

I thought the barbaric ritual died with Father Duncan. Only

Monty was ever interested in it, and no way would the Orpheans try anything with the media attention on them. And yet...

I stare down at the bag in my hands. It's half-filled with Leigh's foraging – a bunch of bullace, some herbs and roots I don't recognize, and a pile of wood mushrooms. I press my finger into one of the bloodstains, smudging it a little. It's fresh. Whatever happened here was recent.

I can still save her.

I can still make this right.

"Leigh?" I call out, my voice wobbly, aware that I might be alerting attackers that I'm nearby. "Can you hear me?"

No answer.

I loop the bag over my shoulder and do a quick grid-search of the wider area. I'm higher on the ridge and the ground is hard here, so I don't see any more footprints. I notice snapped branches and places where the plants have been trodden down, but nothing I can use to really track their movements. I remove the knife and carve my own mark in several of the trees so I can find this exact spot again. It's likely a crime scene.

I can't be too late. I won't let Leigh be the next victim.

I start to head back toward school, tossing up my next move. I jog up the path, calling Leigh's name in the vain hope she just dropped her bag and scratched her leg on a blackberry bush or something. Nothing.

I see a shape at the top of the ridge and jog toward it, my lungs burning. Fuck, I'm unfit. Agatha Christie never made Miss Marple go on a keto diet. My foot snags a root and I go down. My hands scrape stone, and I realize I've fallen at the foot of the ancient altar.

The archaeologists have finished their work and reconstructed the altar. The toppled stone has been replaced, creating a flat surface where the Romans sacrificed to their gods. Rain patters on the stone, washing away any evidence. Water dribbles over the edge, stained pink with blood.

Blood.

Blood on the altar.

No.

I scramble to my feet but before I can get closer, a pair of strong arms circle my waist, yanking me back against a cold, hard body.

"Where are you going in such a hurry, Georgie Pie?"

At the sound of the voice, my blood runs cold.

Monty.

46

"*L*et go of me." I kick at Monty's knees, trying to take him down with the martial arts training Claw's evil cousin gave me. But I'm too short – he leans back and holds me upright so all I kick is air. Monty's had wrestling training, and he's got the upper hand. I'm no Tiberius, just a hundred-pound pipsqueak with thighs burning from my run up the slope.

"You don't need to struggle, Georgie Pie. I just want to talk. I thought you might like to know where your friend is, so you didn't have to worry about her."

"What have you done to Leigh?" I yell.

"Before I tell you, I'm going to need you to lie down, take a load off. A 'chill pill,' as you Yankees like to say." Monty throws me facedown onto the stone altar. I scream and kick, but he plants an elbow in my back and ties my ankles together with a rope he just happens to have in his pocket.

Why the fuck does he need a rope? Oh fuck, oh God, any God that's listening, get me out of this...

Monty leans over me, pressing his body into me as he clamps my wrists together and ties those, too.

"Tiberius!" I yell. "Tiberius, get your ass over here and—"

"He won't hear you," Monty says casually as he tightens the knots. "I had him locked in the bunker beneath the cricket pitch. Even if he comes around, no one will be able to hear him."

Shit.

I'm on my own.

Monty leans away, keeping his knee in my back so I can't turn over. His fingers trace the skin on my neck. I try to jerk away, but there's nowhere to go.

"That's better," he coos. "Now we can talk like civilized people. Well, unless you want to do something other than talk. I've heard you have quite a thing about altars..."

"There's nothing civilized about what you're doing," I shoot back.

"And what exactly *am* I doing?" Monty simpers. "I've been on a walk in the forest with my good chum Leigh Cho. She's been showing me the delightful things she's collected for our feast." Monty reaches down and picks Leigh's foraging bag off the ground. "She's already laid out an impressive spread, but I told her I needed her to find me something extra special for Devil's Night."

"What have you done to her? Where is she?"

"I told you, she's getting ready for the feast." Monty opens the bag and pulls out the mushrooms, rolling them in his fingers. "Look at these little beauties. They will go perfectly with my main course."

His main course.

Leigh.

He pops one of the mushrooms into his mouth and chews. "This weather is so dreary. It will wash all the flavor away. In Ancient Greece, they never had to worry about such dreary weather."

My mind whirs as his words sink in. He's talking about the

part of the Tristeria ritual where the victim runs through the woods and is chased down by the maenads in their state of *Mainomenos,* their body torn to pieces and their flesh consumed raw. I have to get away from him somehow. I have to alert someone, get the police here. "Leigh?" I scream, but the only answer I get is the birds.

Monty reaches for me. I roll away but he grabs me around the stomach and hoists me from the altar, throwing me over his shoulder. I kick and scream, but it's no good, no one can hear me, and I can't hurt Monty enough to get him to put me down. He pats my ass. "Don't panic, Georgie Pie. I'm taking you to your dear friend Leigh. Then you'll see everything is peaches and cream and you can stop being so mean to me."

He starts to walk through the forest.

"I wanted to like you, Georgie Pie, really I did. But you became a threat. William is mine. *My* friend. He's the only one in the whole world who understood me. And now he's gone because of you. Only Dionysos will bring him back. If I become the god, then William will be my friend again."

We reach the amphitheater and keep climbing, back up the path I've walked so many times before, across the sodden cricket pitch, through a narrow alley into St. Benedict's Quad. The rain pelts down harder now, creating pools between the uneven cobbles.

Monty carries me across the quad. "Help," I yell to a group of costumed students heading toward The Bad Habit. "Help me!"

A few students laugh. "Up to their old jokes again," someone says. "It's not Devil's Night anymore," another student yells. But most of them frown at us and turn away. No one wants to be associated with the Orpheans anymore. Since William spoke out, the society isn't intriguing and cool, but privileged and sickening and gross.

I don't blame them. I just wish *one* of them would notice the terror in my eyes or the cruel way Monty manhandles me toward the church.

The church.

No.

No no no no.

I know what lays beneath the church – the old Roman baths that have been the center of Orphean worship since Benet's disciples returned to Blackfriars. The altar carved with the Orphic hymns, deep underground where the Tristeria could be performed in private.

Where no one can hear me scream.

Monty drags me through the nave and transept and into the annex. My eyes fall on the door to Sebastian's room, and hope flutters in my chest. But of course he's not there. He's gone. He's gone because of me, because everyone I touch turns to ashes and dust, because my stupid podcast took away his calling, his *purpose*. And there's a new priest but he's probably been paid off to leave the church empty for the day so Monty can...

...dismember me.

...kill me.

...eat my flesh.

...hurt my best friend.

No fucking way.

I fight hard, squirming and wiggling, trying to get him to drop me. But it's like he doesn't even feel my fists rain down on him. His eyes are glazed over as he takes the steps two at a time, and I know he's taken something. Probably more of that magical psychedelic bread.

"You were right," Monty calls out to someone as he drags me between the pools toward the altar room, past a table laden with Leigh's signature foraged dishes and a carafe of her bullace wine. "She found my trail of breadcrumbs. It's a pity the weather is so inclement tonight. I've a yearning to run naked in the woods..."

Who's he talking to? Who else has he roped into this? Did Monty find some poor first year to corrupt with his ideas about becoming a vessel for the god—

"That role is not for you, Montague." A shadow moves at the corner of the baths, emerging from the altar room, their white robe flying out around them with sudden movement. "You are not a maenad, one of Dionysos' chosen disciples. Thank you for bringing her to us. The Bacchic Lord will look kindly on your pathetic life. You will be rewarded."

The voice is familiar, but I don't want to connect the dots. I can't. I won't. It's not possible—

The figure glides toward me, moving under the torches that dot the walls. A familiar scent – vanilla and blackcurrant – perfumes the air. The flames flicker over porcelain skin, kind eyes, and a tumble of gleaming auburn hair.

"Hello, George," Diana smiles, brandishing a long knife.

47

"*D*iana?" I take in my ex-friend in all her glory. *She's still dressed like a maenad.* "What's going on? What is this?"

She twists the knife in her hands. "What do you think it is? My dear, sweet George, we are gathered for the Tristeria."

Shadows move behind her, and more women emerge from the altar room, dressed in the white robes of the Orpheus Society – only the fabric is stained with dirt and grass and other, darker stains that look suspiciously like blood. Deerskins wrap around their shoulders, and many of them hold thyrsus, which they twist in the air.

They're all maenads.

And they look like they've begun their descent toward *main-omenos*. Wide, glassy eyes stare at me through elaborate masks – they dance across the tiles, drunk on cups of Leigh's wine and their own devotion. Amongst the unmasked women, I recognize faces.

The librarian who showed me the frescoes painted in the basement and told Monty I was reading Benet's diary.

Victoria, the porter who refused to take my concerns about Keely seriously.

Madame Ulrich, her dark hair spilling in an obsidian waterfall down her back as she spins her thyrsus in wild circles over her head.

I try to crawl away but Monty holds me firm, forcing me to look at the spectacle of their dance. This is nothing like the languid dancing we did at the temple on the lake. Violence scents the air as the maenads throw their heads back and howl, beat each other with their thyrsus, and kiss each other with the kind of reckless passion that makes me think of the way I kissed William and Sebastian.

"We are the Tristeria, the true worshipers of Dionysos." Diana raises her thyrsus high. "We celebrate the god by honoring the old ways, the ancient ways. We embark on the sacred journey of death and resurrection with none of Benet's Christian trappings."

"I don't understand," I cry. "The Orpheus Society worships Dionysos. What were we doing that night at the temple, during my initiation, if not recreating the old rituals? Isn't it enough? Why do you need to murder? To eat flesh?"

Diana shakes her head indulgently. "Poor, sweet Georgie. That was *nothing*. Anything you felt that night was the result of drink and hallucinogens and base hormones. That's a watered-down ritual written by an old monk who was more concerned with undermining the church than any real *ekstasis*. You haven't felt true surrender until you've given your body and mind to the god."

"All the Orphean Society rituals, the initiations, the Devil's Night pranks... It's nonsense," Madame Ulrich scoffs. "They're inventions of men who wanted an excuse for a party with some cultic trappings to make it seem wild, to make the initiates feel more special. But it's all base posturing. There's nothing godly in it. Not like what we do. These rituals were never meant for men. Only women can truly touch the god. Only women can reach true *mainomenos,* true *ekstasis.*"

"What are you talking about?" I can't believe this. "You *kill* women. You chase them through the forest and dismember them, and you're trying to tell me you're on some kind of feminist crusade?"

"Men ruined the mystery cults," the librarian says. "They took them over and made the rituals about their own mortal fears and political games, as if *that* is power."

"But they've never known real power." Diana crashes her thyrsus down on Monty's back. He yelps and crumples at her feet. I expect him to lash out at her, but instead he crawls forward on his hands and knees and kisses her feet.

"Dear, sweet Monty." Diana pats his head, and he nuzzles against her like a puppy. "Our loyal servant. Our dogsbody. You have served us well, especially tonight. You have brought us not one, but *two* worthy sacrifices, and you shall be rewarded."

Monty staggers to his feet and drags me through into the sacred chamber. I scream as I see the shape slumped on the altar. Leigh.

"No," I cry.

She's dead. She's dead. She's not moving.

"She put up a good fight." Diana lifts her skirt to show me the scratches on her legs. "Even after I cut her up, we had to run for miles through the woods to catch her. This is good. We chose well – the stronger the sacrifice, the more the god is pleased. Keely simply fell down and let us take her."

"So disappointing," sighs one of the women as they gather around the altar.

"It was all silly Monty's fault, really," Diana coos, stroking him. "I told him not to follow us into the woods. But he didn't listen. He wanted to find Keely, wanted to get away with

William's little prize, because that's all the ritual is to him. But what he saw instead filled you with awe, didn't it, Monts? You came face to face with our wild, ivy-covered, thrice-born god."

"So beautiful," Monty whispers.

"So beautiful," Diana agrees. "Montague understood immediately. He threw himself at my feet, reciting the oath of our god that he would keep our secret, that all he wanted was a taste of the power we have. But I know Monty. I've grown up with him. I know that he might run his mouth off at any time, if it suits him. I knew too, that Father Duncan was back at the party, already suspicious of us. We cut up a strip of flesh from Keely, gave the bones to Monty to get rid of, and then we went to the party, with Monty coming later once he prepared the meat to his liking. We shared the gifts of the god with everyone, even that nasty Father Duncan – that way, if Monty did say anything, everyone would be crucified. This ensures their complete loyalty. It worked. They gobbled up the flesh like the greedy little piggies they are – and it was delicious, of course, rather like veal in taste – and when Monty told them what they'd eaten, they all swore a vow of silence, of complicity. Even your precious William made his vow to me."

She places her hands on my shoulders and leans in. I can smell the sweet wine on her breath. She presses her reddened lips to my forehead. "Poor, curious George. You had it all so wrong. All this time, you thought Father Duncan was making Monty dance like a puppet. He was never one of us. He was trying to root us out. He dated one of our previous sacrifices—"

"—dear, sweet Khloe—" the librarian giggles. "Such a silly girl. How she bellowed like a beast when we slit her body open."

"Father Duncan always suspected someone in the society was responsible for Khloe's disappearance. That's why he stayed at the school and remained close to the Orpheans. He's been waiting all these years for us to slip up. And we never have."

Diana's chin trembles. "It was a terrible loss that he had to go. Such a brilliant mind. But he guessed too much. After you found Keely's body, he put it all together."

"He found the altar where we buried Khloe," says Victoria. "He used to bring her offerings. It was so terribly *touching.*"

"And he was going to go to the authorities. But even with all his knowledge of mystery cults, he couldn't see what we were creating. He didn't have the vision, the imagination, to be a truly worthy sacrifice. He thought Monty was behind it all." Diana scoffs. "I overheard him confronting Monty on Saint Benet's Day. They argued, and I saw Father Duncan storm off into the forest. I knew exactly where he was going. I circled around and hid behind the altar. When he bent over to place his little offering, I hit him over the head with my thyrsus."

That produced the wound that Lauren found.

"How long?" I choke out. "How long has this been going on?"

"There has been a sacrifice every two years since the revival of the Tristeria during my school days," explains Madame Ulrich. "Myself and a fellow sister saw the mockery the men made of our god's worship and decided we must forge our own path. While the male members of the Orphean society drank themselves to oblivion, we snuck into the woods. We brewed the sacred herbs, drenched our bodies in sacrificial blood of the god, and we took the god himself into us."

The first victim. A girl who disappeared from school on Devil's Night nearly fifty years ago, thought to have run off to the continent with her boyfriend.

"Sometimes the ritual is performed here at Blackfriars, sometimes in Paris, or in the other ancient places of Orphean worship," Madame Usher continues. "We move it around to avoid suspicion. The society's contacts mean that whenever suspicion emerges, it can be quickly silenced. Only the most devoted women are invited to become priestesses. Diana originally considered you for the position, before it became clear that you lack the vision necessary to understand our mission."

"It's very unfortunate." Diana touches my face. Her fingers are ice cold. "I love you, George. You're brilliant, and you're such a good person. The goodness just shines out of you. But your little podcast has set back our plans. We won't be able to worship the Tristeria at Blackfriars any longer. We must leave our spiritual home here and go into hiding, the way Benet did after his flight from England. To appease the god for our long absence, this year we must make two sacrifices."

They're going to kill us both.

Diana claps her hands. "No more talking. Let us begin."

The maenads surround me, reaching for me. I kick out with my bound feet, socking Madame Ulrich in the gut. She doubles over, crashing into some of the girls and sending them scrambling. I roll onto my knees and manage to hobble to my feet. I start to shuffle across the floor with the tiny steps my bonds allow. The doorway is right there. If I can reach the stairs then I—

SMACK.

I hobble straight into a wall. No, not a wall. A person. A shadow of stone and sinew that blocks the doorway, his perfect body in a white robe, his aristocratic features carved in stone.

William.

48

I'm stunned.

Absolutely struck dumb by his presence. His smell swirls around me, the scent of old books and oil paints that's so uniquely him.

What's he doing here?

Too late I see the cold glaze in his eyes. He's on whatever drugs they have Monty on.

He's one of them. One of their servants.

"William..." I manage to croak out, but I can't find the words to ask for help. To beg. I know it won't do any good. The William who stood on that podium and asked for forgiveness from the world is gone. He's never coming back.

My dark prince, what have they done to you? What did they promise you?

Warm, soft hands drag me backward and throw me onto the altar beside Leigh. I kick my feet, but it's useless. With my hands and feet bound, if I roll off this altar, all I'm going to do is injure myself.

William takes a kylix cup from the table, fills it with wine, and holds the vessel out to Diana's lips. She places her hands over his and tips the cup, her delicate chin moving up and down as she drinks deep of the wine. She tosses her head, her tongue flicking out to lick the claret stains around her lips. "The blood of the god. The fruit of the harvest."

"The blood of the god, the fruit of the harvest," the women chant in Greek.

William moves amongst the ladies, holding the cup while they drink from it in a Dionysian mockery of Catholic mass. Madame Usher spanks William's ass, and he doesn't even react.

What do they have him on?

He comes to stand in front of me, holding the cup out of reach. "William," I whisper. "Please, after everything you said at that press conference, you can't believe in this. I don't care if you hate me, if you want this for me, but I forgive you. I forgive you and I forgive myself, and you can't let them do this to Leigh."

William doesn't blink, doesn't react. I thrust out my hands, trying to knock the wine cup from his grip. He yanks it out of my reach, staring down at me with those blank, empty eyes.

"This is not for you," he says, simply, without emotion.

He turns away and walks to Diana, who takes the cup from his fingers and drains it. She wipes her mouth with her sleeve and smiles at me. "William is *ours*. He's always been ours. He's even more lost than Monty. All those years of loneliness, and the only thing he ever wanted was for someone to love him for himself. But you can't feel lonely with a god inside you. Isn't that right, William?"

"Yes," William says in that toneless robot voice.

"Exactly. And just think, George. Your body will nourish him as he undergoes his *ekstasis*. That's beautiful. That's poetic, and I know how much our William loves poetry."

"How can you do this?" I whisper.

"How can I not?" Diana looks around to her fellow maenads.

"How can any modern woman gaze upon this sisterhood and not be drawn to it, not wish to drink from the same cup? This isn't personal, George. You're a dear friend and I love you. I don't *want* to do this. It makes me cry to think of it. But that is what a sacrifice is. If it doesn't hurt, it's not a true sacrifice. I promise that I'll make it so good for you. Maybe I'll have William here eat you out while I slit your throat. I wonder if that will make your flesh taste all the sweeter."

With that, the dancing begins again in earnest. Victoria bangs the drum while the women gyrate against each other, screaming and ululating in a sensuous rhythm that echoes off the stone walls.

"William, be a dear and get some of those delicious treats for us," Diana simpers as she claws at her own skin, raising trails of blood on her smooth flesh.

Robotically, William moves back to the table. He sets down the cup and returns with platters of Leigh's amazing food, which he holds while the maenads rush him. They claw at the platters, stuffing the foraged treats into their mouths as bits of half-chewed food dribble down their fronts.

While they gorge themselves, I feel something touch my arm. I bite back a scream and crane my neck to see. Leigh groans. While my hands are bound behind my back, hers are tied in front of her. They're caked in blood, and more blood pools on the stone around her body. I can't see where she's wounded, but I know it's bad. Her fingers trail down my spine as she slowly works her way down my body until she can touch my fingers to hers.

"Leigh, it's George," I say. "Hang in there. I'm going to get us out of this, okay?"

Somehow.

Think, George, think.

Leigh's fingers scrape mine again, her nails tugging at the

rough rope. I wince as it digs into my flesh, but then I understand. Leigh's trying to undo the knots in my hands.

That's my girl. Leigh, you're amazing.

I grit my teeth as the rope bites deeper. Leigh tugs and yanks. It's impossible to tell if she's made progress or not. She mumbles with pain, words without meaning. Lines from that William Blake poem about the poison tree.

Is she fading because of the pain? Or have they drugged her, too?

Please, Leigh. I know you can do this. You're so strong.

I didn't know what I'd do with my hands once they were free, but if I can move, it will at least give us a fighting chance.

The maenads dance in a frantic circle that tightens with each circuit of the room. They close in on us with terrifying menace. Every time Diana swings past, the blade of her knife catches the flickering light and glints menacingly, like the money shot in one of Dad's horror films right before the camera pans away and you hear the sickening sound of slicing and squelching.

That's going to be me and Leigh if I don't—

The rope around my wrists slackens. I try to move my hand, cramping my fingers together so I can slip them out. Leigh lightly slaps me away. Not yet, she's saying.

Come on, Leigh. You got this.

"It's time," Diana cries. "I can feel the god's presence. I can feel his horns growing from my head, his body inside mine. Can you feel him, William? Monty?"

"I can." Monty throws himself to the floor, jerking and spasming as he knocks his head against the stone tiles. William does the same. They roll around while the women beat their backs with their thyrsus.

"Enough," Diana cries. She leans over the altar, her knife slicing the air above us, so close that I feel it kissing my flesh. "Ladies, it is time for us to feast."

49

The women gather in a tight circle around the altar, pressing their bodies together as they cackle and spit and smack their lips. Up close, the scent of them turns my stomach – the sickly wine, the dirt, the blood and bodily fluids mingle together into a potent poison.

"I call upon loud-roaring and reveling Dionysos," Diana cries in Greek as she swings the knife through the air. "Primeval, double-natured, thrice-born, Bacchic lord..."

She swings again, like Edgar Allan Poe's pendulum arcing toward our doom. But this time, she wobbles a bit on her feet.

"...wild, ineffable, secretive, two-horned and two-shaped. Ivy-covered, bull-faced, warlike, howling..."

I press my face into the stone altar, bracing for the slice, the cut, the pain. But nothing happens. I dare to open one eye just as Diana lists to the side.

"You take raw flesh—" Diana clamps a hand over her mouth, her eyes growing wide. Her whole body convulses and she doubles over, clutching her stomach.

What's going on?

"I don't feel so good," she moans.

Madame Ulrich rushes to her side. "What's wrong, priestess?"

"I don't know," Diana wheezes as she sinks to the floor, clutching her stomach. "My insides are being torn apart."

"Do you need me to take over your duties?" Madame Ulrich's lips curl with pleasure at the thought. She snatches for the knife, but just as her fingers close around the handle, she opens her mouth and a stream of bloody bile cascades over Diana's head.

"What the fuck?" Diana screeches, shoving Madame Ulrich away. The art don stumbles and falls back into a group of her sisters, who try to catch her but they're all clutching their stomachs and gagging and retching, and she slips on her own vomit and crashes to the floor. Her head cracks against the stone altar.

The maenads howl, but this is no howl of ecstasy – it's the sound of excruciating pain.

The rope around my wrists falls away. *Yes, Leigh, you legend!*

In the chaos, no one notices me sitting up and untying the rope at my ankles.

Once I'm free, I get to work on the ropes around Leigh's wrists and ankles. She doesn't move as I free the knots, and I'm terrified that I've lost her. When I try to roll her limp body over so I can lift her (never going to happen. I'm such a weakling, but I'm hoping to be hit with an emergency jolt of super strength the way characters are in books), she stirs and manages to lift herself onto her elbows.

"Took you long enough to get here," Leigh rasps through bloody lips.

"Stop them," Diana cries, but no one's in any position to obey. The librarian reaches out a trembling hand to grab my ankle, but I kick her away easily. I wrap Leigh's limp arm over my shoulders and pull her off the altar. As she leans against me, I notice the deep cuts across her arms and torso – slashes that look like claw marks. Sticky blood glues her t-shirt to her body. *I have to get her medical attention, now.*

We half climb, half drag ourselves over the writhing maenads. It's then that I notice Leigh is grinning manically. *But why is she—*

It hits me.

"Leigh, you're amazing," I whisper as we navigate our way slowly around the hot pools. "You did something to their food, didn't you?"

"I crushed Jerusalem berries into the wine," she says. "They're going to be too sick to move for a while. You didn't drink any, did you?"

"No, but what about—" I toe a piece of broken platter on the floor.

"Don't touch it," Lee kicks my foot away. "Everything on the platters is poisonous. Not in large enough amounts to be fatal, but it depends on how much they eat. I couldn't be exact, I just knew that when Monty approached me about catering a little Devil's Night shindig, I'd better be prepared. I dropped my bag with the destroying angel mushrooms when they chased me in the forest, so at least no one will die terribly."

Oh.

"You had destroying angels in your bag?" I say. "Not wood mushrooms?"

As I say the words I realize that I found the bag under an oak tree, which Leigh warned me was how to tell the mushrooms apart – destroying angels only grow in the roots of oaks.

"I was scared," Leigh coughs, blood splattering on her shirt. "I didn't know if I'd need them."

"I don't think anyone will blame you. I found your bag in the woods," I say. "Monty ate one of those mushrooms."

Leigh's face pales. "Then he's dead."

She looks gutted, but I don't give a shit. Let them all fucking die. "Leigh, I know you hate my guts, and I don't blame you, but—"

She coughs blood down her shirt as we hobble through the baths. "I thought *you* hated *my* guts—"

"How could I ever hate you? You did the right thing. I thought I was angry at you but really it was myself. Can you ever forgive—"

"George." A voice calls to me over the din, reaching into my chest and squeezing my heart. I long to turn to it, as I've turned to it so many times since I arrived at Blackfriars. But Leigh needs my help.

Not that she seems to realize it. She grips my arm, dragging her feet so I'm forced to stop. "Turn around," she whispers.

Right now, I owe Leigh my life. So even though we desperately need to get to the stairs, even though that voice cuts through my fucking soul, I turn.

William stands in the doorway of the altar room. His eyes are no longer glazed. Now they burn with a fire so bright it razes through my chest.

"George."

He whispers my name like he's speaking to a goddess.

Behind him, Diana raises her head. She bares her teeth and lunges at him, grabbing a discarded thyrsus from the floor as she claws her way over her sisters.

William steps toward me, his hands raised. "I'm not going to hurt you. Get out of here. Now. Call your friend the pathologist. I'll stop them escaping while you get the police over here."

"But, William—"

"*Now*, George."

I don't have time to question why he's here, why he's looking at me like he will burn the world for me.

I run.

50

I tighten my grip on Leigh and shove past the table, scattering poisoned food across the tiles as we sprint for the staircase.

Behind me, I hear Diana scream and William yell. I hear a thump and a thud and more screaming and yelling. I don't stop. I don't look back, even though every atom in my body screams at me to help William.

Leigh and I drag each other forward, up up up the stairs. She trips over the top step and we stumble into the hallway. I head for the church, but I see a shadow move in the transept, white robe flapping.

I change course. I fling open the doorway to the chaplain's empty apartment and shove Leigh through. "Go out the window and through the graveyard," I whisper. "Get help. I'll draw them away."

Leigh nods and slides into the gloom. I fling open the other door and start up the narrow staircase toward the tower roof, stomping as hard as I can on the stone with my old, dependable New Rocks so whoever is after me knows exactly where to follow me. *Far away from Leigh.*

"George, where are you going?" Diana calls in her singsong voice. I glance down to see her clambering along after me. Shit. She must've overpowered William and climbed up that back passage into the church – the one Sebastian took me through on the night of my first Bacchanal.

Is William okay?

I try not to picture him bleeding out in the baths below, and climb faster. I hear her feet on the steps, soft and swift. She stops and throws up over the railing. I reach the bells, and duck and weave beneath them.

I reach the top of the clock face and dare a look beneath me. Diana appears beneath the bells. She stumbles to the edge of the gangplank and spits blood over the side. Her knife glitters in her hand.

I glance around me, realizing too bloody late that I've lured her to a dead end. There's only one way to go once we reach the top of the tower.

A toolbox lies open on the end of the gangway. As Diana reaches the steps, I throw tools and anything else I can grab in her path. A wrench bounces off her cheek. She leers up at me with blood gushing from a wound on her temple, baring her teeth like an animal, a monster.

She keeps on coming.

Shit. Shit. I duck into the tiny space beneath the lock-out mechanism, and squeeze through into the hidden stairwell, pressing myself into the wall as I climb for the roof.

After about twenty steps, my hand slams into the wooden door. I search blindly for a latch and find it. It's unlocked. I kick the door open and stagger onto the roof.

The wind slams into me, knocking me back against the stone spire. I lurch down the narrow platform running around the edge of the spire, looking for *anything* to block the door – a loose stone, a conveniently-placed medieval trebuchet—

SLAM.

The door cracks against stone. Diana's face appears in the gloom, grinning with wild triumph as she advances on me, brandishing the knife.

"There's nowhere else to run, George." She steps onto the platform and staggers toward me. Blood dribbles from the corners of her mouth, making her look like a monster from one of Dad's movies.

I back away. But there's only so far I can go before I'm backed right up against the parapet. Rough stone digs into my skin. The wind whips up from the courtyard below, and I can feel the nothingness pressing against me, begging me to surrender to oblivion.

"Jump." Diana grins, as though she's the one stoking my thoughts. "Go on, do it. Because either you jump, or I push you, and it will be so much better if you jump. Jump, Georgie, and become just what you've always wanted to be – special, anointed, beloved. In those few seconds before you hit the ground, you will defeat death. You will be twice-born, both living and dead. You will be one with the god. That's so delicious. I'm almost jealous."

"You jump, then," I shoot back. "If you're so hot for Dionysos."

"Not me, I'm afraid," she laughs, placing her hand over her heart. "You see, I don't need to find him. He's in here with me. The first time I plunged a knife into sweet Keely's flesh, the first time I tasted her blood on my tongue, I felt him inside me. And now that I know what's required to keep Dionysos with me always, I'll never stop. I'll perform the ritual every two years and pass the knowledge down to my daughters, to the worthy women who understand what true power means. Tristeria will live forever—"

CLONK.

Diana's words trickle away. Her face bends, twists. She turns to the side, her eyes widen.

She crumples.

A dark shadow stands behind her, the gilded reliquary of Benet in his hand and an expression of utter perplexity on his beautiful face.

Sebastian.

"Holy *bollocks*," he says.

Sebastian.

Sebastian is here.

Diana's eyes narrow. "*You.* I thought we got rid of you." She tries to crawl to her feet and lunge at him, her knife pointing at Sebastian's throat. But she trips on the corner of her robe and goes flying.

Right over the side of the parapet.

The sound is like nothing I've ever heard before, like the slap of a brush into wet paint mixed with a crunch of bones shattering. From the quad below, someone screams. I know it's not Diana. I know Diana is gone.

I hope she saw her god on the way down.

My legs buckle under me. Sebastian lurches forward, catching me in his arms. "George, I've got you."

"You have to call an ambulance," I say. "Leigh—"

"I found Leigh." He strokes my hair. "And we let Tiberius out of the bunker. Don't worry. Everything will be okay."

"Monty ate a destroying angel mushroom."

Sebastian makes a growling noise in his throat. I hear sirens in the parking lot, commotion in the quad below. More screams. Someone yelling Diana's name. It's all a dull hum, background noise in the epic climactic scene. I nuzzle into Sebastian's neck, breathing deep and trying to convince myself that it's really truly him and not a mirage of my fear-soaked mind.

"I'm here, my girl." He holds my face and kisses me, his lips on mine an act of devotion. His hands cup my cheeks the way he holds the chalice of the Eucharist – as if I'm a sacred and holy thing that has been entrusted into his care. "I'm here and I'm never leaving you again."

"Where did you go?" I manage to untangle my tongue from his long enough to ask.

"Oh, sweet George." He holds my cheeks. "I tried to tell you. I asked you to come and see me before I had to catch the train. I left Blackfriars because I left the Church."

"You...what?"

"I left the Church," he says. "It's a whole process. First, my deacon had me go to a silent retreat in the Scottish Highlands. That's typical when a priest misbehaves as I've done, or when someone is considering leaving holy orders. That's what I was going to tell you when I asked you to come to my rooms, but you didn't show up and I couldn't miss the train."

"That's where you've been? The Scottish Highlands?"

He nods. "I'm sorry I couldn't contact you. Scottish monks don't kid around – no mobile phones, no internet. Not even a decent coffee machine. Three months of solitude, just me and God. I walked the mountains, I asked questions and God gave his answers in the ways only he knows. I threw my collar into the loch and came back for you." He swallows. "For you and him."

"You...threw your collar into a loch?" I can barely get the words out. "You littered?"

"Shhh." Sebastian puts his fingers to his lips. "God is listening. He doesn't need any more sins from me."

"Father Pearce, I'm shocked and horrified—"

He shakes his head. "I'm not 'father' any longer."

I look into his eyes, brimming with love. My head fills with all his precious words. What he's giving up. Even if we decide one day that we want to get married, he will not be allowed to wed in the Catholic Church. They consider his vow of celibacy to be a lifelong commitment.

"It turns out that breaking a vow is as easy as making one," Sebastian says. "In the end, the vow was never made to God but to an institution of man, and God doesn't hold me to it. I think I had to leave the Church to understand that."

There are sounds on the stairs behind us. I barely register it until a familiar head of russet hair pops into view. William. He rushes toward me but when he sees Sebastian, he freezes in his tracks, his blue eyes as wide and clear as the ocean.

"You came," he says simply.

"For you, William," Sebastian says. "I would walk across water for you."

William flies at us. Sebastian captures him in his arms, collecting both of us into his embrace, kissing us both until we're dizzy and laughing. Teeth scrape my neck and nibble on my earlobe, tasting, devouring, enjoying each other. We're too much a part of each other for a god to come between us. William's lips wrestle with Sebastian before finding mine. I taste blood on his tongue, but it's not the taste of a sacrificial lamb.

It's our communion.

51

*M*onty doesn't make it.

His death is horrible to witness. I've seen a man boiled alive, and yet watching Monty writhe in his hospital bed, a sheen of sweat on his aristocratic forehead, is the worst thing I'll ever see.

There's a period of latency with destroying angel poisoning – for hours after ingesting the mushroom, Monty was deceptively fine. He chatted animatedly all the way to the hospital, asking Leigh if there's any more food, "since I didn't get to eat anything except this blooming spore," and generally being his usual Montyish self.

By the time he's wheeled from the ambulance into the ER, he's experiencing violent nausea and clutching his stomach. The doctors perform gastric decontamination and fluid replacement in an attempt to protect his liver and kidneys, but it's too late.

Cruelly, the next phase of the poisoning is a false recovery, where Monty seems to rally. He sits up in his bed. He looks brighter. He meets with Inspector Baddeley and Lauren and myself, and answers every question we fire at him with as much truthfulness as Montague Cavendish is capable of.

Claws texts me at hour sixteen to tell me that the Emperor Claudius was done in by mushroom, too. Trust my best friend to bring the grisly Roman factoids at a time like this.

Monty's parents decline to attend his death vigil. Monty takes the news with unusual stoicism. Then he asks if I'd like to play a game of chess with him, and I don't have the heart to deny him.

He sets up a magnetic board on the over-bed table, and I sit gingerly on the side of the bed so I can reach the pieces. William and Sebastian take the opportunity to duck away and visit the others – Leigh's being stitched up in the operating room, but most of the Orpheans are in the same ward, dealing with the aftereffects of their various poisons. Madame Ulrich doesn't look so much like a goddess now, not with a million tubes sticking out of her.

Monty chooses black, which I try not to draw symbolism from. This means I get the opening move. I place one of my pawns in the center of the board, and we trade turns in silence for a while.

"You did me in, George old boy," Monty says as he moves his knight across the board to take one of my pawns.

"I didn't mean to. I don't know enough about mushrooms to see Leigh had picked destroying angels instead of—"

He shakes his head. "I'm not bitter about it. I was always going to go like this. A quiet game of chess with a worthy foe, followed by jaundice, seizures, coma, and death."

Monty swipes my queen and lies back on his pillows, a self-satisfied smirk playing across his blotched face. "When William first started getting sweet on you, I never considered you worthy of him. You weren't like us. But I see now that was my mistake – I underestimated you. I truly believe that if we had the chance to start over, we could be the best of chums."

"I would love to have been your friend," I say, castling to protect my king from his knight. "If you let me."

"It's better this way. Your move, George."

I let him win. It seems only fair.

I DON'T GET to see the maenads carried off by the police at the end of their hospital stay, but I do see it all unfold in the headlines. Inspector Baddeley even got hold of the authorities in France. They were able to locate the remains in the Orphean temple and ID the victim by a strand of hair as an Iranian student who'd gone missing from a nearby French Language school. She also heard from the authorities in the Maldives and Monaco about murder victims with a similar profile linked to locations near where Orpheans had their second homes. It seems that the maenads spread their biannual Tristeria across different locations.

Father Duncan hadn't been behind the deaths of Keely and Khloe after all. He'd been trying to *solve* them. He loved Khloe, and had always suspected the Orpheus Society had a hand in her death – he kept close to them and close to the school in case they ever let their guard down or revealed something he could take to the authorities. When Keely died, he saw the chance to find out once and for all what happened to Khloe twenty years ago. That's why he had that murder wall in his cupboard. He befriended Monty who he rightly assumed was the weak link, and eventually convinced him to show him the altar in the forest. Father Duncan dug around and found that finger bone and realized he was standing on the grave of his love. But he couldn't dig up her remains with the Orpheans so close and so powerful. He was building a case of his own against them, plying Monty with lavish attention in exchange for information he could take to the authorities, information they wouldn't be able to ignore or sweep under the carpet. But of course Monty went straight to his real masters, Diana and her maenads, and they made sure Father Duncan was silenced.

If I hadn't mistrusted him so much, we might've been able to work together. Maybe he wouldn't have had to die.

Justice came too late for Keely, for Khloe May, for Father Duncan and the other victims of Tristeria. But with heavy murder convictions hanging over their heads, many of Diana's fellow priestesses forsake their vows of silence. Madame Ulrich makes a deal for a reduced sentence and gives up the names of all the high ranking officials in the British government who had once been members of Tristeria or who knew of their activities and turned a blind eye, all the way back to the first women who decided to kill for power. Victoria hands over the records she's meticulously kept for this secret society within a secret society. Thanks to these, several other victims are uncovered and their remains recovered and returned to their families.

The country's elite is due a reckoning.

About fucking time.

" ... *A*nd that's the story of how I poisoned a bunch of toff Hannibal Lecters and lived to tell the tale."

I raise my chipped coffee mug, and Shane clinks his against it. We sip from the bullace wine I brought into the studio – a parting gift to the strange, silent artist who has invaded my dreams for the last three years. It's the last day of tutorials before graduation, and we've just spent three hours cleaning the place, scrubbing my doodles and Shane's chemical formulas off the walls and dumped our waste materials into the college skip. Shane's power tools are stacked in carry boxes beside the door, next to a portfolio containing my working sketches.

Today, my Bachelor's degree is officially over. I'll never see Shane Kelly's glorious green eyes again.

Which is pretty gutting, but there are some boss things, too. No more Orpheus Society, for one. George and I are friends again, and the bizzies (that's the police if you don't speak Scouse) aren't charging me for picking the shrooms Monty ate or poisoning the maenads. I'm free from the law.

Not from my own conscience, though. When William came to me and told me a bunch of birds dressed up in deerskins would try to kill and eat me, I didn't think about much except not becoming scran. But Monty *died*. He died because of me, and sometimes I'm okay with that and sometimes I'll be sitting in the pub with a bevvy or in the gallery looking at art and I realize he'll never get to do those things again and I want to punch a hole in a wall.

I haven't been able to eat a mushroom since. And I love mushrooms.

Fucking Orphean toffs. They ruin everything.

So yeah, my feelings about Devil's Night are complicated, right? But that's not what I tell Shane Kelly. Because I like the way those moss green eyes light up when I tell him how I brought down Tristeria.

"I must admit," he nods at me across the empty workbench as he knocks back his wine and reaches for a top-up. "I'm impressed. That was not the story I expected when you came in here."

I wink at him across the table. "I'm more than just a pretty face, y'know. I've got all kinds of tricks up these sleeves."

I jokingly show him my arms, which are completely bare under my vest. Maybe it's because I know this is the last time I'll see him, or because I just got out of the Ozzy after narrowly surviving being shishkebabed by a bunch of rich young cannibals, but I'm feeling sassy. Instead of avoiding Shane's penetrating gaze, like normal, I walked in here with my head high and a bottle of my finest wine under my arm, and we're having what might be the first real conversation we've ever had.

(Sure, it's a conversation about the school's resident cannibals, so that's not fucking normal, but beggars can't be choosers, eh?)

"Oh, I know all about your tricks."

Shane says it in this *way*, cocking one eyebrow in a

dangerous arch as he drinks his wine, that my lady parts go all wobbly.

"So, now that we're free, what are your plans for next year?" he asks as he tops up my cup.

Interesting. Another personal question. I wish I had a boss answer for him, but that's not how my life works.

I swallow. "I'll be here."

He raises a thick red eyebrow. "At Blackfriars?"

"Yup. Probably with my arse on this exact same stool." I pat my steed affectionately. "I signed on for my Masters. You're looking at Leigh Cho, professional student."

Shane's mug freezes halfway to his lips. "You got sucked into the machine too, then?"

"Not you?" I couldn't be more shocked than if he told me he was moving to California to take the starring role in a Lady Gaga video. Shane Kelly may be one talented artist, but he's always sagging off tutorials and getting into fights on campus, not to mention his extracurricular art fakery. I'm honestly surprised they didn't kick him out on his arse a long time ago, let alone allow him back to read for his Master's. "You know you have to write a thesis? That's like a boss amount of words."

"I'll manage." Shane shrugs. "I've feck all else to do."

Which, weirdly, is the same position I'm in. I don't have to write a fuck-off long thesis. I don't have to be in college. My folks are always asking me to come home and bum around with them. But that's where the similarities between Shane and I end. I'm here because I have something to prove. He's here because...

I have no fucking idea.

I raise my cup to my mouth, but only so I have something to do with my hands because they're fucking shaking. Shane Kelly is going to be at Blackfriars again next year. Shane Kelly just asked me a personal question. Shane Kelly is going to be up in my grid while I try to get through the most important year of my life.

Shane drops his cup on the bench and stretches his hands above his head. His shirt rises over his stomach, revealing a line of toned, tatted skin and a hint of that delicious V of muscle extending into his boxers. My mouth dries.

"I'd best be off." He kicks his boxes as he yanks open the door. "One of my lads will be by for the tools. Nice arting with you, Leigh Cho. Maybe I'll see you around next year."

The door slams behind him.

Maybe you will, Shane Kelly. Maybe you will.

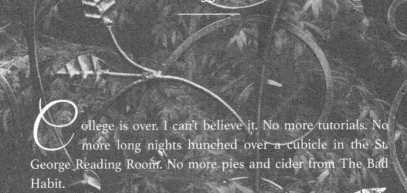

Ollege is over. I can't believe it. No more tutorials. No more long nights hunched over a cubicle in the St. George Reading Room. No more pies and cider from The Bad Habit.

Absolutely, positively, no more Orpheus Society.

William and I sit together in a pew in the back of the chapel, watching as Sebastian sweeps the marble floor, his broad shoulders tugging against his tight-fitting sweater. I arrived at Forsyth Hall by train an hour ago, not sure what to expect. I certainly didn't expect to see Sebastian fussing about in the chapel, his neck oddly bare without his collar. I thought he'd want to avoid this building that represented everything he lost, but he seems to find peace in tending it, keeping it ready for the next priest to take over.

He settles the broom against an ancient statue of one of William's ancestors and brushes his hands on his dark designer jeans. "All done." He turns to me and William. "Now, what was it my prince wanted?"

"I don't know," I say. "He's kept me in the dark, too."

"I want to show you something," William rises from the pew

and collects the backpack resting on the floor beside him. "Will you walk with me?"

He sounds so gentle, so unlike himself. Sebastian and I fall into step behind him. Sebastian takes my hand, happy for once to go wherever William leads.

We exit through a narrow side door and cross the east courtyard. As we cut through the formal gardens, I see Sir Henry and Carmilla chasing each other around the fountain. She wears a flowing dress with puffed sleeves – like the heroine in a gothic novel – and he wears a smile so bright it could melt the sun.

"They've been like this all summer." William pretends to barf, but I can see the corner of a smile tugging at his lips. "It's sickening. They're getting married, you know. After all this time, my father found the peace within himself that comes with forgiveness. He can let go of my mother's ghost. And it's all thanks to you."

I shake my head. "I can't take credit for this."

"If you hadn't torn up my life like a hurricane, destroying everything that felt safe to me, then I never would have known what was on the other side." William edges the backpack higher on his shoulder as his green eyes ripple with emotion. "Two years ago, seeing him like this would have been a betrayal of my mother. But that's not fair to her, or to him. She would have wanted to see him smile like this."

"She also would have wanted to see *you* smile." I elbow him in the ribs. William plasters an enormous, goofy grin on his face. It's faked for my amusement, but it's also real. I can tell because his blue eyes are smiling, too.

He leads us down the path and through the meadow bursting with color from the summer flowers. Down to the edge of the lake, where he pushes out a boat and we all climb aboard. I know exactly where we're going.

We glide across the crystal waters, past the abandoned

temple that will never see another Orphean ritual, until we reach the other side of the lake. I expect William to row us into the shore, but instead he puts down the oars and picks up the pack. He pulls out a small wooden box, clutching it in his hands like it contains his still-beating heart.

"Monty came to Forsyth Hall for last summer," he says. "None of the other Orpheans even so much as texted me after the press release, but I guess Monty didn't have anywhere else to go. He was very strange. He acted as if nothing at all was wrong. He was taking a lot of drugs, and on the nights I stayed up with him, rambling around the estate the way we used to do as kids, he babbled all sorts of things – strange and wild things."

"Tristeria," I whisper. William nods.

"I listened, and I figured out many truths I hadn't before. That was why I contacted Leigh, and we concocted a plan to have her poison the revelers on Devil's Night. I knew that anyone who showed up at school trying to revive Devil's Night had this evil in their hearts. I had no idea there would be so many of them. I'm sorry, George, that I let you believe the worst of me, that I put you in danger. But I had to make them believe I was one of them so I could bring them down. But in the end, they did it to themselves."

"It was Monty," I say. "I think, even though his mind had been corrupted by them and he wanted so badly to be one of them, deep down some part of him knew the Tristeria was wrong. That's why he came here. He trusted you to do what he couldn't."

"I think so, too. He also gave me this," William hands me the box. "Open it."

I lift the lid from the box. Inside is a stack of letters and a roll of film.

Sebastian holds up the letters, frowning at the handwriting. "What are these?"

"Monty was always wandering off around the estate at all hours, filming or taking photographs of nonsensical things," William says. "It makes perfect sense he'd be out that night, pointing his camera at the lake, at the beautiful woman rowing her boat out to her private island. Apparently, he's kept this box for me ever since that night, and even made provisions for it in his will. His solicitor gave it to me last week."

"You've watched it?" I tap the film. William nods.

"She didn't kill herself."

His words suck the air from my lungs. Sebastian makes the sign of the cross.

"And these letters?"

"They're from my mother." William pulls one from its envelope and hands it to Sebastian. "She wrote one for me every year on my birthday. They tell stories, offer advice. Some of them are word games or poems that make me think of her. I was supposed to open them all when I turned eighteen. That night, she was paddling out to the temple to bury this box for me. But she wasn't alone."

"Monty," I whisper. William shakes his head.

"Monty's father," Sebastian breathes, his fingers tightening on William's shoulder.

"Yes. He saw her head out all alone, looking so beautiful and innocent in the moonlight, and he had to have that beauty for himself. But when she didn't acquiesce, he became violent. He held her under until she stopped moving. And Monty saw all of it," William says. "Ever since that moment, he saw himself as my protector. He knew that evil people would try to take things I love away from me, and he wouldn't let them do it. He kept the film as a reminder."

I want to ask why Monty didn't tell William about this sooner, but I know it's pointless to question a mind that worked like Montague Cavendish's. Monty didn't want his only true friend to punish him for his father's crime, and that's exactly what William in his rage and hopelessness would have done. I squeeze my eyes shut as a single tear – the only tear I will ever cry for Monty – falls between my lashes and splatters on my shirt.

"He was so achingly lonely," William says as he puts the box away. "I know that he did wrong things, but I miss him."

"You forgive him," Sebastian's voice wavers, and I know he's not only asking about Monty.

William nods. "I forgive him."

Sebastian pulls William's face to his, licking William's tears from his cheeks before claiming his mouth in a deep, possessive kiss. The two of them kiss long and hard and slow, saying with tongues and lips all the things they've needed to say ever since that day so many years ago.

They draw back, their eyes locked, their breath ragged and gasping. They come for me together, their heads crashing as they fight to kiss me. I squeal as the boat rocks precariously.

"What the hell do you think you're doing?" someone yells from the shore, startling me so much that I accidentally bite William's lip.

"Ow," he yells.

"What's that?" Sebastian whirls around, pitching the boat sideways.

"That will be my other surprise." William smiles, blood dribbling down his crisp dress shirt.

"What?" I jerk around, gripping the edges of the boat for dear life as I scan the shoreline. Two figures stand beside the boathouse, waving frantically. That almost looks like...

"Dunk them both in, George," Claws yells, cracking up laughing.

"Georgina Fisher." Mom shakes her fist in the air. "You bring that boat back here right now before I have a heart attack. None of you are wearing life jackets. That lake could be filled with piranhas. Is that what you want? To be eaten alive by carnivorous fish?"

William and Sebastian and I look at each other, and burst out laughing.

EPILOGUE

"O of, heels were a bad idea." Leigh grips my shoulder as her stilettos sink into the soft grass.

"I told you. I'm doing just fine." I hold out my foot, showing off my brand new bright red New Rock boots.

My old pair fell to pieces last week. Even the most beautiful things have to come to an end. Like my time at Blackfriars University.

It's over. I can hardly believe that my three years at Blackfriars are done.

And it's not the only thing that's ending. Sebastian is officially a layperson. No more priest collar. No more sacrilegious text messages during sermons. No more naughty altar sex (okay, we might still do that at Forsyth Hall when no one is around).

Leaving the priesthood has been hard on him. I think – and don't tell him I said this – that he got off a bit on the prestige of the collar. It may not be very godly, but Sebastian Pearce loved being a priest in part because when he walked through a room, people took notice.

My kinky ex-priest still gets his authority kicks bossing me and William around, and when he commands me in that deep, resonant voice of his, I jump to obey. But I know he's still searching for his purpose. Some things are hard for him – he's forgotten how to deal with money, how to talk to the electric company when there's a power cut in his apartment, how not to lose his savings to telephone scams.

He's spent the last year building a support circle for ex-priests. This group of lovely, lonely men meet once a week to talk about the challenges of living as laity. They are putting together a petition for Rome to reform the priesthood – allowing women to become priests, priests to marry, and same-sex marriage to be recognized by the Church. Sebastian is hoping to travel to Rome in the summer to present it to the Pope, and William and I are going with him. We're making it a proper adventure, visiting the Vatican and all the ancient sites of Rome and Greece – six weeks of ruins, pasta, and Renaissance art. I can't wait.

But first, I need to make it through graduation without tripping.

Leigh and I wave goodbye as we cross St. Benedict's Quad to line up with the rest of the students in alphabetical order. I check my gown is straight and the tassel on my cap hasn't come unraveled. Above my head, the bells of St. Benedict's cathedral toll the hour. We enter the church, marching two by two past the pews of our family and friends, and line up in the choir.

It's sad to see a strange priest standing where Sebastian should be, delivering a sermon about going forth into the world to glorify God's Kingdom. I hope he doesn't mean the kingdom of human sacrifices – I've already hung out there too much.

One by one names are called, our degrees announced, and each student walks on stage to receive their award. I shift my weight from foot to foot, nervously ticking down the list of names as I wonder if I should have gone with my red tartan skinny jeans instead of this black skirt and don't the steps look a little rickety and isn't that a horned god hiding in the shadows behind the organ—

"Georgina Fisher."

Shit, that's me! I step onto the stage, basking in the applause echoing through the church. It took everything I had to make it to this moment alive. The Master squeezes my hand. "Congratulations, Georgina."

I look out into the audience. There's Mom, tears streaming down her cheeks. There's Claws, beaming with pride. Beside her, Sebastian smiles his dark, alluring smile and William stares stoically ahead, his hands folded in his lap and his face relaxed and serene.

I move my tassel to the right.

I'm done.

Blackfriars University is behind me, but it will always be part of my story. Despite all the terrible things that happened here, this place was good to me. It brought me William and Sebastian. It made me realize that I have strength inside me I never knew possible. It gave me a lifelong appreciation for beef and Guinness pies.

After the ceremony, the graduates mill on the lawn, while our families stream from the church and the bells toll overhead. I stand at the fountain where I first saw William all those years ago (fountains feature prominently in my meetings with paramours, it would seem) surrounded by all the people I love most in the world.

"Your father would have been so very proud of you." Mom holds me tight, crushing my ribs in the best possible way.

"Hey, look at you being all clever." Claws hugs me. It's a little harder because she's five months pregnant and there's a definite belly in the way. "You sure you don't want a job back in Emerald Beach? I'm in need of a nanny who also doubles as an assassin."

"Thanks but no thanks." I shake my head. "I've had enough of chaos and mayhem to last me a lifetime."

"Be serious," Claws scoffs, touching her hands to her protruding stomach. "By the end of summer you'll be so bored of being normal you'll beg me for some excitement."

She goes in to hug me again, her lips brushing my ear as she whispers. "It's taken care of."

When a mafia queen asks what you want as a graduation gift, it would be silly not to ask for the Earl who killed your boyfriend's mother to meet a grisly end. "You're the best friend a girl could ask for," I whisper back. "How did you do it?"

"Tiberius stretched him to death on the rack in his very own sex dungeon. It'll be on the news tomorrow."

I step back, my mood made brighter by Claws' news. William presses an enormous bunch of roses into my hands and bends to graze my cheek with his lips. "Congratulations, George."

"What would the graduate like to do now?" Sebastian asks, looping his arm in mine.

I raise an eyebrow. "Pub?"

AFTER SLEEPING off our hangover the next day, I say goodbye to Leigh and her crazy family (seriously, they're a story for another day), and Claws and Tiberius – who stopped by with his wife and daughter to wish me good luck for the future – and travel with Mom and Sebastian and William to Forsyth Hall. We have one more special event to attend before we start our trip.

We sit in the back of the car while Sir Henry's driver winds us through the countryside. Sebastian has been unusually quiet. Usually, car trips are the perfect opportunity for him to discuss some arcane aspect of scripture or the latest article he read in

The Guardian. But he's been staring silently at his clasped hands for over an hour.

I nudge him in the ribs. "What is up with you?"

Sebastian's head jerks around. For a moment, he looks startled, like he'd forgotten I was there. I feel bad. I realize he wasn't moping. He was praying. I start to apologize, but he cuts me off with a gentle hand. "I was going to tell you both over dinner tonight," he says. "But I can't wait any longer. I've decided to convert."

William holds out his drink bottle. "You mean you're finally going to use your special Jesus powers for something useful, like turning this water into a giant glass of Prosecco?"

"I'm converting to Church of England," Sebastian says. "I've already accepted a position – as editor for the Church's publishing arm here in England. It's mostly remote work – I'll be commissioning essays and devotionals, and I'll get to continue my scholarly research. In order to take up the job, I must be an ordained priest. I'll miss some of the rituals, and all of the Latin, but I won't miss the misogyny. I'll be working under a very progressive deacon, and she has some amazing ideas for bringing the church out of the sixteenth century."

"Plus," I point out with a jolt of excitement. "You'd get to wear the collar again."

"Kinky girl."

"While we're talking about the future," William passes me his phone. "What do you think of this?"

I stare at the screen. It's a real estate listing – for a strange and wonderful old Victorian house with elaborate moldings and chimneys sticking out everywhere. It's even got a little turret.

"It's beautiful," I breathe.

"I'm glad you think so, because I just brought it," William says.

I turn to him in surprise. He smiles that enigmatic, princely smile.

"It's true. I've purchased most of the old furniture as well. It's perfect – there's this bright room on the first floor overlooking the trees that I thought we could turn into your office and podcast studio, and there's a little folly beside the duck pond at the back garden that will make a wonderful studio for me. Sebastian can use the library for his *Lectio Divina* or whatever else he wants—"

"—library sex dungeon." Sebastian pumps his fist in the air, and I can't help cracking up laughing.

"It's in this tiny village called Argleton, which has had all these murders, so I knew it's just your kind of place. And—" William hands me a business card "—on the subject of murders, I got Professor Hipkins to put some feelers out for you, and she came back with this. It's the number of one Jo Southcombe, the local pathologist, who needs an intern, if you're interested."

"Hell yes, I'm interested." I take the card. "But William...what about Forsyth Hall? Don't you want to live there, near your mother's memories?"

"I think we should get our own place," he says. "It's not that I don't love the hall, but I think I need to live my own life for a while."

As we pull into the *Jurassic Park* gates of Forsyth Hall, I rest my head on his shoulder, my heart swelling with love that threatens to burst from my chest. "I can understand that."

"Wow." Mom rubs the back of her neck as she stares at the centerpiece of the buffet table – a roasted suckling pig surrounded by poached pears. "I don't think that's vegan."

"No, but it's delicious." I heap my plate high with food as we wait for the guests to gather. I thought you usually did food after a ceremony, but Forsyths don't do things the way normal folk do. This initial reception has already been going on for hours because foreign dignitaries need to be greeted and famous pop stars need to make their Tiktok dances.

A bell tolls, signaling for the party to move venues. Champagne flutes are quickly downed, cheeks stuffed with the last of the salmon puffs. I turn to William and check him over. Perfectly-tailored suit, check. Cufflinks that cost more than a small house, check. Un-Williamlike smile lighting up his face, checkidy-check.

He takes my hand, squeezing it a little hard. He's nervous. Too late to run now. We join the throng of people moving into the chapel.

The Forsyths' private chapel is packed to bursting with people. All around us, wild stories about William's father in his youth fly on the breeze. I spot a couple of famous TV stars and... is that a Royal? *Holy shit that's Prince...*

"Come on." William squeezes my hand. "We should find our seats."

Our seats are in a special area of the choir reserved for family. I sit with Mom while William takes his place in front of the altar. He touches his pocket several times, checking the ring box is still inside. Sebastian strides past him, lighting the altar candles, and pinches William on the arse. William's cheeks flare with heat, and it's so wonderfully adorable.

Sir Henry strides in, wearing a suit of armor because that's the kind of guy he is. The whole room falls silent as he takes his place beside William. Sebastian plays the wedding march as his mother Carmilla enters in a flowing, champagne-colored dress bedecked with glittering beads.

The priest who performs the ceremony is – as I suspect all priests will forever be to me after Sebastian – a disappointment.

Sebastian does a reading from Song of Songs. His voice soars through the lofty space. It feels like he's saying goodbye to this place, but also raising his eyes in greeting to something else. William hands over the rings and comes to stand with us while the couple makes their vows.

"Do you take this woman to be your wife?" the priest asks Sir Henry.

"I do." He gazes down at Carmilla in awe and wonder as the kitten winds between his legs.

"And do you take this man to be your husband?"

"I do." Carmilla's smile is radiant.

I stand between Sebastian and William, holding their hands as their parents bind their love forever, a love that has lain dormant but unbroken for many long years.

That could be us next, making our vows to each other.

We've talked about marriage – what that might mean to us as a polyamorous partnership. We don't have any answers, but I'm okay with that. I don't want to rush things. I want to enjoy this beautiful place we're in right now. I want to live in the poetry with my priest and my prince.

The faintest scent of black coffee and latex wafts under my nose. *Hey, Daddy.* I lay my head on William's shoulder. "Do you think your mother is watching this from heaven?" I ask.

"She is," he whispers back. "And she's happy."

"Did you know that feta cheese has existed since Homer wrote the Odyssey," William says as he accepts a delicious-smelling takeaway bag from a street vendor. "The story goes that the cyclops, Polyphemus, stored the milk from his sheep into bags made of animal skin. One day he opened a bag to discover the milk had curdled, and—"

"Be quiet and eat your spanakopita," Sebastian scolds him, a light tease in his voice. To make his point, he brings his hand down on William's ass. Hard. William makes a face, but a broad smile spreads across his features.

It's our second day in Athens. We've spent every moment since we touched down running from ruin to ruin, where Sebastian and William try to 'out-nerd' each other by reciting obscure facts about Ancient Greek culture and philosophy while I snap pictures of all the well-fed street cats to text to Claws.

We're now standing on a busy corner in the Plaka, eating amazing street food and watching sellers tempt throngs of tourists with brightly painted replicas of Ancient Greek drinking cups.

Greece is nothing like I dreamed it to be. It's hot and noisy and the smog burns my eyes. The modern city butts right up against the edges of the ancient – panels in the subway reveal the archaeological remains of Socrates' city, and if you walk down an alleyway between two restaurants you may find yourself in an ancient temple. The people are friendly and bossy, and take life at a slower pace. Smug, well-fed cats lounge on the ruins in flagrant disregard to the 'Do Not Touch' signs, so much so that it seems as if the city has thrown up its hands in defeat and bowed to their feline overlords.

It's perfect. I'm not sure I ever want to leave.

We finish our food, wipe yogurt off our sticky hands, and walk toward the Acropolis – the landmark of the city. We drag our weary, jet-lagged joints to the top of the Acropolis just as the sun is setting, and stand beneath the towering columns of the Parthenon – one of the grandest temples ever built in the Ancient World and a symbol of Athens' power and democracy.

"This is where it happened," Sebastian says. "This is where all the great minds of our age came to think, to pray."

It's beautiful. History seeps from every crack. There's something humbling about being in a place that's only ever existed for me in books, like Narnia or Middle Earth, but it's *here*, it's real, it's carved in stone. We know so much about what these temples meant to the people who built them and worshiped in them, and yet, we know nothing at all.

"Here?" Sebastian turns to William.

"It's as good a place as any."

"What are you two conspiring about?" I demand, but before I can try to get it out of them, they've both dropped to their knees on the ancient marble. My hands fly to my mouth, my heart into my boots.

"George," William swallows. He looks like he's about to cry. He looks up at me and swallows again. He opens his mouth and quotes one of his favorite Greek poems:

"Λέγουσιν

ἃ θέλουσιν

λεγέτωσαν

οὐ μέλι μοι

σὺ φίλι με

συνφέρι σοι

"They say

what they like.

Let them say it

I don't care.

Go on, love me

It does you good.

Without another word, he draws a small box from his pocket and holds it out to me. Inside is the most perfect ring – a thin band of gold formed into a tiny skull with red garnets for eyes.

"I don't offer poetry." Sebastian draws out his own box. "Instead, I offer scripture. 'Kiss me, make me drunk with your kisses. We will laugh, you and I, and count each kiss, sweeter than wine.'"

"Marry us," William whispers, his words whipped into a fury by the fierce Athenian wind.

"Marry us," echoes Sebastian, holding up his box. His ring is perfect, too. It's a signet-style ring, stamped with the impression of a medallion of Benet. Behind the Black Monk's head, there are even tiny flames licking from the windows of the burning refectory. A reminder of what brought us together – the beginning of our story.

"But...but we can't get married," I choke out between my tears. "I mean, obviously I want to, but legally there's no way for us—"

"We'll move to Utah," William says. "It'll be fine."

"No thank you." I make a face.

"We have options," Sebastian says. "We do not have to be married in the eyes of the law to commit to each other."

"What about the eyes of your Lord?"

"In the eyes of my God, you're both already mine." Sebastian cups my cheek in his hand, his fingers so strong and yet so perfectly gentle. "What do you say, sweet George?"

"Yes," I laugh through my tears. "Yes, and yes. A thousand times yes."

From his bag, Sebastian produces a bottle of red wine. "I thought we should pour a libation. For Dionysos."

We pour the first of the wine to the ground. I hold the bottle to my lips and drink, long and deep. I drink my communion.

Later, at the hotel, we will fall between the sheets and turn water into wine.

THE END

———

Want to get inside the heads of Sebastian and William? Sign up to Steffanie Holmes' newsletter and get two alternative POV scenes from George's men, along with a collection of other bonus material from Steffanie's worlds. Sign up here: http://steffanieholmes.com/newsletter

---

"I was baptized in bloodshed. To the bloodshed, I return."

Discover how George's friend Claws became who she is in the complete Stonehurst Prep dark contemporary reverse harem series. Start with book 1, *My Stolen Life*:

http://books2read.com/mystolenlife

Turn the page for a sizzling excerpt.

FROM THE AUTHOR

University was one of the happiest times of my life. I'm a lot like George in that I'm a big nerd for learning and weird old stuff. I spent far too much time during my degree sitting in the back of lectures I wasn't enrolled in and reading random books that caught my eye in the vast library.

I studied Ancient Greek (and Egyptian hieroglyphs, and a few other useless dead languages to boot) in a sunny room in the Classical Studies department filled with overstuffed chairs and shelves of haphazardly-stacked books. The department itself was an old Victorian house covered in vines in the furthermost corner of the university. To get to my classes there, I would take this shortcut through crumbling stone archways and back alleys that always made me feel like I was a character in a dark academia novel.

Greek is a difficult language – lots of cases and tenses and irregular verbs – but it's also graceful and beautiful. I never quite got to the point of fluency, but I loved the satisfaction of staring at a page of complete nonsense and, with time and my handy Liddell & Scott, puzzling out a line of poetry or wisdom. It felt like uncovering a delightful secret. (And we all know how much I love secrets and mysteries :)).

At the end of my studies, I was one of 20 students selected for a field school in Greece and Crete. We spent six weeks visiting the archaeological sites we'd spent four years studying, drinking raki, and cracking obscure jokes only Classical scholars would get. I made friends on this trip I still have to this day.

When I sat down to write the Dark Academia series, I had all these ideas about Bacchanals and hidden rites and ritual murders bobbing around in my skull, but I *also* wanted to tap in to all of these things I loved about university. George struggles to fit in, but she experiences a lot of joy, too. My love of knowledge and learning and hidden things permeates these pages. Of all the characters I've written, George is probably the most like me, and many of her experiences are mine (I've never met a hot priest, though), so I really hope you enjoy her story.

I've taken some liberties with my Greek mythology. While some parallels can be drawn between Dionysos (Bacchus) and Christ, and these parallels would have been understood by contemporaries of Jesus when they heard the stories of the apostles, the symbology of wine as Dionysos' blood that can purify and cleanse is entirely my own invention – inspired by a common mistranslation of *Euripides*. I hope you'll forgive me this narrative indiscretion.

I've also taken some other liberties – one example is that 'fruit of a poison tree' doctrine isn't part of the UK legal system. But I thought it sounded poetic, so I kept it. If you're a reader and a lawyer, I hope you can forgive me.

Writing this duet has been a joy and a pleasure, but as always, it takes a village to bring a book to life. I'd like to thank my cantankerous drummer husband, for reading this manuscript and giving me so many ideas to make it better. And for being my lighthouse. And for making me so many bacon butties and keeping the house stocked with chocolate during lockdown.

To Meg and Eveis for the epically helpful editing job, and to Stefanie Saw for the stunning covers. To Bea Paige, EM Moore, Laura Lee, Rachel Leigh, Caitlyn Dare, Becca Steele and especially my main girl Daniela Romero for killing it with the *Brutal Boys on Devil's Night* anthology, where this story first appeared.

To Sam and Iris and Amy and all my bogans for the FB and Zoom shenanigans that kept me sane while I spent my writing days stuck at home covered in cats.

To you, the reader, for going on this journey with me, even though it's led to some dark places. If you're curious about George's friend Claws and how she became who she is, then you need the complete Stonehurst Prep dark contemporary reverse harem series. Start with book 1, *My Stolen Life*: http://books2read. com/mystolenlife

If you want to read more from me, check out my dark reverse harem bully romance series, *Kings of Miskatonic Prep*. HP Lovecraft meets *Cruel Intentions* in this dark paranormal reverse harem bully romance that's definitely not for the faint of heart. Hazel is the most badass FMC I've ever written, and I think you'll love meeting her. *Read Shunned now.*

If you want to keep up with my bookish news and get weekly stories about the real life true crimes and ghost stories that inspire my books, you can join my newsletter at https:// www.steffanieholmes.com/newsletter. When you join you'll get a free copy of Cabinet of Curiosities, a compendium of bonus and deleted scenes and stories. It includes two chapters of *Pretty Girls Make Graves* rewritten from Sebastian's and William's POV.

I'm so happy you enjoyed George's story! I'd love it if you wanted to leave a review on Amazon or Goodreads. It will help other readers to find their next read.

Ἐὰν ᾖς φιλομαθής, ἔσει πολυμαθής. Thank you, thank you! I love you heaps! Until next time.

Steff

ENJOY THIS EXCERPT FROM MY STOLEN LIFE

PROLOGUE: MACKENZIE

I roll over in bed and slam against a wall.

Huh? Odd.

My bed isn't pushed against a wall. I must've twisted around in my sleep and hit the headboard. I do thrash around a lot, especially when I have bad dreams, and tonights was particularly gruesome. My mind stretches into the silence, searching for the tendrils of my nightmare. *I'm lying in bed and some dark shadow comes and lifts me up, pinning my arms so they hurt. He drags me downstairs to my mother, slumped in her favorite chair. At first, I think she passed out drunk after a night at the club, but then I see the dark pool expanding around her feet, staining the designer rug.*

I see the knife handle sticking out of her neck.

I see her glassy eyes rolled toward the ceiling.

I see the window behind her head, and my own reflection in the glass, my face streaked with blood, my eyes dark voids of pain and hatred.

But it's okay now. It was just a dream. It's—

OW.

I hit the headboard again. I reach down to rub my elbow, and my hand grazes a solid wall of satin. On my other side.

What the hell?

I open my eyes into a darkness that is oppressive and complete, the kind of darkness I'd never see inside my princess bedroom with its flimsy purple curtains letting in the glittering skyline of the city. The kind of darkness that folds in on me, pressing me against the hard, un-bedlike surface I lie on.

Now the panic hits.

I throw out my arms, kick with my legs. I hit walls. Walls all around me, lined with satin, dense with an immense weight pressing from all sides. Walls so close I can't sit up or bend my knees. I scream, and my scream bounces back at me, hollow and weak.

I'm in a coffin. I'm in a motherfucking coffin, and I'm *still alive*.

I scream and scream and scream. The sound fills my head and stabs at my brain. I know all I'm doing is using up my precious oxygen, but I can't make myself stop. In that scream I lose myself, and every memory of who I am dissolves into a puddle of terror.

When I do stop, finally, I gasp and pant, and I taste blood and stale air on my tongue. A cold fear seeps into my bones. Am I dying? My throat crawls with invisible bugs. Is this what it feels like to die?

I hunt around in my pockets, but I'm wearing purple pajamas, and the only thing inside is a bookmark Daddy gave me. I can't see it of course, but I know it has a quote from Julius Caesar on it. *Alea iacta est. The die is cast.*

Like fuck it is.

I think of Daddy, of everything he taught me – memories too dark to be obliterated by fear. Bile rises in my throat. I swallow, choke it back. Daddy always told me our world is forged in blood. I might be only thirteen, but I know who he is, what he's capable of. I've heard the whispers. I've seen the way people hurry to appease him whenever he enters a room. I've had the lessons from Antony in what to do if I find myself alone with one of Daddy's enemies.

Of course, they never taught me what to do if one of those enemies *buries me alive*.

I can't give up.

I claw at the satin on the lid. It tears under my fingers, and I pull out puffs of stuffing to reach the wood beneath. I claw at the surface, digging splinters under my nails. Cramps arc along my arm from the awkward angle. I know it's hopeless; I know I'll never be able to scratch my way through the wood. Even if I can, I *feel* the weight of several feet of dirt above me. I'd be crushed in moments. But I have to try.

I'm my father's daughter, and this is not how I die.

I claw and scratch and tear. I lose track of how much time passes in the tiny space. My ears buzz. My skin weeps with cold sweat.

A noise reaches my ears. A faint shifting. A scuffle. A scrape and thud above my head. Muffled and far away.

Someone piling the dirt in my grave.

Or maybe...

...maybe someone digging it out again.

Fuck, fuck, please.

"Help." My throat is hoarse from screaming. I bang the lid with my fists, not even feeling the splinters piercing my skin. "Help me!"

THUD. Something hits the lid. The coffin groans. My veins burn with fear and hope and terror.

The wood cracks. The lid is flung away. Dirt rains down on me, but I don't care. I suck in lungfuls of fresh, crisp air. A circle of light blinds me. I fling my body up, up into the unknown. Warm arms catch me, hold me close.

"I found you, Claws." Only Antony calls me by that nickname. Of course, it would be my cousin who saves me. Antony drags me over the lip of the grave, *my* grave, and we fall into crackling leaves and damp grass.

I sob into his shoulder. Antony rolls me over, his fingers pressing all over my body, checking if I'm hurt. He rests my back against cold stone. "I have to take care of this," he says. I watch through tear-filled eyes as he pushes the dirt back into the hole – into what was supposed to be my grave – and brushes dead leaves on top. When he's done, it's impossible to tell the ground's been disturbed at all.

I tremble all over. I can't make myself stop shaking. Antony comes back to me and wraps me in his arms. He staggers to his feet, holding me like I'm weightless. He's only just turned eighteen, but already he's built like a tank.

I let out a terrified sob. Antony glances over his shoulder, and there's panic in his eyes. "You've got to be quiet, Claws," he whispers. "They might be nearby. I'm going to get you out of here."

I can't speak. My voice is gone, left in the coffin with my screams. Antony hoists me up and darts into the shadows. He runs with ease, ducking between rows of crumbling gravestones and beneath bent and gnarled trees. Dimly, I recognize this place – the old Emerald Beach cemetery, on the edge of Beaumont Hills overlooking the bay, where the original families of Emerald Beach buried their dead.

Where someone tried to bury me.

Antony bursts from the trees onto a narrow road. His car is parked in the shadows. He opens the passenger door and settles me inside before diving behind the wheel and gunning the engine.

We tear off down the road. Antony rips around the deadly corners like he's on a racetrack. Steep cliffs and crumbling old mansions pass by in a blur.

"My parents..." I gasp out. "Where are my parents?"

"I'm sorry, Claws. I didn't get to them in time. I only found you."

I wait for this to sink in, for the fact I'm now an orphan to hit me in a rush of grief. But I'm numb. My body won't stop shaking, and I left my brain and my heart buried in the silence of that coffin.

"Who?" I ask, and I fancy I catch a hint of my dad's cold savagery in my voice. "Who did this?"

"I don't know yet, but if I had to guess, it was Brutus. I warned your dad that he was making alliances and building up to a challenge. I think he's just made his move."

I try to digest this information. Brutus – who was once my father's trusted friend, who'd eaten dinner at our house and played Chutes and Ladders with me – killed my parents and buried me alive. But it bounces off the edge of my skull and doesn't stick. The life I had before, my old life, it's gone, and as I twist and grasp for memories, all I grab is stale coffin air.

"What now?" I ask.

Antony tosses his phone into my lap. "Look at the headlines."

I read the news app he's got open, but the words and images blur together. "This... this doesn't make any sense..."

"They think you're dead, Claws," Antony says. "That means you have to *stay* dead until we're strong enough to move against him. Until then, you have to be a ghost. But don't worry, I'll protect you. I've got a plan. We'll hide you where they'll never think to look."

Start reading:
http://books2read.com/mystolenlife

MORE FROM THE AUTHOR

From the author of *Pretty Girls Makes Graves* and *Shunned* comes this dark contemporary high school reverse harem romance.

Psst. I have a secret.

Are you ready?

I'm Mackenzie Malloy, and everyone thinks they know who I am.

Five years ago, I disappeared.

No one has seen me or my family outside the walls of Malloy Manor since.
But now I'm coming to reclaim my throne:
The Ice Queen of Stonehurst Prep is back.

Standing between me and my everything?
Three things can bring me down:
The sweet guy who wants answers from his former friend.
The rock god who wants to f*ck me.
The king who'll crush me before giving up his crown.

They think they can ruin me, wreck it all, but I won't let them.
I'm not the Mackenzie Eli used to know.
Hot boys and rock gods like Gabriel won't win me over.
And just like Noah, I'll kill to keep my crown.

I'm just a poor little rich girl with the stolen life.
I'm here to tear down three princes,
before they destroy me.

Read now:
http://books2read.com/mystolenlife

OTHER BOOKS BY STEFFANIE HOLMES

Nevermore Bookshop Mysteries

A Dead and Stormy Night

Of Mice and Murder

Pride and Premeditation

How Heathcliff Stole Christmas

Memoirs of a Garroter

Prose and Cons

A Novel Way to Die

Much Ado About Murder

Kings of Miskatonic Prep

Shunned

Initiated

Possessed

Ignited

Stonehurst Prep

My Stolen Life

My Secret Heart

My Broken Crown

My Savage Kingdom

Dark Academia

Pretty Girls Make Graves

Brutal Boys Cry Blood

Fallen Stars Burn Bright

Wild Nights Hide Sorrows

Manderley Academy

Ghosted

Haunted

Spirited

Briarwood Witches

Earth and Embers

Fire and Fable

Water and Woe

Wind and Whispers

Spirit and Sorrow

Crookshollow Gothic Romance

Art of Cunning (Alex & Ryan)

Art of the Hunt (Alex & Ryan)

Art of Temptation (Alex & Ryan)

The Man in Black (Elinor & Eric)

Watcher (Belinda & Cole)

Reaper (Belinda & Cole)

Wolves of Crookshollow

Digging the Wolf (Anna & Luke)

Writing the Wolf (Rosa & Caleb)

Inking the Wolf (Bianca & Robbie)

Wedding the Wolf (Willow & Irvine)

Want to be informed when the next Steffanie Holmes paranormal romance story goes live? Sign up for the newsletter at www.steffanieholmes.com/ newsletter to get the scoop, and score a free collection of bonus scenes and stories to enjoy!

ABOUT THE AUTHOR

Steffanie Holmes is the *USA Today* bestselling author of the paranormal, gothic, dark, and fantastical. Her books feature clever, witty heroines, secret societies, creepy old mansions and alpha males who *always* get what they want.

Legally-blind since birth, Steffanie received the 2017 Attitude Award for Artistic Achievement. She was also a finalist for a 2018 Women of Influence award.

Steff is the creator of *Rage Against the Manuscript* – a resource of free content, books, and courses to help writers tell their story, find their readers, and build a badass writing career.

Steffanie lives in New Zealand with her husband, a horde of cantankerous cats, and their medieval sword collection.

Steffanie Holmes newsletter

Grab a free copy *Cabinet of Curiosities* – a Steffanie Holmes compendium of short stories and bonus scenes, including alternative POV chapters from William and Sebastian – when you sign up for updates with the Steffanie Holmes newsletter.

http://www.steffanieholmes.com/newsletter

Come hang with Steffanie
www.steffanieholmes.com
hello@steffanieholmes.com